THE FINE ART
OF
FORGIVENESS

J.S. EADES

Eades, J.S.
The Fine Art of Forgiveness / J.S. Eades
ISBN: 978-0-9939582-2-9

Website: www.jseades.com
Facebook: AuthorJSEades
Twitter: @JS_Eades
Instagram: @jseadesauthor

Editorial Assistance: Dina Bielby, Gina Sweet-Ellis, Colleen Ferrier, and Kirsty Madden
Cover Design: Heather D. Murray

Edition: Amazon Paperback May 2023

I want to thank Heather, Dina, Mara, Gina, Kirsty, Colleen, and of course my husband and son. But most of all I want to give a huge thank you and shout out to my writing partner, Eva. This sequel has been a long time coming, and I never could have finished it without all her help.

Part 1

Chapter 1

Amelia

HOOOONK

With a shriek of tires, the car swerved around me, jolting me back to the world.

"You gotta fucking death wish, lady?" the driver shouted through his open window as he sped away.

I stumbled backward onto the sidewalk, mouth agape, hands quivering. That voice. I craned my neck to try to see the car, but it was now too far down the street.

It wasn't a sky blue Mustang, that much I knew for sure. It wasn't him. It was just my distracted mind playing tricks on me.

I blew out a long breath, looked both ways this time, and then rushed across the road. Contrary to that guy's snarky comment, I did *not* have a death wish.

Not anymore, anyway.

Is it possible to mourn someone who's still alive? I still mourned the death of my father, still missed him like crazy, but this wasn't like that. It was like nothing I'd ever felt before, this abject hollowness. This *grief*. No longer fresh, hot, wet grief, but months-old, dry, deep, ache. The kind of grief you're able to hide from others. The kind that slowly eats you away inside.

I didn't know how to define it, so I couldn't identify it. Not until later, when it was pointed out to me by my therapist. I just knew that, like a persistent yet apathetic vampire, it was slowly sucking the life out of me.

Speaking of my therapist, it had been several months since my last appointment so I felt a bit nervous walking into her office on a cold, wet, early November afternoon. As I sat down across from her, the first thing she said to me was not what I'd expected.

"Hello Amelia. You've changed your hair." Debbie Westwood smiled warmly at me and I felt myself relax a little.

A few weeks ago, I'd cut my hair short. My whole life it had been long and brushed straight, but now it sat just above my shoulders and I let it do its own thing, which tended to be wavy. I'd also, for the first time ever, dyed my natural auburn shade a rich brown. My mother hated my new look, but that was no surprise.

"I did," I replied without elaborating. My hair wasn't all I'd changed. I now wore my glasses almost every day, my contacts case gathering dust in the apartment in Richmond I shared with my friend Dee. Glasses were easy to remove during teary moments. Thankfully, I didn't have as many of those as I used to, but they still hit me sometimes. I'd quit wearing makeup for the same reason.

"It suits you," she said and I was surprised to realize she meant it.

"Thanks."

Debbie moved on. "So, how're you doing these days?"

There it was. The question I'd been waiting for, the one I always got. How was I doing? It seemed everyone asked it: my friends, my mother, even my ex-husband the rare times we were in contact. Truthfully, I didn't know how to answer. Sometimes I was okay, managing to get through the day like a fairly normal person; sometimes I was only hanging on by the thinnest of threads. But I couldn't very well say that to people who cared about me, could I? They would only worry, and I didn't want them to worry. I knew they were just asking to be polite.

So I lied. I told them I was fine, and, with the occasional exception of Dee, who knew me far too well, they believed me. It was what they wanted to hear, after all, and gave them

2

permission to move on to the next subject. And that was always my goal. To move on.

I didn't lie about my wellbeing as much as I used to, not all the time to everyone now, but I still did. The most recent lie I told Dee just this morning: "I hardly think of him anymore." I *wished* it were true, *wanted* it to be true more than anything, but it wasn't. I still thought of him every day. Not every waking moment of each day—there was at least that much improvement—but every day. I knew it was pointless and needed to stop, but I couldn't seem to help it.

Debbie Westwood, however, was not a loved one. She was my therapist. I was paying her to listen, so I decided to edge a little closer to the truth.

"Oh, you know. Good days and bad days. To be expected, really." I shrugged to emphasize how normal I assumed I was.

She nodded, jotting something on her notepad. "Are you working?"

I frowned. This was the second most common question I got, although it was often phrased as: 'are you looking for work?' or 'how's the job hunt going?' I hated having to answer this, too. Because the truth was that I wasn't, at least not in the way people seemed to expect I should be.

"Yes. Sort of. I mean, I'm taking on some accounting work, and doing the books for my roommate's business. But that's more in exchange for my share of living costs. If you mean 'am I earning a steady income?' then no. Not really. But I still have my dad's inheritance, so I'm getting by okay for now."

She made another note.

"Tax season's coming up in a few months, so I'll have a lot more work soon," I added. I'm not sure why I needed to justify my lack of consistent employment, but as I'd done my whole life, I felt obligated to prove myself worthy.

"That's good. You haven't been searching for employment at another company then?"

I shook my head. After how things at the last place had gone, I wasn't eager to jump back into the office environment. Too many stressors still. My current goal was to have my own accounting business someday, so that's what I was working toward.

"And how are you feeling about your separation? It's been a few months now. Are things still civil?"

I bit my lip. "Yes. But we rarely communicate now." I sighed. And then the truth I'd been holding so closely, not just from my therapist, but from nearly everyone in my life, slipped out. "I…uh….I cheated on him."

Debbie looked up at me impassively. Why didn't she seem more shocked? Even *I* was shocked to hear those words come from my mouth. She tilted her head to one side and gave me a compassionate smile. "Is that why you ended your marriage?"

"Yes. And no. I…we, uh, we weren't together anymore by the time I left Scott. And I know I should've told him months before that—I *really* meant to—but I could never bring myself to actually do it. And after my…after my affair ended—*God* I hate that word, it sounds so *ugly*—I finally made myself tell Scott we were over. And then I moved out."

She wrote something else down. "Why do you think it sounds ugly?"

I flushed. How could I possibly explain in any way that would do our relationship justice? But I had to try. "What we had wasn't ugly. Not to me. Not to either of us. But I know everyone else would think it was. I cheated and lied to my husband. That was completely unforgivable. But I don't regret being with…him."

"You loved this man?"

I hesitated for a moment. Then I nodded. "Yes. And he loved me. His part in it wasn't as deceitful as mine. He was separated from his wife when we were together. But then she came back, and she got pregnant, and…and…I mean, it's not like I ever expected him to put me before his kid—*kids*, although the baby isn't born yet—but…"

"But he chose to stay with his family?"

"Yeah."

She looked at me with such sympathy that I was a bit taken aback. I didn't expect anyone to feel anything but scorn for me after hearing what I'd done. I deserved scorn far more than sympathy. "That must have been devastating."

A lump had risen in my throat. "It was," I nodded.

Glancing up at the clock, her brows drew together. "Unfortunately, our time is nearly up. However, I think it's important that we continue with this particular topic. Are you able to book an hour with me next week?"

Since I didn't have health benefits, I could no longer afford one hour appointments. Once a month for a half hour was all I could manage, and even that was pushing it. "I can't. I don't have coverage anymore. I wish I could."

Debbie picked up her desk phone and dialed out to her receptionist. "Clara, please book Ms. York for an hour next week. Schedule it into my pro bono slot."

"Really?" I asked once she'd replaced the receiver. "You'd do that for me?"

"In this situation, yes. I strongly feel we should continue this conversation as soon as possible. I know it's difficult for you to talk about, and I must say I'm quite proud of you for finally telling me the truth today about what happened. I think getting all this out into the open may be healing for you."

Swiping away the moisture pooling in the corner of my eye, I nodded.

"Do you have anyone else you can talk to? Your roommate, perhaps?"

I nodded. "Yeah. She's awesome."

"Good." Debbie got to her feet and escorted me to the door. "I'll see you next week, Amelia."

Thanking her, I went out to speak with her receptionist to pay for this week and schedule my next appointment.

When I walked out into the parking lot, I was glad to see the rain had stopped. The droplets on my old blue Honda glimmered like crystals in the brisk autumn sunshine. I didn't need to head back to Richmond yet, and since she lived nearby, I decided to go see my mother.

The house I grew up in was on a tree-lined street in an older part of Swann's Landing. Though my father had passed away from a massive coronary a little over a year ago, my mom still lived there. It was too big for one person, but so far she'd shown no sign of wanting to move somewhere smaller.

My heart clenched as I walked up the steps to the front porch, like it did every time I came home now. A part of me would always be expecting my dad to fling the door wide and greet me with his usual smile. I didn't think I'd ever get used to him being gone.

Knocking first to give her warning, I used my key to let myself in. Mom was coming down the stairs carrying a half-filled laundry basket. From my angle, it looked nearly as big as she was. "Oh, Amelia! You didn't say you were coming by."

I shrugged. "I had some free time after an appointment." Dropping my bag on the bench, I took the basket from her.

"How about I throw these in for you while you put on some coffee?"

"I've actually stopped drinking coffee. It's bad for my blood pressure."

I raised an eyebrow. Brenda York was always worried about her health, and it wasn't unusual for her to quit eating or drinking or doing something after reading an article saying it was bad for you. She inevitably resumed said activity before long though, so I tended to brush off such announcements.

"How about tea?"

"Tea is fine." She went into the kitchen, and I headed down to the basement to start the wash.

When I returned, she set my old *Virginia is For Lovers* mug in front of me, the teabag still submerged in the steaming water. That mug had been a gag birthday gift from Scott not long after we'd started dating back in high school. I looked at it with a frown, wondering if Mom remembered how we got it. Knowing her, she probably did.

"So how's the job search going?" she asked before I could take a sip.

"Nothing to report." Did I sound defensive? Maybe a little.

Her mouth fell open to chide me about not having full-time work yet, but before she could launch into her usual lecture, I held up a hand. "Let's not get into this again. I know you're worried about me, but I'm fine. I'm trying to build up my accounting business. The minute I accept a job offer somewhere, I'll call you. I promise."

She exhaled a small huff and took a swallow of tea. "It's been months already. Don't wait too long, or you'll end up—"

"Mom. Seriously. I can manage my own career."

Holding my gaze, she folded her hands on the table. "I ran into Scott and Liv at the grocery store the other day."

Oh, here we go, I thought. Pasting on a smile, I replied, "Oh yeah? How're they doing?"

Liv Webb was the other of my two best friends. At least she used to be. I wasn't sure where we stood these days. We hadn't really spoken since I'd left Scott. They were seeing each other now Dee had told me, which hadn't been any huge surprise. It also explained why she'd been keeping her distance.

"They seem happy. Apparently she's moved in."

I nearly spit out my tea. "*What?*"

"I take it they haven't told you?" Mom arched a brow.

I shook my head.

"It's still your house, too. Is Scott planning to pay you out for your half of it?"

Still in shock, I muttered, "I have no idea."

"Well, you'd better talk to him then. You two should really put it up for sale and split the proceeds. I'm sure you could use the money right now."

I sighed and put down the mug Scott had given me so many years ago. Initiating that conversation with my ex was not something I wanted to do. But if he and Liv were cohabitating now I was going to have to suck it up and call him.

To my mom, I just said, "I'm glad they're happy. And yes, I'll talk to him about the house." Both of those were true. No matter how awkward things were these days, I still loved them and wished them only the best.

I didn't stay much longer. Mom didn't like to talk about my dad unless she had to, and I was no longer in the mood to socialize. I spent the majority of my time alone these days, and I'd come to relish it. Prefer it, even. Alone meant I didn't have to pretend. After thanking her for the tea, I got on the road and headed back to Dee's.

Weirdly, though I'd been living there for almost five months, I still didn't think of Dee's as home. And I no longer considered the house I'd lived in for the previous six years with Scott home. Nor the house I'd grown up in. The truth was, I didn't really feel like I had a home anymore. Mostly, I just felt like I was adrift. And I didn't even know what I was searching for.

In the thirty years I'd been alive, the past one had been the roughest, bar none. But I'd survived. I wasn't the same Amelia I used to be, but I was still kicking. I'd lost my dad, my job, my marriage (all right, those last two I walked away from, but that's just semantics) and, most devastating of all, my…God, I didn't even know what to call him.

My Declan.

My love.

Declan

To someone on the outside looking in, I supposed my life looked nearly perfect: successful career, nice house, flashy car, hot wife, adorable daughter, and a new baby girl on the way in a couple of months. Yeah, I had it pretty damn good.

Or so it seemed.

I was a salesman, and a damned good one, so I was adept at controlling my outward reactions. But ever since one particularly massive ball of shit hit the fan this past spring, I'd had to work extra hard at faking happiness. Truthfully, it wasn't that difficult. Most people failed to see the ugly, jagged bits hiding beneath the shiny surface. They tended not to look too hard in case they didn't like what they found. And I got that.

A prime example of the less than pleasant things I had to deal with: my dad—my real dad, not my adoptive one—had an incurable brain tumor. Groundbreaking new treatments had slowed its growth and extended his life, but a ticking time-bomb still lurked inside his head. It hadn't been that long ago that James had come into my family's life, but in the fifteen months I'd known him, I'd grown to love him like he'd always been here. So had my daughter, Alexis. We would be devastated if—when—he passed away. So, although we were enjoying the time we had with him, knowing an end-date was coming sooner rather than later pretty much sucked.

And I'd also only recently reconciled with my wife after a shitty period that had cumulated in us taking a timeout from our marriage for several months earlier this year. We were trying to be a happy family again, but it wasn't easy. Things between us were still a bit off, still kind of tense sometimes. It was more me than Laura, but I had more things to work through than she did. Complicated things. Mind-fucking things. Although I tried my damnedest to push them deep down inside and move past them, they often refused to stay buried. I'd promised both my wife and myself that I'd be there for my family though, and I did the best I could. I had a temper, and she knew just how to push my buttons, so I won't try to pretend I didn't fail sometimes.

Laura co-anchored the Swann's Landing News at Six, so as per usual, I left work to pick up Alexis from the babysitter's. Mrs. Haverford had looked after her since she was small, and now that she'd started kindergarten still watched her for a couple of hours after school. School had been a major adjustment for Lex. She was very clingy when either of us dropped her off in the mornings, and so far that showed no sign of improving. Some of it was probably due to her mother leaving us for three months this past spring for a work assignment in New York. I couldn't help worrying that Lex was developing abandonment fears like the ones I'd harbored since my own mother passed away when I was seven.

8

As I came down Fort Avenue in Lynchburg, some dickwad decided today was a good day to cut me off. He was wrong. I drove a sweet Mustang Boss convertible. Though a few years old now, she was still as mint as the day she rolled off the lot. And this asshole nearly took off her left front fender.

Rage erupted within me. Though I'd gotten better at controlling it, it was never very far from the surface these days. This time I didn't tamper it down. I slammed on the gas pedal and caught up to the offending vehicle at the next set of lights. Throwing my car into Park, I reached for the door handle. I had no clue what I was going to say or do, but I had a nearly insatiable urge to confront him.

Luckily, common sense won me over at the last second as an image of Alexis waiting for me to pick her up popped into my head. With a sigh, I settled back into my seat and flicked the indicator to signal my turn instead of following that prick. My hands were a bit shaky on the wheel, but I pulled myself together, as I had so many times over the past few months.

I couldn't afford to lose my cool. Not now, not at work, and definitely not at home. Losing my cool in the wrong situation could mean losing my daughter—sorry, my *children,* plural— and that was *not* an option.

When I pulled into the babysitter's driveway, the door flew open and Alexis rushed out all smiles, her brunette curls bouncing off her shoulders as she ran to my car. Before she reached it, I threw open the door and scooped her into my arms.

"How was school?"

"S'okay." She kissed my cheek. "Ow! You're all scratchy, Daddy!"

"Did my stubble scrape you? Sorry, sweetie. Maybe my beard grew extra fast today."

She giggled, and I opened the back door for her to climb inside, buckling her safely into her booster seat. The drive to our house at the other end of the street was a short one, but as always, she insisted I turn on the radio.

I used to be a big music fan. Any time I was alone in my car Radiohead, or Pearl Jam, or the Chili Peppers, or some other great band would be blasting. Now I listened mostly to talk radio or left the stereo off completely. However, I made an exception when Alexis rode with me.

When I hit the button on my dash, the sweet, yet mournful notes of Jim Coltrane singing "Ain't No Place Like Home (In

Your Arms)" filled the car, burrowing straight down to the part of me where I'd buried that box of memories. The one that refused to stay sealed.

My eyes squeezed shut, a useless barrier against the rush of emotions that flooded me. I swatted blindly at the controls, switching the music off only by sheer luck. I could handle a lot of stuff, force myself to stay cool through nearly anything, but not Coltrane. Not anymore.

"Why'd you turn it off?" Alexis asked with a slight whine.

I sighed, waiting a beat to make sure I could reply in a steady voice. "We'll be home in a sec," I told her.

My heart was pounding, and once again my fingers trembled against the leather steering wheel.

Chapter 2

Amelia

Sometimes my brain played tricks on me. Like my cell phone would ring, and I'd get this flash of surety that it was him calling, like I just *knew* it was. When I'd answer, there'd be silence, a hum on the line, and then a click and gone. The screen always said Unknown Caller. I tried not to read too much into it—they were probably just telephone solicitors—but I couldn't help wondering.

I didn't tell anyone about weird stuff like that. Not Dee, and especially not Josh. Josh was the only other person who knew what really happened between Declan and me. Although he was one of my closest friends, he was also Declan's *best* friend. I loved and trusted Josh, but tried not to burden him too much with my issues. I didn't want him to feel disloyal.

But I had Dee, and she was always willing to listen. I chose not to tell her some things—things I thought might make me sound like I was losing my mind, but whenever I needed her she was there. And she didn't complain, at least not much. She did tell me I spent too much time listening to The Cure's "Pictures of You" on repeat, but I knew she was only teasing. It's funny—Scott had never understood why I loved that song, as I'd only been a kid when it came out, but we had different taste in music.

Thinking of Scott reminded me of what Mom had told me. I'd been putting off contacting him about the house, but I had to do it. With a sigh, I picked up my phone and texted him.

I need to talk to you. Please let me know when works.

About an hour later, he texted back: *What's up?*

Maybe I'd just try to do this over text. At least that way there would be no need for small talk.

I think we should put the house up for sale.

He didn't respond for about ten minutes. Then: *Why?*

I sighed, debating whether or not to tell him I knew Liv had moved in. He might've assumed I knew, but neither of them had bothered to tell me themselves, which still kind of irritated me. I decided not to mention it and see if he'd say anything.

I hate to ask you to move, but I could really use the money from my half. We should talk to a realtor. Do you know anyone?

Again, he didn't reply right away. Maybe he was ticked off. If so, I understood, since I'd just asked him to find a new place to live. But I still needed an answer. Twenty-five minutes later, my phone pinged. *Give me a few days? I'll talk to the bank about a loan to pay you out.*

That would mean we'd need to get an appraisal of the property to determine how much he'd have to pay me. I wondered if he knew that. Clearly he wanted to stay in the house. With Liv. Which he still hadn't mentioned. I didn't really mind, but I did wish they'd just tell me the truth.

With a rueful laugh, I realized how hypocritical *that* thought was. Yes, I would have preferred Scott and Liv to be honest with me, but the fact was that other than my share of the house, Scott owed me nothing. Certainly not loyalty. Or honesty. Or even friendship.

Sighing softly, I responded: *Sure. Let me know soon.* Before I hit Send, I added, *Hope you're doing okay.*

His last message just read: *I will.*

In hindsight, it might have been better to call him after all. Maybe we would've connected better, even if it was awkward. I hated that things were still so weird between us, but there was a good chance they always would be. I was the one who'd broken his heart. I was the one who'd lied to him. I regretted it deeply, but what was done was done. I had to live with the consequences.

This whole thing was my fault. Maybe not every crappy thing in my life was my fault, but I knew most of it was.

Declan

Bolognaise sauce simmered on the back burner sending its delicious aroma throughout the entire lower level of the house. I'd just dropped noodles into a pot of boiling water when I heard Laura come in.

Alexis beat me to the entryway. "Mommy!" she shouted, flinging her arms around her mother's waist before she could even remove her jacket.

A year ago, Laura getting home in time to have dinner with us was more of an anomaly than the norm. She often had meetings and needed to stay well after she went off the air. There were many evenings she didn't come in until after Alexis was already in bed, a fact that used to annoy the hell out of me. But these days she made a conscious effort to get home earlier as often as she could. I knew she was trying to do her part to repair our formally fractured family. And I appreciated it. Not as much as Alexis of course, but I did.

"Hey. How was your day?" I asked.

"Okay." She sounded exhausted, as she often did these days. Being pregnant didn't agree with her very well this time around. The nausea had finally let up, but she still felt tired most of the time.

This pregnancy hadn't been planned any more than Alexis had been. And the timing couldn't have been worse, as our marriage was just about ready to be declared D.O.A. Just when we'd reached the breaking point, when I'd accepted that we were over and was starting to plan a life without Laura, Fate decided to throw another fucking curveball my way. This past April, we'd spent a weekend in Vegas—a trip I'd intended to use as a catalyst for a mutual agreement to divorce. Instead, after a night of drinking, we ended up pregnant again. Now don't get me wrong—we were both happy about the impending arrival. I'd wanted another child for years, but Laura had been so focused on her career she'd kept putting it off. She took this pregnancy as a sign that we were meant to repair our relationship, and after some soul-searching on my part, that's what we were trying to do.

I hung her jacket in the closet for her. "Why don't you go upstairs and lie down? I'll call you when dinner's ready."

"Thanks, hun." She flashed me a grateful smile and headed up to our room.

13

It didn't come easy, this reparation phase we were in. At least not for me. My feelings toward my wife were complicated. It's not that I didn't love her anymore—I still did—but it wasn't the same. She was the mother of my daughter and unborn child. She was also the woman I used to be madly head over heels for, the woman I used to think I'd spend the rest of my life with, the person I used to consider my closest friend. See the problem? Too much had changed over the past couple of years, and the love I felt for her was more of the 'nostalgia for the past' kind than the 'throw her down and make passionate love to her' kind. I cared about her, and I certainly didn't wish anything bad for her, but I knew deep down I wasn't *in* love with her. Not the way she wanted me to be. I'd hoped maybe I could rediscover those old feelings, but I was wrong. They weren't coming back. Not as long as I was in love with someone else, anyway.

I'd cut all ties with Amelia, as Laura had insisted upon. And you know? Laura hadn't brought her up to me since. Not once. Not a single question if I'd heard from her, no snide comments, no nothing. She clearly considered the matter closed. Which meant one of three things: I was doing a fucking Oscar-worthy performance of hiding how much I missed Amelia, Laura was a lot more oblivious than I would've thought she'd be, or—and this is the most likely—she just didn't give a shit. She'd won. She had me. Amelia didn't. And Laura knew I'd keep my promise to her. I wasn't going anywhere.

Alexis was filling water glasses to set on the table when Laura came into the kitchen, one hand absentmindedly rubbing her belly. "Smells great," she said, stifling a yawn.

"You fall asleep?"

"For a few minutes. I wish I could shake this constant exhaustion. One of these days I'm going to nod off right in the middle of my news report."

I chuckled. "It's only gonna get worse before it gets better. But don't worry; I'm sure you'll be back to your old self in about…oh, three years or so."

She glared at me. "Gee, thanks. *That's* a comforting thought."

"Good thing you've got me around to help you out then, huh?" I winked at her. "Just remember: you *could* be stuck with one of those husbands who expects his wife to not only work full time, but also take care of the kids and do all the cooking and cleaning."

Rolling her eyes, she said, "Yes, I guess I'm lucky I married Mr. Domestic. Which is something you never fail to remind me of."

"Who? Me?" I set a bowl of steaming pasta on the table and pulled out her chair for her.

Light, teasing moments like these I could handle. With Laura, I could deal with light; most of the time now I could slip into it like an old pair of gloves. It was the more difficult, serious subjects I avoided. If I let myself dwell on that stuff for any length of time, I'd get angry. And getting angry would accomplish nothing.

"When's your next OBGYN appointment?" I asked. I always tried to free up my schedule so I could take her to these. At the last one, she'd had the ultrasound that showed us we were having another girl, much to our delight.

"Um, next week. Friday morning I think? I can text you."

"No need. I'm sure it's in my phone."

Lex's eyes lit up. "Will you get to see inside your belly again? Can I come? I wanna see my baby sister."

"Not next week, no. But I'll let you know if my doctor wants to do any more ultrasounds. If he does, I'll see if they'll let us bring you along."

"Yay!"

Laura took a bite of pasta and then turned to me. "Is James coming over tonight to watch the game with you?"

Before I could answer, Alexis jumped in "Yes! Grandpa promised to play Barbies with me."

I laughed. "He's probably already on his way."

After we finished dinner, Laura helped me clean up, although I tried to convince her to go sit down with Alexis. She finally agreed after she finished making Lex's school lunch.

"If it's not too late when he leaves, come up and spend some time with me," she said, pushing a loose strand of red hair behind one ear. I detected an unnatural note of hesitation in her voice. Instead of turning to look at her, I stiffened, then immediately made myself relax. For a long time after we'd reunited, I'd continued to sleep in the spare room. Once I finally agreed to move back into the master bedroom, I thought it might be easier, but I still couldn't shake my discomfort. We both knew I usually came to bed after she was already asleep.

Before I could reply, she added, "We could watch that new detective show. If I can manage to stay awake for it."

This time I turned and shot her what I hoped was a believable grin. "Sure," I agreed.

Apparently I failed at credibility, or more likely, she just knew me too well. Her hopeful look fell away, and she arched one perfectly tweezed eyebrow. "Or not. Do what you wanna do." She turned on her heel and walked away.

I knew she felt rejected, but I didn't go after her. No matter what I told myself, I couldn't seem to help how I reacted to her come-ons. Even pregnant, she was one hell of a sexy woman. Lots of guys would kill to be in my shoes. Yet I still maintained this distance between us. For once in my life, I didn't even wonder what was wrong with me. I knew damn well.

A few minutes later, the doorbell rang, and I heard Alexis run to open it.

"Hi Grandpa," she said brightly as I came into the entranceway. The minute my dad saw her, a wide smile stretched his face. I loved how much they'd grown to love each other, right from their first meeting. He bent down to give her a hug, looking up at me over her shoulder.

"Hey guys. Hope I'm not interrupting dinner."

"Nope, we're all done. C'mon in."

Alexis led him off to play while I caught up on some work in my office in the upstairs spare room that I used to sleep in. Laura had come down to say hello, but then went back to lie down again. When it was Lex's bedtime, we let James read her a story before the three of us took turns tucking her in.

James and I returned downstairs and put on the hockey game. I'd only been vaguely interested in the sport before I met him, but since we'd been hanging out I'd gotten a lot more into it. Until recently, he'd spent most of his adult life living in Buffalo, so he was a big Sabres fan. Though not the worst team in the league by any stretch, most years they weren't exactly Stanley Cup contenders. I got a perverse pleasure in seeing them lose; it was fun to rub in my dad's face what a shitty team he supported. I didn't have a favorite team myself, but I told him it was the Pittsburg Penguins, knowing me cheering for Buffalo's rival would annoy him the most.

Neither team was playing tonight, but I poured us some drinks and we watched the game companionably.

"Laura not feeling well?" James asked soon after we sat down.

I shrugged. "Nah, she's fine. She's always tired these days. This pregnancy's taking a lot out of her."

"Ah." He nodded. "But everything's okay with the baby, right?"

"Oh yeah, all good."

He didn't say anything more for a few minutes. Then he asked, "So how're things between you two?"

I looked at him, a small frown tightening my brows.

"We're okay. Just doing the best we can."

James raised his eyes to mine. Our blue eyes were so similar that when I looked at him it sometimes felt like I was staring into a magic mirror at my older self. And I couldn't help hoping older me would be a lot happier with his life.

"You sure?"

I sighed. "It's not perfect. We still have a long way to go, but we're working on it."

"No one said it'd be easy. But you're still not happy." It wasn't a question.

I took a sip of my whiskey and turned my focus back to the television. "I'm trying to be."

"Have you seen her?" He meant Amelia, although he didn't know her name.

"Nope."

"Been in contact with her?"

"Nope."

"That must be difficult. I know from experience how hard it is to let go of someone you love. Especially when you blame yourself for it." I knew he was thinking of my mom. They had both been young, and he'd gotten scared and left her when she'd been pregnant with me. He'd regretted that choice every day of his life since.

Picking up my glass again, I downed the rest of my drink. Then I heaved another long, low sigh. "It sucks. But we have to live with the consequences of our actions, don't we?"

James opened his mouth as if he were about to argue this point, but then he shut it again. It didn't matter; I knew what he was thinking. He didn't want me to have to live with the same sort of regrets he did. But this wasn't the same. I was standing by my wife and children. I was doing the right thing for my family. I just needed to keep telling myself that.

Later, after James had left, I went upstairs to get ready for bed. A twinge of guilt hit me when I walked into the bedroom, but right along with it came a rush of relief.

Laura was already asleep.

Chapter 3

Declan

Was it the worst day of my life? It was certainly right up there with the day my mother died, and that was over twenty-eight years ago. So, yeah. No fucking contest. But looking back, if I'm being honest, that day was merely the catalyst for many god-awful days. Which one earned the ultimate title of Worst Day? I couldn't even guess. There were more than I could count. But every facsimile of a perfect life that anyone might've thought I had shattered that day.

I don't actually remember a large chunk of it. Probably on purpose. It's funny how the mind sometimes blocks stuff out to protect itself. As if there was any protection to be had.

I do remember that, though the skies were gloomy, the day started out pretty good. I was working with Josh Marshall, which was always the best way to pass time at the office. Josh was our Senior Accountant at Baker, Wright, and Kavanaugh. He and his fiancée, Holly, were getting married in three months and I was his best man. We spent most of the morning working out numbers for a big meeting in the afternoon, but over lunch we discussed plans for his bachelor party. He wanted something simple and local, but I was still trying to convince him to go big. Not Vegas-big—I had no urge to *ever* return to that city—but I wanted us to at least get the hell out of Lynchburg.

The first hint that my day was about to take a free fall happened shortly after three o'clock. One of my most lucrative clients called to move our meeting to five. Thing was, Alexis' babysitter couldn't keep her late tonight. She needed to be picked up by five-thirty. Now there was no chance I'd be able to get her by then.

Heaving a deep sigh, I picked up my cell and frowned at the screen. Laura was going to be pissed, but I needed her to help me out with this one. So I called her at work.

"Laura Logan," she answered after the fourth ring. She sounded distracted.

"Hey. How're you feeling today?"

"Uncomfortable. I'm always uncomfortable. Being pregnant sucks. What's up?"

"Well... actually I need you to do me a big favor. My meeting with Frank from ConnectAssure just got pushed to five, which means I can't pick up Lex today. Is there any way you could come grab her and take her back to the station with you? Mrs. Haverford has a thing tonight—she made me swear on my life I'd get her by five-thirty."

"I can't, Declan. I have to be on air at six. You know that. Can't you ask Ryan or Josh to take her for an hour?"

Ryan's my brother—well, half-brother, as I'd discovered last year when I met my real dad—and also an Account Executive at BWK. Unfortunately, I already knew he couldn't help me with this particular problem.

"Josh's in the meeting with me, and Ryan's out of town," I told her. "But if you leave now you could pick her up and still make it back with time to spare."

"But—"

Before she could argue, I continued, "Look, I know you're busy, too, and I hate to ask, but ConnectAssure's my biggest client. They're being courted by another agency and I need to convince them to stay with us. It's kind of a huge deal."

"And my career isn't?"

I sighed. "I didn't say that. You know I wouldn't ask if I had any other options. *Please*?"

There was a pause. I heard a long huff. Then: "Fine."

I leaned back in my chair, swiping a relieved hand over my eyes. "Thanks. I owe ya. Text me when you guys leave the studio and I promise to have dinner ready the minute you get home."

"You owe me is right." Another pause, longer this time. "Good luck with your meeting."

"I'll need it. Hey, I really appreciate this."

"I know. Love you."

I hesitated a second. I couldn't help it; saying those three words to Laura didn't come easy anymore. But she was doing me a solid and she knew it. "You, too. See you guys later." I hung up.

The truth was that Ryan wasn't actually out of town. He was helping his ex-wife-slash-current-girlfriend Diana move back in to his house. Diana was the Accounting Department Manager which made her Josh's boss. We worked together on the regular, but I was far from her favorite person. The feeling was mutual, however because of Ryan we tolerated each other. Most of the time.

Did I mention nepotism had not gone out of style at BWK? My own career was a prime example. Ryan's father and my adoptive father, Patrick Kavanaugh, was one of the partners, and though we were both skilled salesmen now, we had gotten in here because of him. My relationship with both Ryan and Patrick used to be...well, *strained* might be a good way to put it. It was vastly improved these days though, proving not everything in my life had gone to complete shit over the past six months.

Since Ryan and Diana's reconciliation, my brother had been in a much better place. He was a recovering addict, and his drug of choice wasn't heroin or crack, but prescription painkillers, which in many ways were just as bad. They were a hell of lot easier to get his hands on, something he knew all too well. Last fall, the stupid bugger had nearly offed himself by ODing. In the parking lot at work, no less. Luckily, Diana had discovered him in time, and he'd landed his ass in the hospital for the pleasure of getting his stomach pumped. Then he'd done a stint in rehab. Fortunately, neither Diana nor I had seen any signs of him slipping over the past year, and believe me, we kept a close eye on him. It was one of the few things we agreed on.

Yesterday, Ryan had mentioned Diana wanted to get her stuff moved over this afternoon. Though I'd never be her biggest fan, I knew she loved him and was good for him, so I figured them shacking up again made sense. Hell, maybe they'd even remarry. As long as he was happy and sober, I was all for it.

I still had another half hour before I needed to head down to the boardroom for the meeting, so I grabbed the case file for ConnectAssure and began reviewing their last three years' history. As I flipped pages, I found a print ad quote from a little over a year ago. The accountant who'd prepared it was Amelia York.

It wasn't unusual to still run across her name in the case files. I mean, she'd only quit a little over six months ago; I'd probably still be spotting her work for a while yet. My normal reaction was to divert myself from sliding down that treacherous path by focusing on some other aspect of what I was working on, but this time my mind refused to let go. An image of a pretty woman with long auburn hair and big brown eyes flashed into my head. She was smiling; I always pictured her smiling. I couldn't bear to imagine her any other way, although the guilt I felt at having taken away that smile, at having hurt her so badly, gnawed at me.

We'd had a lot of amazing times together and I chose instead to remember those: when I'd been the reason for that smile, when we'd shared a laugh, or, best of all, those too few, yet unforgettable moments when I'd caused her to make much more pleasurable sounds. Sometimes I swore I still heard her voice and I'd turn, expecting to see her face light up when those amazing doe eyes met mine.

Picking up my phone again, I scrolled through my contacts until I found her name. I hadn't deleted it, although I often told myself I should. Without thinking, I hit the Call button. It rang twice, and then I heard a soft voice say "Hello?" She sounded guarded, and I didn't blame her. I hung up without speaking.

Whether I wanted to or not, I still loved Amelia York. The hardest choice I'd ever made had been to let her go.

And every minute of every day it killed me inside.

"Hey."

I looked up from my painful and utterly pointless reverie to find Josh in my doorway.

"Catch you in La-La Land?" he teased.

Heat rose to my cheeks as I closed the file. I attempted to laugh it off. "Nah, just going over how we're gonna convince ConnectAssure to stick around."

Josh looked unconvinced. Tilting his head, he asked, "Sure that's all?"

He knew me far too well, but where my mind had wandered was a subject that was strictly off limits these days, a fact of which he was well aware. I nodded. "That's all."

He dropped into one of the guest chairs across from my desk. The same one she always used to sit in. *Nope.* I mentally swatted that memory away.

"Look outside lately?"

I turned to my window. The blinds had been drawn all day. Pushing apart two of the slats, I peered out into swirls of white. My eyes shot wide. "Holy shit! Was that in the forecast?"

Josh shook his head. "Freak November storm took a turn south. Down from Canada, apparently. Glad I don't have to drive to Swann's Landing anymore."

Frowning, I thought of Laura heading this way to pick up Alexis. She was a good driver, I reminded myself. And she had the Rover, which had excellent traction. She'd be fine. I debated texting her to drive carefully, but stopped myself, realizing making her phone beep was a distraction she didn't need if she was focused on the road.

Glancing at my computer monitor, I noticed it was ten to five. "C'mon," I said to Josh. "Let's head down. The coffee should be fresh, and I'm gonna need some serious caffeine to get through this."

Patrick was already in the boardroom, and a few minutes later our receptionist escorted in Frank from ConnectAssure. As I'd presumed, the meeting went long, but the end result was worth it. We agreed to some pricing reductions, and they agreed to stay on for another year. I considered it a win.

When my phone rang about halfway through negotiations, I put it on Mute. It flashed several more times before the meeting ended just after six, but I didn't check my messages until after we'd said our goodbyes and I was on my way back up to my office to grab my jacket.

The first message was from Mrs. Haverford, wondering why Alexis hadn't been picked up yet. So was the second one, her tone irritated that she couldn't reach either Laura or myself.

The third message was from Officer Braxton of the Lynchburg Police Department.

Amelia

Though I'd gone to bed early, I slept poorly, my sleep disrupted by overlapping dreams that fluttered out of my memory's grasp each time I woke. Just before nine, I heard the vibration of my phone against the dresser. Stretched out a blind hand out to grab it, I squinted at the small screen. It was my mother.

"Hi Mom," I answered, my voice rough, unable or maybe unwilling to disguise my irritation.

"Did you hear?" She sounded breathless, even a little excited.

I pushed myself up into a sitting position. "Hear what?"

"Oh Amelia, it's just so awful! I feel so bad for her family. She was the same age as you! And pregnant, too. Just horrible."

Suddenly I was wide awake. "Who was? What happened?"

"Laura Logan was killed last night. She had a head on collision with a truck on the road to Lynchburg."

I didn't respond at first. It was like my brain regressed, all ability to speak forgotten. Finally I just muttered, "No."

"I know, I know. I can hardly believe it myself. I watch her every day on the news. It's so tragic. Did you know her? She went to high school with you, didn't she?"

A stab of fear shot through my haze as I thought of something. "Wait. Was anyone else in the car with her?"

"No, she was alone. On her way home from work. And the truck driver wasn't even injured. Just goes to show..." She continued to talk, telling me more details, but I'd stopped listening. All my thoughts were of Declan.

"I hafta go," I told her, my voice no longer raspy, but still nothing close to normal. I think she protested, but I ended the call anyway. I'd call her back later, once I could think straight.

Stumbling to the bathroom, I splashed cold water on my face. My heart was racing, and a thick lump had risen in my throat. I had that all-too-familiar feeling like I was about to cry. But no tears came.

I began to pace around the apartment. Dee had already left to go open her salon, so I was mercifully alone. My mind still felt like it was submerged in water, everything around me muffled and distant.

Poor Declan.

I tried to imagine how he must be feeling, losing his wife and unborn child in one horrific blow, but I just couldn't wrap my head around it. Then I thought of Alexis. The poor girl was only four and a half: far too young to be without her mom. I felt terrible for them both.

Part of me wanted to reach out to him, needing more than anything to find him and wrap my arms around him. But a bigger part knew contacting him was a bad idea. I couldn't make any of this better. In fact, I was probably the last person he'd want to hear from right now.

I tried calling Josh, but it went straight to voice mail. Maybe he was with Declan. He probably was, and I was thankful. Much as I wished it could be me, I was glad to know Josh would be there for him when I couldn't.

I got dressed, although I didn't notice which clothes I threw on. Stuffing my phone and keys into my pocket, I grabbed my coat and left the apartment. The snow from yesterday's freak storm was melting away, but though the sun shone, a chill lingered in the air. I turned up my collar and started walking. My stomach growled, demanding nourishment, or at least coffee, but I ignored it.

I must've walked for hours. I don't remember where I went, which streets I crossed, which green spaces I cut through. My thoughts swirled almost like I was drunk. They were fleeting, unimportant and quickly forgotten. Mostly. There *was* one that forced its way to the surface—one selfish, unwanted, yet painfully honest thought. As awful as it sounds, I suddenly wondered if this could end up being a positive for me. Without Laura in the picture, might there at last be a chance for us? Could Declan and I eventually have a future together after all?

Ugh, stop!

I shoved that thought away, hating myself for even thinking it. There was nothing good about this situation. Nothing.

I kept going. Waves of guilt washed over me at intervals, but that weird sense of numbness remained.

I'm not sure what time I returned to the apartment, but Dee wasn't back yet. I tried to nap, but couldn't. I tried to eat, but though my stomach continued to rumble, I couldn't do that either. I craved a drink, even going so far as grabbing a glass and opening the cupboard where we kept the vodka. But after staring at it blankly for a few moments, I put it back. Instead, I curled up on the couch in front of the television, no clue what was on, just staring into space with my arms around my knees.

Dee walked in the door shortly after six and found me in the same position. The moment she saw me, she came over and sat beside me. "I heard," she said. "Liv messaged me, and it's all over Facebook." She rubbed my shoulder. "You okay?"

I didn't know if I was, but I nodded.

"I texted you a few times. Were you sleeping?"

Had she? I hadn't even noticed. I slid my phone from my pocket and saw I'd missed not only Dee's messages, but also one from Liv, and another call from my mother. All wanting to talk to me about the same thing. With a sigh, I said, "Sorry. I wasn't checking my phone much."

She scrutinized my face, frowning. "I can see you're upset, but I hope you don't feel guilty. I get why you might, but you shouldn't. It was an *accident*. A horrific accident, but still. An accident."

"I know."

"You wanna talk about it?"

"Not really," I told her. "I think I'm just gonna go to bed."

I didn't think I'd be able to sleep, but I drifted off right away. The nightmares persisted, and once again I woke late feeling exhausted and out of it. I still wasn't too hungry, but I forced down some crackers and dragged on my coat for another walk.

Dee returned that evening with her girlfriend, Terri, and once again found me lying in front of the television.

"Aw, sweetie," Dee said. I shifted upright so she could sit beside me. The sudden change in position after being horizontal for so long made me light-headed.

Terri took the nearby chair. "How's it goin'?" She was a short, free-spirited Texan, very laid back and in many ways the opposite of Dee, but I really liked her. They'd been dating for a few months and in my opinion seemed great together.

I shrugged.

"Is it okay if I tell her?" Dee asked quietly.

Shrugging again, I said, "Go ahead." I wasn't in the mood to rehash my sordid history, so I dragged my butt off the couch and went to take a much-needed shower while she filled Terri in.

When I emerged, smelling significantly better but still as out of it as ever, they both looked up at me with sympathy.

"That's rough. Seriously rough," Terri said.

"Yeah."

I went to reclaim my spot on the couch, but before I could sit, Dee said, "We were thinking of going down to The CP for pizza. Come with?"

I shook my head. "I'm not really up for going out."

"C'mon. Fresh air would do you good. Let us distract you for a bit."

I thought of telling her I went for a two hour walk earlier. I considered saying I wasn't really hungry. Instead I just sighed. "Fine. Give me a minute to change."

After throwing on clean jeans and a hoodie, and running a brush through my hair, I rejoined them. We walked a block down the street to Dee's favorite pizza pub, The Cheesy Pint. Spotting an empty curved booth in the corner, we slid in. I ended up sandwiched between them instead of the two of them side by side like usual. I asked if either wanted to switch places with me, but they declined.

Dee ordered a pitcher of beer for them. I stuck with water, still not sure alcohol would be a smart idea.

Once the server disappeared to the kitchen with our food order, Terri turned to me. "How you doin' now?" she asked.

"Still pretty numb," I sighed.

"Hmm." Her eyes darted to Dee, then back to me. "Mind if I ask a few questions?" The word *ask* came out like *axe*. "If you don't wanna answer, just say."

"Sure." I took a sip of ice water. It was too cold on my throat, but at the same time felt wonderful.

"How were you the night of the accident? Sleep okay?"

I thought about it, and then shook my head. "I haven't been sleeping very well lately. Loads of weird dreams."

"That's no good. You feel sad?"

"Of course!" I was a bit offended. How could she even ask that?

"The other night, though? Before you heard?"

I shrugged. "I guess. A bit. But I get like that sometimes." My eyes shot to Dee's and she reached over to squeeze my hand. After five months of living together, she was pretty used to my messy emotions.

"Other than sad, how d'you feel now?"

I didn't know where Terri was going with this, but I tried to play along. "Pretty spaced out, honestly."

"Hold on," Dee cut in. "Ames, you didn't even *like* Laura. In fact, I think it would be fair to say you pretty much hated her. I know you feel bad for *him*, but this seems a little extra. Why're you so mopey?"

I turned to look at her, eyes wide. "I didn't hate her!" Dee started to protest, but I held up a hand. "And even if she wasn't exactly my favorite person, none of that matters. She had a daughter and…and a husband, and I'm completely devastated for them."

Dee arched an eyebrow. "Okay, sure. I get that. I do. But I mean, isn't a part of you secretly a little...you know… kinda happy? Not to be callous, but the biggest obstacle to you two being together is out of the way now."

My face felt like it was on fire. I broke eye contact and stared down at my glass. "I'm *not* happy about this. I feel *horrible*," I muttered, glancing back at her. "And guilty. How could I not after what I…we…did? I'm sure he does, too. Oh God, he must be just shattered!" That last word came out in a rasp. My throat had become tight and sore.

I heard Dee sigh. "Happy was the wrong word," she said. "It's not like I thought you'd be dancing on her grave or anything. I guess I meant more like *hopeful*."

Swallowing hard, I shook my head. I wasn't about to admit that exact thought had occurred to me yesterday. I'd already been selfish enough and felt bad enough. And I kind of hated myself for it.

"Not that getting back with him, like *ever*, would be a good idea," she added. "Far from it. But it's totally natural you might see it as a possibility now."

I didn't reply; I just had another drink of water, wishing more than ever that the liquid in my glass was vodka. At least the cold eased the pain in my throat.

Terri glanced between us. She looked like she was debating something.

Dee noticed. "What is it, babe?"

"It's clear how upset you are," Terri said to me. "Maybe you should reach out? I'm sure he'd appreciate it." She flashed me a reassuring smile.

"Bad idea," Dee stated emphatically before I could reply. She glared at her girlfriend. "I know you mean well, but you weren't there when all the shit went down. You don't understand. No matter how bad Ames feels right now, she needs to keep well away from that man."

"Well now, don't you think that's up to Amelia to decide? Maybe letting him know she's thinking of him could ease some of this helplessness she's feeling?"

My eyes darted between them, watching them discuss me like I wasn't even there. Dee had been protective of me since I'd moved in, which made sense as she was the only one who knew how badly I'd taken the breakup. It was clear she hadn't shared my most private, most shameful part of that day with Terri, and I was deeply grateful for her discretion.

"No, Dee's right," I said. "Contacting him is a terrible idea. I'm sure I'm the last person he'd want to hear from anyway. But his best friend is a good friend of mine. I'll call Josh tomorrow and see how things are."

That seemed to settle the topic and a minute later the waiter returned with our pizzas.

I felt a bit better after hearing Dee and Terri's thoughts and knowing how much they cared about me. But they didn't understand. They thought they did, especially Dee, but she didn't. She couldn't. If there were other women that had gone through what I was going through, I would never know about them. Because the reason I felt the way I did was because of the awful choices I'd made. There was no one else who could get it. I was alone in this.

I hadn't lied to them, though. I did want to talk to Josh as soon as possible. But not to find out how things were. I already knew.

The man I loved whether I liked it or not was in sheer hell.

And there wasn't a single thing I could do to make things better.

Chapter 4

Amelia

The next morning I was much more functional. I still felt awful for Declan, but that weird haze that had clung to me the past two days had finally lifted. The guilt remained, but then again, it never really went away anymore; it just swelled and faded depending on what each day brought.

I had just sat down to run some numbers for Dee's salon when my phone rang. It was Josh, at last returning my call.

"Hey," I answered. "Thanks for calling. I know you're probably slammed right now."

"Pretty crazy, yeah." He sighed. "So, how're you doing?"

I exhaled a rueful laugh. "I'm okay, but that's not important. I'm just really worried." I paused. "I know he's not even slightly okay, and I know there's nothing I can do to help, but..."

Before I could go on, Josh said, "You are so important, Amelia. Don't ever think that. And yeah, he's pretty messed up. He's ...well, he's as you'd expect. I'm trying to be with him as much as I can. So is Ryan. And his dad. He's not alone."

"Good," I breathed. A lump rose in my throat. "I wish I could be there, too."

Another soft sigh. "I know you do. So far, he hasn't had to do too much heavy lifting. He's letting Laura's parents take care of

29

all the arrangements. The funeral's gonna be in Swann's Landing, at the same place your dad's was."

"Blair and Sons?"

"Yeah, that's it."

I remembered Declan telling me a few days after my father's service that he'd had a panic attack in the parking lot and hadn't been able to bring himself to come inside. He had a deep loathing of funeral homes since his mom passed away when he was a boy. Not that anyone really liked them—I'd be happy if I never stepped foot inside one again—but this was going to be extra hard on him.

"When is it?" I asked.

"They're having a private funeral just for family and close friends on Monday, but there's a public visitation Sunday afternoon from one to four. I expect it'll be busy."

"I don't doubt it."

"Will you come?"

I paused to consider my response. "No, I don't think so. I don't think it'd be appropriate."

"Well I think you're overthinking things. But if you're not comfortable, I understand. Just know Holly and I will be there for the whole thing if you change your mind."

"Thanks."

"No problem. Look, I've gotta run, but we'll chat soon, okay?"

"Sure. Hey Josh?"

"Yeah?"

"Take care of him."

"You know I will." He hung up.

I set my phone down and went back to my calculations, but I could no longer concentrate very well. Maybe Josh was right. Maybe I *was* overthinking things. But I still didn't want to go to Laura's visitation. As sorry as I was for the pain Declan and Alexis were going through, Dee had been right last night. I hadn't liked Laura. Not even a little. And I'd feel like a giant hypocrite if I had to hear everyone gushing about what a wonderful person she'd been. Unfortunately, I knew otherwise. It just wasn't going to happen.

I had no idea I was about to be overruled.

A few minutes later, my phone buzzed again. This time it was my mother.

"Hi Mom."

She didn't bother with pleasantries; she just dove straight in. "I've got Laura Logan's service information. They're using Blair and Sons."

"I heard."

"Can you pick me up at twelve-fifteen on Sunday? I think there'll be a line to get in. Everyone I've spoken to is planning to go."

"Oh. I, uh, I wasn't really planning on going."

"Nonsense. You're from Swann's Landing. You even went to school with her. Of course you're coming with me."

I sighed. The two key words there were *with me*. She didn't care if I wanted to go; she just wanted me to take her.

"Can't you just go with one of your friends?" I suspected any protests would be ignored, but I had to try.

"Possibly, but that's not the point. With your father gone, we're the only two Yorks left, and our family has been here even longer than the Logans. We *both* should go. Together."

Closing my eyes, another sigh slipped out. I already knew I was going to be stuck doing this whether I liked it or not.

"Do I have any choice?"

"No, you do not. See you on Sunday, Amelia. Come over early for lunch first, if you like."

"Fine." I hung up the phone and dragged a hand through my hair.

Crap.

On Sunday morning, I padded into the kitchen a good two hours earlier than usual. Again, I hadn't slept well, but this time I knew exactly why. I'd tossed and turned most of the night, unable to stop worrying about what this afternoon might bring.

Dee was already up, sitting at the counter in front of her laptop. The tantalizing smell of fresh coffee lured me toward the carafe. Yawning, I poured myself a cup and slid onto the stool beside her.

She scrutinized me. Clearly deciding against telling me I looked like crap, she instead turned her computer to face me. "Look what I found."

A professional photo of Laura, presumably taken for work, stared back at me, all toothy smile and perfect curls. It looked like Laura the news anchor, but it sure as heck didn't look much like Laura the person I'd actually known.

"Great," I said, turning away. I blew on the surface of my coffee and took a tentative sip.

"Oh come on." Dee flashed me a wicked grin. "You don't want to read it? A perfectly fake-ass o-*bitch*-uary for a perfectly fake-ass bitch?"

I couldn't help it; I burst out laughing. Slapping a hand over my mouth to stop the giggles, I said, "Mean!"

"Sure. But it's true." Her eyes were twinkling. I knew just what she was doing. She was trying to relax me and lighten my mood, knowing the stressful day I had ahead. And I appreciated it.

"Still. Not appropriate."

"But true."

I pretended to glance around as if there was anyone there to overhear us. "She *was* kind of a bitch," I admitted. "But loads of people loved her. I'm sure I'll be hearing about what a saint she was all afternoon."

Dee narrowed her eyes. "You know, you don't have to go."

Sighing, I muttered, "Yeah. I do."

"You're a grown-ass woman, Ames. You don't have to do anything you don't want to."

With a small chuckle, I replied, "In theory, that's true. In actual practice, not so much." I set down my mug. "Mom really wants me to. I guess it'll be okay."

Dee looked doubtful. "I'm just worried about your emotional well-being. I don't think you seeing him is good for you."

"Today's service is open to the public, so I'm sure it'll be a total madhouse. I won't have to talk to him. He probably won't even see me. I'll just find Josh and Holly and hang with them while Mom works her way through the condolence line."

She arched an eyebrow. "You've got this all figured out?"

I snorted. "No. Not even slightly. My plan is to just keep my head down and get out of there as soon as possible."

"And what will you do if you *do* run into him?"

My eyes shifted away from hers. "He'll be too busy with everyone else to even notice me." I insisted stubbornly.

"Maybe." Dee still looked skeptical. "But for the record, I think this is a terrible idea."

"Duly noted," I smiled, getting to my feet. "I guess I'd better get ready." I was trying my best to act like this was no big deal, like I was just doing a favor for my mother, but inside my anxiety was already climbing.

Once I'd showered, fixed my hair, and put on enough makeup to cover the bags under my eyes, I had to decide what to wear. A lot of my dressier clothes were at my mom's, hanging in the closet of my childhood bedroom where I moved them from the house I used to share with Scott. It was a cool day, so I just threw on jeans and a sweater, figuring I'd change at Mom's.

My eyes shifted to the dresser and the wooden jewelry box on top, nearly hidden beneath stacks of books and envelopes. I walked over and pulled out the drawer, removing a square blue box tucked into the back. Inside was a silver ring on a chain. Not just any silver ring, but one with a little twist along the circumference. A Möbius strip, Josh had told me the night of my thirtieth birthday party. The twist made the ring only have a single infinite surface, he'd explained. I used to run the pad of my finger around the inside and outside of it when I was feeling stressed, which, let's face it, was most of the time.

No one but Josh knew the ring had been a gift from Declan. I didn't know if Declan had understood the symbolism of the Möbius strip when he'd bought it. Probably not. Knowing what I know now, I doubted he'd meant it to represent endless love. I assumed he'd just thought the ring was cool. But it didn't matter. Although it still meant something to me, why he'd chosen it was no longer of any importance.

I hadn't even looked at it in over five months, but for reasons I couldn't quite explain, I fastened it around my neck, letting the ring fall inside my shirt to its familiar place against my chest.

The smell of eggs and bacon frying hit me the moment I opened the front door. I hadn't been feeling very hungry—I assumed due to my apprehension about the service, but as soon as I walked in my stomach started to growl.

I went straight into the kitchen to help Mom. To my surprise, I not only cleaned my plate, but I even went back for seconds, something I hadn't done in a very long time. My mother only ate one egg with toast, but that was normal. She was a tiny woman, and had always had a tiny appetite. I took more after the York side of the family. At least I used to, back before I upended my life.

Mom was right about the amount of people at the funeral home. It was only a little past twelve-thirty, and a lineup already extended around the side of the building and into the parking lot. I lucked out and snagged one of the last two spots. Everyone else would have to park on the street or around the block.

"This is insane," I told her as I turned off the engine. "How about I just drop you off and come back and get you in a couple hours?"

"Don't be silly, Amelia." Mom stepped out of the car, scanning the crowd for any familiar faces. The day was breezy, and the thick clouds blocking the sun promised that winter was just around the corner. As we joined the back of the line, I looked around nervously for Josh or Holly, but didn't spot them. They were probably already inside with the family.

When Blair and Sons opened the front doors, the line surged forward, but it still took us nearly a half hour to reach the entrance. Some of Mom's friends were behind us and she mostly talked with them, leaving me to my thoughts. My anxiety surged and ebbed, surged and ebbed as we inched along; each surge shooting higher, each ebb relaxing less, until my entire body felt like it was resonating.

By the time we got inside the salon sweat dampened my back. Turning my head, I scanned the line stretching outside and thought I spotted the top of Scott's head. I couldn't tell if Liv was beside him or not. She probably was. Great. More people I wasn't sure I wanted to run into.

"Hey."

A hand landed on my forearm. I whipped around to find Josh looking down at me with a tight grin. "Thought you weren't coming?"

I shrugged, indicating my mother, who was still chatting with her friends. "No choice," I mouthed.

"This line is to pay condolences to the family. That's why it's moving so slow," he murmured.

Although my memories of my dad's service were fuzzy, I recalled people doing the same for us. That line hadn't been anywhere near as long as this one, but then again, he hadn't been a small town celebrity.

"I assume you're not up for that. C'mon," Josh urged. "We're hanging out over there beside the coffee station."

Relieved, I told my mom where I'd be and followed him. We worked our way to the back of the room where Holly waited with two paper cups. She handed one to Josh as we

34

approached. "You said she wasn't coming," she scolded him, but she looked pleased to see me.

After giving her a hug, I poured myself some coffee. At first I just focused on Josh or Holly or my coffee, but much as I tried not to, I couldn't seem to stop myself from scanning the room. Ryan and Diana were standing along one wall talking to guests. Patrick Kavanaugh was on the far side of Ryan. Past him stood the Logans. They looked tired, yet stoic. I even saw them smile a few times, and I wondered if the kind things people were undoubtedly telling them about their daughter bolstered their strength.

I could see no coffin. Before I could ask, Josh leaned down and whispered, "She was cremated. The urn is on the dais behind her parents."

My chest tightened with renewed remorse for Declan and Alexis. But I admit I was also a little relieved. Open caskets were the worst, and this particular situation would have been extra brutal. It was one less thing I had to worry about.

Speaking of worrisome things, I couldn't spot Declan. I listened close to see if I could pick out his voice from the cacophony, but I couldn't. I didn't see Alexis either, and wondered if he'd taken her to another room for a break.

"Where's Alexis?" I asked Josh.

"He didn't want to subject her to this, so she's at home with his sister, Miriam. You ever meet her?"

I shook my head. I'd seen Miriam once from a distance, when Declan and his family were having lunch at Finnegan's here in town, but we'd never met. Unfortunately, Declan and I hadn't had the sort of relationship where we could introduce each other to family or friends.

Just as I decided he wasn't here, the lineup surged forward again and I spotted him through the crowd. My gut clenched when I saw his face. Drawn and haggard, he looked like he hadn't slept in weeks. No amount of makeup could have concealed the dark circles around his eyes. As I watched, he dragged a hand through his dark hair, but his fingers couldn't muss it more than it already was. I knew him well enough to realize he'd been doing that for hours.

I didn't think my heart could break further, but I was wrong. This time it had nothing to do with me. It was all about him. The pain I felt was not because of him, but *for* him. I wanted nothing more than to rush to his side, to assure him that I'd always be there for him no matter what.

But I didn't.

I couldn't.

Not anymore.

When he glanced our way, I froze. Those familiar blue eyes at first looked glazed, but they seemed to come into focus when they landed on me. Then the throng of people between us shifted again, blocking my line of view. I couldn't tell if he'd recognized me or not.

I turned to Josh, alarmed. "Oh God. He looks awful," I whispered.

Josh nodded. "Yeah. And this is a *good* day."

"You're kidding?"

"No decisions to make, and he has people to drive him, tell him where he needs to be." Josh bent closer to my ear. "He's also drunk."

My eyes widened. Years ago, before I'd met Declan, I knew he'd had some issues with alcohol, including a DUI that had almost cost him his job. But I remembered how I'd felt the day of my father's service. I could definitely empathize with his choice to numb his senses today.

"Shouldn't you go stand with him?"

"Not yet. He's got James there for support. Hopefully not for literal support before this is over. I'll take my turn in a bit."

I took a sip of coffee and grimaced. It was lukewarm and bitter, so I set the cup on a nearby table. On the other side of the room, I saw my mom clasping hands with Laura's mother and talking intently. I couldn't recall them being friends, but Swann's Landing was a small town so it was no surprise they knew each other.

"We have some news for you, actually," Holly said to me, her eyes darting toward Josh.

"Don't tell me you're pregnant?" It was the first thing that popped into my head. Again, not really any surprise.

She laughed. "No, not ready for that just yet. But we're postponing the wedding."

Their wedding was supposed to be on Valentine's Day. It was less than three months away, and I'd been expecting to receive my invitation soon. Why were they were delaying it?

Before I could ask, Josh bobbed his chin in Declan's direction. "It seemed like the right thing to do, considering."

I nodded. "Right. So, when will it be?"

"We're aiming for next fall." Holly said. "We haven't nailed down a date yet, but we'll let you know once we do. October, I think. The leaves are pretty at that time of year for photos."

"That's a great idea."

Before I could continue, Josh said, "I think your mom's trying to get your attention."

The crowd had parted again and I saw my mother waving frantically at me. She was standing in front of a surprised-looking Declan. "Amelia, come here," she called, her waves now beckoning gestures.

"Crap." I turned to Josh. "What do I do now?"

He looked sympathetic. In a low voice, he said, "As I see it, you have two choices: you can run out the door and hide, or you can suck it up, walk over there, and say hello."

I sighed. "Sometimes being an adult sucks." Then I straightened my spine and worked my way through the crowd until I was standing beside my mother.

"There you are." She put a hand on my shoulder. "Amelia, this is Laura's husband, Declan."

My heart raced as I looked up at him. This was the first we'd been face to face since before everything went horribly wrong. The last time we'd looked into each other's eyes, we'd still been hopeful for a future together. We'd still been in love.

"We, uh, we've already met," I said to Mom in an attempt to stop her from telling me anymore about him. "We used to work together at BWK."

"Really? You never said. I'll let you two catch up, then." To my relief, she moved along to talk to Declan's father.

He and I just stared at each other. I felt like that proverbial deer caught in the headlights, only in my case, the headlights were a pair of somewhat bloodshot blue eyes. Eyes that still stubbornly haunted my dreams.

Finally I just let instinct take over and did what a part of me had wanted to do since the moment I heard the news: I stepped forward and embraced him.

It was a quick hug, the kind old friends who haven't seen each other in a while might share. I could smell the aftershave he'd splashed on, but it wasn't enough to conceal the bitter scent of whiskey beneath. Josh was right; he was drunk. And barely holding it together.

It was stupid, I guess. I probably should have kept my mouth shut. But the smell of him, the nearness of him—it was too familiar. It was too much. I could feel his pain radiating off him, and I just couldn't help it. "I know you're not okay," I whispered. "And I know I'm probably the last person you wanna see right now, but...if you ever need me...I'm here."

I stepped back and offered him a wobbly smile. Declan didn't say a word, but I swear I saw a flicker of gratitude in his eyes.

I told Josh and Holly I'd come visit them soon, said a quick hello to Ryan and Diana, found my mother, and then got us out of there as fast as I could.

On the drive back to Mom's, she kept glancing at me.

"What? Do I have something on my face?"

"Why didn't you tell me you knew Laura's husband?" She sounded reproachful.

I sighed. "I don't know. It didn't seem important."

Mom was quiet for a bit. Once I pulled into the driveway, she turned to me. "Do you know him well?"

"I guess." I shrugged. "I used to, anyway. We haven't kept in touch."

"He's very handsome."

My brows bounced up. "Um, yeah?" All of a sudden I didn't like where I suspected she might be heading. "Mom, I really don't think—"

"I'm not saying right *now*, or anything," she cut in. "It's obviously much too soon. But you're single, and now *he's* single, and perhaps, in a few months, you could—"

"No," I stated emphatically, "that's not gonna happen."

She frowned. "If you say so. You know I just want you to be happy, Amelia."

"I know. And I will be someday, I promise. But it's not going to be with Declan Kavanaugh."

When I got back to Richmond, I went straight to my room and took off the necklace. I put it back in its little box and tucked it beneath some papers and other cases inside my jewelry box. I never should have put it on this morning. It was all too clear that necklace no longer stood for anything, and I was definitely no longer the gullible woman who used to feel such happiness when wearing it.

It was high time to move on.

Declan

Afterward, that entire day merged into one big fucking blur. Well, almost all of it.

I was drunk. Not completely shitfaced—those nights came afterward, and frequently, whenever Alexis stayed at her grandparents, or at a friend's house, which with everyone offering help seemed to be at least once a week—but buzzed enough to take the edge off, yet still appear functional. Miriam had offered to stay home with Alexis the day of the public visitation, for which I was immeasurably grateful, and James drove me to Swann's Landing. So yeah, I was drunk before it began. To get me through. Zero fucks given.

All those damn people. All those somber faces offering meaningless condolences, telling me their favorite memories of Laura, grasping at my hands. None of it meant shit to me. None of it mattered.

The only bit that stood out clearly among all that white noise was Amelia's sudden appearance, her gentle brown eyes drilling into mine and sobering me, at least for a few moments. Seeing her was the last thing I'd expected that day. She even wore the necklace I'd given her for her birthday, although I had no clue why. It was just another layer of guilt to add to all the others. Not only did her being there shock the shit out of me, but what she said shocked me even more.

She didn't offer pointless platitudes. She didn't try to make me feel better. She just understood. She put her arms around me— that in itself something I'd been missing for far too long— and told me she was there.

If you ever need me.

It played over and over in my mind. When I remembered nothing else, I remembered her voice whispering those five words.

Because, God help me, I did. I needed her—hell, I *wanted* her—so bad I thought I might turn inside out. Though I would've given my left arm to turn back time and prevent the accident, to my shame, I wanted her even more than I wanted my dead wife back.

Yeah.

I know.

It was just another reason why I was a total asshole.

I wanted her. But I didn't deserve her. Or, to be clearer, she didn't deserve *me*.

I was a total wreck of a man, bad luck to any woman who had the misfortune to get close to me. Laura and my unborn child were gone because of me.

The only thing that kept me going was Alexis. She needed me. For now. Until she grew up and realized what a shitty excuse for a human being I was, which she inevitably would someday. Then she'd leave me. And I wouldn't even try to convince her to stay. Because leaving me would be the best decision she'd ever make.

I deserved to be alone.

Laura had deserved a better husband.

Alexis deserved a better father.

And Amelia? Amelia deserved to spend her life with a man who would always put her first and make her happy.

I wasn't capable of making anyone's life happy.

I was only capable of destruction.

Chapter 5

Amelia

The months after Laura's death passed with a weird sense of monotony. They drifted along in painstaking increments, yet at the same time seemed to whip by faster than I could comprehend. I know that makes no sense, but that's how it felt. Time passed. And I barely noticed.

The grief that had overwhelmed me back in June was still there, clinging on deep inside, but I'd learned to live with it. It didn't control me anymore. I had switched to taking St. John's Wort, an herbal remedy that was supposed to alleviate depression, as I could no longer afford my anti-depressants without a benefit plan. It seemed to help, although not as well as the prescription pills had. I also still saw Debbie Westwood when I could, but as my therapy appointments were also not covered, I'd reduced the frequency of my visits.

I spent Christmas Day with my mom, but I didn't really feel like celebrating. To me, Christmas wasn't just a holiday so much as it was its own feeling, a unique blend of emotions that only came over me at that time of year when I was surrounded by my loved ones sharing not just gifts and food and laughter, but creating new memories together. Without my dad, without Scott, without Declan in my life, there was no laughter, no happiness. I went through the motions for my mother's sake, but I could no longer feel Christmas. So I put in the necessary time with her, but otherwise tried to hide until it was over.

Other than the holiday, I hadn't made an effort to go see Mom much since the funeral. I didn't want to talk about my ex, or my lack of employment, or—least of all—Laura's death, and she didn't want to talk about my Dad, or selling the house, which limited our conversations to awkward small talk. It felt like too much effort to avoid all these meaningful subjects, so I made a conscious choice to stay away.

In February, Dee and Terri tried to set me up with a friend of theirs. At first I was resistant, but after a few weeks of pestering I finally gave in. His name was Jorge, and he was the web designer who had built Dee's salon's site. He picked me up in a silver Mercedes and took me to The Happy Tomato, assuring me it was one of the best restaurants in Richmond.

Jorge was tall, with straight dark hair, and eyes even deeper brown than my own. He opened my doors for me, pulled out my chair, and was generally sweet, but there was no spark. At least not on my end. He was cute and nice, but it was too soon. I was still too numb inside. When he drove me home and asked if he could see me again, I was honest with him. I told him I really liked him and hoped we'd stay in touch through Dee's social circle, but that I was sorry but I wasn't in the right place emotionally to date yet. He was a total gentleman and said he completely understood. Then he got out of the car, opened my door for me and walked me inside.

I suppose I was lucky to have such a nice guy be interested, but after that one date I knew I needed to stay single. At least for now. Maybe for forever. At this point, it seemed like forever alone was my future. After what I'd done to my husband, it was probably what I deserved.

My thirty-first birthday rolled around in March, but I didn't care. It just made me melancholy for how happy I'd been the previous birthday. It fell on a Saturday this year, and my Mom invited me over for lunch. Afterward, I promised Josh and Holly I'd drive into Lynchburg and visit them.

Mom gave me a sweater and a bottle of wine. Not that I'd told her, but I barely drank anymore. I'd realized during one of my periods of reminiscing and writing about the past year and a half that I tended to lean on alcohol in times of stress. Which, in hindsight, was pretty often. So I'd cut back on drinking, raising a glass with Dee and Terri at New Year's Eve, but not much more.

After lunch, I didn't linger. I helped my mother with the dishes, then thanked her for the gifts and headed out. Driving north between Swann's Landing and Lynchburg made me think of Laura's accident. Though the pavement was dry and the day was clear, my anxiety spiked and I cut back my speed.

My friends' new house was a wide blue bungalow with neatly trimmed hedgerows bracketing their front yard. Josh saw me pull into the driveway and came out to greet me wearing a red polka-dotted party hat, which made me laugh.

"There's the Birthday Girl," he said as he pulled me into a hug. Holly stood in the doorframe, smiling.

"Your house is adorable. Give me a tour?"

My absolute favorite thing about their place was the cute little backyard. They had a wooden deck with cozy chairs on it and it seemed like a relaxing place to hang out. Once the weather warmed up, they promised to have me over for a barbeque.

An hour or so later, Josh had gone to the store, and I stood at the kitchen sink peeling potatoes as Holly seasoned pork chops for dinner.

"So, Amelia…do you mind if I ask you a personal question?" Holly said, clearly attempting to sound casual.

I stiffened. I had no idea how much, if anything, Josh had already told her, but I had a pretty good idea what she was about to ask.

"Go ahead," I replied, also trying to keep my voice light.

"I know it's none of my business, and you absolutely don't have to tell me if you don't want to, but Josh has dropped a few hints, and I've been curious for a long while now." She paused, closing the oven door and turning to me. "Did something happen between you and Declan last year when Laura was in New York?"

Heat flooded my face. "Um…" I looked down at the potato I was holding and sighed. Was I willing to admit what I'd done and risk Holly thinking less of me?

Her eyes widened. "It's okay. Just forget I asked."

I cleared my throat and muttered, "No, I…it's just not something I like to talk about. But…yeah."

Although I was deeply ashamed that I'd cheated on Scott, I decided to tell her what happened. It wasn't fair to expect Josh to keep such a huge secret from his fiancée. So I started in on the long, sordid story while we prepared dinner. Once everything was cooking, we continued our conversation in the living room. Josh returned before I was finished and he seemed relieved that Holly was finally in the loop.

After I explained why and how Declan had ended things, deliberately leaving out the most private bits, Josh returned to the kitchen to check on dinner.

Holly shifted closer to me on the couch and hugged me. "That must have been awful."

"It was," I sighed. "I hope you don't think I'm a horrible person. I know what I did to Scott was unforgivable. I know I should have ended things with him first."

She seemed surprised. "You're not a horrible person. I could never think that."

"Yeah, I kind of am. I swear I never meant to fall for Declan, though. We both resisted for a long time, but eventually we just…we just couldn't any longer. He was separated, and I knew my marriage was over, but I still should've waited until I was separated, too, but… I didn't. We didn't."

"You fell in love. Your timing sucked, but these things happen. It also sucks that people got hurt, of course, but that was pretty much inevitable."

"Yeah," I nodded. "It sucked all right. It still sucks sometimes."

Josh came back into the room. "I'm glad you told Holly. I didn't like keeping this from her."

"Me too." I paused, biting my lip. Then I met Josh's eyes. "So, how's he doing?"

His face grew serious. "Not so great. He's drinking way too much, at least whenever Alexis isn't there. Laura's parents take her overnight most Saturdays to give him a break, and he drinks himself into a stupor pretty much every time."

I frowned. "That's worrying."

"Yeah. I'm gonna go see him later tonight. I try to keep him company most Saturdays, at least when I can. If I'm busy, his dad usually goes over. Did I tell you James and I keep in touch these days? We think it's best if he's not left alone too much."

Swallowing hard, I remembered my lowest moment, when my own depression combined with alcohol had led to some very dark thoughts, and a very dumb decision. Fear gripped me. Josh was right, Declan shouldn't be left alone. "You don't think he'd do anything stupid, do you?"

Josh shook his head. Though that was one secret of mine he didn't know, he understood what I meant. "Nah. And even if he did sink that low, he'd never do that to Alexis. He adores that kid. She's pretty much his entire life now."

"Are you sure? Grief really messes up your head." I never would have thought I was capable of it either, of doing that to Scott and my mother and my friends, but I hadn't been thinking straight at all that day.

He frowned. "I'm pretty sure. But James and I are keeping an eye on him."

"Good," I said firmly. "Because..." I trailed off with a shudder, not able to even voice the words.

"Don't worry. He's got a circle around him. Ryan keeps tabs on him, too. Even Patrick is being super supportive. I just don't like him getting loaded alone. It gives him too much time to dwell on shit."

"I know all about that."

"Kinda figured you might."

I gave him a weak smile, grateful for both his friendship and the friendship he provided to Declan that I couldn't.

Holly had been quiet while we talked, but now she piped up. "On a lighter note, we've got a new wedding date."

I turned to her, happy for a change of topic. "Oh good! When?"

"September 29th. Same church, but the reception is going to be at the Hilton downtown now. I hope you can still make it."

"It's not like I have a busy social schedule anymore," I laughed. "Of course I'll be there. I wouldn't miss it."

But inside, I wasn't so confident. It was still a little over six months off, and a lot could change in that time, but the thought of spending the day at an event that Declan would also be at caused panicky tendrils of anxiety to tighten. Anxiety that stubbornly commanded: *Stay away!*

Declan

I tried my damnedest to be Mr. Responsible Dad all week, but once Alexis went to her grandparents on Saturday afternoons, I admit I felt a sense of relief. I missed her when she was away—don't get me wrong, I loved my daughter more than anything—but I allowed myself one night a week of self-indulgence. Or self-pity, as the case tended to be. When I was alone, there was no need to suck it up and pretend I was fine.

Lately Josh had started dropping by to hang with me on Saturday evenings. I wasn't an idiot—I knew why he did it, but I didn't mind. He was one of only two people in my life that I could let loose around. The other was my father. There used to be a third, but as seemed to be my habit, I went and fucked up that relationship beyond repair.

I'd just popped the cap off my third beer when Josh rang the doorbell. I was in a rare half-decent mood. Drunk or sober, those were few and far between anymore, and I relished them. I flung open the door and waved him past me with a, "Duuude!"

He pointed at the beer in my hand. "Started already, huh?"

I turned on the drama, rolling my eyes and shaking my head. "You expected me to wait for you?"

Josh laughed, probably relieved I wasn't my usual grumpy-ass self. Handing him a beer, I led the way to the family room where I'd been watching hockey. Buffalo was playing New York, and at the moment they were getting their ass handed to them. I knew full well James would be watching this game too and probably bitching at the television.

Josh sat on the couch beside me. "This one looks to be already over," he observed with a chuckle.

"Yeah, but I still like watching the Sabres take a thrashing. Gives me something to rib Dad about tomorrow."

He picked up his bottle with a snort. But instead of taking a drink, he just held it, his other hand drumming his fingers against his knee.

I had a swig of my own, enjoying the buzz that had now settled over me like the embrace of an old friend—one of those tricky friends whom you couldn't always trust, but an old friend nonetheless.

"So what were you guys up to today?" I asked.

Glancing at me, Josh hesitated. His expression seemed cautious, which made me wonder what he was hiding.

"What?" I teased. "Something secret? Spend all afternoon in bed?"

"No. No secrets." Josh laughed with a shake of his head. After a beat, he added, "Amelia came over to see the new place." He had turned to look at me now, scrutinizing my reaction. "Today's her birthday."

At first, I just stared back at him and tried keep my face neutral. Then I muttered, "I know."

It had been in the back of my mind most of the day. Shortly before Josh had arrived, I'd even picked up my phone and begun to text her a happy birthday. But for once in my life, common sense prevailed. No matter how awesome it might seem at the time, drunk texting an ex is *never* a good idea. I'd closed the text, wondering yet again why I hadn't been able to bring myself to delete her number. No good could come from contacting her.

"How's she doing?" I lifted my feet onto the coffee table as if none of this was any big deal.

Josh arched a brow. "Is this the type of question where I'm just supposed to say 'great' and we move on? Or do you want the truth?"

I sighed. Damn him. He knew me too well. "She okay?"

He paused to take a drink of beer. "The truth then. She pretends otherwise, but she's doing about as well as you are. I'm worried about her, same as I'm worried about you."

Shit. That wasn't good.

At that moment, my phone beeped and Laura's parents' number popped up on the screen.

"Hey," I answered, expecting my mother-in-law. "Everything okay?"

"Daddy?"

I tried to sober up and switch into Dad-Mode. "Hey Lex. What's up? Why aren't you in bed?"

"I had another bad dream."

Uh oh. I couldn't exactly drive to Swann's Landing and pick her up in this state. She often had nightmares since her mom died, but they nearly always happened when she was home with me. She usually slept pretty well at her grandparents' house. "Oh pumpkin, I'm sorry. Do you wanna tell me about it?"

"It was scary. Mommy was in it. And you. And it was dark. I heard you yelling, but I couldn't find you. I was crying." She sniffled as if to prove her point. "But I don't really 'member."

"That does sound scary. I wish I was there to give you a hug and make you feel better."

"That's okay. I jus' wanted to talk to you. Gramma said I could call."

"Aw, I like to talk to you, too. Of course you can call me. Anytime you want. And I'll see you tomorrow morning and give you a great big hug then."

She sniffled again. "Promise?"

"I promise. You think you can go back to sleep now?"

"I think so. Love you, Daddy."

"Love you, too, kiddo."

I disconnected.

"Everything okay?" Josh asked.

"Lex had another nightmare. I was hoping they would've started to let up by now."

"Are you still taking her to her therapist?"

After the accident, I'd started taking Alexis to see a child psychologist a couple of times a month. From the feedback I'd gotten, and from what I'd seen myself, it seemed to be helping her. Although it felt like a lifetime ago, I remembered how messed up I was after my own mom died of cancer. I lost my childhood that day. There was little time for grief; I had to step up and help take care of my kid brother. I learned way too young to bury all my sadness deep inside. It changed me, and I was never the same carefree boy again.

Because of this, I couldn't help worrying about Alexis growing up too fast. But I also knew children were often more resilient than adults in times of tragedy, and in my opinion my five year-old daughter was a lot stronger than I was. She got that from her mother.

"Yeah," I replied.

"How's she doing these days? Other than the dreams?"

"Actually, she's mostly okay. We talk about her mom a lot, and I know she misses her like crazy, but that's to be expected. I worry about the nightmares, but otherwise, yeah. She's good. She's better than I thought she'd be."

"Great." He leaned back against the sofa, returning his focus to the game. "What about you?"

Instead of answering, I picked up my beer and downed the rest of it, setting the empty bottle back on the table with a thump.

A minute or two passed, and I guess Josh assumed I wasn't going to reply. "So, pretty much the same, then?"

With a sigh, I mumbled. "Pretty much."

Chapter 6

Amelia

Like every other month since my life imploded, April blew by without me really noticing. I kept myself busy doing taxes for Dee and her friends, and a few of my mom's friends back in Swann's Landing. There was little time to dwell on stressful thoughts, which was a blessing. The extra money all this work brought was also a blessing. Although Scott had secured a loan to pay me out for my half of the house a few months ago, I hated that I'd been depleting my savings so much. Unfortunately, once tax time finished at the end of the month, the extra work vanished along with it.

Though I still worried about him, I waffled over whether or not to reach out to Declan. For a long time, I was able to resist. But one night in May, lying awake in bed, I realized it had been a year since my last day at BWK. What a nerve-wracking, emotionally tumultuous day that had been. Remembering it got me thinking of him again, and this time I fumbled in the dark for my phone and opened my texts. I had no idea if he'd want to hear from me—I suspected the answer was negative—but I sent him a short text.

Thinking of my time at BWK and wondering how you're doing?

A not-insignificant part of me hoped otherwise, but mostly I knew he wouldn't reply.

June was an especially difficult month, as it had now been a full year since the worst day of my life. The day my dad died came pretty close, and that anniversary last fall had been rough, too, but this one was even worse. I could no longer think thoughts like: *a year ago, everything was still fine.* I'd been 'not fine' for over a year. Don't get me wrong; I wasn't still wallowing in self-pity—those days were few and far between now—but that deep, unshakeable sense of grief remained, always just below the surface. It had become of part of who I was now, a fact I didn't love, but had grown to accept.

At the beginning of the month, Scott filed divorce papers. I wasn't all that surprised when I received them, but I did feel a melancholic pang once I signed and mailed them back to his lawyer. Another era of my life was ending. I realized Scott and I had been over for a long time, and it was silly for me to feel sad about it at this point. But soon it would be official. So many doors to my past were now closed, sealed shut, never to be re-opened. Though I knew I wasn't, I felt very alone.

The day after I returned the papers, Scott called me. After a moment's hesitation, I answered. "Hey."

"Hey, Ames—Amelia. So, I, uh, had my lawyer send you over some papers to sign."

"Yeah, I got them yesterday. Don't worry, I signed them."

"Oh. Good." There was a brief pause. "Thanks."

I bit my lower lip. "Sure." I wondered if there was any other reason for his call. "How're you doing?"

"We're...I'm... Fine. Everything's fine."

"Got a good group of kids this year?" Scott was the auto shop teacher at Swann's Landing High, a job he both loved and excelled at.

"Yeah, they're awesome. Can't believe the year's almost over." Now I could hear the smile in his voice.

"Yeah."

"Yeah." He paused and I assumed he was about to sign off. "How 'bout you? Doing okay?"

I wanted to tell him I missed him. I wanted to ask him to tell Liv I missed her, too. But the truth was that I wasn't up to opening the door to that particular line of conversation today. I was just too mentally exhausted for confrontation, even if it was a much needed one that might actually lead to some sort of tentative resolution.

Another time, I told myself. As I thought this, I realized how often I did this. Procrastination of unpleasant discussions seemed to be one of my defining traits now. Yet another aspect of the New Me I didn't love.

"I'm good," I assured him. I had no idea if he could tell I was lying, but he didn't question me further.

"Great, great. Well, I gotta run. It was good talking to ya."

We ended the call, and I leaned back and closed my eyes with a long sigh. I wondered if a day would ever come when things would feel comfortable between us again.

Declan

It was June. It was fucking hot as hell. And I was at home on a work-mandated vacation.

Apparently some of my co-workers had been bitching about my 'stress levels' lately. Patrick had come into my office last Thursday, shut the door behind him, and told me in no uncertain terms that I was taking this week off. When I tried to protest that I had clients I needed to visit, he just said to reschedule them. Then his face had softened into that expression I'd come to recognize all too well since Laura died: pity. More goddamned pity. I didn't want it. I didn't need it. Not at the time, and definitely not now. But since Patrick had refused to take no for an answer, here I was with a week off stretching out in front of me.

For possibly the first time in my entire life, I would've rather been at work. Selling and servicing my clients kept my mind occupied, kept me feeling like I was working toward a productive goal. Home, especially with Alexis still in school, although this was her last week of it, left me feeling aimless. I didn't need to clean. I had a cleaning service come in every Friday, and we hadn't done much to mess it up over the past two days. Laundry was done and put away. In the back of my mind I knew there *were* a few things that needed my attention, but I wasn't particularly interested in tackling them. Not sober, anyway. And since I had to pick my daughter up from school at three o'clock, I needed to stay that way.

Alexis was actually doing pretty well. Most days, she seemed her usual joyful, rambunctious self. We'd had a rough Mother's Day last month, but that was to be expected. Although Mother's Day itself turned out a lot better than the week leading up to it, when my poor girl had to watch all the other kids make paintings for their moms in school and hear them all talk about what they were planning for their mothers on the big day. I had a very sad, quiet little girl that week, and though I tried to cheer her up, there wasn't much I could say or do to make her feel better. We just had to get through it like we got through everything else: together. We spent Mother's Day in Swann's Landing with Laura's parents, and I was relieved to see Alexis perk up, laughing and smiling with them. They were missing Laura themselves, of course, but they hid their sadness well, and all in all the day went a lot smoother than I'd worried it might.

Which reminded me, the day before Mother's Day I'd woken up to a text from Amelia asking how I was. I knew it probably wasn't a great idea to reply, that the best thing for her would be to stay far, far away from me, but I won't lie—hearing from her made me smile. I was incredibly tempted to text back. However, before I could, Alexis cried out for me and I jumped up and went to comfort her from what I assumed was yet another bad dream. I never did end up replying, but it was for the best. I'd just had a moment of weakness. I wouldn't let it happen again.

The doorbell rang, interrupting my reminiscing. To my surprise, I found Ryan on my front steps, a bound stack of flattened cardboard boxes in his arms.

"What the hell are *you* doing here?" I asked him, eyeing the boxes with trepidation. I had a feeling I already knew. "Shouldn't you be at work?"

He smiled, stepping past me into the front hallway and leaning the stack against the wall. "Thought I'd come help you pack up some of Laura's stuff to donate to the auction."

I arched a brow. "What makes you think—"

He held up a hand to silence me. "Look, I know it's not exactly a task you're eager to dive into, but it has to be done at some point. Why not now, when we're collecting donations anyway? Alexis is at school, and you've got me for a couple hours to help you out. What d'ya say?"

I paused, eyes narrowed. My brother had a point; I *did* need to start packing up Laura's stuff. I just hadn't gotten around to going through any of it yet. Actually, scratch that. It's not that I hadn't found time to do it; I'd been deliberately avoiding it. The thought of that particular task made me want to get very, very drunk. But since BWK had an annual charity auction every June to raise money for cancer research, I had to admit, now would be an ideal time to sort through her mostly-designer clothes and shoes at least.

Though it was pretty fucking low on the list of things I wanted to do today, I muttered. "Fine."

"Great!" Ryan flashed me an encouraging grin. Then he picked up the boxes and headed for the stairs. After a moment's hesitation and a deep sigh, I followed.

The master bedroom was at the far end of the upstairs hall. Slipping past my brother, I pushed open the door to let him through. I'd been sleeping in the spare room at the top of the stairs, and my former bedroom had a definite disused feeling about it. Though the air conditioning was blasting, it smelled musty. I pushed open a window to let in the breeze.

Ryan set the stack on the floor, pulled a pair of box-cutters from his back pocket, and cut through the twine. "You got any packing tape?" he asked. I went to find some, and when I returned with it, he started assembling boxes.

I opened Laura's closet and peered inside with a frown. The easiest place to start was probably with her vast footwear collection. Dragging a box toward me, I sat on the floor and started tossing in shoes, sandals, boots, even an old pair of slippers that probably should have gone in the trash. Before long, the box was full and I taped down the flaps. "One down…" I paused, glancing up at the racks of clothing. "And a shit-load more to go."

My brother set aside another box and gave me a long look. "If you don't need to sort them, how 'bout you let me pack up her clothes? I'm sure there're other items that need your attention more."

I looked up at the rows of colorful dresses, jackets, blouses, and skirts, contemplating. Turning back to him, I nodded. "Sure. Have at it."

I shifted over to kneel on the floor by Laura's dresser and began pulling out drawers. They were filled with undergarments and pajamas. I didn't even look at them closely; I just grabbed great handfuls and threw them into an empty box. Once the second box was taped up, I decided to go down to the kitchen to grab us a couple of beers. I figured one drink wouldn't prevent me from driving in a few hours, and air-conditioning or not, this was turning out to be sweaty work.

Ryan took the bottle from me gratefully and took a deep swig before taping up a full box and pushing it beside the others. A

53

minute later, he said, "Soooo…what d'you wanna do with the wedding dress?"

I shut my eyes, my head dropping. Somehow I'd completely forgotten about Laura's gown, zipped up in a dry-cleaner's bag in the very back of the closet.

Before I could reply, he added, "Maybe you should save it for Alexis, in case she wants it for her own wedding someday?"

That hadn't even crossed my mind. A weird queasy sensation came over me and all of a sudden, I didn't feel like going through Laura's stuff anymore. I had to get out of this room. Right the fuck now. Dropping the handbag I'd been looking through onto the bed, I got to my feet and headed for the door.

"Uh, just leave it." I dragged my fingers through my hair, looking around the room wildly. "Actually, you know, just leave all of it. I'll pack up the rest later."

He frowned, examining my face. I didn't care what he was looking for, or if he found it; I just needed him to go.

"You sure?"

"Yeah."

"Should I take these with me?" He indicated the four boxes we'd filled.

My heart was racing, my head spinning. I couldn't think straight. "No, just…I'll drop them off later."

Ryan stood and took a step toward me. "Declan? You okay?"

I braced both hands on the doorframe and dragged in a deep breath. Meeting his eyes, I nodded. "Yeah." It was a lie and we both knew it, but he didn't press. We went downstairs and I escorted him to the front door.

"I can stay for a bit if you like. We could sit out back and finish these." Ryan tilted his half empty beer toward me, his face the picture of brotherly concern.

I shook my head. "Another day. But thanks for your help."

With a shrug, he put his bottle on the side table. "Not a problem. I'll call ya later."

When he was gone at last, I went to the living room and fell heavily onto the couch, upending my own bottle and emptying it in one long swallow.

It would be over a year before I looked at any of Laura's stuff again.

Amelia

My divorce became final at the beginning of September. I couldn't help feeling a bit sad, but I also knew Scott was much happier now. Much to my surprise, a few days later Dee told me that he'd proposed to Liv and they planned to wed as soon as possible. This hurt more than the formal ending of my own marriage. Two of my life-long best friends were getting married and they hadn't even told me. I was no longer a part of their lives, and although I completely understood why, it still stung.

Though I didn't expect an invitation to that wedding, the invitation to Josh and Holly's had arrived a month ago, and it still sat on top of my dresser untouched. I knew I had to attend, that my anxiety and complicated feelings for their best man were no excuse to let them down. But I still hadn't returned the reply card.

One sunny morning a few days later, my phone rang. It was Josh.

"I know why you're calling," I answered, grinning.

He laughed. "Do you? Good. I guess that means your reply card didn't get lost in the mail. You *are* coming, aren't you?"

With a small sigh, I said, "I want to. I really do..."

"Then come. It'd mean a lot to me—to *us*—for you to be there."

"I know." I was quiet for a few seconds. "Okay. But you won't hold it against me if I end up sneaking out of the reception early?"

"Of course not. Although I'm hoping any awkwardness you might feel will pass so you can relax and enjoy yourself. I'll sit you with Evan and Sam and Kaitlyn, so you'll be among friends. Okay?"

"That sounds good. Thanks." I paused, debating whether to or not to ask. But of course I couldn't help myself. "So how's he doing, anyway?"

It was Josh's turn to sigh. "Still not great. He's still drinking too much, whenever he doesn't have Lex. And he's grouchier than ever here at work. He and Diana got into a full-on shouting matching in the hall last week."

"You're kidding?"

"Nope. I'd hoped maybe there'd be some improvement by now, but so far I'm not seeing much. I'm worried about him, Amelia. I wish he'd go to counselling, but he refuses."

"Well, take it from me: no one can make him go if he doesn't want to. It has to be his choice. I know you're worried—I am, too—but I don't think there's much else you can do. He just needs you to be there for him, and you are. That's the most important thing." I paused, snorting, "You're not making me feel any more confident about going to your wedding, you know."

Josh chuckled. "Honestly? I kinda think it would do him good to see you. If you're up for it, that is."

"And that's the question I'm struggling with most: am I up for it? But you know what? I'm a big girl. I can handle seeing him. I promise I'll be there. For you and Holly, though, not for him. Just to make that clear."

"Understood. Well, either way, we're glad you're coming."

I hung up and sat back in my chair, sighing heavily. I would go. For Josh and Holly, I could do this. They had always been supportive of me, I loved them, and I'd given Josh my word. But I won't deny that hearing how deeply Declan still grieved for Laura hurt. He clearly loved her a lot more than I'd believed. After they'd reconciled, they must have rediscovered the love and passion they used to share, before things had gone downhill. Before he'd met me.

When Dee got back from work, I told her about my conversation with Josh.

"It would do *him* good to see *you*?" she repeated, incredulous. "What about the fact that it would not do *you* any good to see *him*? What about that?" She was fuming.

"It's okay. I want to go. Some of my old friends from BWK will be there, and it'll be nice to catch up. I'll just avoid him. And if I can't avoid him, I'm sure I'm capable of being civil if I have to."

She rolled her eyes. "What day is the wedding again? The twenty-ninth?"

"Yeah."

Pulling out her phone, she examined her schedule. "Can you bring a guest? How 'bout I come with you?"

I frowned. "You'd do that? Even though you wouldn't know anyone?"

"I've met Josh and Holly. C'mon. I'll keep ya out of trouble."

"That's actually not a bad idea. It'd be a lot more fun with you along."

Dee grinned. "Then it's settled. Where's the reception being held?"

"Um." I picked up the invitation, scanned it, and handed it to her to review. "The Lynchburg Hilton. Downtown."

"Cool. Let's get a room so we can have a few drinks. My treat."

"No need. I haven't really been drinking much these days. I can drive us."

"Nah, it'll be fun." She opened her browser and found the Hilton website. "I'm booking it. This way if you need a break from the reception, you have a place to go." She looked up at me with a reassuring smile. "We'll have a blast!"

I shrugged, agreeing that maybe this way it could end up being a good time. Then at last I completed the reply card, indicating I'd be bringing a Plus One.

It was all settled. The wedding was in three weeks, which gave me lots of time to mentally prepare. At least that was what I told myself.

Chapter 7

Amelia

The day of Josh and Holly's wedding dawned hot and sticky. Mid-afternoon temperatures were expected to soar into the eighties and, though it was now officially autumn, it felt like summer. Unfortunately, instead of chirping birds through my open bedroom window, I woke to the not-so-pleasant sounds of someone vomiting in the bathroom next door.

Concerned, I got up and knocked on the door. "Hey? You okay in there?"

I heard Dee groan.

"She's definitely not okay."

Whipping around, I found Terri at the kitchen counter in her bathrobe, a cup of coffee in one hand.

"Oh no. Did you guys get into the wine last night?"

She shook her head. "I'm pret' sure it's the flu. She was running hot 'n cold all night. And my wee nephew just got over a bad bout of flu."

My first thought was: *Poor Dee.* My next was: C*rap! There goes my date for the wedding.*

The bathroom door creaked open and Dee emerged, her normally rich bronze complexion ashy and damp with perspiration. One hand clutched the doorjamb.

"Oh wow," I said as Terri went over and slid an arm around her waist to support her. "You look awful."

"Gee, thanks," Dee muttered. Then she sighed. "Looks like you're gonna hafta to go solo today after all." She gave me an apologetic half-smile.

"Don't even think about it. You just get back in bed and get some rest."

She coughed. "Sorry, Ames."

"Don't be. I'll be fine. You just work on feeling better."

"Don'tcha worry, I'll take good care of her," Terri assured me.

I turned back to Dee. "You think I could squeeze in a quick shower? Will you be okay for, like, ten minutes?"

"Go ahead. I've got an emergency bucket by the bed." With that, she shuffled into her room and closed the door.

I returned to my room and sat on my own bed, staring at the wall. There went my wedding support system. I mean, I knew I'd have friends there, but they didn't know my secret. Only Josh and Holly knew, but this was their day. I couldn't bother them with my issues. However, I still had the hotel room Dee had booked. If I needed to escape from the reception, I could go up to the room for a breather.

It was a good plan. And I refused to let myself think about all the various ways it could go wrong.

It took me a bit longer than I expected to find the church, and by the time I arrived, the parking lot was full. After a drive around the block, I managed to squeeze into a small spot on a side street. I was wearing heels so I couldn't run, but I hurried as fast as I could, much to my dismay working up a sweat in the heat. Thank goodness I'd been smart enough to wear a sleeveless dress. Once I stepped inside the church, I realized with chagrin that the ceremony was about to start. No ushers remained in the lobby to seat guests, so I slipped through the doors to the nave and slid into a back pew.

The old building wasn't air conditioned, and although hanging fans whirled overhead, and there were strategically placed oscillating fans in each corner, the crowded room was stifling. I craned my neck to see around all the heads until I caught a glimpse of Josh and Declan standing to the right of the alter. Josh's head was tilted toward his best friend in whispered conversation. They wore dapper gray tuxedos with deep orange ties, and both looked very handsome. Suddenly they straightened as the minister said something to them, indicating toward the doors I'd just come through. Declan scanned the crowd, and I quickly shifted out of his line of sight. Just as I did, the organ started playing the opening notes of the familiar Wagner piece signaling the bride was about to make her grand entrance.

We all turned to watch as Holly began her slow procession arm in arm with her father. The dress she'd chosen was a slim, floor-length, cream brocade, and it suited her perfectly. As she locked eyes with Josh waiting at the far end of the aisle, her entire face lit up. She absolutely beamed from ear to ear. I had never seen her look more beautiful and I knew Josh was undoubtedly thinking the same.

The ceremony was short and simple. My heart swelled with love for my friends as, with tears in both their eyes, they kissed and made it official. Holding hands and grinning, they returned down the aisle towards me, catching and holding my gaze for a second before continuing out the doors. Holly's sister and Declan followed a few seconds after, but I scooted back from the edge of the aisle and since he was staring straight ahead, I don't think he saw me.

The church emptied backward, the pews at the front filling the aisle first, and I realized I would be one of the last to exit. I deliberately waited until everyone else had left before re-entering the lobby. A sticky layer of sweat coated my entire body at this point, so I made a detour to the ladies' room to freshen up.

Once I came out, I noticed an Exit sign pointing down the hall. I following it and emerged into the parking lot through a side door, successfully avoiding the main entrance where I assumed the wedding party would be greeting guests.

The sun reflected pinpoints of light into my eyes from the windshields of the many vehicles. It felt unbearably bright compared to the dim interior. I pulled my sunglasses from my handbag and stood there for a few moments to adjust and just breathe. Then I made my way to the rear of the crowd gathered in front of the church.

My assumption was correct; the wedding party stood at the top of the steps posing for photos. I pulled out my phone, and with my zoom took a picture of them as best I could. It wasn't the greatest photo, but I somehow managed to catch them all smiling. Declan's smile even looked genuine, and it made me happy to see it, remembering what Josh had said about his state of mind these days.

I knew I should go over and congratulate my friends, but as there were loads of people in front of me wanting to do the same, I figured Josh and Holly would forgive me if I waited until the reception to give them my best wishes. So, with that in mind, I turned on my heel and headed for the relief of my air conditioned car to go check into my air-conditioned hotel room.

The room Dee had booked for us was simple, but nice. It was on the third floor, and had only one queen-sized bed instead of two, but since she hadn't been able to come, the sleeping arrangements didn't matter. And even if she were here, neither of us would've minded sharing a bed, nor would Terri have been annoyed. We were all pretty laid back about stuff like that.

I didn't need to go down to the ballroom for the reception for a couple of hours. If I'd thought to pack my swimsuit, I would have gone up to the rooftop pool for a nice, cooling swim. But since that wasn't an option, I slipped out of my dress, and as I hadn't gotten much sleep last night tossing and turning and worrying, I crawled beneath the covers.

Much to my surprise, I dozed off right away, but I woke feeling more groggy than refreshed. Rolling over, alarm cut through my fog when I saw the time. I'd been asleep for over two hours and I needed to get downstairs pronto. Tossing back the sheets, I dashed to the bathroom to dress and fix my hair. Examining my reflection, I decided I looked presentable enough. It was time to go.

As I stepped off the elevator into the lobby, I heard someone calling my name and spotted my ex-coworker, Sam, hurrying toward me. Sam was Declan's brother Ryan's Administrative Assistant at Baker, Wright, and Kavanaugh, and we used to eat lunch together a lot. She was with her boyfriend, Evan, who worked with Josh in my old department.

"Long time no see! God, you look amazing! I love your hair! And your dress is to die for! Have you lost weight?" Sam gushed, barely pausing to breathe between exclamations.

"Uh, a bit maybe? Thanks. You look amazing, too." I gave the tall blonde a one-armed squeeze. Any weight I'd lost hadn't been intentional, but I wasn't about to mention my depression, especially not at my friend's wedding.

People were filtering into the ballroom, and I figured dinner was about to start. Remembering what Josh had told me, I said, "I think we're sitting together. Let's go find our table."

"Oh, we already found it. C'mon, I'll show you." She linked her arm through mine and led me through the doors.

Inside, clusters of people stood drinking, chatting, and munching on hors d'oeuvres. The lineup for the bar wound all the way down the right wall. Sam pointed to a table near the back where I spotted Kaitlyn and Evan. Thank goodness we were seated as far as possible from the bridal party's long table. Maybe Josh did that on purpose so I wouldn't have to constantly look at the best man.

"Hey, Amelia. Long time no see." Evan told me when we got to our seats. "I took the liberty of getting you a margarita when I got drinks for the table. But if you don't want it, I'm sure Sam will be happy to make it disappear for you." He winked at his girlfriend.

Since I didn't need to drive until morning, I took the glass he offered. I had no intention of getting loaded, but a drink or two might help me get through this. "Thanks," I told Evan, taking a sip.

He smiled. "No problem."

I leaned in to give Kaitlyn a hug before sitting down. Holly's sister was Master of Ceremonies, and she choose that moment to grab the microphone and announce that everyone should take their seats as dinner was about to be served.

Besides the four of us, according to the place cards our table was also supposed to include my former boss Diana and her boyfriend—and Declan's brother—Ryan. I scanned the ballroom, but couldn't spot either of them.

"Where're Diana and Ryan?" I asked Kaitlyn.

She shrugged. "No idea. I didn't see them at the church, either. Maybe something came up."

I knew they were only invited because Diana was Josh's boss. She was demanding, egotistical and not very well-liked at work, and I suspected everyone at my table was probably relieved she wasn't there.

Dinner was excellent, and so was my margarita. Before dessert arrived, I'd emptied my glass. Once we were finished eating and the dishes were being cleared, everyone's favorite part of the night, speeches, begun. Holly's sister went first, and then it was the Best Man's turn. I craned my neck to see the podium as Declan approached the microphone. To my surprise, he looked uncomfortable. He was a salesman, and used to presenting to large groups of clients and potential clients. Public speaking should've been a piece of cake for him.

"First of all, I'd, uh…I'd like to thank you all for coming out to support the, uh, the lovely couple…Josh and Holly…today." He stopped to clear his throat. "As some…as many of you know, Josh and I…" He trailed off, looking down at the cue cards he held in one hand. His other clutched a beer bottle by the neck. "Josh. Josh is my homeboy. My main dude. My brotha-from-anotha-motha." At that last bit the audience tittered appreciatively. I didn't laugh; my brows narrowed in confusion. Never once had I heard him refer to Josh like that before. To me, his words sounded forced.

Declan took a swig of beer, seemed to re-find some of his confidence, and continued. "When he first started dating Holly, I didn't really take it too seriously. Much like myself in my younger days, Josh'd had girlfriends before and none had lasted very long. So I didn't expect this one to any different." Again, he stopped to take a drink. "But it didn't take long before I realized I was dead wrong. And one time when we were shootin' the shit at work, he told me he was taking her away for the weekend, and I could tell by the look on his face that Holly was special. He'd fallen for her big time. He even said he thought she was The One. Which she is. Clearly." Declan looked down at his cards again and somehow fumbled them, scattering them on the floor.

"Fuck. Sorry." He snorted, then sighed. "Really sorry. What I'm trying to say, not very well apparently, is that my bro over there is the happiest I've ever seen him. And it's all because of Holly. And I'm really happy for him that he made the smartest decision he'll ever make by asking her to marry him. They found each other, and that's a pretty rare thing. Let's have a drink to Josh and Holly, the luckiest couple I know." He raised his bottle, but before he took another swig, he added, "I know these two have what it takes to make it. Congrats, buddy." With that he tilted his bottle toward Josh and took a long draught.

Josh got to his feet, grinning, and came over to Declan, clapping him on the shoulder as he stepped down from the podium. He leaned in to whisper something into Declan's ear. I knew Josh was thanking him, but I couldn't help wondering if he'd also asked him to slow down a bit with the beer.

I didn't need to be near him to know that, just like at Laura's visitation, Declan was loaded. Josh told me he'd been drinking too much, and this was the second time I'd seen it with my own eyes. In public. I was worried about his mental state, but I knew there was little I could do to help.

Declan returned to his seat, and Holly joined Josh at the podium. Together the newlyweds gave the final speech, raising a glass to their wedding party and once again thanking everyone for coming. When they finished, the D.J. put on a slow song and Josh led Holly to the center of the dancefloor, taking her in his arms for the first dance of the night.

About halfway through the song, the wedding party coupled off and joined them on the floor. Josh and Holly didn't even seem to notice them. As I watched them whispering and smiling at one another as they danced, I felt a pang of jealousy. Declan was right; they *were* lucky. They'd found each other at the perfect time in their lives. No matter how independent I was, I couldn't help yearning for the kind of loving, committed relationship they shared. Twice I'd thought I'd found it and both times I'd been wrong. Maybe I was just meant to be alone.

Once the song was over, Evan stood up and announced, "I'm heading to the bar. Anyone need a refill?"

I glanced down at my empty glass. "I think I'll join you," I told him, getting to my feet and following him across the room.

We got to the bar just in time, as a crowd of thirsty guests soon formed a messy line behind us. After Evan placed his drink order, the bartender turned to me. He had thick, black hair, golden skin, and brown eyes that twinkled when he smiled at me. "What can I get for ya, hon?"

I smiled right back. His name tag read *Pedro*. "A margarita, please, Pedro."

"Comin' right up." He was actually pretty cute, and I assumed flirting with customers earned him good tips. "That your husband?" he asked, tilting his chin toward the back of Evan's head as he poured tequila into the blender and turned it on.

I laughed, shaking my head and waggling the fingers of my ring-free left hand. "Been there, done that. Not with him, though. He's just a friend."

"His loss." Pedro flashed me another grin as he grabbed a clean glass and poured out my margarita. "A pretty chica like you? You must get hit on on the regular." Pedro was clearly in no hurry to serve the next person in line. "You know, a wedding's pretty much the perfect place for a hook up. If that's your scene." He winked as he slid my drink into my waiting hand.

My mouth dropped open, but before I could formulate a reply, I heard a snort beside me and I turned to find myself face to face with Declan. I was surprised to note silver streaks in his dark hair and many more lines around his eyes. His cheeks were drawn and it looked like he'd lost weight. The trauma of losing his wife had aged him. He arched a thick brow. "Beer me," he instructed Pedro, but his eyes never left mine.

"So? Is that your *scene* these days, Amelia?" he asked with that cocky grin I remembered so well.

I felt my face turn red. This was *so* not how I'd imagined our next face to face meeting would start. Forcing myself to laugh, I said, "Of course not."

His grin fell away. Reaching for the fresh beer, he took a sip. "Yeah. I didn't think so."

On impulse, I grabbed hold of his shirt sleeve and tugged him away from the bar so we weren't blocking others. Or being overheard. To my relief, he followed willingly.

Once we reached the side of the room and could speak in relative privacy, I released my grip. I could feel my pulse racing. "It's good to see you," I said, trying to act natural.

Declan's smile returned. "You, too."

"Where's your brother tonight? He and Diana were supposed to be sitting at my table."

With a shrug, he said, "No idea. Something probably came up. He didn't text me."

"Well, it's not like I'm missing having to make small talk with her." Diana and I had never really gotten along. When I worked at BWK, Declan and Josh used to refer to her as the B.F.H., meaning Bitch From Hell. Based on what Josh told me a few weeks ago, Declan and Diana still clashed often, and it sounded like their conflicts were more volatile than ever. She'd always been able to set him off, but I assumed his increased stress levels were the reason for the escalation.

"Yeah, their no-show is probably a win for everyone."

Looking him straight in those mesmerizing blue eyes, I asked, "So how're you doing?"

His face closed down, and I knew instantly that his answer would be a lie. Shifting his gaze away, he said, "I'm good. How 'bout you?"

"Don't bullshit me, Declan."

His eyes flew back to mine, startled. The Amelia he used to know rarely swore. Then he laughed, a genuine laugh that made my heart flutter. "Guess you know me too well."

"I know you well enough to know you're not doing so great. And I know you probably don't really wanna talk about—"

"It's my best friend's wedding, Mel. I'm celebrating. To the happy couple." He raised his bottle and clinked it against my glass before taking a drink.

I hesitated a moment, then took a sip, too.

"Tonight, it's all good." He flashed that disarming lopsided grin I'd been missing so much.

I sighed softly. "Fine. How's Alexis then?"

"She's doing really well. Awesome, actually. A few rough moments sometimes, but kids are a lot more resilient than we give them credit for."

"That's great. But still. It must be so hard on her. I've been worried about both of you."

He smiled again, but this time it didn't quite reach his eyes. "No need. We're doin' fine. But tonight is not for dwelling on that stuff. As I said, I just wanna celebrate Josh and Holly."

It seemed every time I managed to get through his defenses for a moment or two, he shut me back down. Our dynamic felt…not exactly wrong…but *off*. I wished we could be as easy with each other as we used to be. Maybe this weirdness was to be expected, but I didn't like it.

Before I could say anything more, he added, "Speaking of whom, I should really go find him. It was great to see you." He touched his bottle to the edge of my glass again, and without another word turned and made his way back toward the head table.

I had mixed feelings as I watched him walk away. He was obviously not okay, but he'd also made it clear that he didn't want to talk about it. Not tonight, anyway. Knowing him, probably not at all. On the plus side, while our conversation was kind of awkward, it wasn't as uncomfortable as I'd feared it would be. Maybe I was being naïve, but it felt like our connection, though fragile, still existed. And then there was the small but significant fact that he'd called me Mel. Mel had been his nickname for me when we were together. No one else had ever called me that. Not before. Not since. I'm not sure if he'd said it on purpose, or if it had just slipped out, but its effect on me was instantaneous. One little word, probably no big deal, but hearing him use such a personal and intimate reference both thrilled and cut me.

I was trembling as I made my way back to our table.

"Everything okay?" Kaitlyn asked with a frown.

"Yeah." I took another sip from my glass.

"I saw you talking to Declan at the bar," Sam cut in. "Did he tell you where Ryan and Diana are?"

"He hasn't heard from Ryan. Have you texted him?"

"Yeah, earlier." She picked up her phone and looked at it. "Oh, look, he's finally responded." She paused to read the text. "Okay, it's no biggie. Diana's just sick."

Just then a new song came on. Evan asked her to dance and they headed for the dancefloor. Kaitlyn hadn't brought a date, so we chatted quietly for a few minutes about what had been going on at the office since I left.

"Amelia!"

I turned to see Josh approaching me with a wide smile.

"Hey," I greeted him. "Awesome party you're putting on here."

"Thanks. Care to dance?"

"Will Holly mind?"

He laughed, pointing toward the edge of the floor where she was dancing with Declan. I held out my hand and Josh led me to a spot near the middle.

"You look very pretty," he said, taking me in his arms. It felt a little weird to be dancing with Josh. I couldn't remember if we'd ever even hugged before. But it was an excellent way to have a private conversation for a few minutes.

"Thanks. You're looking pretty dapper yourself."

"I noticed you and Declan talking. Everything alright?"

"Yeah. It was a bit awkward, but that's no shock. He doesn't want to talk about anything meaningful; he just wants to get drunk."

"So I noticed."

"Hey, so, with Ryan not here and you super busy being one half of the guests of honor, do you want me to keep an eye on him for you tonight?"

Josh shifted his head so he was looking down at me. "Seriously? You'd do that? Seems to me that'd be the last thing you'd wanna do."

I bit my lower lip. "Well, I couldn't do much if he gets out of control, but I could find you and let you know. I want you to be able to relax and have a fabulous time tonight, and not have to worry too much about him."

He frowned as he considered my offer. I know he was thinking of my own emotional well-being. I was, too.

"It's okay, Josh. Just for tonight, I don't mind. I don't need to spend every moment at his side. I'll just kind of keep a watchful eye his way to make sure he doesn't get too sloppy."

"If you're sure. You already know I think you spending time with him could be good for him. I just don't want it to stress you out too much."

I chuckled. "I'm fine. Honest."

Before I realized what he was doing, Josh had maneuvered us beside Holly and Declan. "Mind if I dance with my beautiful bride?" he asked. "Tradesies?"

Holly smiled at me. "Oh hey, Amelia," she said before Josh slid his arms around her and spun her away. Declan and I were left facing each other. At first he seemed hesitant, but two seconds later he held out his arms to me and I stepped into them. Although we had never danced like this before, it felt weirdly natural.

"You again," he teased. He smelled like beer and aftershave.

"Me again."

He bent his head close to my cheek. "I probably should've said this earlier, but you look gorgeous." His breath ticked my ear, sending tingles up my spine. Some things between us clearly hadn't changed.

"Thanks. You too."

There was so much I wanted to say, but I didn't. I just allowed myself to enjoy the moment as we danced. Our fingers were entwined, our palms pressed together. His other hand rested on my waist, and at one point he started rubbing circles on my lower back. Maybe it was just a reflex. I tried not to read too much into it.

The song ended and he stepped away. "Thanks for the dance," he said, before turning to go back to his table and presumably find his beer.

"Welcome," I muttered, although I knew he didn't hear me.

I returned to my own table, my mind swirling. What had I just done? Why had I offered to watch Declan tonight for Josh? Had I just made a massive mistake?

Chapter 8

Amelia

Keeping an eye on Declan during the reception turned out to actually be pretty boring. He drank. Chatted with a few people. Left for the washroom. Came back, went to the bar, sat by himself, and drank some more. From what I could tell, his cheerful mood had departed. Now he looked like he'd rather be anywhere else.

I could sort of relate.

Not that I wasn't enjoying hanging out with my former co-workers, but they were drinking and dancing, and I'd stopped both after I'd made my promise to Josh. Holly came over and sat with me for a few minutes, but she couldn't stay long as her grandparents were leaving and she had to go say goodbye.

Sometimes when I looked over at Declan, I caught him staring back at me. When our eyes connected he would glance away, and I wondered if he'd noticed how much I was watching him. I thought about just going over there and sitting with him, but I couldn't bring myself to do it. If only we were still as comfortable with each other as we used to be. But we weren't, and I needed to remember all the reasons why.

By ten o'clock, most of the older guests had left and the DJ had started playing more upbeat, current music. Josh, Holly, and Holly's sister were dancing with Kaitlyn, Sam, and Evan, plus a few of their cousins I didn't know. I was enjoying watching them goof around on the dance floor when I noticed Declan again returning to the bar.

At first I didn't pay too much attention. He'd been back and forth several times over the past couple hours. This trip seemed different, though. Something about the tilt of his head, the way he'd squared his shoulders, told me he was agitated. Frowning, I pushed back my chair and began to make my way around the dancers toward the bar.

I heard both Declan's and Pedro's voices rising when I was still about twenty feet away, and I picked up my pace. Then suddenly Pedro came around from behind the bar, and before anyone could step in, swung a fist at Declan's face. Beer had slowed Declan's reflexes; he dodged, lost his balance and went down. I'm not sure how I managed it, but I slid to my knees and somehow caught his head in my lap before it hit the ground.

He landed with a grunt, but he didn't stay down for long. Swearing, he scrambled to his feet and looked around for his assailant. One of Josh's cousins now stood in front of Pedro holding his arms out between them.

"Don't know what the problem is, but you dudes both need to back off." He bobbed his chin at Declan. "Y'okay, buddy?"

Declan's face was red. "Fine. But this asshole—"

"Get him out of here," Pedro said, turning to me. "He's completely loaded. I told him he was cut off, and he started getting mouthy. Made a rude comment about my sister."

I stood up with a sigh. "Sorry about that." Turning to Declan, I asked, "You have a room here?"

When his eyes focused on me, his anger seemed to dissipate. He nodded.

"Great." I led him by the arm to the salon doors. "Wait here. I'll be right back once I tell Josh I'm taking you upstairs."

That earned me a drunken leer. "Thought you said that wasn't your *scene*?"

I rolled my eyes. "I'll make sure you get into your room. That's all. The rest is up to you. Do. Not. Move."

I hurried back to my table and grabbed my handbag, then made a beeline for the head table where Josh stood talking to Evan. After I explained what happened and assured him I didn't need help, Josh handed me Declan's jacket.

I returned to find him leaning against the wall, arms crossed and eyes shut. "Declan?"

"Huh?" he mumbled, opening his eyes a slit.

"C'mon. What's your room number?" I took his elbow and tugged him toward the elevators.

"Uh…it's…oh yeah, like the jeans. 501."

We got on the elevator with an older couple who might have been Holly's aunt and uncle. They glanced at Declan disapprovingly as I pushed the button for the fifth floor. Once more, he leaned his head against the wall and closed his eyes. The car had barely begun moving when he slid an arm around my waist, tilted his head against mine and groaned, "Don't feel so great."

His face had gone an unlovely shade of green, and it didn't take a medical degree to know what was about to happen. Without even thinking, I punched the button for floor three. My room was right in front of the elevator bank, and he needed a toilet, stat.

When the doors opened, I dragged him across the hall, ignoring the muttering of the couple behind us. Let them judge. I had other things to concern myself with right now. Quickly, I swiped my card and opened the door, shoving Declan in front of me and into the adjacent bathroom.

We were just in time. I heard the toilet lid bang up and then the unpleasant sounds of his stomach violently emptying. With a sigh, I draped his jacket over the chair, sat on the edge of the bed, and waited it out.

After it had been silent in the bathroom for a couple of minutes, I tapped on the door.

"You okay in there?"

There was another groan, then: "Yeah." Next came the sound of running water and seconds later he opened the door, no longer green but definitely still pale. Beads of sweat stood out on his forehead.

As he came out, I slipped inside. "Just give me a sec to pee, then I'll take you up to your room."

"Promises, promises."

I had to smile. Typical Declan. Even when he was at his worst, mere moments after barfing his guts out, he still managed to make flirtatious innuendos.

He hadn't left a mess for me to clean, so I considered myself lucky. After the events of the evening, I was tired and just wanted to get him settled so I could go to sleep myself.

Much like the rest of this day so far, things didn't go quite as planned. When I emerged from the bathroom, the first thing I noticed was his dress pants pooled on the floor, the belt still wound through the loops. Beside it was his white button-up. And beneath the covers of my bed lay Declan. Sound asleep.

Are you frickin' kidding me?

For a long moment, I just stared at him in disbelief. Heaving a deep sigh, I walked over to take a closer look.

"Declan?"

No response.

"Declan?" I called louder, shaking his shoulder.

This earned me a moan and he rolled onto his side. But he didn't wake.

Crap. Now what was I supposed to do? I couldn't lift him, and he clearly wasn't going anywhere on his own anytime soon. I turned on the bedside lamp and took a seat in the chair, leaning forward to brace my chin on my palms and contemplate Declan's sleeping form.

As far as I could see it, I had two options. I could go downstairs, find Josh and Evan, and ask them to come carry him up to his room and put him in his own bed. I couldn't help chuckling as I pictured them flanking him with their arms around him, struggling to maneuver him into the elevator clad only in his underwear.

Or, there was the less embarrassing, far easier physically, but much more problematic emotionally solution: I could just leave him where he was and attempt to sleep beside him.

I sighed again, immobilized with indecision. Sleeping in the same bed as Declan was not a great idea. But maybe it was a better option than bothering Josh and Evan, and humiliating Declan in the process? He might not mind too much about Josh, but he'd be furious about Evan knowing an embarrassing secret, and possibly telling Sam and other co-workers at BWK.

At that realization, I knew I was stuck.

Crap. Crap crap crap. Shit!

For a long time, I just sat there, playing on my phone and hoping like crazy that he'd awaken. After a series of increasingly longer yawns, and realizing I could barely focus on my screen, I relented. I grabbed my nightgown from my bag and headed back to the bathroom to brush my teeth.

When I came out, I switched off the lamp and went around to the far side of the bed. I could still see him in the dim light seeping around the edges of the curtains. His face had softened, all his stress and frustration eased. He looked peaceful, even child-like, lying there.

"Declan?" I tried again, knowing it was pointless but needing to give it one last shot. When he didn't respond, I gave up and slipped beneath the blankets.

I thought I wouldn't be able to sleep with him beside me, close enough to touch, yet to me still as distant as a star, a bright twinkling one that enchants you, the kind you know if you ever got near it, it would burn you to ash. But it had been a long day, and my exhaustion crept over me in increments, until my dream-self and waking-self were so entwined I could no longer tell them apart.

Like I had so many times since we'd met, I dreamed Declan and I were making love. I felt his hands caress my body, gliding along my arms, over the curve of my hip, down my leg, before reversing direction, moving all the way back up to cup my breast. Drawing a sharp breath, I rolled to face him, raking my fingers into his hair and dragging his lips to mine.

It all seemed so familiar, like countless dreams before it. Yet I sensed something was off. He tasted funny, like…beer? That wasn't right.

Our kisses intensified, his tongue pushing against mine. His hand ran up under my nightgown, his fingers tracing patterns over my bare back. I shuddered with pleasure.

Hold on. There was something I needed to focus on. Beer. Why did he taste like beer? And why could I feel stubble scraping my chin?

My eyes flew open with a start. This was no dream. Declan was here. In bed. With me. Kissing me.

At first, I tried to pull away, but his arms only tightened around me, pulling me closer, mashing my chest against his. His lips were still on mine, and I still kissed him right back. Through my fog, through my desire, I tried to recall the reasons why I should stop this. It was like grasping at mosquitos, buzzing in my face one second, out of reach the next.

Focus, Amelia! Think.

One, he'd broken my heart. He'd…he'd thrown me away like yesterday's trash. It had nearly destroyed me. I could not go through that again.

Great. That's a huge one. Remember how much he hurt me. What else?

73

Two, although he was single now, he hadn't made any effort to get in touch. Because he was depressed or because he just didn't want to, I didn't know.

Meh. I could forgive that one. Anything else?

Three, he was so drunk he probably wouldn't even remember this. It would mean nothing to him.

Bingo! That's it. Best reason yet. But...

But it meant something to me. No matter what my logical mind tried to tell me, deep inside this was what I wanted. I still missed him. I still wanted to be with him. I still loved him. Those were facts, whether I liked them or not. The truth was that I didn't really want to stop.

So, God help me, I surrendered. No matter the consequences, I wanted this. I knew we'd have to deal with the aftermath in the morning, but right now tomorrow seemed unimportant and far away.

Our kisses became more desperate. He started pushing up my nightgown, and we broke apart just long enough for me to drag it over my head. His questing fingers found my breast and he rubbed a thumb across my nipple, making me gasp, making me want him even more than I already did, which didn't seem possible.

I could feel the evidence of his arousal pressing against my stomach, and a few seconds later his hand left my breast to slip below the elastic of my panties and pull them down my legs and off. My own fingers scrabbled at his boxer-briefs, and he helped me remove them, too.

This was not like the other times we'd been together. We were desperate for each other, so eager we couldn't wait another second. He rolled on top of me and positioned himself. I heard him suck in a sharp breath as he pushed inside. My mouth fell open and a gasp slipped out, but otherwise I didn't make a sound.

I'd waited far too long for this. And no matter if it was wrong, still wrong, had always been wrong, probably always would be wrong, it felt absolutely right.

We didn't speak. We kissed, we touched, but we didn't speak.

But...

But don't get me wrong. It wasn't beautiful, or graceful, or probably even very sexy. He reeked of beer. His kisses were sloppy. We were out of synch with each other more often than we were in harmony. It was awkward and frantic and didn't last very long.

I didn't care. None of those things mattered to me. I just wanted him. Any way I could get him.

Until he said what he said anyway.

After, when he'd finished—I didn't, but I didn't mind that either, not really—Declan collapsed on top of me, burying his face into the curve of my neck.

For a long moment, he didn't even move, and I felt his chest heave against mine as he tried to catch his breath. Then he pulled away a few inches and planted a wet kiss on my collarbone, whispering against my skin, "*God*, I missed you so much."

And I knew in that moment that this wasn't at all what I so badly wanted it to be. He was half asleep, he was drunk, and he was clearly under the illusion that he'd just made love to his dead wife. He thought I was Laura.

A sick feeling washed over me and I pushed him off, rolling to my side so I faced away from him. I curled up in a protective ball and waited to see if he'd touch me again, or say anything more.

But I needn't have worried. Soon I heard soft snores behind me. He'd fallen back asleep. To dream of his lost love, no doubt.

You might think I was irrational to jump to the conclusion that he'd thought he was with Laura, but it wasn't just the words he'd spoken that convinced me.

His cheeks had been wet with tears.

Declan

The bitch of a hangover I woke up with was annoying, but not surprising. I'd gotten pretty used to those fuckers. What I didn't get for a moment or two was where the hell I was.

I was not in my bed, and I definitely wasn't at home. Bracing myself for the worst, I pushed up on one elbow and looked around groggily. My eyes flared when I spotted the woman in bed beside me, her dark hair splayed out in sharp contrast to the white pillow. Though her back was to me, I recognized her instantly.

Amelia.

All the memories, both amazing and awful, from last night washed over me, and I smiled. Hell, I probably grinned like a fucking loon. My head throbbed, my body ached, and yet I felt like a massive weight had at last been lifted. The emotion swelling inside me had been absent for so long that it seemed almost foreign. But I knew what it was: happiness.

I was happy.

Amelia was finally beside me again. And I was happy.

I shifted closer to her and leaned over. At first I just watched her sleep, sappy grin stuck firmly in place. But then I just couldn't resist. I gently ran the pad of one finger over her cheek, brushing away an errant strand of hair. At some point over the past year, she'd changed her hair style. It was darker now, and shorter. I liked it, although I hadn't told her that yet. Shit, there were so many things I needed to tell her. When she woke, we would have to discuss some stuff, foremost being the massive apology I owed her.

But first, more urgent matters demanded my attention. To put it bluntly, I needed to piss like a fucking racehorse. I pushed back the sheets and dragged my sorry ass out of bed, making a point to shut the bathroom door before I turned on the light so as not to disturb Amelia.

This morning's mirror was not my friend. I looked like utter shit. Happy shit, but shit is still shit. My eyes landed on her toothbrush and toothpaste. I ran my tongue over my teeth and grimaced. My breath probably smelled like the bottom of a dumpster. Dragging my fingers through my hair, I turned away from my bedraggled reflection and took care of business.

When I came out of the bathroom, I sat on the bed and looked over at Amelia's sleeping form. It was seriously tempting to crawl back in with her, but I knew I wasn't the most pleasant thing to wake up to in my current state. I badly needed to brush my teeth and shower, and my pounding skull begged for ibuprofen. With a small sigh, I reluctantly got dressed. I figured I could dash up to my room, take care of my personal hygiene issues, and return before she even woke up.

My plan was to be beside her again when she opened her eyes. Yes, we needed to talk, but unless she wanted to hash things out immediately, I had some other ideas of how to welcome the day. Talking could come after.

It took me a few moments to locate my jacket, but I spotted it draped over the back of the chair, my tie tucked into one pocket. Had Amelia carefully put them aside for me? Picking my jacket up, I went into the hall and gently pulled the door closed behind me. Both elevator cars groaned in their shafts, but it felt like forever before one stopped.

Once I reached my own room, I tossed the jacket onto the bed and stripped off my clothes. None of them seemed damaged or stained, which seemed like another win. The rest of me not so much. I walked naked to the bathroom and dug around in my toiletry bag until I found the bottle of painkillers. Tapping three of them onto my palm, I shoved my face under the running tap and sucked back water. While it got the pills down, it did little to quench my dry throat. I wandered back into the main room to see if the hotel had left a complimentary bottle of water. They had, and I chugged it down. That turned out to be a bad idea. As soon as all that water hit my stomach, a wave of nausea came over me and I ran, belly sloshing, to the toilet and puked it back up.

Christ. How much did I drink last night anyway?

Too much. That seemed clear. Did I owe Josh an apology? Hopefully I hadn't embarrassed him. But knowing me, there was a good chance I had. Then, with chagrin, I remembered that asshole bartender taking a swing at me and knocking me flat on my ass.

Oh yeah. He cut me off. And he'd been flirting shamelessly with Mel. Dick.

I sighed. Yep, an apology was definitely in order. The list of people I'd pissed off seemed to grow longer by the day. All because of my temper. I frowned, reconsidering. It was also because of my drinking. I needed to do something about both.

I got to my feet and turned on the shower, my stomach already starting to settle. I didn't even give the water time to warm up, I just jumped in, shivering as the cold spray hit my skin. It didn't matter; I'd warm up just fine once I was back where I belonged: in bed with Amelia.

As I was toweling off, I heard my phone beeping and after a few frantic seconds located it inside my jacket. I wondered if it was Amelia wondering where I'd gone, but instead saw my in-laws' number on the small screen. I hit Talk hoping nothing was wrong with Alexis.

"Hello?"

"Hi Daddy."

"Morning sweetie. What's up?"

"Gramma said I could call and ask how Uncle Josh's wedding was. Did you take lotsa pictures?"

"It was great! They had an awesome day. I didn't take too many pics because I was standing with Josh a lot of the time, but I did get a few good ones. I'll show you later when I see you."

"Did you tell them I said hi?"

"I sure did. What did you guys do last night?"

"Went to Finnegan's and watched a movie. Don't tell Gramma I said this, but it was really boring!"

We talked for a few more minutes. I was in such a great mood, and hearing my daughter's cheerful chatter only boosted it. Once I said goodbye, I hurried to throw on jeans and a t-shirt so I could get back down to Amelia.

I stepped off the elevator and was standing in front of her door when it hit me. I had no key card. I couldn't let myself back in.

Way to go, idiot! Now you'll have to wake her after all. Awesome way to not piss her off.

As I raised my fist to knock, a bellhop came around the corner and spotted me. "I'm afraid you've just missed her, sir," he said as he approached.

"What?" I turned to him, confused. "What're you talking about?"

"The woman in room 308 just checked out."

"She did?"

"I'm afraid so. If you hurry down, you might still catch her in the lobby. Would you like to me to call the front desk to ask her to wait for you if she's still there?"

With a sinking heart, I shook my head, all hope and happiness evaporating. "No. That's fine."

She hadn't been drunk last night, so I had no doubt that she remembered everything in perfect detail. Which meant she didn't want to see me. And who could blame her after all I'd put her through? No one. And really, it was for the best. I should've been relieved one of us was smart enough to put a stop to this before things went any further.

I should have been. But I wasn't.

Those deep, dark wounds that had finally begun to heal once more ripped open, more ragged and raw than ever. And I was pissed off. Not at her for leaving—she was right to leave—but at myself, because I'd foolishly allowed hope to bloom. Fickle fucking hope: the most useless of all emotions. What good is hope, if it always lets you down? But never again. I swore with everything in me that I'd never allow either of us to be put in a position like this again. As I knew she was fully aware, it was in Amelia's best interests to stay far, far away from me.

The ibuprofen I'd taken hadn't done a lick of good. It felt like my throbbing brain was trying to batter its way out of my skull. I jabbed the call button for the elevator and leaned against the wall, pressing a sweaty palm against my forehead as I waited to go back up to my room so I, too, could check out and go home.

Chapter 9

Amelia

The morning after the wedding I awoke to the soft thump of my hotel room door closing. I rolled over to find myself alone. Declan had fled. Without waking me, without texting me, without even leaving a note. I wasn't particularly surprised. A little disappointed maybe, but not surprised. To be completely honest, there was a part of me that was relieved. Having to face him after what had happened would've been awkward. Presumably for both of us. He'd obviously wanted to avoid any confrontation.

Maybe I should've been grateful he left. Much as I worried about his state of mind, my own mental health needed protecting. If I wasn't careful he could set me off again, spark another downward spiral. The last one had led me to a very bad place and I didn't want to risk another.

I got up and began packing up my stuff. Looking back at the rumpled bed, I recalled how he'd woken me in the night, how we'd made love…

No.

We hadn't made love. We'd had sex. And he hadn't even realized he was with *me*. He'd thought I was Laura. Maybe because he was drunk, or maybe he'd assumed he was dreaming. Either way, it wasn't me he'd wanted. That stung a lot more than him sneaking out this morning.

I decided to skip showering or even brushing my teeth. I could do those things once I got back to Dee's. I just zipped up my bag and headed down to check out.

"So, how was it?" Though the day was warm, Dee lay on the couch beneath a fuzzy blanket.

"Fine," I replied dismissively. "More importantly, how're you feeling?"

Her wan smile told me she was still under the weather. "Better, thanks. Come sit down and tell me all about it."

I perched on the edge of the nearest chair. Shrugging, I said, "There's not much to tell." Pulling out my phone, I showed her some photos.

"Wow! Holly's dress is just *divine*! I'd wear something like that."

Raising my eyes to hers with a smile, I teased, "Something you're not telling me?"

"No, no." She waved me off. "Not yet anyway." With a rough, nervous laugh, she added, "Can you *imagine* the look on my Hindu parents' faces if I told them I was marrying a woman? The sheer horror? They'd totally lose their shit!"

"They'd come around eventually, wouldn't they? They know you're gay."

"Yeah, but I think Mommy Dearest is still holding onto the hope that it's just a phase I'm going through, and that I'll come to my senses and meet a nice Indian boy and not embarrass my family." Dee chuckled again. "*That's* never gonna happen."

"No kidding. But they love you. I'm sure in time they'll accept it."

With a wry smile, she said, "I wouldn't be so sure. But hey clever girl, you managed to lead me off topic. Back to the more important stuff. So did you talk to him? How was it?"

I felt my cheeks grow warm. "A little." I shrugged again. "He was loaded. And more interested in drinking than chatting."

She frowned. "He's an ass. You okay?"

"Yeah, I'm fine." I could have also told her nicer things, like dancing with Declan, and him saying I looked gorgeous, but I decided not to. Instead, I got to my feet to signal I was done with that particular line of conversation. "I'm gonna go jump in the shower. I could really use one."

Dee nodded, but asked no more questions. I think she was just too under the weather to pursue the topic further.

Ten minutes later I stood beneath the steaming spray, eyes squeezed shut, fighting back useless, idiotic tears for what felt like the thousandth time. The water drummed against my upturned face, as I tried to cleanse myself of my grief, my pain, and—most important of all—my sins.

Then I came to a decision.

No more wallowing, I told myself. This had gone on long enough, and I was sick of it. It was no way to live. I couldn't let myself be weak, miserable Amelia any longer. She was pitiful. Actually, she was pathetic. I hated it. I hated *her*. I had to move on with my life.

It was time to toughen up.

The following week, I had my monthly therapy session. I wasn't sure if I'd tell Debbie what had happened the night of Josh and Holly's wedding until I was sitting across from her. She asked me how my weekend had gone, and before I could stop myself it all just came out, flooding from my lips in a great gush. I barely paused to breathe. She took it in passively, as she always did. After I finished, I sat in silence for few moments while she jotted notes.

When she raised her eyes back to mine, she asked, "How are you feeling now?"

For once, I had an answer to this. I didn't even hesitate. "Strong," I said. "Believe it or not, I'm okay. At first, I was naturally a bit disappointed he'd left, but then I realized I was also kinda relieved." I straightened my spine and met her eyes. "You know what? It was what it was. We had sex. I wanted to. He wanted to. But now it's behind me. And so is he."

Debbie's brows rose ever so slightly. If I hadn't been looking her in the face, I wouldn't have even noticed. "Is he?" Her voice was soft. "Behind you?"

I nodded. "I won't sit here and try to convince you that it didn't hurt, him ditching me again without a word. It did. But I…" I paused and took a deep breath. "I've moved past it."

"I'm glad. That's a very healthy attitude."

"Thanks. It's not always easy, but I'm trying. I'm not the useless, broken woman he dumped last year anymore. I'm stronger now. He didn't break me this time. I won't let him."

She made another notation before changing the topic to my mom for the last few minutes of my appointment. I wasn't sure if she was convinced by my assurances that I was fine, but it didn't matter.

I would be. In order to get on with my life, I had to be.

I'd promised my mom I'd stop by Finnegan's after counseling to pick up dinner for us. As I stood at the bar waiting for my order, I was startled to hear a familiar voice behind me.

"Amelia?"

Instantly recognizing the voice, I spun around with a nervous smile. "Hey Liv."

A petite woman with wavy honey-blonde hair stood in front of me. She looked as apprehensive as I felt.

"Hey. Waiting for takeout?"

"Yeah, I'm on my way to Mom's. You picking up, too?"

"What else?" She paused, then added, "How're you doin'?"

"Good. Not much to tell, really. Still staying at Dee's, but you probably already knew that."

Liv nodded. "Yeah." She took a deep breath. "So...I don't know if you've heard or not—"

Before she could continue, I reached out and grabbed her left hand, lifting it up so I could see her engagement ring. It was simple and pretty, not entirely dissimilar to the one Scott had given me eight years ago. "I did. Congrats. I mean it." I grabbed her by the shoulders and embraced her. At first she stiffened in my arms, but then I felt her hands slip around my waist as she squeezed me back.

"I'm sorry I didn't tell you sooner. We just weren't sure..."

Stepping away, I decided to just cut to the chase. "It's awkward, I know. I know all too well. This whole situation is super weird. And it sucks. I miss you. I miss you both. And I wish you guys nothing but happiness, honest."

Spotting tears in the corners of Liv's eyes, I dug in my bag for a tissue and handed it to her.

"Thanks." She dabbed at her eyes. "That means a lot. I'm sorry things are so weird between us. I wish they weren't. Maybe someday they won't be."

"Yeah, hopefully. And I'm sorry, too." I gave her what I hoped was a reassuring smile.

"We both still care about you. You know that, right?"

"Ditto," I said.

"Order for York?" The bartender placed a large, delicious-smelling paper bag in front of me. I slid him my credit card, and once he processed it, I turned back to Liv.

"I'm glad I ran into you. Please give Scott my best, okay?"

"I will. Hey, Ames?"

"Yeah?"

"Maybe it's just me over-analyzing the whole weirdness factor, but you seem a little off. You sure you're okay?"

I shrugged, picking up my takeout and flashing a tight grin. "I'm good. I'm just hungry. Text me sometime, okay? Maybe we can grab a drink next time I'm in town?"

"I'd like that. Talk soon."

I actually wasn't all that hungry, even with the enticing odor of hot french fries wafting from the bag, but it was an easy excuse to use. It seemed even after so much time apart, my best friend still knew me far too well.

I couldn't sleep. My overactive brain kept going over my conversation with Debbie Westwood, retracing my chat with Liv, and both were intermixed with replays from the night of Josh's wedding. I tried my best to put that particular memory out of my mind when I was awake, but during the long hours lying in that weird state between sleep and wakefulness, I was helpless to keep it at bay.

After about an hour of tossing and turning, I got up and went to sit at my desk, opening my laptop in hopes that browsing Facebook might help me feel sleepier.

It didn't.

I'd unfollowed both Liv and Scott months ago. Scott posted mostly football stuff, but Liv was an over-sharer on social media. Though I was happy she was happy, I didn't need to see regular reminders that she was now living the life I once had. After our conversation at Finnegan's, I decided to refollow. Her most recent post was a cute shot of her and Scott laughing about something I didn't really understand. And why would I? It's not like I was a part of their lives anymore.

Josh had also uploaded a bunch of photos of himself and Holly in New Orleans, where they were currently on their honeymoon. Both couples looked smiley and blissful and madly in love. Don't get me wrong—I wasn't jealous. Their posts just made me wistful. Maybe someday I'd find that kind of love again, too. Although I wasn't so certain I deserved it.

With a sigh, I closed the screen.

Maybe I'd try writing a bit. It often helped relax me. I switched on the lamp and pulled open my desk drawer to get my notebook. My birth control pills sat on top of it, and I reached to move them aside. But my fingers stopped in midair before touching the packet. Though I'd already taken my daily dose hours ago, my eyes lingered on them.

Why bother?

Well, they helped regulate my periods; that was a plus. But they cost me money every month, money I could definitely use for more important things. And it's not like I was having sex. My night with Declan had been an anomaly; I definitely didn't see sex in my future anytime soon, as I was nowhere near ready to meet someone new. So why should I continue putting hormones into my system and taking money from my wallet? Maybe deep down I'd been holding onto to some insane hope that eventually Declan and I would reunite, but last weekend proved that was never going to happen. So why bother?

I grabbed them and tossed them toward the wastebasket in the corner. In a rare perfect throw the packet clattered to the bottom. Grinning, I fist-pumped the air.

Just like *he* used to.

Declan

Last week, Josh had been away on his honeymoon, but I was pretty sure he'd be back to work today. I gave him most of the day to get caught up on all the shit that had undoubtedly piled up in his absence, and around three-thirty wandered over to Accounting. He was in his office, brows all furrowed over whatever he was reading on his monitor.

I knocked on his doorframe, startling him, but when he saw it was me, he broke into a smile. "Hey! How goes it?" He gestured toward one of his guest chairs. "Have a seat."

"Welcome back to Hell. How was the Big Easy?"`

"Big. And easy." He laughed. "It was awesome. Can't wait to go back. Y'ever been?"

I shook my head.

"You'd love it."

"Yeah, I'll hafta make the trip someday. Can you spare a few minutes?"

"Sure. What's on your mind?"

I took a deep breath. "So…you know I don't really do apologies much, but…" I trailed off.

Josh's eyes flared and he laughed. "Bullshit."

"Shh." I put a finger against my lips. "I have a reputation to maintain." I reached over and shut his office door. "Seriously, though. About what happened at your reception…"

"You got shitfaced and you started a fight with my bartender and you're really sorry and you'll never do it again?" He arched a skeptical brow, but he was grinning. "Does that about cover it?"

"Something like that, yeah."

"Dude, I'm not pissed at you. Not gonna lie—Holly was, but she's over it now. We both know you're still not in the best mental space. And seeing Amelia probably threw you even more." He paused and sighed. "But you've gotta get a handle on your drinking. You know that, right? I'm telling you this as your friend."

I nodded sheepishly. "I know. Sorry if I embarrassed you guys."

Josh waved that off. "It's fine. I tipped Pedro an extra Benjamin at the end of the night. He's used to drunken assholes. I'm sure he's forgotten it already. But Amelia won't have. Have you spoken to her since then?"

My face grew hot. "No. Not since she helped me back to the room." I chose not to elaborate. Telling him what had happened that night would just be inviting a lecture I didn't need. I already knew I'd fucked up.

"You should apologize to her, too, you know. And thank her. She didn't have to look after your sorry ass, but she volunteered. Because she cares about you. So do I, but sometimes it seems to me like you don't care very much about yourself anymore. And that worries me."

I wasn't in the habit of lying to my best friend. Avoiding his questions sometimes, sure, but not outright lying. However, this time I felt like I had no choice. "I will. And I know. No need to worry."

Another sigh. "No, you probably won't. But you should. She deserves that much."

I bristled. "She deserves a helluva lot better than anything I could ever offer her."

At first he didn't reply. He just looked at me, his fingers tenting below his chin as he studied my face. Finally he said, "You may be right. But right or wrong, it doesn't matter. It's not about what she deserves or what you deserve. Love doesn't work that way."

I was becoming extremely fucking uncomfortable with this conversation. My fight or flight response kicked in strong, and since I had no desire to fight with Josh about this or anything else, I chose flight.

Pushing back my chair, I got to my feet and opened the door. "Thanks for the advice. Glad to hear you guys had a blast down south." I didn't meet his eyes as I stepped into the hallway, but I was far too familiar with the expression I knew they'd be holding: pity.

Chapter 10

Amelia

The summer-like weather had gone, replaced by typical autumn drizzle. Wind rattled the glass in the living room windows, and I tugged a blanket off the back of the couch and wrapped it around myself. I hated gloomy days—they did nothing for my mental state. Mostly, I just wanted to crawl back into bed and sleep them away.

Sighing, I saved the spreadsheet I'd been updating, turned down my music, and picked up my phone. Josh had been back from his honeymoon for a week now and it was time I checked in. His office phone rang four times and I was just about to hang up and text his cell when he answered.

"Accounting Department, Josh Marshall speaking." He sounded distracted.

"Hey, it's Amelia. Is now a bad time? You can call me back later if—"

"No, it's fine. I was just out in the hall talking to Evan when I heard my phone. I'm pretty sure he won't mind if I give you a few minutes."

"So generous," I laughed. "How was your trip?"

"New Orleans is literally the coolest city ever. Did you see the pics Holly posted on Facebook?"

"I saw a few. It looked pretty amazing. Glad you guys had fun."

"We really did. You'll have to go someday."

"Yeah, maybe. So…" I stopped. Did I really want to ask? Was this the real reason I'd called? I was clearly a terrible friend.

"So?" Before I could continue, in an understanding voice Josh added, "Let me guess. You wanna know how he's doing, right?"

I sighed. "Yeah. I know, I know. Pathetic, aren't I?"

"Not at all. I saw him a few days ago…uh, I think it was Monday afternoon. He popped in to apologize for being a drunken idiot at the wedding. But I haven't heard from him since. I've been pretty slammed this week though, and I think he's been busy with clients. I haven't seen his car in the parking lot in days. So, in answer to your question: I don't really know. About the same, I think. I told him he needs to get a handle on his drinking."

I felt myself nodding, although Josh couldn't see it. "It must be so hard for him, though. He really misses her."

"Who? Laura? Yeah, I guess. I know he blames himself for what happened. But it isn't just about that. You know that, don't you?"

I was quiet. I didn't want to tell Josh what Declan had said when he'd thought I was Laura that night. Then I'd have to explain what had happened and that was one secret I had no urge to share.

I was just about to try to change the subject when I heard another voice in the background, possibly Evan, and then Josh telling them to hold on. "Amelia? I'm sorry but I hafta go. We'll talk soon though, okay?"

"No problem. Tell Holly I said hi."

"Will do." He disconnected.

I put my phone back in my pocket and turned back to my laptop. I had to stop asking Josh about Declan. If I was going to move on, I needed to stop talking about him, dwelling on him. I needed to stop giving him so much of my mental energy.

But that was a lot easier said than done.

By mid-afternoon, the clouds had parted and the sky was once again a clear, bright blue. I decided to get out of the apartment and go for a walk. Walking helped me to focus my scattered thoughts, and I'd gotten into the habit of regular walks over the past year. Ever since I was a small girl holding my dad's hand, I'd always been a walker. Now that I lived in Richmond, I'd lengthened my strolls to the point where I sometimes went out and explored the city for hours until every muscle in my lower body ached. Especially on days when I didn't want to interact with others. Which, if I'm being honest, was most of them.

The wooded trails in Washington Park were a bit muddy from the rain, but I didn't mind. Bright orange and yellow leaves surrounded me, and as I strode along, my shoes crunched through drifts of them along the path. No one else was around at this time of the day, and it was very peaceful.

As I crossed a small bridge over a babbling stream, my mind drifted to Liv. It had been several weeks since our awkward run-in at Finnegan's, but before we had gone our separate ways, she'd asked me to let her know when I'd be in Swann's Landing again and maybe we could meet up for drinks. No matter the weirdness, I was eager to at least start the complicated process of repairing our friendship. Since I was planning to visit my mom this weekend, I decided to text her.

Going to be in town Sat. Time for a drink later?

I hit Send, and tucked my phone into my pocket. As I zipped it closed, a wave of dizziness hit me, and I lurched forward, bracing my hands on my knees to steady myself. After a few deep breathes, my head cleared and I tried to continue walking. I took a few more steps, but then I stopped again. My breathing was labored, and it felt like my heart was racing. I realized with dismay that I felt exhausted. Clearly my body was telling me it was time to turn around and head back.

This wasn't the first time a sudden bout of fatigue had hit me recently, but as I'd done before, I tried to push through and ignore it. It also wasn't the first time I'd noticed my heartrate going faster than normal.

I reduced my pace, but by the time I climbed the steps and entered the apartment, I was beat. I didn't even eat dinner; I just went right to bed and fell into a dreamless sleep.

The next day, I woke up super groggy. I barely had enough energy to get up to pee, and I definitely didn't feel up to the hour's drive to Swann's Landing. Opening my eyes just wide enough to peer between my lashes, I groped for my phone and called my mom to say I couldn't make it. While I'd been asleep, Liv had replied to my text saying she was busy tonight. Instead of feeling disappointed, I was relieved. As our friendship was in that fragile, rebuilding stage, I didn't want to have to cancel on her.

Re-settling into my pillow, I drifted back to sleep. I wasn't too worried about my health. I figured I was just over tired. It didn't feel like I was coming down with a cold or the flu, so I just put the fatigue down to too much stress and not enough truly restful rest.

On Sunday, I felt a lot better, although my appetite was still minimal. I had enough energy to go for a walk, but I kept it short, just going once around the block. Again, I went to bed early, but this time it wasn't dreamless. I had many overlapping dreams, filled with strange images I couldn't quite remember in the morning.

About a week later, I was at the kitchen counter in front of my laptop when I heard Dee's key in the lock. When she stepped inside, she took one look at me and narrowed her eyes. "What's up with your face?"

"What?" I asked, confused. I went into the bathroom and looked in the mirror. There were several big red pimples on my left cheek, my nose, and a huge one on my chin that hadn't been there when I brushed my teeth that morning.

Great, I thought. *An explosion of zits. Just what I need.*

Opening the cabinet behind the mirror, I pulled out some acne cream and dabbed generous dollops on each spot. I sometimes got pimples when it was nearing my time of the month, although not usually this bad. Which reminded me. Hadn't my period been due several days ago? I figured since I'd tossed my pills, the timing was likely messed up. I'd read that could happen.

"Looks like my hormones are in overdrive this month," I told Dee, shaking my head and chuckling as I re-entered the kitchen.

She came over to examine me more closely. "You still feeling wiped out all the time?"

"Yeah, a bit." I shrugged. "It's no big deal. I should be getting my period any day now."

With a small frown, she said, "If you say so. But if this exhaustion continues, I really think you should see your doctor."

"Duly noted," I smiled. "By the way, have I ever told you you're gonna make a great mom someday?"

She laughed. "If I didn't know your sex life was non-existent, I'd be wondering if *you* were about to be one."

I sobered. "I'm not pregnant. I can't be. I was on the Pill…"

Dee's eyes shot wide. She grabbed me by both shoulders. "What the ever-lovin' fuck, Amelia! You slept with someone? No, wait. *Shit!* You slept with *him*, didn't you? After the wedding?"

Heat flooded my face. Biting my lower lip, I broke eye contact and nodded.

"*Why* didn't you tell me?" Her voice softened. "Sorry. I'm sorry. I won't yell at you." She tugged me over to the couch and sat down with me. "Tell me what happened. Please."

Staring down at my hands, I told her about Josh and Holly's reception and what went down that night. When I finished, she took my hand. "Why are you so sure he meant Laura? Maybe he meant he missed *you*?"

"You weren't there. You didn't see him. He's really depressed. He…he loved her a lot, and now she's gone and he blames himself for what happened to her. I *know* he regrets being with me. I know it."

Dee was quiet for a few moments. Then she asked, "Are you sure?"

"I'm sure."

"Okay. And…he didn't use a condom?"

I shook my head.

"And you hadn't missed any pills?"

"No. I was always pretty careful about that stuff "

She frowned. "Was? Past tense?"

"I actually tossed them out a few weeks ago. I figured it's not like I'm ever gonna have sex again, at least not anytime in the near future. And they're expensive."

"Well, okay. Maybe it's just stress making you so tired. And maybe your face broke out because you're about to get your period. Do you have that bloaty feeling?"

I rubbed my stomach. "Yes, for sure. Even my boobs are sore."

Dee looked at me sharply, eyes narrowed. "I hope that's all it is."

"Me, too."

About an hour later, she knocked on my bedroom door. When I opened it, she was holding up my bottle of St. John's Wort from the bathroom. "You still taking these every day?"

I nodded, reaching for the bottle. "Yeah, they're supposed to help with depression. Why?"

"Dude. You ever read the warning on the back?" Her deep brown eyes were huge.

Frowning, I turned it over and examined the back label. At the bottom in bold type it read: *Caution: taking St. John's Wort may decrease the effectiveness of the birth control pill.*

I went completely still. "Shit."

"Yeah."

Thirty minutes later, I sat on the toilet staring at the pregnancy test stick in my hand. I knew Dee was just outside the door waiting for me to tell her the results, but I had no idea how to process the information before me.

I closed my eyes in disbelief, hoping as hard as I could that maybe I'd read it wrong. But when I reopened them, there was still a bright pink plus sign in the little window.

Dee had bought a two-pack of tests for me at the drug store around the corner. I grabbed the other one and ripped open the package.

After repeating the process, the read-out was the same: a plus sign. Which meant...

Oh God.

I was pregnant.

"You've *got* to be kidding me!" I moaned.

I couldn't accept it. The parallels were just too unbelievable. Laura had gotten pregnant after a drunken tryst with Declan in a hotel room. While they were technically separated no less. And now the same thing had happened to me. How was that even possible? Laura might have wanted this, but I definitely did not.

With a groan, I tossed the used tests in the garbage and dragged my fingers into my hair.

What was I supposed to do now?"

Chapter 11

Amelia

"I'll make an appointment for you at Planned Parenthood. It's just up the street from the salon."

I looked up at Dee in confusion. I was still in shock, not even slightly able to wrap my head around this.

This isn't happening.

How can I be...? How? I couldn't even think the word.

She sighed and wrapped an arm around my shoulders. "Hey, hey. It'll all be okay. Don't cry."

Was I crying? I swiped a finger below one eye and, sure enough, came away with moisture. I hadn't even noticed I'd begun to cry.

"I know, Ames. It sucks. Big time. But sometimes shit like this happens. It doesn't have to be the end of the world. We'll deal with it, but you need to go see them."

"I..." I stopped, swallowing hard. "I don't...I just...need a few days. Can I have a few days to just...?" I had no idea what I wanted. I only knew I needed time to process.

"Of course." She gave me a squeeze. "Take a day or two. Research your options. There's bound to be loads of info on the Planned Parenthood site. And I bet there's online forums where you can ask other women questions who've gone through this, or are currently going through it."

I nodded. "Yeah. Okay."

"If you want to talk things over, you know I'm right here. I'm with you for this. All the way."

"Thanks," I croaked, pulling away from her to grab a tissue.

Another one of those waves of exhaustion came over me, and I told Dee I was going to go lie down. But as I huddled under my blankets, eyes squeezed shut, sleep was nowhere to be found. My tears had dried. My throat no longer felt constricted. But I still had an ache deep in my chest. I knew that neither my tears nor that ache were caused by sadness. They were because I was scared.

No. Not scared, completely terrified.

Then I remembered what I'd promised myself, what I'd told Debbie Westwood: I wasn't going to be weak, pathetic Amelia anymore. No more crying. What I needed to do right now was to be strong and practical and figure out my next step.

I rolled onto my back and opened my eyes, staring at the ceiling. When I'd had a tough decision to make, I usually made a Pros and Cons list. This time, the Cons were obvious.

There were so many reasons to not do this. (I couldn't think of it as a baby. I wouldn't let myself. Not then.) The first and most important one was that Declan wasn't in the picture. He'd made it clear by his continued silence that he wanted no part of my life now. If we were a couple, this situation would be a lot different. If we were still together, maybe we'd even be excited about it. Maybe. I didn't know. But there was no point in speculating. We weren't. I was alone in this.

Which brought me to my next point: I could barely picture myself as anyone's mom at all, let alone a single mom trying to raise a child on my own. The very idea of it felt alien. I was still in my rebuilding stage, and so far the rebuilding wasn't going all that well. My pathetic life plus single motherhood—those two things just did not mesh.

And even if my life *was* going the way I wanted, I wasn't sure I'd be onboard with a pregnancy right now anyway. So far, I'd never felt any yearning for kids. When Scott and I had been together, it had always been him who'd wanted babies; he'd just been waiting for me to get there, too. I'd never been the type of girl to fantasize about becoming a mom and raising children. I guess I'd always figured one day I'd be ready. But that day hadn't yet arrived.

My own mom wasn't the warm and fuzzy nurturing type, either. I'd always assumed she'd resented my arrival, as it had put an end to her career. As an adult, I knew that had been her choice and wasn't my fault, that she could have chosen to go back to work whenever she'd wanted, but a part of me had always felt like she blamed me for having to give up her dreams. What if I was like her? What if I ended up resenting my child for holding me back? But holding me back from what? I had no job, no money, and was living in Dee's spare room in her small apartment. My friend circle was the smallest it had ever been, and my mother would undoubtedly not be super supportive about me becoming a mom right now, let alone her becoming a grandmother.

Having a child at this point in my life would be a terrible, horrible, awful idea.

But.

There was one major But. The only reason I had to consider keeping it.

This was a part of him. And a part of me. This was a new life that we'd created together. Sure, at the time of conception, it hadn't exactly been about love, at least not on his part. But he used to love me. We used to love each other. And now, maybe this was all I had left of that. Of him.

All of the Cons I'd come up with still applied, and I knew wanting to hold onto this small piece of him like a living souvenir of our broken relationship was absolutely *not* a good reason to bring a child into this world. Especially with me for a mother. I knew this. But still.

It did matter. It mattered a lot.

I realized I was unconsciously rubbing my belly. It was still flat. There was no outward sign of the secret within. Only Dee and I knew. And if I decided not to keep it, no one else ever would.

I didn't know what to do, so I did nothing.

The next day when Dee got home from work, she silently handed me a stack of pamphlets she'd picked up from Planned Parenthood. She didn't mention my situation, not over dinner, and not while we watched television together later. We drank hot chocolate, shared a fuzzy blanket on the couch, and giggled at stupid sitcoms. To my surprise, Terri didn't come over. Maybe she had to work late, or maybe Dee had asked her not to. I didn't know, but I was grateful to spend some time just the two of us, even if we were pretending like everything was normal, like I didn't have a massive decision I soon needed to make.

Later in bed I carefully read through each of the brochures. Most of them were about either abortion or adoption. All I knew by the time I set them aside and turned off the lamp was that adoption was off the table. If I decided to have it—and that was still a huge *if*—there was no way I could give it away to strangers. I would raise it myself. I knew that as well as I knew anything.

Which truthfully didn't feel like much at the moment.

My heart is pounding. Where is Declan? I need to find Declan. It's important.

I run down the narrow hallway. It's all white, with blank walls and a high ceiling. I turn left, then a quick right. He's around here somewhere, I know it. If I just keep looking, I'll find him.

Picking up speed, I turn another corner. I can hear music in the distance and head toward it. I go through a set of double doors into a darkened room. They remind me of the ones into the cafeteria at work.

Yes, I'm in the cafeteria. The lights are off, but faint light comes through the windows. A radio sits in the middle of one of the long tables. It's playing Radiohead's 'High and Dry.' As I walk toward it, my body casts a long black shadow on the floor.

I scan the large room for him. It's empty.

The music stops, startling me and I catch my foot on a chair leg and stumble. I go down on my knee, grabbing the edge of the table with one hand while I cover my stomach with the other. Protecting it. I have to protect it.

My belly is round and bulging. I can feel movement beneath my fingers. Kicking. The baby is twisting and squirming inside me. His baby.

Where is he?

I drag myself to my feet and look around and—oh God!—my heart leaps as I spot him. He's at a table in the far corner by himself, his face half-concealed in shadow. Although I can't see him well, I know it's him. I'd know him anywhere.

Though we're the only two people in here, he hasn't noticed me.

"Declan?" I call, but he doesn't look up.

I run toward him, cradling my belly, dodging to avoid sharp corners as I wind through the maze of tables. My breath comes in ragged bursts.

He's still so far away. "DECLAN!" I try to shout, but it comes out as no more than a sigh. Frustrated, I raise one arm and wave frantically at him. He still doesn't react.

This room seems to be as long as a football field. It's no longer the BWK cafeteria. It's more like an airport. Why are we in an airport? Is he leaving me again?

He can't leave me! Not now. Not when I need him the most.

In a burst of speed, I propel myself forward until at last I reach him.

"Declan," I say for the third time, hoping against hope he'll hear.

At long last he looks up, and my heart skips a beat as he grins at me. He's pleased to see me. Thank goodness. Thank God. Thank fuck.

"Amelia?" He gets to his feet and comes toward me. Some of my apprehension ebbs away at the sight of his face. "What are you doing here?"

"I needed to see you. I have to tell you something."

He reaches me at that moment and throws his arms around me, pulling me tight against him. But just as quickly, he steps away, staring down at my protruding belly in shock.

Fear grips me again. I go still, waiting for his reaction. I stop breathing, even.

Long, long moments crawl by. His hands, which had been around my waist, slide forward to cup my stomach. He falls to his knees and kisses the curve of my belly gently, reverently.

Then he looks up at me and smiles. "It's a girl," he tells me with confidence. "A sweet little girl."

"How do you know?" I ask, but I accept it as truth.

Declan shrugs. He gets to his feet and looks into my eyes. "I just do. The same way I know I love her already. Another beautiful daughter. This is the best news ever."

My tension finally releases and I smile back at him. "I'm so glad you're happy. I was so worried about telling you."

"Why wouldn't I be happy? I can't wait to meet her." Then he leans close to my ear and whispers, "We'll name her Laura."

I woke up with a start, my eyes flying open as I sucked in a sharp breath.

What the hell was that about?

Pressing my head back into my pillow, I sighed. My hand went to my stomach, rubbing soothing circles over my skin.

Could it be a girl?

I didn't want to think of it as a girl. Or a boy. Just an 'it' was better. I couldn't let myself imagine it as an actual child, and certainly not as *my* child. Not now. Not yet. Not unless I decided to keep it.

And if I did decide to keep it, I'd have to tell him. I'd have no choice.

We'll name her Laura.

I shuddered. Though I knew it was just a dream, a bizarre manifestation of my fears, I still recoiled inside at the thought of having that conversation with him. Sure, in real life, he wouldn't know if it was a boy or girl, and I was certain there was no chance he'd want to name it Laura, but...what if he didn't want anything to do with it? Or me? What if he was so messed up that he just couldn't deal with this and pushed me away yet again? Could I handle that? Would it break me again?

It could. There was a definite risk.

But I also understood something else. No matter what happened with Declan, I wouldn't really be alone. I'd have Dee and Terri. And Josh and Holly. And, at least to some extent, my mom. And maybe, just maybe, Liv as well. I'd be surrounded by people who would care about me and my...it.

I'd raise it without him, if that's what he wanted. I'd figure out this mom-stuff not by myself, but with the help of my friends. And we'd be okay.

We'd be just fine.

And I suddenly realized I'd made a decision after all.

Chapter 12

Amelia

I awoke the next morning to the sound of wind rattling my windowpanes in their frames, and with a shiver rolled over to go back to sleep. That blissful oblivion of first waking didn't last long, though. My eyes shot wide as I remembered the shocking, life-altering decision I'd come to last night.

Everything was about to change. Again. There had been so many major life changes over the past two years; it was hard to believe I was now facing yet another. And though the others had completely altered the trajectory of my life, I knew this change would be the biggest one yet. I had no idea what my future would look like, but I understood nothing would ever be the same.

The prospect of all this was beyond terrifying, and I allowed myself some time to just lie there and be scared. Fear was normal in my situation, but I was determined that I wasn't going to let it control me. So, I took a deep breath, threw back the blankets and got up, determined to embrace this as best I could.

The first thing I had to do was see a doctor. This pregnancy wouldn't feel real to me until it was confirmed by an actual medical professional. I thought about calling Dr. Fleming's office back in Swann's Landing, but decided against it. If I did that, I'd have to drive an hour each way for every appointment, even if I felt crappy. I could ask Dee for the name of her doctor, but then I'd have to wait until she got home, and first I'd need to explain my decision to her. I didn't want to sit here all day and do nothing. I wanted to be proactive and get a confirmation as soon as possible.

I got up and went to the bathroom. When I returned, my eyes landed on the pamphlets Dee had picked up for me. Flipping one over, I found the phone number and as she'd been bugging me to do since I told her the home pregnancy test results, I called Planned Parenthood. The polite young woman who answered was able to book me an appointment to see their on-site doctor this afternoon.

Stifling a yawn, I sat back on the bed. I still had several hours before I needed to get showered and go out. I could go online and do some work, or research more, or…I glanced down at my pillow. It was still dented from where it had cradled my head. Sighing softly, I crawled beneath my sheets and went back to sleep.

The doctor who saw me was tall, with pale blond hair and a baby face. He flashed me a kind smile. After closing the door of the examination room, he immediately told me, "Your urine test came back positive," Glancing down at his clipboard, he added, "Ms. York."

I'd provided a sample to the nurse before being brought in here to wait, and I was a bit surprised the doctor already had the results. I pictured them using the same type of drug store test that I'd used, and couldn't help wondering why I'd bothered coming in. Confirmation and information, I reminded myself. Not to mention a doctor's assurance that this was real.

"Right." I nodded grimly. "That's why I'm here, Dr. Zane."

He smiled again. It was a kind smile. "You can call me Steve." He took the chair opposite me. "Is this your first pregnancy?"

I nodded again.

"How are you feeling? Any tenderness? Morning sickness yet?"

Steve looked at least five years younger than me. Maybe more. How could he possibly be a doctor? Maybe he'd just graduated and was doing volunteer work at a non-profit to gain experience? I wasn't sure how comfortable I felt discussing my

101

pregnancy with a doctor who looked like a boy I used to babysit, but then again, I really didn't have much choice if I wanted to get things rolling today.

"No, not really. I've been super tired, though. Will I start feeling sick soon?"

"Tired is normal. You need extra rest right now. Morning sickness could start any day, last a few weeks, or last throughout. Or you might not get it at all."

Puking the entire time? That would seriously suck. I sighed, but didn't reply.

Dr. Steve's expression turned serious. "Have you made a decision about what you want to do?"

Frowning, I asked, "About what?"

He cleared his throat, looking a little uncomfortable. "About the baby. I don't mean to be insensitive, but…are you planning to keep it? Or?"

"Oh. Uh, well, I've gone over my options—it's pretty much all I've thought about since I found out. Yes, I'm going to keep it." It was the first time I'd voiced my choice out loud, and it sounded strange, like some other woman, one with no doubts in the world, was speaking through my mouth.

Dr. Steve smiled again. "Okay, good. Then we can get down to the important stuff. Do you know the date of your last period?"

"I know the date of conception. Is that good enough? It was September thirtieth." I counted it as the day after the wedding. It had happened after midnight, after all.

He did a calculation, then looked up at me and said, "Your due date will be June nineteenth next year. Although that's just an approximation. Babies aren't very good at keeping to schedules."

I offered him a weak grin. The thought of giving birth scared the living crap out of me. June still seemed very far away, but I had a feeling the months between now and then would zip by a lot faster than I wanted.

"Do you have a family doctor? You'll need to be referred to an OB-GYN."

"I do, but I recently moved here and my family doctor is an hour's drive away. So seeing someone local would be a lot easier."

"No problem. I can give you a referral for an OB-GYN nearby. Dr. Middleton's office is only two blocks from here. Would that be okay?"

"Perfect." I smiled. "Thank you."

He then asked me if I had any allergies, and about my and my family's medical history. After he jotted some notes, he asked about the baby's father's history.

With a sigh, I looked down at my hands and shrugged. "I don't really know. We're not... He's not in the picture anymore." There went the self-assured stranger. One question about Declan and I went right back to sounding insecure. I mentally chastised myself. I didn't know what he'd say when he found out, but if he chose to walk away, then he ceased to matter. Only we did. Not me—I realized I was no longer just me, I was now a we.

Dr. Steve's voice brought me back to the moment. "Okay. Do you have support to help you through all this?"

Though I hadn't actually asked, I was confident I would, so I just nodded.

"Good, good. That's super important."

He gave me a list of pregnancy books I might want to read and instructed me to start taking folic acid right away, as it helped prevent birth defects of the baby's brain and spinal cord. He also wrote out a requisition for blood work, and sent me over to the blood clinic next door.

After giving blood, I picked up a bottle of folic acid from the same pharmacy where Dee had gotten the pregnancy tests, and then headed back to the apartment. Putting my earbuds in, I listened to music as I walked and tried very hard to focus on the song instead of my reality.

I wasn't sure if talking to Dr. Steve had made this feel more real or not. In some ways, it had. But a part of me still felt like I'd somehow gotten stuck in someone else's life. And I had no idea how to find my way back again.

When I emerged from my bedroom on Saturday morning, the smell of freshly brewed coffee hit me like a punch to the gut. I darted into the bathroom, just making it to the toilet in time.

Great. Is this what my mornings are gonna be like now? Please let this only last a few weeks, and not all the way to next June!

I sat on the floor for a moment until the nausea passed, then splashed water on my face and brushed my teeth.

When I came into the kitchen, Dee looked up at me with an arched brow. "Morning sickness already?"

"Guess so." I said, leaning against the wall. "Not fun."

She reached for a clean mug. "Coffee?" My face must have blanched, because she frowned and replaced the cup as I shook my head.

"Not this morning. That's what did it, I think. Which is so weird, because I normally love the smell of fresh coffee." Though it was chilly out, I went over and cracked a window to help clear the air, then popped a slice of bread in the toaster.

"Well, at least you won't have to deal with it for long."

I didn't reply or even turn to look at her. I knew I had to tell her, but I wasn't sure how to explain or how she would react. After I'd buttered my toast and sat down beside her, I said, "So, about that."

Dee looked up at me over the top of her laptop. "About what?"

"About my...situation."

"Did you make an appointment yet?"

"I saw a doctor at Planned Parenthood a couple days ago, actually."

Her eyebrows flew up. "You did? Why didn't you tell me? I would have gone with you! Jesus, Ames. You shouldn't have had to go through that by yourself. How're you feel—wait. Why're you having morning sickness if you already took care of it?"

I looked down at my toast. "I, uh, I didn't have an abortion."

"Oh. Okay. Did you make an appointment then?" She grabbed her phone. "Let me put it in my calendar."

"No, I..." I stopped, sighing. "I'm not going to get one."

Dee froze, eyes narrowed. "You're not?" She came around the counter to stand in front of me. "You're gonna give it up for adoption?"

Shaking my head, I held her gaze. "Would you support me if I...?"

"If you *what*? Had a baby? Are you being serious right now?"

I just nodded. I tried to smile hopefully, but I'm not sure I managed it.

"Whoa. You *are* serious. You're really, really serious." She turned away and braced both hands on the countertop, dragging in a deep breath.

I stayed quiet, letting her process. Then, in a soft voice, I asked, "Do you think I'm a total idiot? You do, don't you?" Her reaction had me worried. Was I was making a huge mistake?

Dee raised her head and looked back at me. "This is what you want? You're sure?"

Biting my lower lip, I nodded again. "I know it's crazy, but...I'm sure."

To my immense relief, she threw her arms around me and squeezed. "Okay," she whispered. Stepping back, she looked me straight in the eyes. "Okay. I'm in. We'll do it. We'll figure this out."

"Thank you." Tears were forming in the corners of my eyes. "You don't know how much that means to me."

With a smile, she shook her head incredulously. "Holy shit, Ames. You're gonna be someone's mommy. I'm gonna be an auntie. Who would've thought?"

"I know, right? It's totally nuts. But it feels right. I thought about it long and hard, and this is the right choice. I know it is. Even without Declan."

Dee's smile vanished. "Have you told him?"

"Not yet. I have to, though." I sighed. "I'm not exactly looking forward to it, but I'll try to get a hold of him next week. And I guess at some point I'll have to tell my mom, too."

She brightened. "I'm going to see my parents today. Why don't you come with me and I'll drop you off at your mom's for a few hours? And I'm meeting Liv for a drink later—you should come, too. It'll be like old times!"

I thought about it for a moment. My stomach had settled, at least for now. I wouldn't have to drive. And it definitely would be great to hang out with Dee and Liv like we used to. I wanted to take any chance I got to work on repairing my friendship with Liv. As long as I could stay awake for it, this could be fun.

"I guess I could. Would I have time for a nap before we go?"

She smiled. "Of course. We'll head out after lunch."

"Amelia?"

I'd just stepped inside my mother's house after Dee dropped me off. "Yes, sorry I didn't call first. Dee was coming to visit her parents, so I decided to tag along."

Mom came into the front hallway to greet me. When she saw me, her smiled turned to a frown. "Goodness! You look terrible."

"Thanks," I said wryly as I shrugged off my coat.

She came closer to examine me. "Your face is all broken out, and you have huge dark circles. Are you sick? Your colour looks off, too."

I took a step back and forced a smile. "I'm fine. Just haven't gotten enough sleep lately. And it's just a few pimples. No big deal. They'll clear up in a few days."

"You haven't had a break-out like that since you were a teenager. Are you eating properly? Getting your vitamins?"

Sighing, I said, "Yes and yes. Honestly, I'm totally fine."

"You need to start taking better care of yourself, Amelia. You'll never find a husband if you just let yourself go."

I rolled my eyes. "Finding a husband isn't exactly on my priority list right now."

Her lips pressed into a line. Then she turned and went into the kitchen to put the kettle on. I shook my head as I followed, grateful she decided to drop it.

Over dinner, I tried my best to make small talk, but the whole time I couldn't help wondering how Mom was going to react once she found out my news. Probably not well. I was sure she'd tell me I was making a very stupid choice, and that a baby would scare off any man who might want to date me. And hey, maybe she'd be right. Maybe it would. If so, those were men I'd be better off avoiding.

Thankfully, I didn't plan to drop that bomb on her tonight. I'd read that the risk of miscarriage reduced significantly after twelve weeks, so I figured I'd wait at least another month before telling anyone but Declan. I wished I could put off telling him, too, but no matter how much I dreaded it, he deserved to know as soon as possible.

As I was trying to picture what this house would be like with a baby crawling around in it next year, the doorbell rang. I pulled it open and was surprised to find Liv standing there.

"Oh hey." I craned my head to look around her. "Is Dee in the car?"

Liv flashed an awkward smile. "She's running late, so she asked me to pick you up. Apparently her mom insisted she cut her brother's hair. She said she'll meet us there."

"No problem. Just let me grab my coat."

I said goodbye to Mom and, as I had so many times in the past, walked down the porch steps with Liv. Scott's truck was parked along the curb. I didn't mention it; I just got in the passenger side. The door hinges creaked as I pulled it open, as I knew they would. Familiar odors of old leather and WD-40, washed me in nostalgia. Though I'd sat in that seat hundreds of times before, the familiarity it brought back made me feel strangely isolated. I felt not just out of place, but out of time. This truck, and what it represented, was part of my past.

On the short drive to Finnegan's, neither of us said much. I think we both felt the distance wedged between us. It had shrunk a little, but it was far from gone.

Once we went inside and found an empty booth, Liv turned to me. "I'm heading to the bar. You want a Blue Hawaii?"

I was taken aback for a moment. I hadn't even considered the fact that I couldn't drink now. "Um, I'll actually just have a ginger ale, please."

She looked incredulous, one brow arching comically. "Yeah, right."

"I've kind of quit drinking. At least for a while."

"Seriously?" she laughed.

I nodded. "Yeah. Sorry to be a party-pooper."

Shrugging, she said, "No, it's cool. I'm just surprised. Back in a sec."

I checked my phone while I waited. Dee had texted saying she'd be another twenty minutes. Hopefully in that time, Liv and I could talk our way through the awkward factor.

Liv returned a few minutes later carrying two glasses. She set my ginger ale on the table and sat across from me, sipping from her bright blue drink. With a grin, she said, "I figured just 'cause you weren't drinking didn't mean I couldn't."

"Of course. Have as many as you like. I can always drive you home." I stopped, remembering that Liv's current home was my old home. Which I was totally fine with, I reminded myself.

Her expression grew serious. "It's kinda weird, drinking when you're not. Why'd you quit?"

The answer to that was complicated. I tried to simplify it. "I realized after a few months of living with Dee and reflecting on my life that maybe I drank too much."

"No, you didn't. You drank in moderation, when you were with friends, just like I do."

Shaking my head, I said, "I drank a lot more than you saw, especially in the last year before…" I trailed off, unable to voice the rest. "Before I moved to Richmond," I finished lamely.

"Well, you were probably under a lot of stress. I assume. It's not like you told me about it or anything."

Nodding, I said, "I was. A *lot*. And I'm sorry for not confiding in you. I didn't tell anyone, really. Not until the day I moved out, anyway."

She had another sip. When she set her glass down, she said in a soft voice, "I thought I was your best friend. But you never said a word to me. Not a single word. I found out you'd left him and moved in with Dee from Scott."

Oh God. Here it comes. And I deserve every bit of it. "I'm so sorry, Liv. About all of it."

"You really hurt me. You hurt Scott, too, obviously. But we were *best friends*. And you shut me out and moved away and now we barely talk to each other and it really sucks." Her voice choked.

I reached across the table and squeezed her hand. "You're right. I suck. I hurt everyone, and I deserve your anger."

"Yes, you did." Liv glared at me. Actually glared. It stung, although I tried to hide how much that look pierced me. "And you've never even told me *why*."

"I feel horrible about it, if that makes you feel any better. I hate that I hurt you guys."

Sighing long and low, she said, "I know. I know you well enough to know you must've had a really good reason for walking away."

"I did."

"I mean, I get that you needed some space from Scott while you guys both dealt with the separation, but I don't get why you froze me out. Was it because Scott and I were growing closer? Is that it?"

I frowned. "Maybe a little. But there was other stuff going on that I simply couldn't talk about. It was…complicated." And there was still stuff going on with me that I couldn't tell her yet. My life was still complicated, just in different ways.

"*Complicated*? Too complicated to confide in your best friend?" She shook her head, but she didn't look as angry as she had a few minutes ago. "Okay. Fine. Will you at least tell me now?"

Biting my bottom lip, I shook my head. "I'm sorry." God, I was already so sick of that word. "I can't. I just can't. Maybe someday I'll be able to talk to you about it, but—"

"Let me ask you one thing," she cut in. "If I wasn't married to your ex—and holy shit, how trashy does *that* sound to say out loud?—would you tell me then?"

I felt like I was under a spotlight. Suddenly I wanted to be anywhere else. She was asking me very valid questions that I didn't have any adequate answers for. "I—"

To my relief, Dee suddenly appeared beside our table. "Sorry I'm late." She stopped, glancing between us, and her smile faltered. "What did I just interrupt?"

I forced a smile. "Liv was just giving me much deserved crap for dropping off the planet. But hopefully she can forgive me?" I gave Liv a pleading look, complete with eyelash batting.

She raised one eyebrow at me as if to say *we are far from finished here*, but then smiled. "Of course I forgive you. That's what friends are for."

Dee slid onto the bench beside me. "So you guys are good then? Please tell me you guys are good again."

Liv snorted. "Yeah, we're good. I can't stay mad at her. Never could." She picked up her glass and downed the rest of her blue drink in one swallow. As if on cue, a waitress showed up at our table.

"Talk about good timing," Liv told her. She and Dee both ordered drinks, and then Dee started telling us about her day with her family.

I looked at my two friends, both laughing and relaxed, and for a moment it almost felt like the old days. Though there would probably still be weird moments in our future, I felt a huge relief that Liv and I were both anxious to repair our friendship. And she would be so excited once she found out about the baby. I could just see her dragging me shopping and planning a baby shower. I was grateful for the support of my friends. No matter what happened with Declan, I wouldn't be alone.

Monday was Declan's birthday. Before I went to sleep Sunday night, I sent him a quick text: *Happy Birthday. Is it OK if I call you? What time works?*

It was late, but I hoped he might still be up to see it. If not, he could respond tomorrow. Part of me knew there was a huge chance I wouldn't hear back at all, but before I tried a more insistent way to reach him, I figured I'd see if he'd reply. If he wanted to talk to me, he'd text me back. If he didn't, after a few days, I'd call him.

This conversation was going to happen Even if neither of us wanted it.

Chapter 13

Declan

My hope for my thirty-seventh birthday was that it would pass just like any other day. I intended to simply ignore it. The past month—hell, the past *year*—I'd spent a lot of time and energy trying to ignore painful things. Most of them refused to let me, but I figured this one would be easy.

As usual, I was wrong.

When I picked up my phone that morning, to my surprise I found a text from Amelia. I wasn't surprised she'd remembered what day it was, because of course she would, for the same reason I'd remembered her birthday back in March. What surprised me was that she'd actually taken the time to wish me a good one. After the morning after Josh's wedding, I'd figured she wanted nothing more to do with me. Yet in her message, she'd asked if she could call.

My curiosity was piqued, I admit. But that persistent little voice in my head piped up, the one that always insisted we should stay far away from each other. And, perhaps a bit grudgingly, I knew that voice was right. So, with a regretful sigh, I put down the phone and went to grab a shower.

I hadn't reminded Alexis in the preceding days that it was my birthday, but someone had obviously given her a head's up. When I came out of the bathroom, she threw her arms around me and began singing "Happy Birthday to You" at the top of her lungs.

I couldn't help laughing as I picked her up and swung her around, sending her brunette ringlets flying out from her head. My mood instantly lightened. Sometimes it's the little things, you know?

No one at work knew it was my birthday except my Admin Assistant, Colleen, and my brother. Ryan was out at client meetings all day, and I'd made Colleen swear she wouldn't mention it. After lunch, she slipped a chocolate chip cookie from the cafeteria onto my desk, but otherwise didn't say a word. It brought a smile to my face, which was a rare occurrence at work anymore. Things like this were one of the many reasons I was glad I'd hired her.

After work, I planned to pick up Lex from the sitter, order in pizza, and we'd have a mini celebration at home, just the two of us. If she insisted I blow out candles, there were Twinkies in the cupboard that could substitute for birthday cake in a pinch.

Before I left the office, I got a text from James. It read: *Happy Birthday. I've already picked up Alexis. Meet us at Alessandro's at five-thirty?*

Alessandro's was one of the most popular Italian restaurants in Lynchburg. It was always crowded with a line of people waiting to get in, although on a Monday evening it probably wouldn't be too bad. It had also been one of the places where the three of us—Laura, Lex and I—used to go if we had something to celebrate. Back when we were a normal family.

With a frustrated sigh, I texted him back that I'd see him there. It's not like I had any real choice in the matter. And truth be told, I didn't mind spending my evening with James as well. He probably would have dropped in to watch the game with me later anyway, birthday or not.

So when I pulled into the parking lot at Alessandro's, I was surprised to spot my brother's candy-apple red Jag parked down along the side. I knew it was his car. The personalized license plate KAVANAW gave it right away. I rolled my eyes, as I always did when I saw it. Ryan loved it, but I thought that plate made him look like an idiot. Which I'd told him more than once.

For fuck's sake.

This meant Ryan and Diana were inside waiting for me, too. I glanced around until I spotted Patrick's SUV in the far corner. Great. A surprise party. Just what I fucking needed.

Not gonna lie. A part of me was seriously tempted to get back in my car and go home and text James saying I'd see them after dinner. I really wasn't in the mood to celebrate anything, and I *definitely* had zero interest in being the center of attention. But that wouldn't be very fair to Alexis, who was probably super excited to surprise Daddy. And it wouldn't be fair to the rest of my family either. I knew they only wanted to see me happy. It's not like I could tell them I just needed to be alone, that all I really wanted to do on my birthday was to hide away from the world and drink myself into a stupor.

So I pasted on a grin, squared my shoulders, and walked inside.

I would play along. For their sakes. Just like I always did.

After dinner, throughout which I fake-smiled and tried my best to pretend to enjoy, Ryan asked if they could come back to my place for a bit. I declined, citing it was a Monday night, and both Lex and I needing to get up early the next day. My brother frowned, but didn't push it.

Later, after I'd just kissed a yawning Alexis goodnight, I heard the doorbell ring.

I trotted down the stairs and was confused to find my step-father on my front step.

What the fuck is he *doing here?*

Patrick, like Ryan, was several inches taller than me. I was forced to look up at him. "Hey. What's up?"

He ran one hand over his silver hair. A bottle of bourbon was clutched in the other. An expensive bottle of bourbon. Was it just me, or did he look a little uncomfortable?

"Sorry for showing up unannounced. I know you told Ryan you didn't want company, but I thought maybe you and I could have a little birthday drink. Is Alexis in bed?" He thrust the bottle my way and stepped past me into the foyer.

"I just tucked her in." My brows drew in tight. Patrick never just showed up at my house to talk.

"Mind if I join you for a bit? I won't stay long." He was already removing his jacket.

I looked down at the bottle of bourbon in my hand with a small frown. "Sure, why not?" I planned to have a birthday drink tonight anyway, and this stuff was a hell of a lot better than the beer in my fridge.

I detoured into the kitchen to grab glasses and then Patrick followed me back to the living room where I poured us each two fingers of bourbon. The liquor was smooth, and I relished both the burn and the caramel-y aftertaste. I used to drink bourbon all the time, but after the accident, I'd switched mostly to beer. No idea why. Maybe I was punishing myself. This was a hell of a lot better than beer.

Picking up the remote, I flicked on the hockey game. Then I remembered hockey was what I watched with James. Patrick had no interest, so I flicked over to football.

"Did you enjoy your surprise party?" he asked.

I glanced at him. His face was impassive. "Sure," I shrugged.

He snorted. "No, you didn't."

I arched a brow. "What makes you say that?"

At first Patrick didn't respond. He set down his glass and though his gaze was trained on the television, I got the distinct impression he wasn't watching it. A minute or so later, he began to talk. "Your mother passed when you were seven, and your brother only two. It may have been a long time ago, but I still remember it like it was yesterday. So I know a thing or two about grieving. And trying to raise a child without their mother."

My eyes flared. How had I not made this connection before? I was a colossal idiot, because of course Patrick had gone through this. I knew he had. And yet it had never once occurred to me. Until now, when he was spelling it out for me like I was still that seven year-old kid.

He continued. "It's not the same, obviously. Kathleen wasn't pregnant, so I didn't have that loss to contend with, too. But she was my wife, and I loved her dearly. And I imagine the coping mechanisms—or lacks thereof—that you're experiencing are similar." He turned his head slightly to look at me. "You're a great father to Alexis, and you take excellent care of your clients, but I don't think you're taking very good care of yourself these days."

I frowned. "I'm doing the best I can."

"I know you are. But I also know you're pretending you're fine so people don't worry, so everyone thinks you're getting on with your life. Aren't you?"

Exhaling a sigh, I said, "Is it that obvious?"

Patrick smiled a thin smile. "If your goal is to keep us from worrying about you, then you're failing. Your brother and I are both concerned. The anniversary is fast approaching—"

"I'm well aware." I cut in. My tone had grown frosty. Like I didn't fucking know that. Less than a month away now, and I dreaded it with every fiber of my being.

"And we know it's going to be tough on you. But you won't let anyone in. I completely understand why you wouldn't choose to confide in me. I know our relationship over the years has been…tenuous, at best, and I realize that's mostly my fault. But you and Ryan had become so much closer in the months before Laura's passing. I was thrilled you'd repaired things and seemed to be acting like brothers again. But since the accident, you've pulled away from him, again. Grief can be overwhelming, and it's perfectly natural to want to withdraw and hide. I understand that, because I did it, too, for a long time. Too long." He paused to reach for his bourbon and take a sip. "You reminded me *so* much of your mother. Every time I looked at you, she was all I saw. And I regret that I retreated from you when you needed me the most. I'm sorry about that."

A lump rose in my throat, but I choked it back down. I wasn't used to him talking to me so frankly about personal stuff. Usually we discussed business, or I listened while he reprimanded me for something. Thirty-plus years, and we'd never talked about my mom like this. Not once. And honestly? It freaked me out a little. After a large swig from my own glass, I turned to face him. His dark eyes felt like they were boring holes in me.

"S'okay. It's all in the past."

"It's not okay. But hopefully we can put it behind us now." He sighed. "My point is that I'm worried you're pushing away the very people you need the most."

I opened my mouth to protest. Then I shut it again. He wasn't wrong.

"You need them, Declan. More than any other time in your entire life, maybe. And it's hard as hell to let people love you when you don't think you deserve it. Why do you suppose I've never let another woman into my life in all these years?"

For a few minutes, we sat in silence, staring at the television, although I doubt either of us even knew the score. After a while, I turned back to him. "Can I ask you something?"

"Of course."

"Did you blame yourself? For Mom's death? I mean, I know she had cancer, and it was no one's fault, but…did you?"

He flattened his lips and looked away. I didn't think he was going to reply, but at last he said, "Yes. Like you said, it wasn't anyone's fault, but I still felt guilt. I always thought I could have done more for her, could have found better doctors, could've made her more comfortable, happier in her last months. I know it was irrational, but I did blame myself for a very long time. I couldn't help it."

"Laura's accident was totally my fault."

Patrick turned back to me. "Don't be silly. There was a snow storm. The state troopers were about to close the highway."

"I had a big meeting—ConnectAssure—and it got pushed back," I continued like he hadn't spoken. "Lex's sitter had something going on and she couldn't keep her late. Neither Ry nor James was around. You and Josh were in the meeting with me. So I called Laura and asked her to come pick up Lex for me and take her back to the studio. She wouldn't have been on that road if it wasn't for me."

Sighing, he said, "That's rough. There was no way you could've known. But I'm aware me telling you the facts won't ease your guilt. Have you talked to anyone else about this?"

I shrugged. "Not really. Josh knows, I guess."

"I mean a professional. A grief counselor. Your insurance will cover it."

"Uh, no. But I'll think about it."

Patrick picked up his glass again and swallowed the rest of the contents. "You do that. Talking about stuff like this…heavy stuff…it's not easy. But it might come a wee bit easier with a stranger."

"Maybe," I relented.

"Take it from me, who dealt with his own demons far too late in life." With that, Patrick got to his feet, clearly ready to head home.

I looked up at him. "Thanks for sharing. I appreciate it."

"Hope it was helpful."

Shrugging again, I repeated, "Maybe."

I walked him to the front door and saw him out. Then I returned to the couch and poured myself another two fingers. I had to work in the morning, but it was my birthday. And this was no cheap-ass bourbon. This was the good shit.

I thought about what Patrick had said. And I thought about the choices I'd made, and was still making. Maybe he was right. Maybe it was time I made some positive changes in my life. I could look into contacting a grief counsellor. Alexis had seen one for kids for about six months after the accident, and she seemed to have helped my daughter. I resolved to give it some more consideration in the morning.

What Patrick didn't know, what none of them knew, was that what weighed me down was more than just grief over losing Laura and the baby. It was so much more mind-fuckingly complicated than that. And, stranger or friend, I didn't know if I could bring myself to voice those feelings out loud to anyone.

Chapter 14

Amelia

At my first appointment with Dr. Middleton, the OB-GYN to whom I'd been referred by Planned Parenthood, I was nervous, with no idea what to expect. She started off by asking me lots of questions about my health and my family's health history. Many of them were the same ones I'd previously answered for Dr. Steve. Other than again having to explain that the baby's father wasn't involved, that part was pretty easy and some of my anxiety lessened.

Next she had me lie on the examination table and put my feet up in stirrups so she could do a pelvic exam. Never the most pleasant experience, I was glad it didn't take long.

"Based on your conception date, you're nearly nine weeks along. Would you like to hear the baby's heartbeat?"

My eyebrows shot up. "Really? You can do that already?"

"I can try. No guarantee I'll find it, but if not this time, then we will at your next appointment." She reached behind her and grabbed a tube of what looked like lubricant. "This is ultrasound gel," she explained. "It acts as a conductor to help the fetal Doppler transmit waves inside you. I'm going to squeeze some onto your stomach. It'll probably feel a little cold. Is that okay?"

"Go ahead."

Dr. Middleton lifted the paper gown I wore to expose my midsection. When I'd examined myself in the mirror after my shower this morning, I'd thought I could detect the beginning of a slight bump. I wasn't sure, though; it could have just been breakfast. Lying on my back, I couldn't see any curve greater than normal. The doctor squeezed a big blue blob just below my belly button and used the end of the wand to swirl it around until my entire lower stomach was covered in cool, clear gel. It felt weird, and I already couldn't wait to wipe it off.

Re-positioning the wand to just above my pubic bone and tilting it slightly, she began to glide it slowly back up. Back and forth, she moved it over my skin, until suddenly she stopped. A low, fast throbbing sound burst from the speaker at the end of the Doppler's cord.

She broke into a smile. "Ah. There we are."

I held my breath, entranced by that rapid flutter. *Holy crap! That's its heart. Beating inside me. This is actually happening. I'm gonna be someone's mom!*

Finally I exhaled. "Wow," I murmured. "That's really my baby?" The heartbeat seemed faster than I expected. I had to ask: "Is it…normal?"

Laughing, she replied, "Oh yes, completely normal. It's more rapid than an adult's because the baby is so small. Nothing to worry about."

"Oh okay. Good. How big is it?"

"It's only about the size of an olive right now." She held up her fingers about an inch apart. "Very tiny."

Dr. Middleton let me listen for a bit longer, then removed the Doppler and gave me some paper towels to clean myself off while she wrote down some notes. Before she left to let me get dressed, she told me that I should see her once a month until my third trimester and after that more frequently.

She seemed like a kind woman, and I was relieved she'd be guiding and helping me along this crazy adventure. I'd become unexpectedly protective of this little life inside me. There might be plenty of obstacles yet to overcome, but at least with Dr. Middleton I knew I'd be in good hands.

As I walked home, my thoughts were preoccupied. I kept trying to picture this small pink olive with that rapid heartbeat growing inside me. No matter how hard I tried, I couldn't reconcile the weird image in my head with reality.

118

When I turned the corner, I stopped in my tracks. An abrupt wave of sadness hit me, and I had to scramble for a tissue as my eyes welled up.

There was a photography studio across the street, and their front windows prominently displayed blown up examples of the types of photos in which they specialized. The largest, the one I couldn't tear my gaze from, was of a happy couple. The man stood behind her, one arm around her waist cradling her rounded belly. The woman was looking up at him with a serene smile. They both radiated love and happiness.

My heart clenched as I swiped my tears away. I'd never in my life wanted that before—the joy and anticipation that couple had both for each other and their future child. Yet suddenly I did. Suddenly I wished more than anything that Declan and I were together, and happy, and over-the-moon excited for our baby's arrival.

I had to turn away. I knew, deep down, that my life was never going to look like that couple's. He didn't even want to talk to me. As I'd expected, he hadn't bothered to respond to my text. I'd waited a few days, and then tried again. Still nothing.

Whether I liked it or not, I was going to have to corner him somehow and tell him in person. Which was going to suck. I didn't want to do it. But I would. I'd do the right thing. And after I made it clear I wanted nothing from him and he was under no obligations, I'd walk away and never look back.

My little olive and I would be just fine without him.

Declan

"Mr. Miller? The doctor will see you now."

James and I got to our feet and followed the woman down the hall to the oncologist's office. We were back at the U. of V. Cancer Center to discuss the results of my father's most recent MRI. Dr. Wong was an elderly Chinese man who'd been studying the human brain and its various diseases for nearly half his life. He stood at the rear of the room with his back to us, examining the MRI scans as we sat down.

Turning to look at us, he flashed a tight smile that didn't reach his eyes. "How are you feeling, James?"

"Same as usual, doc. Maybe a bit more tired some days, but I put that down to plain ole aging."

"You had a dizzy spell this morning," I reminded him.

"Oh right. Yeah. I don't get them that often, though."

Dr. Wong's smile faded. "You may start experiencing increased balance issues going forward."

"The results aren't what we'd hoped for, then?" James asked, exhaling a soft sigh.

"Unfortunately it looks like the tumor has begun growing again." He took a seat behind his desk. "We expected this might happen, though I was hopeful that with the treatments it would remain inert for a few more years."

Dr. Wong continued speaking to James about various side effects he might see return or worsen, and the new round of drugs the doctor wanted him to start on to slow the growth. I barely heard the rest of their conversation. It felt like I'd been punched in the gut.

Fuck. This is not happening. It can't be. I can't lose him, too. I can't.

But it was clear it was just a matter of time now. No prognosis or time-frame was specifically mentioned, but all three of us understood this was the polar opposite of good news.

So. That happened. My father was dying. Not just vaguely at some point, but soon. We had no idea when yet, or how to prepare. It could be a few months. It could be as long as another year. But however much time he had left, it wasn't long enough. And there wasn't a single goddamn thing I could do about it.

And the day before had been the one year anniversary of the accident. I'd hid myself in my office and tried not to interact with anyone, but it still weighed heavy on my mind. Heavier than usual, I mean. Alexis didn't know what day it was, and I didn't tell her. But after she'd gone to bed, I chugged back a few more beers than usual on a work night. The buzz they provided hadn't eased my pain in the slightest. If anything, it had only made me dwell on it more. I would have given anything to be able to go back in time and change things. I'd make better choices. I'd fix it all. All the shitty things that had happened to me and my family over the past few years were my fault. Every last goddamn one of them.

I was the fucking kiss of death.

The drive back from Charlottesville took just under forty-five minutes. It should have taken an hour, but I was stressed and my foot pressed heavy on the gas. Driving too fast with a distracted mind was not a great combination. I was damned lucky we didn't get pulled over.

James knew I was upset. He attempted to lighten things with conversation, but stopped when it became clear I wasn't in the mood to chat. In hindsight, I should've been asking him how *he* felt about this development, and trying to lighten *his* mood. I should have, but I didn't. I was too stuck in my own head to talk to him about what all this meant. Selfish as fuck, I know, but I couldn't help it. We'd discuss everything we needed to later, once I had some time to process it. Though we'd only known each other a couple of years, we'd become really tight. I think he understood.

After dropping James back at his apartment with a promise I'd see him later tonight, I headed to work. Before I went into my office, I stopped at Colleen's desk to let her know I again didn't want to be disturbed unless it was urgent. Then I closed my door, threw my coat on a chair and began responding to e-mails to try to distract myself. I tried to focus on my client's concerns, but it didn't work very well. All I could think about was James.

Around three o'clock, my desk phone rang.

It was Josh.

Amelia

After another week of silence, I gave up hoping Declan would respond to my text. One day around lunchtime, I was feeling particularly fed up with the way he'd been ghosting me. I just wanted to get this over with. So I got in my car and drove to Lynchburg. I didn't have any specific plan in mind. I was just going to wing it and hope I got lucky. Or unlucky, depending how it went.

When I pulled into the lot at Baker, Wright, and Kavanaugh, I turned left to park in the staff parking area like I used to. Then I remembered I didn't work there anymore. I drove around to the front entrance and parked in the visitor section.

So far my luck seemed to be holding. I'd spotted Declan's blue Mustang along the back of the staff lot. That meant he was somewhere in the building, unless he's gone to an off-site meeting in someone else's vehicle, which was unlikely. Declan loved his car, and he loved to drive it.

I looked at the frosted glass front doors and frowned. After some consideration, I decided against going inside. Instead, I dug for my phone and called Josh's extension.

"Accounting Department. This is Josh Marshall."

"Hey, it's Amelia. Sorry to bug you at work, but I really need a favor."

He laughed. "I'm fine, thanks. So's Holly. And how are *you* doing?"

I exhaled a self-conscious chuckle. "Sorry. I'm glad you guys are good. I'm okay. Just a little bit…uh…preoccupied at the moment."

"Oh yeah? What's going on?"

"The thing is, I need to talk to Declan. He won't return my texts, so I was wondering if you could transfer me to him. That way he'll see the call coming from you and hopefully pick up."

There was a pause. "Can I ask why?"

"I, uh, I can't tell you. Not right now. But I promise I will. Just…later."

"Now you've got me intrigued."

With a soft sigh, I said, "Again, I'm sorry, Josh. But I really need to speak to him. Will you please put me through?"

I heard another laugh. "Whatever it is, it's clearly important. No problem. Hold on."

There was a click, and then I heard instrumental music.

My hands had broken out in a cold sweat. Would he be willing to talk to me? Even if he tried, I was not going to let him blow me off this time. I was going to do this. Today.

Soaring trombones and trumpets filled my ears. A piano joined in. I didn't recognize the song, but it seemed to be never-ending.

Suddenly Josh was back. "Still there?"

"Yep."

"Go ahead." Another click and Josh was gone.

"Hello?" I said hesitantly.

"Amelia."

I decided to start the same way I had with Josh. "Look, I'm sorry for bothering you at work, and I know you don't really wanna talk to me, but you won't return my messages and I have to tell you something."

Silence. Then: "What's up?"

"Not over the phone. I'm in town. Can you come meet me? It'll only take a few minutes."

I heard a sigh. "Now's not a really good time."

"It's important. And it can't wait. Ten minutes?"

A long pause. For a moment I wondered if he'd hung up on me. At last he said, "Fine. If it's that important."

"It is. Meet me by the park on Fillmore Street? Where we—"

"Yeah, okay. Be right there."

Declan

After replacing the receiver, I stared down at the phone for a moment, my thoughts swirling.

I was still reeling from the news about James' brain tumor. I wasn't sure I could deal with any other stressful situations today. Getting up, I braced both hands on my desk, lowered my head and closed my eyes, trying to force my over-stressed brain to function like a normal, rational human being.

Okay. Amelia had texted me a couple of times over the past few weeks. Though she'd asked if she could call in the first message, they'd been worded pretty casually and, though I admit I'd been tempted, instead I had done my damndest to put them out of my mind. I didn't recall her saying it was urgent that she speak with me. I was trying to stay strong and stay away from her. For her own good.

What could be so damned important that she couldn't tell me over the phone? That she had to say to me face to face? Seeing Amelia was going to be another level of torture I absolutely was not up for right now. But I'd already agreed to meet her.

Why? Because I was an idiot when it came to her. I made stupid choices. I fucked things up. This hellish merry-go-round was killing me. I needed to put an end to it. For good.

Sighing, I grabbed my coat and headed for my car.

Thick clouds obscured the sun as I turned into the small parking area by Fillmore Park and pulled in next to Amelia's navy Honda. I could see her silhouette through the side window, staring down at her phone.

My heart was racing. I ached—a real, physical ache that throbbed insistently deep in my chest—to just go to her and pull her into my arms. Yet at the same time, I also had a massive urge to throw my car into reverse and speed away without looking back. Insidious doubts were creeping in, like old frenemies I could never truly escape from.

Ten minutes. Ten fucking minutes. You can handle being around her for that long. Just man up and go find out what she wants.

I got out of my car. My fingers trembled against the metal as I pulled open her passenger door and slid onto the seat. Just like I had so many times in the past. It all felt so familiar. And it took everything in me to not reach for her. To not touch her. To not kiss her.

You can do this. Just stay strong.

Amelia turned to face me. Her normally shining hair hung limp and listless against the sides of her face. She was pale and drawn, with angry red pimples marring her forehead. Even her eyes didn't hold their usual sparkle.

"Are you okay?" I blurted, feeling a stab of fear. *Shit. Please let her be okay. I can't take any more bad news.*

She flashed a small smile. To me, it looked like a sad smile. "That depends on your definition of *okay.*"

"Are you sick?"

With a nod, she said, "Off and on." Her voice was softer now, less confident.

Now I was really worried. "What's wrong?"

Tearing her eyes from mine, she gazed out the windshield. "I'm only telling you this because you deserve to know, not because I want anything from you. I just need to make that clear."

"Telling me what?" My tone had become more urgent, more demanding. "What the *hell* is going on?"

"I'm…" She stopped. "God. This is even harder than I thought it would be…and I knew it was gonna be hard." She turned back to me, and I could see she was fighting back tears. "I'm pregnant."

Amelia

Though his expression had been guarded, at my admission his eyes shot wide. Those sky blue eyes had haunted me nearly every night in my dreams since the day we met two and a half years ago.

124

Almost comically, his mouth fell open a little. I could tell he was trying and failing to formulate words. At last he managed: "You're...? *What?*"

I sighed. "You probably don't even remember. You were pretty drunk."

He shook his head a little. I didn't know if he was negating my suggestion that he didn't recall or just trying to clear his thoughts. He blinked a few times, but remained silent.

"It's okay. You don't have to—"

"Are you sure?" he blurted.

Snorting, I tried to meet his eyes, but they were darting around, refusing to land on anything, most of all me. "Very sure."

Silence filled the space between us. Overwhelming silence. Every passing second gave my overactive mind more time to analyze his reaction, more time to convince myself that he was repulsed by the idea of having a child with me.

The longer Declan didn't say anything, the angrier I got. At last I couldn't contain myself any longer. "Look, I know you want nothing to do with me anymore. You've made that pretty clear. And I know you don't want this. I just—"

Before I could continue, he cut in. "I remember." His voice was so soft I almost didn't hear. He still wasn't looking at me.

"Okay." Well, that was something anyway. He remembered. But that meant he knew we'd had sex that night and made a choice not to speak to me after. I sighed. "You clearly regret it."

Finally he turned to me again. I wasn't sure if he was seeing me or not. His eyes looked so glazed it felt like he was looking right through me. The Declan I used to know wasn't behind those eyes. That Declan was gone. Maybe he didn't even exist anymore. I missed him. But I knew I had to let him go.

"I..." He stopped. "I don't..."

My hand crept to my belly and cupped it protectively. "I know you don't. And it's fine. I don't expect anything from you."

Pain was etched on his face. "It's all my fault," he muttered. Then, louder, "I'm just...I'm so sorry. Just send me the bill. I'll pay for everything."

I blew out an exasperated puff of air. "I don't want your money," I spit out. "I don't want anything from you. I just thought you had a right to know."

Then I thought further about what he'd just said and realized something. He assumed I was getting an abortion. He hadn't even considered the fact that I might want this child, *our* child.

Because *he* clearly didn't. Tears began to rise again, and I broke eye contact with him. I would not cry. I refused to show him any weakness. Not anymore.

"Are you sure?"

I was so angry I could barely speak, so I just said, "Yes." I was afraid if I tried to say more I might choke on the words.

Declan

It was too much. Total information overload. My mind flat out refused to process any of it. It had shut down to avoid certain meltdown.

I think my mouth fell open, but no words were coming out.

Amelia raised her head to look back at me. When the dark curtain of her hair fell away, I saw bright red spots of color had appeared on both cheeks. She was pissed. No, scratch that. She was absolutely furious. She was on the edge of her own meltdown, but for very different reasons. Because of me.

She cleared her throat. "Just have your lawyer draw up something saying I waive you of any financial or personal obligations. I'll sign it, and then you'll never have to hear from me again." Her voice sounded ice cold. Not like the Amelia I knew at all.

"No, I…I'm just…this is just…" Stupid brain had fucked right off. White noise filled my head every time I tried to speak.

"You need to go now." She was fucking livid. And I didn't blame her. I was little more than a useless lump right now.

I tried again. "Wait. You don't understand."

"Get out of my car, Declan. We're done."

I was pretty sure I hadn't told my body to move, but it did anyway. It obeyed her command of its own accord. Pushing open the door, I stepped outside and was immediately damp. It had begun to rain. I hadn't even noticed.

I couldn't let Amelia leave like this, thinking I didn't want anything to do with her, or the baby. Thinking I'd abandoned her the same way James had abandoned my mother all those years ago. I needed to try to explain myself. But I also knew there was zero chance I could do that until I had some time to pull myself the fuck together.

"Call you later?" I said. It came out as a whisper. I wasn't sure she even heard me. But she had.

"Please don't."

Then she put her car into Drive and took off.

Part 2

FIVE YEARS LATER

Chapter 15

Amelia

"Hello Amelia. It's been quite a long time. How've you been?" Debbie Westwood asked as I took a chair across from her.

She was right. It had been a little under five years since my last visit. I was lucky she was even willing to see me again. So much had been going on in my life, and I hadn't been able to justify the time nor the expense. At least that's what I'd told myself. And once I could afford therapy again, I'd just kept putting off making an appointment, feeling guilty about how much time had passed. I felt guilty about a lot of things, but these days it was easier to bury those thoughts. I had more important stuff to focus on.

I took a deep breath. It was time to catch her up. "I'm good, actually. There's been lots of changes since we last saw each other. Well. One major change that's affected my entire life."

She smiled "Oh? And what's that?"

"By any chance do you recall me telling you at our last appointment that I slept with my ex after my friend's wedding?"

Debbie glanced down at her notes. "Yes. And you'd said you were planning to put him behind you going forward. Were you successful?"

"I was." I nodded. "Well. Sort of."

"Sort of? Can you elaborate?"

"So, the thing is, I, uh, I actually ended up pregnant. I have a four year-old son. His name is Liam."

I'd managed to surprise her. She was quiet for a moment, as if she was collecting her thoughts. Then she smiled again. "Belated congratulations. That's wonderful."

"Thank you. He's a great kid. I know all moms probably say that, but he really is. I totally lucked out."

"Are you and Liam's father back together? Or can I assume from your *sort of* comment that his current role in your life is just about your child?"

"No, we're not together. And he has no role in our lives. I just said sort of because Liam is his son."

"Did he choose not to be involved in Liam's life? That must have been painful."

Biting my lower lip, I broke eye contact. "He doesn't know," I mumbled.

"You didn't tell him?" Her forehead furrowed and she wrote something on her notepad.

"He knows I got pregnant. I did tell him, but..." I trailed off, shrugging.

Debbie's face was serious, but not judgmental. "Can you tell me how your conversation went?"

I sighed. "I made it clear I was only telling him because it was the right thing to do, that I didn't want anything from him. I said he should get his lawyer to draft a document waiving his obligations and I'd sign it."

"I see." She jotted another note. "Was he upset by the news?"

"He clearly wasn't very happy about it."

"How did he respond?"

I snorted derisively. "He said to send him the bill for the abortion."

"Ah. That must've been very painful to hear." Her eyes were soft and sympathetic.

I didn't want to remember the pain. Only the anger. "Let me be clear," I stated firmly. "Letting him think I terminated the pregnancy and then later choosing not to tell him he had a son—these were *not* decisions I took lightly. I thought long and hard about all of it. But even though Liam wasn't planned, and I wasn't exactly at a great place in my life, ultimately..." I paused, trying to think of how best to explain it. "I know this sounds kinda cheesy, but I guess I just knew in my heart that keeping him and raising him without his father's toxic influence was the right choice. Not just for me, but for both of us."

"It doesn't sound cheesy. It sounds like you considered your options and after careful deliberation made a conscientious decision."

"Yes. That's exactly what I did. It was far from easy, deciding to raise a baby on my own. I mean, I'd never fantasized about having kids or anything. When I was with Scott, I definitely wasn't ready. I had no interest in them. But after I learned I was pregnant, I was surprised by how much I wanted it. Being Liam's mom—it was meant to be. He's the best thing that's ever happened to me. And we have a good life now. We don't need Declan."

"Okay." She nodded. "Returning to your conversation with Declan. What else did he say? Did he say he didn't want to be involved?"

"Yes. Well. He started to. I think I cut him off." What had he actually said? I tried to remember his exact words. I'd gone over our conversation, or lack of, so many times, but still, it was a long time ago. Frowning, I told her, "He didn't really say much. He seemed uninterested. And he'd made it clear he didn't want to talk to me. I know I got really mad and told him to get out of my car and not to contact me."

Debbie again made some notes. When she looked back up at me, her face was impassive. "Why were you so angry, Amelia? Try to remember. Was it because he assumed you'd get an abortion? Or was there more to it?"

Why *had* I been so furious? Was it his weird non-reaction? Could it have been the pregnancy hormones heightening my emotions? No, I knew there was more to it than just that. "I guess I was feeling protective. Of both the baby and myself." I sat up straighter in my chair. "He left me. Twice. And the first time seriously broke me. I couldn't trust him to not leave again. I couldn't go through that another time. And I didn't want my child to suffer because of him. Ever."

She nodded. "It makes sense that you'd be protective of your baby and your own mental health. After what you went through with him, that's understandable. But you have to know, as the father, he has rights, too."

"I do know. He could fight me for custody if he found out. But I don't intend to tell him. When Liam gets older and asks me about his dad, I might tell him the truth then. But right now, he's better off with me. And it's not just me. We share a house with my best friend Dee and her girlfriend Terri. Liam loves them like family."

Debbie smiled. "That's good. But aren't you worried he might find out from someone else? A mutual friend perhaps?"

My face grew hot, and I looked down at my hands. "I, uh, I thought about all that, too. I haven't been in touch with Josh since then, either. He's Declan's best friend. I couldn't have asked him to keep such a massive secret for me. It wouldn't have been right. I needed to start fresh, so that's exactly what I did. I changed my phone number, I deleted my social media accounts, and I stopped communicating with everyone but my mom and my roommate. I basically disappeared. I've made a few new friends—acquaintances, really—through Dee and Terri, but mostly it's just us four. We've become a tight, happy, little family. I kinda like it like this."

"That seems pretty drastic. Cutting out all your friends but your roommate? You must've felt like your ex posed a major risk."

I frowned. A rare flash of uncertainty came over me. "An emotional one, yes. He'd never hurt either of us physically. And I do feel guilty about not telling him, because I know how much he loves being a dad, but I just couldn't take the chance that he might trigger me into another major spiral like the last one. I refuse to do that to Liam. He needs me, and I swore I'd be there for him. It was the right decision for us."

"Letting him be a part of your son's life doesn't mean you have to get back together with him."

Breaking eye contact again, I sighed. "I know."

I didn't add more and after a few long, silent seconds, she seemed willing to let that topic go for now. "Okay. Can I ask about your financial situation? Are you working now?"

With a relieved smile, I said, "Yes, I got a job a few years back as a receptionist at a local law firm. There's no chance for promotion, but the hours are good and the money, well, it covers the bills. We don't have much extra, but we get by."

She jotted more notes on her pad. "That's an awful lot of change in your life. How are you handling it all? Do you still get bouts of depression?"

I shrugged. "Not too often. Sometimes, I guess. When it's late at night and I can't sleep and I'm all alone with my thoughts. But it's manageable."

"That's good to hear. No need for medication, then?"

"I don't think so."

Debbie glanced up at the clock. "Well, I'm sorry to say our time is almost up." She got to her feet. "Unfortunately thirty minutes goes by quickly, especially when there's so much to catch up on. I'm really glad to hear things are working out for you. Please let my assistant know if you'd like to book another appointment."

"Thanks for listening." I shook her hand and left her office, but I didn't stop to book another session.

When I opened my mother's front door, I heard a child's voice yell, "Mommy's back!" Mere seconds later, a fresh-faced boy with unruly dark hair ran down the hallway and into my arms. He always greeted me with a hug when I returned after being away for any length of time longer than a few minutes. I kind of loved it.

Mom came out of the kitchen with a damp dishrag in one hand. "How was it?"

I shrugged. "It was okay. Kinda strange after so long, but overall fine. Was he good for you?"

She smiled down at Liam. I had no memory of her ever looking at me with such open adoration when I was young. "He was a perfect angel. As always."

I gave Liam's hair a ruffle. I had given up even trying to comb it into any sort of organization in the mornings. It did what it wanted. He made a hooting noise and ran back to the living room, presumably to see what he was missing on *PAW Patrol*.

"I ran into Liv at the grocery store the other day. Her little boy is getting big, nearly as big as Liam."

"Oh yeah?" I followed my mother into the kitchen. I knew Liv and Scott had also had a son less than a year after Liam was born, but I'd never met him. Dee had showed me a picture once that Liv had posted on Facebook. The child had pale blonde hair and reminded me of Scott's baby pictures. I was happy for them and knew how ecstatic they both must be, but seeing that photo had caused a deep ache in my chest. I didn't reach out to congratulate them—yet another thing on the long list of things I felt guilty about.

"She asked after you," Mom said.

I stilled. "What did you say?"

"What I always say when someone asks: that you're fine. Don't worry, I didn't say anything else." She began wiping down the counter.

"Thanks."

"I still don't understand why I have to keep my only grandson a secret from all my friends, and yours, if I run into them. I'll keep my promise to you, but I do hope you straighten out whatever the reason for all this secrecy is soon. I'd love to put some photos of you two up around here. It would brighten up the place."

"You can put up a photo, Mom. I didn't say you couldn't. But maybe just in your bedroom."

She sighed. "As soon as you give me one, I'll get right on that."

"Liam starts kindergarten soon. I'll get you a school photo in a nice frame this fall."

"See that you do." She rinsed out the cloth and turned back to me. "Are you two staying for dinner? Or do you have to head back straight away?"

Before I could reply, I felt a tug on my elbow and looked down into a pair of earnest blue eyes. "Can we stay for dinner, Mommy?"

"Of course," I smiled.

I was just putting the last of the dishes away when the doorbell rang. As Mom was in the living room with Liam, I went to get it. When I opened the door, my eyes widened in shock.

"Hey stranger," Josh said with a smile. "I thought I recognized your car."

"Who is it?" Mom called.

"It's for me," I told her, slipping out onto the porch and pulling the door shut behind me. "Holy crap! It's great to see you." Without even thinking, I threw my arms around him and gave him a hug. When I stepped back, I looked behind him toward the street. "Is Holly in the car?"

"No, she's at home with our daughter."

I turned back to him with wide eyes. "Oh wow. You guys have a little girl? What's her name? How old is she?"

"Her name is Emily, and she's three. But you'd know that if you hadn't fallen off the planet a few years back." My mouth dropped open, although I wasn't sure what to say, but he held up a hand to stop me. "And I assume you had a really good reason for doing what you did—I assume it, but it doesn't mean I have to like it. I also assume your reason is about five-foot-nine, a grumpy pain in the ass, and calls himself my best friend?"

My face felt like it was on fire. I broke eye contact, sheepishly mumbling, "I'm really sorry."

"No, no. Believe it or not, I tracked you down for a good reason of my own, and getting an apology and the truth out of you wasn't it, although I'm happy to listen if you decide to share." He pointed toward the porch swing. "Mind if we have a seat? There's something I want to discuss with you."

I did owe him an apology and the truth. I felt awful for shutting Josh and Holly out. But the only explanation I could give would mean telling him that the little boy inside this house was Declan's son, whom he didn't even know existed. And that would mean forcing Josh to keep a massive secret from his best friend. I couldn't ask that of him. So I kept my mouth shut.

"Of course." I sat down beside Josh. "What's up?"

"A lot has changed since last time we talked. Diana left BWK last year."

"No way! She did? Where'd she go?"

Josh shrugged. "Some other company. I don't remember. But you're looking at the new Accounting Manager."

I gave him a wide smile. "That's awesome! Congrats! Kaitlyn and Evan must be thrilled."

"Evan left a few years ago, too. Kaitlyn took my role as Senior Accountant." He shifted to face me. "The thing is, our client base has really grown, and I need to hire a second one." Now he was looking at me pointedly.

My brows flew up. "You're joking? You can't possibly want me to come back?"

"Before you say no, just hear me out. With Diana gone, you'd have a *lot* more autonomy. And I'd have your back with the Account Execs. Things aren't like they used to be. Morale seems to be much better now, at least I think so."

"I don't know. There were other reasons why I left."

He nodded. "I'm well aware. But listen, I don't know where you're working now, but I'm prepared to offer you more. How would eighty thousand a year to start sound? Four weeks' vacation? And you'd get full benefits with no waiting period."

Holy crap! That wasn't just a little more than I was currently making, that was a *whole lot* more. More vacation time to spend with Liam. Full benefits would mean we'd have any prescriptions covered, and I could take him to the dentist more often. As it was, if he fell and broke a bone I'd probably have to take out a loan to pay the hospital bill. And with that kind of income, I could even afford to get our own place.

"He's still there?" I asked hesitantly. I'd definitely need health benefits to pay for my therapy if I had to work with Declan again.

Josh didn't need to ask who I meant. "He is, but not in the same role. He's a Senior Account Manager now. I won't sugar coat it—you'd still have to do cost quote for his clients sometimes. But you'd split the workload with Kaitlyn. And me, if you guys needed me. If—when—he pushes back, I don't mind stepping in to mediate. I've been working with him for a long time. I can handle him."

Josh's words made my heart sting with regret. Declan and I used to work so well together. We'd loved being able to solve problems for BWK's clients. We'd respected each other and enjoyed each other's company. But that was years ago. The thought of stepping back into those kinds of back and forth negotiations with him again made me shudder. This was a terrible idea. Especially now. "This all sounds too good to be true," I said with a sigh. "Working with you again, and Kaitlyn, too, would be amazing. But I'm not so sure—"

"I know. But at least just say you'll think it over. That's all I'm asking. I could really use your expertise, and I'd make it worth your while. And, selfishly, I'd love to have you back. I've missed you." A sad look came over his face, and that rush of guilt flooded me again.

"Okay. No promises, but I'll consider it. When do you need an answer?"

"You can take a few days." Josh smiled as he pulled a business card from his pocket and slid it into my hand. "Give me a call or e-mail and come in for an informal interview next week. You can make your decision after that. What do you say?"

With no small amount of trepidation, I nodded and said I'd be in touch.

I had difficulty sleeping that night. Not long after I'd turned off the light, Liam shuffled into my room asking to sleep in my bed and I'd pulled back the blankets for him, as I usually did. But his soft snores weren't the reason I couldn't fall asleep.

My thoughts were swirling. Josh's job offer seemed to be everything I wanted. It was almost perfect. Almost. Except for one minor and one major drawback. The minor one, leaving this cute little house I shared with Dee and Terri and moving back to Swann's Landing or even Lynchburg, I thought I could handle. But the major one, being forced to not just see but interact with Declan again, I wasn't so sure about.

And of course there was so much more to it than that. It wasn't just having to work with him, it would be risking him discovering my most guarded secret. I didn't see how I'd be able to keep it from Josh if I accepted this position. If I returned to BWK, at some point my friends there would find out I had a son. I'd have to tell Josh and Holly for sure, and soon, which would put them in the awkward position of having to hide it from Declan. I knew they'd keep my secret if I explained why, but it felt wrong to even ask it of them.

If Declan found out, he'd be furious with me, not that I'd blame him. I had no doubt he'd want to be part of Liam's life. In fact, I'd expect it, and I might even be able to handle that if I had to. But Declan and Liam knowing each other wasn't what terrified me most, what made me want to hide my son away. My biggest fear, the thing that gripped me with panic and kept me awake at night, was that he would want shared custody and I'd lose Liam every other week.

I turned toward him, sliding an arm over him and pulling his warm little body against mine. I couldn't lose him. Not for half the time. I couldn't even imagine not seeing him for a weekend. He was what kept me going every day. Without him, I'd be miserable. What if I fell into a really dark place again?

That couldn't happen. I was his Mommy. I gave birth to him, and with a little help from my friends, I was raising him. I was the one who held him when he cried. I was the one who found his first tooth that fell out after he'd spit it into the grass. I was the one he had crazy dance parties with in the kitchen to the music of my favorite bands, which had now become his favorites, too. I was the one who read him stories every night and tucked him in and made sure he felt safe and loved. I was his whole world. He needed me. And I needed him. But we didn't need Declan. So far, we'd done just fine without him.

I knew to others my reasoning probably sounded selfish. But I was terrified that if I slipped into another depression, I might not be able to take care of him. Sure, I had Dee and Terri and my mom, but what if it happened when they weren't around?

What if I couldn't pick myself back up this time? I could not fail him. I would not.

All I wanted was to be the best mother I could be. That was why staying away from Declan was necessary. I needed to do what was in Liam's best interests, and keeping myself mentally healthy was absolutely best for both of us.

But the money, and the benefits, and the security, and being around the friends I'd been missing so much…all these things mattered, too. Creating a good life for Liam was important. I buried my nose into his soft hair and inhaled the familiar scent of his lavender shampoo. Just the smell of it calmed me.

Was there any possible way I could take this job and still feel like I was in control of our lives and our future? Josh had asked me to at least come in for an interview and discuss it before I made up my mind. So, with some reluctance, I decided I'd text him in the morning to set up an appointment. Exploring this option completely would help me make a more informed choice. And going back to BWK for an hour just to chat wouldn't kill me.

Would it?

Chapter 16

Declan

With a barely suppressed sigh, I lifted Nicole's arm from my waist, pushed off the sheet and sat up. I scanned the floor for my boxer briefs, finally spotting them crumpled beside the dresser leg. Carefully I got up and grabbed them on my way out the door.

After taking care of business, I braced a hand on the bathroom counter and pushed my hair off my forehead, glaring with bleary eyes into the mirror.

Jesus.

I looked old. I mean, maybe not, like, *ancient*. Maybe not to others. Women still seemed to find me attractive. The sexy naked chick currently asleep in my bed was proof of that. And a sexy, naked chick fifteen years my junior, no less. More than one guy at the office had high-fived me for that one. They all thought she was hot shit, and I supposed I was lucky she even wanted to fuck a geezer like me. In a few months I'd be turning forty-two, and right now I looked every day of it. There was a lot more gray at my temples. The creases around my eyes seemed deeper. When I shaved off the scruff, now liberally sprinkled with silver, I thought my face looked haggard. And even if I *was* being too hard on myself, looks-wise, I definitely felt my age these days. I knew I had plenty to be happy about:

my successful career, my bright and beautiful ten year-old daughter. And Nicole, of course. But somehow none of those things ever seemed to be able to completely fill the hole inside me.

The hole left by Laura.

By each of the babies I never got to hold.

By James.

And the biggest one, the one I rarely let myself even think about anymore, the one left by *her*.

The hole I'd dug myself.

I frowned at my reflection, glaring at the blue eyes staring back at me. *What the fuck are you even doing with your life?*

"Declan?"

Shit. She was awake after all.

"You coming back to bed?"

I sighed again. Instead of returning to her, I went downstairs to grab a beer. Standing in the open fridge door, I popped the top and chugged down a long swallow. I felt kind of blah. I wasn't really in the mood for company anymore. And Alexis was sleeping over at a friend's, which meant Nicole probably assumed she'd be staying the night.

Clutching my bottle, I went back up to my room.

"You didn't bring me one?" she pouted.

Raising a skeptical brow, I said, "You don't like beer."

"I'd take a hard lemonade. Or a glass of wine."

I snorted. "I don't buy alcopop. I do have a few bottles of wine, but they're expensive and I don't really feel like opening one tonight."

A frown crossed her features. But even frowning, she was still smokin' hot. She lay on her side with her head propped up on her palm, hair all disheveled in that just-been-fucked kind of way, tits on full display above the sheet. I knew it wouldn't take much to initiate round two.

Jesus, what the hell is wrong with me? Instead of appeasing that kissable pout and diving back in like any normal red-blooded guy would, all I wanted was for her to go home.

"Fine. I'll bring my own next time." She leaned closer, sliding her free hand up my chest. "I'm sure we can figure out plenty of other ways to enjoy ourselves." She pressed her lips to my bare shoulder. Her fingers ceased their northward journey and began to travel south. To my amazement, I had no reaction. Not a single twitch. When even my cock was apathetic, there was clearly no point.

"I'm pretty beat tonight, Nic. I think I'm gonna call it a night."

She retracted her hand, her eyes narrowing. "You just wanna roll over and go to sleep? *You*? That's gotta be a first."

"Maybe" I chuckled. "Hey, don't get pissed, but I think I could use some alone time."

Her head jolted back, chin lowering in surprise. "You're kidding? You want me to leave?"

Instead of replying, I just sighed.

Nicole threw off the sheet and leapt from the bed. The lamplight threw strange shadows over her skin as she bent to grab her bra. "Seriously, Declan? You got your rocks off and now you're dismissing me like some kind of cheap slut? What the hell's gotten into you tonight?" She pulled on her skirt, dressing in a rush.

Irritation surged in my chest as I got out of bed. "Now don't get your panties all in a knot. I'm not dismissing you. I'm just not in the mood for a sleepover. It's no big thing, so don't make it into one. I'm tired. I'll call you tomorrow."

Her eyes were downcast, but I heard her huff as she buttoned up her top. "Whatever."

"How about I take you out somewhere nice for lunch next week to make up for it?"

Nicole paused, her eyes darting to mine. I smiled what I hoped was an apologetic smile. I knew she thought I was being a dick for no apparent reason, and she wasn't exactly wrong. Her mouth was set in a hard line, but after a few seconds it curved upward at each corner. "Fine. You can take me to Alessandro's."

"You got it."

I walked her down to the door and kissed her goodbye. I even tried to put a little oomph into the kiss. The grin she shot me before heading to her car confirmed I was no longer on her shit list, which was a relief, if only a small one. Though I wouldn't be heartbroken if she dumped me, I wasn't quite ready to end this…whatever it was—the word *relationship* didn't seem to fit, but we were more than just fuck-buddies—yet.

Amelia

Butterflies flitted about in my stomach as I pulled into the parking lot at Baker, Wright, and Kavanaugh. It had been years since I was last here, but unlike me, the wide, two-storey brick building hadn't changed. As I nosed my Honda into an empty spot in the Visitors section, I couldn't help remembering the last time I'd been here, the day I told Declan I was pregnant. But I refused to let myself think about that right now. Today I had much more important things to consider.

At first, I just sat there, my fingers gripping the wheel so tightly they went white. I took a deep breath and released it slowly, deliberately. Then I reached for my phone to text Josh.

My nerves somewhat calmer, I stepped out of the car and couldn't help smiling up at the chickadees chirping in the big maple at the corner of the building. As I walked inside, I recalled my first day of work seven years ago, impatiently waiting in this very room for Diana to come and take me to my desk. The award plaques on the wall had several new additions. The clock above the door had been replaced with a more modern one. But the receptionist was the same.

"Hello. Amelia, right? Long time no see." She smiled brightly. "Are you here to see Josh Marshall?"

I nodded. "He knows I'm here. I'm sure he'll be right out."

As I finished speaking, Josh came through the door that led to the offices. "Hey. Welcome back." He made a beckoning gesture. I followed him back and we headed to the meeting room in the corner, the same one Diana often used for our department meetings when I worked there. Tall windows on two sides made the room bright and cheerful. I came in behind Josh and was surprised to see Declan's younger brother Ryan already at the table

A grin stretched across his face as he stood to greet me. I'd forgotten how tall he was. "Great to see you again, Amelia. How've you been?"

I could ask you the same thing, I thought. Ryan had suffered from a secret prescription painkiller addiction back when I'd worked there. Only Declan and Diana had known about it, but Declan had filled me in shortly after Ryan accidently OD'd, just making it to the hospital in time to save his life. Instead, I replied with the usual. "I'm great. Living in Richmond now. How are you?"

"Good, good. Can't complain."

Josh and I sat down. "Ryan is here to represent the Sales department, since, as you know, Accounting works closely with them."

"Also to answer any questions you might have about how things have changed since you left." Ryan added.

141

"We're just waiting on Nicole from H.R.," Josh told me.

"Speak of the devil," Ryan said loudly, smiling as a brunette woman in a pink dress entered the room. She took the empty chair opposite me and flipped open a folder.

"Morning," Josh said to her. "Nicole, I'd like you to meet Amelia York."

I turned my attention to her. She was maybe a decade younger than me, and had thick, dark lashes and sparkly pale pink eye shadow that made her brown eyes look huge. She stood, reaching out a hand across the table to shake mine. "Nicole Reagan, Human Resources. Nice to meet you, Amelia. I've heard so much about you."

From the corner of my eye, I noticed Josh's mouth twist. I tried to focus on Nicole as she sat back down. "Good things, I hope?"

She laughed, and it made her whole face light up. She was quite pretty. "Definitely."

I glanced back at Josh again, but his expression was neutral. Maybe I'd just imagined the grimace.

We chatted about what my role would look like if I returned, and Ryan and Josh filled me in on some of the process changes as well as name-checking many of their new clients.

Before long, the meeting was over and I said goodbye to Ryan and Nicole. Once they'd gone, Josh turned to me. "Do you want to go over to Accounting and say hi to Kaitlyn?"

I frowned. "I do, but since I haven't made a decision yet, I think it might be best if I just slip out quietly."

"Your call." He led me back to the Reception area. "I'm really glad you decided to come in today. Any idea how much time you might need?"

I knew he needed my answer soon so he could look elsewhere if it was a no. "A few days maybe? Would that be okay?"

"That's fine. Is there anything I could do to help sway you?"

I snorted. "You've already made a pretty tempting offer. If I decline, please know it wasn't because of anything you did."

Josh smiled. "I'm still hoping for a yes." He leaned in and gave me a one-armed hug. "Promise me you'll at least come over to the house to see Holly and meet Emily soon?"

Squeezing his wrist, I said, "Definitely. No matter what I decide, we'll get together again soon."

It normally took about an hour to drive between Lynchburg and Richmond. Today, however, was not a normal day. I ended up stuck in traffic the moment I hit the outskirts of the city. Not much fun, but it gave me plenty of time to think.

I was getting frustrated with myself. Why was this decision so difficult? It should've been easy. Just say no, like that old anti-drugs slogan. It should have been easy to turn Josh's job offer down. There were so many reasons not to take it. Good reasons. Valid reasons. I knew them all well, as they'd weighed on my mind for years.

But I could provide a better life for Liam if I returned to BWK. And, for the most part, I thought I'd be happier. I'd enjoyed working there and felt productive and useful, even on the crappy days. It wasn't that I was unhappy at my current role, but it didn't challenge me. It would never lead to anything better. It certainly didn't leave me feeling fulfilled or particularly useful at the end of the day. It would be nice to feel confident and proud of the work I did again. It would be even nicer to have benefits and some extra cash and be able to spoil my son a little. With that salary, I might even be able to afford to take him to the beach on vacation next summer. He'd never seen the ocean before. An image popped into my head of Liam and I building a sandcastle at Virginia Beach while the surf crashed against the shore. He'd love it there. Maybe I could even bring Mom along.

With a rapid shake of my head, I put a stop to that thought. I was getting way ahead of myself, letting myself get all excited about future plans that would probably never happen. I glanced at the traffic and saw that my off ramp was at last in sight. At the speed I was inching along, it might take another ten minutes to get there, though.

On impulse, I tapped the Bluetooth button and called my mother.

"Hello?" She sounded distracted.

"Hey Mom, it's me. Did I interrupt something?"

"No, I was just reading. What's that noise in the background?"

Closing my windows, I replied, "Just road noise. I'm stuck in traffic, but almost home."

"You're calling me while driving? That's dangerous. And illegal, Amelia."

I chuckled. "I know, Mom. I've got you on hands-free. Don't worry."

"I always worry. Is Liam in the car with you?"

"No. But if it makes you feel any better, I'll keep it quick. I'm just coming back from a job interview in Lynchburg. At BWK, where I used to work."

"Oh really?" Now she sounded interested. "For your old role?"

"No, Senior Accountant, actually. But I haven't decided yet if I'm going to take it."

"They already offered you the position? Is the money good? Why wouldn't you take it?"

"The salary's great. I wouldn't want to commute from Richmond, though. If I do say yes, would it maybe be okay if Liam and I stayed with you for a few months until I could save up enough to get our own place?"

She was quiet for a few moments. Not long, but long enough for me to know she was thinking it through. I wasn't annoyed, though. If we did move in for a while, I wanted her to consider the implications of having a four year-old running around her neat and tidy home.

"Of course. I'd enjoy the company. I could clear out the spare room and put in a little bed for him, so he wouldn't have to sleep in with you."

"You mean it? Because I don't want to impose. If I actually do this, I swear we'll only stay for a little while. Not for years or anything."

I heard a soft exhalation. "You wouldn't be imposing. I'd love to have you both. And jump starting the career you let slide is the smartest thing you could do right now. For both of you."

Suppressing my own sigh, I said, "You're probably right. And thank you. I'll let you know what I decide."

"You realize if you two move in, people will notice. You'll have to be willing to let our friends and neighbors know about Liam. Are you prepared for that now? Can I tell people I have a grandson?"

I bit my lower lip. I wasn't sure I'd ever truly be prepared for that. "I…I'll call you later. I'm at my exit. Gotta go." Punching the call release button, I blew out a puff of air. Mom was right. If I did this, there'd be no more secrets. I'd have to tell Josh and Holly. And Liv and Scott, at some point.

But I still had no intention of telling Declan. Not now. Maybe not ever. Hopefully Josh would understand. I pulled off the clogged highway with relief, anxious to get back home and see my son.

"At long last, the sleepy little lion cub closed his eyes. 'Night, night' whispered Mommy Lion."

"Night, night," Liam parroted back to me, as he always did when we read this book. It was starting to get a little babyish for him, but he still loved it and I still loved reading it to him.

I shut the book and tucked it into the shelf below his nightstand. After switching off the lamp, I lay down beside him. "So, I have a question for you, little man."

"What?"

"If Mommy took a different job in a different city, and it meant we had to go live with Gramma for a bit, what would you think about that?"

"I like it here." He snuggled up against me. Five years ago I never would have guessed that this would become the best part of my day.

"I know you do. I like it here, too."

"Don't wanna leave. Auntie Dee and Auntie Terri would miss us."

I exhaled a soft sigh. "Yes, they would. But we'd still come visit them all the time. And they'd visit us, too. Aunt Dee's family lives not far from Gramma, remember?" I felt Liam nod against my chest. "You're starting school in another month. What if you started school in Swann's Landing instead of here? Would you be okay with that?"

"I'd miss Quentin." Quentin was the little boy two doors down. Liam played with him sometimes.

"I know. I'd miss everyone here, too. But we'd make new friends. And we'd get to see Gramma every day. That would make her happy." At least I hoped so.

"Yeah."

"If we stayed with Gramma for a while, maybe in a few months we could get our own place, just you and me. And if I took this job, maybe next summer you and me and Gramma could go on a trip together. That would be fun, wouldn't it?"

Liam yawned. I could tell this conversation wasn't going to last much longer. "Can we go to the beach?" he asked, his voice now foggy with sleep.

"Yes. We could definitely go to the beach." I brushed his hair aside and kissed him on the forehead. "Get some sleep, little man. Love you loads."

Another yawn, this one longer. "Love you loads, Mommy."

I stayed there with him until his breathing deepened. No matter what kind of day I had, I always felt better once I was snuggled up with my son. Our cuddles calmed my overactive brain like nothing else could.

I wanted to give Liam the best possible life I could. He deserved it. Even if that meant taking some risks. And making some personal sacrifices.

After another five minutes, I carefully got off the bed and slipped out of his room, going across the hall to my own. My phone was on my dresser plugged into the charger. I sat on the side of my bed and stared at it for a long time, thinking, deliberating, weighing everything for the hundredth time.

Finally I picked it up and opened a text to Josh: *You win. I'll come back. Give me a call tomorrow to discuss details. And let's make a date for a visit soon.*

I pulled on my pajamas and went to the bathroom to brush my teeth. My mind was reeling and it felt like my heart was beating way too fast. What had I just agreed to? I splashed cold water on my cheeks to try to clear my head. A long sigh escaped through my nose

My face in the mirror looked like a stranger's. Not because I'd changed my hair, not because I looked older, not because of any superficial stuff like that. Because when I stared into my own eyes, I could no longer see the Amelia I used to be, back when I'd worked at BWK the first time.

I stepped away from the mirror and considered. Maybe that wasn't a bad thing. Maybe I didn't miss her anymore. My life was finally on the path I'd been telling myself for years that I wanted. And I liked the woman I was now. Weak, pathetic Amelia was in the past. Going back to BWK didn't mean I would end up sliding back into old habits. No matter how complicated this decision might end up making things, I had to do what was best for Liam, best for both of us.

It was time for a change.

Chapter 17

Declan

True to my word, on Wednesday I took Nicole to Alessandro's for lunch. It was a beautiful warm day, so I expected it to be busy, but it wasn't that bad. Maybe because we'd arrived just as the lunch rush was clearing out.

Not gonna lie—it felt fucking weird walking inside. I hadn't been there in years. It had been one of Laura's favorite restaurants and after she died, I'd lost interest in returning. The food was good, not amazing, and the atmosphere was kind of over-the-top fake Italian cheesy.

The patio was still full, but we lucked out and got a table by a window. "Sorry again about being an ass the other night," I said after we'd placed our orders.

Nicole shrugged. "It's fine." Which I knew meant it still wasn't.

I put my hand on top of hers. "I don't have a good excuse, other than I just wasn't in the mood for company. *Any* company, not you specifically. It doesn't happen as often now, but I still have some bad days. I swear it wasn't anything you said or did."

Her eyes were focused on the fake flower in the vase on the table. She just nodded. "I understand." She pulled her hand from mine and reached for her glass of water.

I sighed under my breath. "Forgive me?"

Nicole raised her chocolate brown eyes to mine. As she stared at me I started to feel uncomfortable. Those eyes looked way too much like a different pair of brown eyes. I had to fight the urge to look away.

She smiled, and to my relief the tension abated. "Of course."

I smiled back. I hadn't realized she was still harboring resentment from the other night, but it seemed it was over now. "So how was your morning?"

"Busy. Lots of paperwork. I sat in on an interview with Josh for a new senior accountant. Ryan was there too, did he tell you?"

"He didn't mention it. I didn't even know Josh was hiring another one. Was the applicant a good fit?"

Nicole tilted her head a little. "Oh yeah. She seems perfect. Actually, you might remember her. She used to work at BWK a few years back."

My brows flew up as the rest of my body went still. *No way. No fucking way.* "What's her name?"

"You know this is totally confidential, right? I shouldn't be telling you this stuff. I could get in deep shit."

"I'm aware." My voice had gone steely. I set my hand on top of hers again. I could feel my tension ratcheting and I cautioned myself to be gentle as I squeezed her fingers. "But you won't. I'm not gonna blab it around. *What was her name, Nic?*"

Her eyes narrowed. "It's not like I have the file with me or anything. Let me think. It started with an A. Amanda? Anita?"

Fuck.

"Amelia," I muttered, letting go of her hand and sitting back.

"That's it!" she said with a grin. "I take it you know her?"

It took me a few seconds to answer. Swiping my hair off my forehead, I blew out a sigh. "I used to. A long time ago."

Assuming we were done with that topic, Nicole moved on to her brother's wedding, which was coming up in a couple of months. I knew she wanted me to go with her, although she hadn't yet asked. She started rambling on about her soon to be sister-in law, but it didn't matter. I was no longer listening.

Instead, my thoughts turned to a conversation I'd had with my father five years ago, the day after the last time I'd seen Amelia.

Mere seconds after I'd finished loading the dishwasher, the doorbell rang. I'd invited James over to watch hockey with me, as had become our habit during the season.

Alexis ran to let him in, grabbing onto his hand before he even had time to remove his shoes. "Grandpa James! Come here! You *have* to see this silly dog on YouTube." She tugged him into the living room where she'd been watching videos on her tablet while I cleaned up and put away the remains of dinner.

As I wiped down the counters, I could hear their laughter. These days, it was hard to imagine our lives without James. Though we'd really only known him for a couple of years, he'd become an integral member of our little family. Alexis had only lost her mother a little over a year ago; I hated knowing she'd soon lose her beloved Grandpa as well. I knew all too well how much these things affect and change you, especially as a child. My daughter was way too young to have to go through losing a loved one even once, let alone twice. And there wasn't a damn thing I could do to protect her from it.

Later, after James read her a story and we kissed her goodnight, we retired to the living room where I poured us drinks and turned on the game. I wasn't much interested in hockey tonight, though. There were more important subjects that needed discussing.

First things first. "How're you feeling?"

He glanced sideways at me. "If you mean about what the doctor said, which I assume you do, then I guess the best word would be *disappointed*."

"Disappointed? Just disappointed? Not, say, devastated? Or terrified? Or maybe pissed right the fuck off?"

James smiled a sad smile. "Sure. Those things, too. But you have to remember I already got this diagnosis once before, and had to process all the emotions that came with finding out I was dying back then." Pausing, he took a sip of bourbon. "I like to think of it this way: I got a few years reprieve that I wasn't expecting. And it's been nothing but a blessing, getting to know you and Alexis. I was hoping for lots of years yet to watch her grow up." He ran a hand through his hair, spiking it up in thick gray chunks. "To be honest with you, I wish I didn't even know that goddamn tumor's growing again. Not knowing's better."

"You think?" My mind shot to Laura. "I'd rather be able to say my goodbyes. Just…being gone just like that, with no warning…" My eyelids slipped shut for a moment as I tried to pull my thoughts together. "It's such a blow to everyone left behind. I mean, I know it's a mind-fuck either way, but…yeah. I'd wanna say goodbye."

"You're right, of course. And we'll have lots of time to say our goodbyes. I still feel fine. I could have another year or more."

We both knew a year was probably hopelessly optimistic, but I didn't correct him. I hoped like hell he'd have another year. Or by some miracle, even longer. "I hope so. You told Miriam?"

He nodded. "Yeah. She's flying down next weekend for a visit. I meant to tell you earlier. Sorry."

I was surprised Miriam hadn't texted me herself, not just about James' condition, but about her planned visit. She usually stayed here, as James lived in a small one-bedroom apartment with a lumpy couch—her description, not mine. I made a mental note to text her later to make sure she knew she was welcome here as always. Alexis would be thrilled to find out her auntie was coming.

"That's okay. You've got a lot on your mind."

"I'm getting more forgetful. That's one of the symptoms, you know." With a sigh, he returned his attention the game. The Sabres were struggling, which was no real surprise, as they'd had a shitty season so far.

Frowning, I didn't reply. Having to bear witness to his memory, his coordination, and eventually his eyesight failing was going to suck. Hard.

For a while we just watched the television in silence. I hadn't told anyone what had happened with Amelia, but it also weighed heavy on my mind. It bugged me that I couldn't recall exactly what I'd said to her. All I knew was that I'd managed to yet again fuck things up big time.

I glanced over at James. He was the only person I really confided in anymore. And although I wasn't proud of my actions, and Amelia's news didn't have the happy ending it should have had, I figured he'd want to know. With a glance his way, I said, "So… something happened yesterday."

He shifted to face me again, looking hopeful. "Please tell me it's something good?"

My face twisted. If I wasn't so goddamn useless, this news could've been amazing. Instead, it was just another kick in the balls. "It's…no, not really. Not the way it turned out."

"Well, tell me anyway. I could use a distraction." He gestured toward the television. "These idiots couldn't find the puck tonight if they tripped over it."

Picking up my tumbler, I threw back a swallow of bourbon. "So, you recall my friend Josh got married a couple months ago?"

"Sure. You were his best man, right?"

"Right. Well, Amelia was there. At the wedding."

James' face went blank.

"The woman I told you about a while back? The one I was seeing when Laura and I were separated?"

"Oh. Right. Yes. Did you spend some time with her?"

"That's one way to put it. I, uh...I had a lot to drink that night. And ended up spending the night in her hotel room."

"Ah," he smiled. His smile fell away as he took in my expression. "That wasn't a good thing?"

With a sigh, I said, "Let's just say we went our separate ways in the morning. I was a fucking mess. I guess I still am."

James frowned, but didn't comment.

"So anyway. Yesterday afternoon after I got back to work, I got a call from her asking to meet because she needed to tell me something." I paused, lifting my gaze to his. "That night? The night we hooked up? I was drunk and stupid and didn't use a condom. I mean, before, when we were together, she'd been on the Pill. I guess she must've gone off it—she didn't say, and like a total idiot, I didn't ask—but anyway, the point is, she's pregnant."

A massive grin erupted, brightening his entire face and making him look at least ten years younger. "That's amazing news!" He looked so happy I wished I didn't have to tell him the rest. Before I could start, however, his eyes narrowed. "Wait. Hold on, didn't the same basic thing happen with Laura? How could it possibly have happened twice? That's a pretty insane coincidence."

Chuckling, I held up my hands, palms forward. "I know. It's totally nuts. Apparently booze makes me uber-potent or something."

"Clearly," James snorted, shaking his head. "Well, I'm really happy for you, son. This is wonderful. Just wonderful."

"You'd think, wouldn't you? You'd think this time, with Amelia, it'd be a no-brainer. But she's..." I paused, taking a deep breath. *Just spit it out*, I scolded myself. "She's not gonna keep it."

His mouth fell open. "What? Why not?"

Because who in their right mind would want to have a child with a waste of space like me? I sure as hell wouldn't.

Sadly I shook my head. "She wants nothing to do with me."

"Oh Declan. I'm almost afraid to ask. What's the problem this time?" A deep frown now creased his forehead. I hated that I'd taken away the happiness I'd just seen on his face. He deserved to be happy about something right now. If only he could have this child to be excited about. He needed something good to look forward to. Hell, so did I.

At first I didn't respond. I had another mouthful of bourbon and held the liquor on my tongue for a few moments, relishing the sharp flavor, then the burn it created down my throat as I swallowed. Finally, I looked back at him. My voice came out rougher than before. "Me. I'm the problem. I'm a fucking train wreck. And she knows it. She probably hates me."

"I'm sure that's not true. Although, as I recall you probably hurt her pretty badly last year." He paused, narrowing his eyes and staring at me. "Let me ask you something: you're head over heels for this woman, right? She's the one you want to be with?"

I blew out a sigh as I nodded.

"Then don't just let her walk away. You need to go after her. Not that I think it'll be easy. It won't. But you have to try to prove to her that you want her. And this baby."

My throat had grown tight. "I wish I could. But I don't think she'll let me." I took another sip and turned back to him. "The thought of having a child with Amelia—it's just the best damn thing ever, you know? But then I remember what a colossal fuckup I am and I wonder if they'd be better off without me to ruin their lives. All I've ever done is cause her pain."

"Then you need to apologize. And grovel. Get down on your knees and beg her if you have to. Do it over and over until she listens. It may take a long time, but if somewhere deep inside she still loves you, she'll be able to forgive you. Eventually."

My hands were clenched in a tight fist over my knees. "I would. I really would. But it's not that simple. There's so many things—"

"Stop." His blue eyes had gone steely. "Just forget everything else for a minute. Forget your guilt. Forget that you think you're a screw-up. This baby is the catalyst you need to turn your life around. You love her. And she's pregnant with your child. It's time to rise up outta this hole you've dug for yourself and fight for her. You need to do everything in your power to fix this. Tell her how much you love her. Convince her you want her to keep the baby, that you want to be a part of its life. Convince her you're worth taking a second chance on so you can raise this child—a child created out of that love—together. Do it for me, so I can meet my second grandchild before I die. Do it for Alexis, so she can be a part of a happy family again with a baby sibling to love. She needs this as much as you do." He reached over and set a hand on my shoulder. "Most of all, you need to do it for yourself. Because, son, you can't keep on the way you've been going. Forgive yourself, and maybe she'll be able to forgive you, too."

I could barely swallow, that lump that grown so huge. Breaking his intense stare, I tried to cough it away, lifting my glass to choke down the rest of my bourbon. I didn't reply; I just got up and took the empty tumbler to the kitchen. Instead of refilling it, I rinsed it out.

When I returned, my father was once again focused on the game. We watched the rest of it, joking about the players and making derisive comments about the refs, but deliberately not mentioning health or babies or broken relationships.

At the end of the night, James turned back to me and simply said, "You can do it. I have faith in you."

I forced a small smile. "Thanks, Dad. Really. I'm gonna try." Though I knew it was ultimately Amelia's decision whether she had this baby or not, I didn't want to let her go without telling her how I really felt about it.

And I'd tried. I'd really tried. I'd tried to call, but couldn't get through. I'd tried to text, but every one bounced back as undeliverable. She'd either blocked me or changed her number, neither of which was much of a surprise. I couldn't go by her house as I didn't know where she lived. I couldn't ask Josh, as she'd ghosted him as well. He'd paid the price for my misdeeds, and our friendship had suffered for a while for it, although we were pretty much back to normal these days.

What I'd told James that night had been spot on. Amelia wanted nothing to do with me. I assumed she'd gotten an abortion and made the drastic choice to cut all reminders of me out of her life. And although it hurt—fuck, it hurt so bad I felt like I was barely holding the ragged threads of myself together some days—I couldn't be angry with her for it. I deserved no better. And she deserved so much better.

My father died having never gotten to meet a second grandchild. I'd failed him, just as I'd failed Laura. And my other unborn child. And the woman I loved.

It can't be! I sat at my desk an hour later, frowning at my monitor. *It's not possible. She'd never come back here.* My chair groaned beneath me as I leaned back, unable to focus on the proposal I was attempting to read. *What in God's name would ever make her want to return?*

But Nic had told me the woman they'd interviewed used to work here. And her name was Amelia. Interviewing for a Senior Accountant position, a role she was definitely qualified for. It *had* to be her. I had no clue why she'd even consider coming back to BWK, but it had to be her.

Which brought me to another thought. Why hadn't Josh told me? Surely to Christ he'd think to give me a head's up if he was meeting with her? Or maybe he didn't want to say anything until it was for sure? Maybe it wasn't a done deal yet?

Abruptly I pushed back my chair, yanked open my door, and walked over to Accounting. When I got to Josh's office, it was empty. Kaitlyn informed me that he was in meetings all afternoon. Fine. I could wait.

The following morning, I found him at his desk, although he was on the phone. I closed his door behind me and took a seat. Luckily I'd brought my coffee along.

Josh glanced up at me, brows raised in question.

"I'll wait," I mouthed.

He frowned, told whoever he was talking to that he'd have to call them back, and replaced the receiver. Then he looked over at me expectantly. "Morning, Declan. To what do I owe the pleasure?"

"Glad to know you consider my company a pleasure," I deadpanned.

Josh rolled his eyes. "Depends on the day. Is this about Merrill and Hogan?"

Merrill and Hogan was a medium-sized law firm that I'd been trying to seduce for weeks. "Nope, although now that you mention it, I do need to talk to you about the ad costs you sent me Friday. But that can wait."

"Okay. So what brings you over here then?"

I looked him in the eyes. "Is there perhaps a certain tidbit of info you'd like to share?"

154

His brows narrowed ever so slightly. "Such as?"

"A little birdie told me you're interviewing for another senior accountant?" I took a sip from my mug and stared at him pointedly.

Josh leaned back in his chair with a sigh. His lips were thin. "That is confidential information. She could get fired if any of the senior partners found out she's sharing this stuff around before any official announcement's been made."

I waved this away. "Whatever. She didn't tell anyone else. And frankly, if what she said is true, I would've really preferred to hear it from you."

"I couldn't. Like I just said, it was confidential."

"*Was?*"

He regarded me for a long moment. "I was planning to go over and see you this morning, actually. Because yeah, I know you deserve a bit of a head's up. But you beat me to it. Or should I say Nicole beat me to it."

"So it's true? She's really coming back?" I was floored, torn between shock, trepidation, and, if I'm being honest, a thin veneer of hope. Fucking hope, such a cruel emotion, yet I couldn't seem to completely squash it.

"She really is. I can hardly believe it either."

I stood up, setting my cup on his desk as I began to pace in the small space. "How did this even come about? You haven't heard a peep from her in the last five years and then just…bam! Out of nowhere she reaches out to you? Or have you two been in touch for a while now and you just neglected to mention that, too?"

Josh frowned. "You can stop with the accusatory tone already. I mean, whose fault is it she dropped off the earth? Sure as hell not mine. Or Holly's."

I stopped in my tracks, turning to stare at him. "You think I don't know that? You guys were just collateral damage. I'm well aware it was all my fault. I'm not a complete idiot."

"You could've fooled me."

Taking my seat again, I chose to ignore the dig. "So what happened? Did she contact you? Or did you just bump into her?"

"Something like that. I know where her mom lives in Swann's Landing. Sometimes I drive down that street to see if I might spot Amelia's car in the driveway. Last week I got lucky. I knocked on the door, she came out, we talked, and she agreed to come in for an interview. The rest, as they say, is history."

"Okay. Okay, but that still doesn't answer the biggest question: why the hell would she want to return after being so careful to avoid us for so long?"

"I can be very persuasive." Josh's smile fell away as he looked closer at me, assessing my level of agitation, I'm sure. "No idea," he admitted with a shrug. "Maybe she needs the money. Or maybe she misses us." Seeing my skeptical look, he added, "Well, *some* of us, anyway. And hey, here's a thought to mull over: maybe she's just ready to forgive and forget and move on with her life?"

I exhaled a long sigh. "Maybe. I guess we'll see. When does she start?"

"August twenty-seventh."

"Ah. Well, thanks for filling me in."

"I would've told you. I hope you know that," he said. "I'm aware this is still a sensitive subject for you. But you're both grown-ass adults. I'm sure you're capable of having civil discourse about our clients when necessary." He paused, chuckling. "Well, I know one of you is."

I snorted. "We'll see. Things around here are about to get interesting again."

Josh's face got stern. "Don't be an asshole and everything will be just fine. I'm serious, Declan."

"Who me? I'm always nice." Getting back to my feet, I pulled open his door before he could make a smart-ass comeback "Catch ya later."

I couldn't stay. I needed some time to myself to think about this. Amelia and I used to have a great working relationship. We'd been so much more than just colleagues; we'd been friends. Before anything else, before we'd ever fallen for each other, we'd been friends. A small and probably insanely naïve part of me couldn't help wondering if we could ever be friends again.

Chapter 18

Amelia

"Is that the last of it?" my mother asked as I started upstairs with what felt to my aching arms like the hundredth box.

Dee appeared in the open doorway, her arms laden with bags. She was smiling. "Nope. But *this* is!"

"Woo hoo!" I shouted.

Liam's small face appeared above me in the second floor hallway. "What woo hoo?"

Dee and I laughed. My mom just looked on, a slightly confused smile on her lips. "All our stuff is now out of the cars," I told him. "We're moved in." We hadn't brought any of our furniture. Dee and Terri had said I could leave all the big stuff at their house until we got a place all our own, so I'd just packed up our personal possessions in bags and boxes. Lots of bags and boxes, considering we were only two people, and one of us was only four. I joined Liam at the top of the stairs and set the box I was carrying on top of stack against the wall. I'd move it into my bedroom later.

Terri came around the corner from the spare room that would now be Liam's room and stood beside him. "Yee haw!" Then she laughed. "I don't usually 'yee haw' like some back-country hick, but this moment seems to warrant it." She wiped sweat off her brow. "Y'all got a cool drink handy by any chance?"

Mom turned toward the kitchen. "Three glasses of iced tea coming up!"

"And apple juice!" Liam added as he trotted down the steps to follow her.

"And apple juice," my mother repeated with a smile. She would get used to having him around all the time, but I worried his excess energy might stress her out.

Later, once we'd had lunch and relaxed a bit, Dee sidled up to me in the kitchen while Mom and Terri were upstairs helping Liam start to organize his new bedroom. "Gonna miss you," she said, taking the dish towel from my hand and grabbing a dripping plate.

"We'll miss you, too," I told her. "But you know we'll come visit. And you guys can drop in whenever you're in town."

"Until you move to Lynchburg, anyway."

"We might not move to Lynchburg. I have no idea yet where we'll end up. I might find a place here so Liam won't have to change schools. Who knows?"

She sighed. "The house just won't feel the same without you guys."

"I'm sure you won't miss Liam waking you up on days you don't need to be in the salon early," I said with a snort. "And you and Terri deserve some alone time. You've had me around pretty much the entire time you've been together."

Tears appeared in the corners of Dee's eyes and she pulled me into a tight squeeze. "I will *so* miss his happy yelling waking me up. I'll miss his not-so-quiet whispers. I'll miss all the times he chatters away at me and I only understand about half of it. I'll even miss the temper tantrums. Most of all, I'm gonna miss his sweet hugs. I never thought I'd love having a kid around as much as I've loved Liam."

I pulled away from her and looked her in the eyes. "Indira Khanna! Are you actually feeling maternal?"

"I guess maybe I am," she chuckled. "Weird, huh? My mother'd be totally over the moon if she knew. Speaking of whom, I guess we'd better get going soon. I promised her we'd be over there before two."

After Dee and Terri left, Liam got it into his head that he needed to find his Battleship game. Together we went through box after box until we finally located it. He promptly took it downstairs and challenged Gramma to a game on the dining room table. Yep, Mom's life was about to change pretty drastically. At least once school and my new job started, she'd have some personal space during the daytime again.

I told them I was going to do some unpacking and returned to his room. His stuffies were carefully organized along the wall side of the bed and there was an empty box in one corner. Another one was only half unpacked, books strewn over the floor below it. I gathered them up and stood them on the shelf above his bed, and then opened an overstuffed garbage bag and began to sort his clothes into the closet and dresser.

Maybe all my worrying had been for nothing. Maybe this was going to work out after all. Maybe my mother would end up enjoying having Liam around every day. It wouldn't be so bad. And in a few months we'd get our own place and give her her space back.

Listening to them play downstairs, I couldn't help recalling Mom's reaction when I'd first told her I was pregnant. Her opinion about me having a child had certainly come a long way since then.

On Christmas morning, I woke up in my bedroom in the house I'd grown up in, just as I had every Christmas for the first twenty-two years of my life before I'd moved in with Scott. For a moment I found myself listening for my dad's voice drifting up from the kitchen as he chatted with my mom while making breakfast.

With a sharp pang, I remembered. He wasn't here. This was our third Christmas without him, yet it still felt as raw as the first.

I turned over with a groan. My head throbbed and the queasiness had already begun. I didn't always feel sick the moment I awoke anymore, but it still happened on the regular. Stretching out a hand from under my warm blankets, I felt around on the bedside table for the small packet of crackers I'd left there. Dry, pasty crackers first thing in the morning did nothing for my taste buds, but they did help suppress the nausea.

Rolling onto my back, I stared at the ceiling while I waited for my stomach to settle. The plaster stucco swirled and peaked in its oh-so-familiar patterns. How many times in the past had I lain here mesmerized by them? This room knew me as well as I knew it.

But I was no longer a kid. I couldn't just stay in my room for hours letting my imagination run wild. With a sigh, I threw back the covers and went into the bathroom. As I brushed my teeth, I examined myself in the mirror. There were dark circles around my eyes and my hair looked like it could use a wash. No matter how often I shampooed, it always seemed kind of dull and limp. I rubbed my forehead ruefully, wishing I could pop an ibuprofen for my headache. But for the next six months I'd just have to tough it out. Maybe breakfast would help. I threw on my robe and headed downstairs.

"Merry Christmas," I greeted my mom as I entered the kitchen. She sat at the table with a steaming cup of coffee in her hands. As I'd predicted, she'd gone back to drinking it.

"Merry Christmas to you, too. Coffee's in the pot."

The pungent smell was doing nothing for either my headache or the lingering remains of the nausea. "No, thanks." I pulled open the fridge door and took out the orange juice. When I turned around with my glass, she was scrutinizing me with a small frown.

"No coffee? That's not like you."

Mom had just given me the perfect opening to tell her my news. But although I'd promised myself I'd do it today, I wasn't quite ready yet. Shrugging, I replied, "I felt like O.J. this morning. Want me to scramble up some eggs?"

"That would be nice." She didn't mention that my dad had always made us a big scrambled eggs breakfast on Christmas morning, but I knew we were both thinking it.

After breakfast, which neither of us finished, we went into the living room to open gifts. This didn't take long, as we'd agreed to keep things simple and just had one package for each other. I gave my mom a deep cerise cashmere sweater that I'd barely been able to afford, but knew would look great on her. She gave me a leather-banded watch. I didn't really wear watches, but it was slim and elegant-looking, and I thanked her for it with as much enthusiasm as I could muster.

I put the watch on my wrist and sat back, looking up at the Christmas tree my mom had erected in its usual place in the corner. All our ornaments from years gone by were carefully and neatly hung. Something caught my eye and I got up to take a closer look. It was a red and green star made from painted Popsicle sticks. It had been a long time since I'd seen

160

that star—I'd made it way back in grade school. With a small frown, I ran a finger over the glitter. Mom hadn't hung any of my handmade ornaments up in years. I took a closer look around the tree and spotted two others: a poorly crocheted yellow bell and a "wreath" of plastic beads strung on a lopsided wire circle. Had she been feeling sentimental this year? I'd forgotten all about these, and I admit, it was kind of touching to see them back on the tree.

I turned to her. "Actually, Mom, there's something else I have—"

"Another gift?" she cut in.

"Sort of," I smiled. "You could say that."

She looked up at me expectantly. When I didn't produce a second box for her to unwrap, her expression changed to confusion. "What is it?"

Okay, now's the time. Just spit it out and get this over with.

Biting my lip, I sat back down beside her. "Well...this wasn't planned or anything, but, uh...so...you're gonna be a grandma."

Mom's eyebrows drew in tight. "Is this some kind of joke, Amelia?"

Shaking my head, I assured her, "It's no joke. I'm pregnant. I'm due in June. For real."

Her mouth fell open, but no words came out. That had to be a first. I'd actually made my mother speechless.

I decided to nip what I assumed would be her forthcoming protestations in the bud. "Before you start in, please just hear me out. I know what you're gonna say: that I'm not employed, that I'm not married, or even in a relationship, that I have no experience with kids, and that I'm gonna ruin my life having a baby right now." The look on her face told me I'd nailed her thoughts pretty much on the head. "There's not a single thing you could say to me that I haven't already thought over a million times. All those things are true, but none of them matter. This is what's happening: I'm having a baby. I'm gonna be a mom. I may not have a partner, but Dee's promised to help me, and hopefully once you get over your shock, you'll want to, too."

Her lips were a hard line. We looked at each other for several long seconds. At last she said, "Who and where is the father?"

I sighed. That was the other bit I'd been dreading. "He's...we're not together anymore. He won't be a part of our lives."

"Does he know about the baby?" She looked like I'd just told her something horrible instead of something wonderful. Which wasn't any surprise, but it still stung.

"I told him."

"And he walked out on you? What kind of man would do that? And why didn't you tell me you were dating someone? Why am I just hearing about this now?"

My face felt like it was on fire. "I didn't...it was...complicated. We were together for a bit, but we split up." I straightened my spine. "Don't worry about him. It's for the best. Really. I don't need him."

She was quiet for a moment. Then she said, "You didn't answer my other question. Who *is* he? Do I know him?"

"No. And it doesn't matter. It's over."

"It's hardly over! You are having his baby! That's *very* far from over." She shook her head, frowning at me. "You should really try to work things out with him. A child needs both parents. My friend Donna's daughter has shared custody with her ex-husband and it sounds like a nightmare. One week she has her son, then the next he's with his dad. So much back and forth. It must be terribly confusing, not to mention stressful, for that little boy."

"I'm sure it is." I agreed, lifting my chin to look right at her. "But my situation is nothing like that. There'll be no working things out. He's out of my life forever. So please drop it. Right now, the most important thing is that I'm pregnant. And I'm keeping the baby. And because I'm pregnant, I'm feeling super headachy right now, so I think I'm gonna go back up and lie down for a bit." I got to my feet and gave her a wan smile. "Just please try to trust me when I say this is what I want. I hope you can be happy for me."

Mom's brows narrowed again, but one corner of her lips edged upward. It wasn't quite a smile, but it was close. "Then I will just say congratulations. I don't feel old enough to be a grandmother yet. But you know? Your father would be in absolute seventh heaven about this."

I smiled back. "You think so?"

"I am certain of it."

The thought of Daddy as a grandpa made me feel simultaneously melancholy and pleased. I tried to imagine how he'd react if he were with us right now. I could just picture his wide, toothy grin. He'd give me a big hug and assure me he'd do everything in his power to take care of me and my child.

Tears rose to my eyes. I quickly turned away and headed for the stairs.

Less than a week after Liam and I moved into my mom's place, I invited Josh, Holly, and their daughter Emily over for a visit. I couldn't put off telling them about Liam any longer. Meeting him was going to be a shock, but they needed to know and I needed to get this over with before I went back to work.

Not long before they were due to arrive, I found myself pacing the front hallway, lost in my thoughts as I tried to decide how best to introduce my son to my friends. Would I need to admit that Declan was his father? Would Josh jump to that conclusion anyway?

"Whatcha doing, Mommy?" Liam asked. I hadn't even heard him approach. He looked concerned, probably sensing my anxiety.

I stopped in my tracks, dropping to my knees in front of him and resting a hand on his small shoulder. "Remember I told you some old friends of mine were coming over?"

He nodded. "Do they have a kid?"

"Yes, a daughter named Emily. I think she's a year younger than you."

"Does she like Spiderman?"

"I don't know," I said with a smile. "But you can ask her. Why don't you run up to your room and put on your Spiderman costume? Do you know where it is?" There were still several full boxes in the hallway and I couldn't remember if we'd unpacked his costumes yet.

"Yep. In my drawer." Liam scooted past me and up the steps. A few minutes later he returned dressed in red and blue nylon, bouncing between the railing and wall and pretending to shoot webs from his wrists. He could not have been cuter.

Just as he reached the foot of the stairs, the doorbell rang and I jumped, my heart throbbing in my ears. *Okay, here goes*, I thought as I pasted on a smile and pulled open the door.

"Hey guys. It's so great to see you." I stepped forward and gave Holly a hug, then turned my attention to the cute blonde girl holding onto her daddy's hand. "You must be Emily," I said, my grin stretching wider. "My name's Amelia."

She glanced up at Josh who gave her an encouraging smile and nod. "Hi," she whispered, her eyes darting back to me as she edged closer to him.

"I'm so happy to meet you, Emily." I gestured past me. "Please come on inside."

As I closed the door behind them, I heard Holly say, "Oh, hi there Spiderman! And who might you be?"

I whipped around. Liam stood there looking up at them. His Spiderman mask concealed his entire head, so just his big blue eyes were visible. "I'm Liam."

"Hello Liam," Josh said. He shot me a questioning look.

Exhaling a soft sigh, I came to stand beside my son and slid my arm around his shoulders. "So, something else happened since we last hung out." I tried to smile, but it wobbled and fell away. "This is, uh, this is my son Liam."

Holly's mouth dropped open. "Your *son*? Oh my God, Amelia. You have a son? Why didn't you tell Josh?"

"It's...I don't know. I was going to when he dropped by a few weeks ago, but then I just...didn't. I told myself I'd tell him later, but then next time I saw him we were in a meeting with other people and mentioning it seemed awkward." I looked up at Josh sheepishly. "I didn't want to just text you. But meeting him is a big reason why I invited you guys over today."

Josh couldn't take his eyes off Liam. When at last he turned to me, he wore a stunned expression. Though he didn't say a word, I knew he had loads of questions.

Liam pulled out of my grip and ran through the living room to the sliding back doors. Pushing the screen open, he went outside. "C'mon out back," I said to my guests. "We can sit on the deck and chat."

Holly picked up Emily and carried her out. None of us said another word until we sat down by my mother below the shade of the overhang. Mom was knitting what appeared to be a sock. I still couldn't help a bit of a double-take when I saw her hands working away with the needles. I hadn't even known she'd taken up knitting until we'd moved in. It seemed like such a grandmotherly hobby, not at all something I'd thought she'd be interested in.

"Mom, these are my friends Josh and Holly, and their daughter, Emily." Emily mostly ignored us, looking longingly across the yard at Liam swinging on the swing my dad had hung from a thick branch of our big oak tree when I was young.

The lure of the swing appeared to be overcoming her initial shyness. "Guys, this is my mother, Brenda York."

Mom set her knitting aside and stood to shake their hands. "So pleased to meet you. Do you both work at BWK?"

"Just me," Josh said, finding his voice at last. "It seems I'm Amelia's boss now, weird as that sounds to say out loud. Holly works at the Lynchburg Historical Foundation."

"Oh, that's great. I've done some volunteer work for our Historical Society here in town. Now did Amelia offer you anything to drink? I've got some homemade lemonade in the fridge."

"Not yet." I turned to Emily. "Would you like a glass of lemonade, sweetie?"

Emily nodded, her gaze still on Liam. My son apparently had great hearing when he felt like using it, because he leaped off the swing and ran back to the deck, tearing his mask off and declaring, "Mommy, I'm thirsty!"

I held my breath as his adorable little face at last came into view. My eyes darted to my friends, and, as I'd anticipated, Josh was staring wide-eyed at Liam. I could nearly see the pieces falling into place in his head. Before Josh could say anything, I announced, "I'll go get us some drinks."

"Let me give you a hand with those," I heard Josh say from behind me as I pulled open the screen door.

"Sure," I mumbled, knowing why he'd offered, but glad we could at least have that conversation in the relative privacy of the kitchen. I kept my back to him as I took the pitcher of lemonade out of the refrigerator.

"So how old is Liam?"

"He's four." I opened the cupboard above me and, one by one, pulled down glasses. Then I grabbed the tray from the top of the fridge and started arranging them on it.

I felt his hand touch my elbow. "Look at me for a minute. Please."

I stopped. With reluctance, I turned around.

"Is there something you maybe wanna tell me?"

I bit my lip, but didn't reply.

Josh's voice dropped to just above a whisper. "That's why you vanished, isn't it? Because of Liam?"

This time I nodded.

"When? Oh man. It was after our wedding, wasn't it? He was completely shitfaced. And you took him up to his room."

I nodded again, breaking eye contact.

"Please tell me it was consensual. Or I'm going to have to kill him. You know that, right?"

"It was. At the time, it was. But he left before I woke the next morning. There was no further contact."

He tilted his head for a few long seconds, considering me. "So you didn't tell him?"

I grimaced, not wanting to dredge up the memory of that particular conversation. I nodded a third time. "I did."

"And what happened?" When I just shrugged, Josh dragged an exasperated hand over his hair. "Goddammit, Amelia. This is major. This is…I can't believe…" He stopped with a sigh. "You should've told me. Holly and I would've been there for you. Even if…Jesus. I'm afraid to even ask, but what did he say?"

Turning back to the counter I started pouring the lemonade. "I don't really wanna rehash it if that's okay. It was hard enough the first time around."

Josh said nothing. I tried to focus on the liquid sloshing into the glasses. I heard another deep sigh as I filled the last one. "I can barely believe this. Did he really want nothing to do with you? With his own child? I know he was pretty screwed up back then, but that's a total dick move even for him."

Putting the now-empty pitcher in the sink, I spun around. "Look, Josh, he doesn't know about Liam. And it needs to stay that way. I need you to promise you won't say a word to him. Seriously. It's important."

Josh frowned. "I thought you just said you told him."

"I did. And he expected me to get an abortion. He even offered to pay for it. I'd already decided I was keeping the baby, but he never once considered that an option. Afterward, I figured it'd be best if I just let him think that's what I did. We don't need him in our lives. We're better off without him. I'm really sorry that meant cutting off you guys, too, but you're his best friend. I couldn't put you in the position of having to keep such a massive secret for me." One of Josh's brows arched at that. "Well, until now, anyway. Since I'm coming back to work with you again, I knew I had to tell you guys."

Josh leaned back against the counter beside me, his arms crossed over his chest. "You're wrong, you know. I would've done it for you if you'd explained why. You're my friend, too. We didn't need to lose five years."

"I know you would have. But it wouldn't have been right to ask you to. Not then." I rested my head on his shoulder, hoping he realized how sorry I was.

"I understand. And I'm pretty sure Holly will, too. But you know, it's been a long time. He's in a different place now. A better place, I think. Maybe things would be different now if he knew?"

"No," I stated firmly. "He's proven again and again that he's no good for me. For us. Maybe someday I'll tell Liam the truth and he can decide then if he wants to meet his father, but...I can't let him back into my...*our* lives." I turned to face Josh and looked up at him pleadingly. "I'm trying hard to build a good life for us right now. Declan just causes upheaval and stress. Neither of us needs that."

Josh still looked unhappy about the situation, but he nodded. "I guess I get that. I won't say a word. Neither of us will. I promise."

With a relieved smile, I reached for the tray of glasses, but Josh picked it up first. "You get the door," he said. "And by the way?"

I turned back to him, another bolt of apprehension shooting through me.

But I didn't need to worry. Josh was smiling. "That kid of yours is super cute. I'm sure you realize if Declan ever sees him, he's gonna know right away."

"I know. He looks just like his father."

Chapter 19

Amelia

I walked into Baker, Wright, and Kavanaugh on my first day back with far more trepidation than excitement. So much had changed since my first day seven years ago. Well, I'd changed. BWK had not. Not much anyway. Diana and Evan had left. And Josh was my boss now, which was a huge plus. He was a lot happier to have me here than Diana had ever been.

I had dropped Liam off in front of Swann's Landing Elementary this morning, giving him a big hug and reminding him that Gramma would be picking him up after school from now on. He was a bit sad to say goodbye, but nowhere near as much as he'd been on his first day. Now that he was starting his second week of kindergarten, to my immense relief he seemed to be enjoying it. As I'd tried to explain to him, it wasn't really all that much different than the daycare he'd attended in Richmond all last year. I was pleased that he'd already made two friends from his class. He talked about Kendra and Mark all the time. I'd have to find out who their parents were so Liam could invite them over to play.

Josh and Kaitlyn soon got me settled into my new office. After I filled out a stack of HR forms for my health and dental benefits, Josh sat with me to show me what had changed since I'd left and what would be expected of me in this role. At lunch,

Sam greeted me with a squeal and a squeeze in the cafeteria, then grabbed me by the arm and practically dragged me to their usual table.

"So," Sam started in before I could even take a bite of my sandwich. "Did Kaitlyn tell you my news?"

"What news?" My eyes shot to Kaitlyn, but she just smiled.

"I'm Samantha Mapplethorpe now!" She proudly waggled her diamond clad finger for me. "I got married last summer. Can you believe it? *Me*? Married? But Joey is *such* a sweetheart. You have to meet him. You'll just adore him!"

"Oh wow! Congratulations, Sam. That's amazing news!"

"I know, right?" She pulled out her phone and began to show me photos from the wedding.

"What about you?" I asked after, turning to Kaitlyn. "What's your love life look like these days?"

Kaitlyn chuckled. "Same old, same old: single and happy. How 'bout you?"

I was tempted to tell them about Liam, but rumors traveled way too fast around BWK and it was a lot safer if no one knew but Josh. "Me, too," I said with a grin. "Single girls for the win!" I held out my fist and she tapped it with her own as we laughed.

"So what have you been up to all this time?" Sam asked.

As I started to tell her, Nicole from HR came into the cafeteria. I'd been keeping a watchful eye on the doors, worried a certain someone might walk in. So far there had been no sign of him, but I kept glancing that way. Spotting me, Nicole smiled, waved, and came over to our table. "Hey Amelia. How's your first day so far?"

"So far, so good," I told her.

"Wonderful. I know you already filled out a bunch of forms this morning, but it seems I missed including the one for your emergency contact. Is it okay if I drop it by your office this afternoon?" She pushed a strand of dark hair off her face and I was again hit by how pretty she was, especially in that cute blue sundress she wore.

"No problem. I'm sure I'll be there. I've got a mountain of case files to review."

"Great. See you later then." She headed over to the food lineup.

I looked back at Sam in time to see her rolling her eyes at Kaitlyn.

"What?"

Flushing a little, Sam leaned toward me and lowered her voice. "I don't know about her. She comes off all friendly, but something's just not right."

Frowning, I asked, "What do you mean?"

Before Sam could reply, Kaitlyn jumped in. "Don't listen to her. Sam thinks something's off with her because of who she's dating. I'm pretty sure she herself has never done anything in particular."

"You just wait," Sam said under her breath. "Bad taste is bad taste, all the way 'round."

I picked up my sandwich. "She seems nice enough. Who's she dating?"

Sam glanced around conspiratorially, her wavy blonde hair swinging down around her face as she leaned in again. "Voldemort."

I laughed. "*What*? What are you talking about?" But then, like a punch to the gut, I remembered. Years ago, not long after I'd started at BWK and had begun regularly having lunch with Sam and Kaitlyn, Sam had compared Declan to Voldemort. It had been the code word she used for him with Kaitlyn, but she hadn't said it around me very much and I'd forgotten. "Oh! Right. Are you serious?"

"As a heart attack. No clue what she sees in him. Maybe she has a thing for assholes."

Kaitlyn and Sam both snorted. I looked over to the lineup but Nicole must have already gotten her food and left. Maybe she'd gone to eat with him?

Setting my sandwich back down, I tried my best to keep my expression impassive. My appetite had fled. I mostly stayed quiet and listened to them talk about work. At last I gathered up the remains of my lunch and got to my feet.

"Heading back already?" Kaitlyn asked, surprised. "We've still got ten minutes."

"I, uh, I forgot I need to make a phone call. See you guys later." I stuffed my garbage in the trash on the way out the door, praying desperately not to run into Declan, or Nicole for that matter, on my way back to Accounting.

He had a girlfriend. A beautiful, way-too-young-for-him girlfriend. Who also worked here. Who I would have to interact with sometimes. *Oh God.* She was stopping by to drop off a form to me this afternoon. I could feel my heart racing. Why hadn't Josh warned me? He must have known I'd find out.

When I got to my office, I closed the door—and boy was I thankful I now had a door to close—and sat down at my desk. I reached for my coffee cup, but realized there was nothing but cold dregs in the bottom. I needed a coffee. Actually, I needed something stiffer. I hadn't touched a drop of alcohol in years, but right now I really wanted a glass of wine. Or vodka and juice. Or even straight vodka would do. Unfortunately none of those was an option.

Leaning back in my chair, I stared up at the ceiling with a deep sigh. This was ridiculous. I didn't need a drink. I didn't need anything. So what if he was dating Nicole? What did it matter? It's not like I wanted to be with him anymore. He had every right to date anyone he liked.

My jerk of a brain suddenly flashed up an image of the two of them together. Naked. A surge of revulsion rose in my throat. I leaned forward onto my elbows and covered my eyes as I shoved that thought away. I didn't care. It didn't matter. It was none of my business who he slept with. It hadn't been for a very long time. Maybe it never was.

I needed to be an adult about this. Declan was a part of my past. Though I knew I'd be forced to interact with him once in a while now, he wasn't going to be part of my present. I was strong; I could do this. And quitting was not an option. I had Liam's best interests to think about. They were much more important than any discomfort of my own.

At the thought of cuddling with Liam later, I felt my tension ease. I could put up with having to see the two of them here, because I had my sweet boy to go home to every night.

I got up to refill my mug from the coffee station back by the file room. When I returned to my desk, I found a form on my blotter with a yellow Post-It note stuck on top. *Please return this to me ASAP.* She'd added a smiley face underneath and a neat letter *N*.

I rolled my eyes at the smiley face, but was pleased I'd lucked out and missed her. I quickly filled out the form and once I was done, instead of walking it over to Human Resources, I put it in an envelope addressed simply to Nicole in HR. I couldn't remember her last name, but I figured there was probably only one Nicole in that department.

As I popped the envelope into the interoffice mail, it suddenly hit me. I'd filled out health and dental benefit forms this morning. Benefit forms that included Liam's information so he would have coverage. That meant Josh wasn't going to be the only one around here who would know I had a son. Nicole would, too. And I couldn't very well tell her he was a secret.

Anxiety squeezed my chest. What if she said something to Declan? Of all the women he could've chosen, why did he have to be sleeping with BWK's Human Resources person? I went back to my office, fingers trembling as I shut my door. *Oh God, what had I just done?* Nicole wouldn't say anything, would she? I mean, why would she? There'd be no reason to. It's not like Declan or anyone else would just happen to ask her if I had any kids. And as far as I understood, all the information I'd provided was strictly confidential. So she couldn't spill my secret even if for some weird reason it did come up.

I took a sip of coffee and tried to relax. This wasn't ideal, but it also wasn't the end of the world.

Hopefully.

No. It wasn't. More than likely she wouldn't even really notice. She entered information like that about employees all the time. She didn't know me. I was just another name.

There was nothing I could do about it now, so I tried to forget about it. It would be fine. Just like Declan having a girlfriend was fine.

Everything was fine.

By the time five o'clock rolled around, I had gone over at least half of the case files for BWK's largest and most lucrative clients, which was where my focus would be. A headache had formed behind my eyeballs and I was anxious to head home. I'd be seeing columns of numbers in my sleep tonight.

Much to my relief, there'd been no sign of Declan today. I assumed he'd probably been out visiting clients. If things went my way, maybe I'd be lucky enough to avoid him all week. Maybe even the week after that. I knew seeing him would be inevitable eventually, but the longer I could put it off, the better.

My luck held. I didn't end up seeing him my entire first week. There was little chance he didn't know I was back at BWK, so I could only conclude he was deliberately giving me space. Which I appreciated.

On Saturday, I took Liam to visit Dee and Terri. It was our first time returning since our move. During the drive, he kept telling me we were "visiting home." I reminded him that Gramma's place was our home now, and in a few months we'd have another new home that would be all our own, but I'm not sure he understood.

Once we arrived, the four of us took a walk to Liam's favorite park where he was happy to find his buddy Quentin. The boys gleefully scampered around the playground equipment pretending the ground below was molten lava and trying their best to avoid it. I let him play for about an hour before I had to insist to my poor, protesting little boy that we needed to go back to the house and start dinner.

After eating, Dee, Terri, and I stayed at the kitchen table chatting while Liam played Candy Crush on Aunt Terri's phone out on the sofa. Boops, zings, and plops like falling water droplets came from the living room. From Liam's groans of frustration, I assumed the game wasn't as easy as he'd expected.

Dee glanced over at him before turning her attention to me. "So have you run into him yet?" she asked in a low voice.

I shook my head. "Not yet. But I'm sure it'll happen at some point."

"And?"

"What?"

Her voice went even softer. "Will you say anything?"

Snorting, I replied, "About what? Our history is history. All I'm willing to talk to him about at this point is work stuff."

Terri looked worried. "What if he finds out about...?" She bobbed her chin toward Liam.

"He won't. No one at work knows except Josh. And he won't tell." I didn't mention the HR situation. I was sure all of my information was private.

Before they could say more, I realized the game noises had stopped. "Liam, honey? Whatcha doing?" I asked as I got to my feet.

His big blue eyes lifted from the phone screen to mine. "Nothin'. Lookin' at pictures."

I went into the living room and sat down beside him. "Pictures of what?"

"Us. Look." Liam tilted the phone my way. On the screen was a shot of Dee, Terri, Liam, and I that a friend of Terri's had snapped for us out in the backyard this past spring. We all looked happy. Well, I looked a little goofy, but still happy. We'd had a few friends over for a barbeque and the weather had been fabulous.

"That's a wonderful photo." I held it up to show the others. "Hey Terri, d'you mind if I steal a copy?"

"Be my guest," Terri said.

"Thanks." I opened a text message to myself, attached the picture, and hit Send.

"Hey, you know what you should do?" Dee piped up. "Print it out and frame it and keep it in your office. So whenever you're feeling frustrated or having a crappy day, you can just pull it out and remember the people who love ya."

At first I thought having a photo of Liam at work was a terrible idea. Then I thought about it more. Though he looked nothing like Dee, if anyone spotted the picture, they would probably assume he was Terri's child if I didn't correct them. "That's a great idea," I told her.

"How 'bout we play a game?" Dee said to Liam. She pulled Trouble out and set it up on the coffee table. My son really loved board games, even if he couldn't always remember all the rules. Dee handily kicked our butts, and by the time we finished, Liam was yawning.

"C'mon, little man. I think it's about time to head home."

He turned to me, eyes suddenly wide. "No! This *is* home!"

"Hey, hey. We've talked about this. You know we don't live here anymore."

His lower lip jutted out. "Yes we do! I wanna stay. Can we sleep here tonight?"

From the corner of my eye, I saw Dee and Terri exchange glances.

"No, honey. I know moving was tough. It was for me, too. I'm sorry, but we have to go back to Gramma's now. You love your new room at Gramma's right? I promise we'll come visit Auntie Dee and Auntie Terri again soon." I rubbed his shoulder but he flinched away from my hand.

"Don't wanna go." His face had turned red and he fisted his eyes and began to rub, a sure sign a meltdown was imminent.

Dee knew the signs as well as I did. She came and knelt beside him. "Liam, sweetie, it's okay. We'll see you again before you know it."

He lowered his hands and looked at her over the tops of his knuckles. "C-can I stay? Pleeeease?" The first tears began rolling down his rosy cheeks.

She glanced at me before turning back to Liam and reaching for his hand. "Another time, buddy. You have to go back to your Gramma's tonight. But maybe next time you come we can have a sleepover. With movies and popcorn and everything."

Liam's face brightened. "Can we do it now? I wanna watch a movie now!"

Sighing, I shook my head. "Not tonight. We'll have to plan that for next time. I know it's never fun to say goodbye, but we'll see them soon." Again, I tried to put my arm around him, but he was having none of it. He jerked away from me, looking at me with such anger that I had to stop myself from recoiling in surprise. With all the emotional control of a stressed-out four year-old, he threw himself onto the carpet and started to writhe and scream. Tears flew from his eyes. Snot ran down his face. He yelled and cried and refused to be consoled for more than five minutes, no matter what I tried to do or say.

Liam didn't have temper tantrums very often, but when he did, they tended to be doozies. This one was no different. And this time it was my fault. I'd been putting my poor son through so much lately: moving to a new town, starting school with a bunch of strangers, living with Gramma instead of his favorite aunties. It was all too much too soon and his frustrations could no longer be contained.

It broke my heart.

I sat on the floor beside him and rubbed his back until eventually he wore himself out. At last he allowed me to gather up his sweaty, whimpering little body and hold him to me. I pushed his damp hair off his forehead and kissed him. It was clear he would be asleep within minutes of being buckled into his car seat.

"Sorry about that," I whispered to Dee and Terri.

"Nothing to be sorry for," Terri said. "He's little. Change is extra tough on him."

Dee came over and put her arms around us both. "I get where he's coming from. I'm sad to say goodbye to you guys, too."

"Love you lots," I said, my eyes darting between Dee and Terri.

"We love you, too." Dee planted a kiss on my cheek and on the top of Liam's head, and Terri patted my shoulder as I got up headed for the door with my son in my arms. I missed living here, maybe even more than Liam did, but I didn't want to admit that out loud in front of him. He needed to know I was all in with this choice. It would help him come to grips with it faster.

During the drive home, I kept the music low. Soft snores provided accompaniment from the backseat. A smile curved my lips as I remember all the nights I'd fallen asleep to the sound of those gentle snores when he'd felt lonely in his room and crept into my bed.

Liam's little outburst at Dee and Terri's had worn him right out. It was tough at his age to handle intense emotions. They overwhelmed him sometimes. And, like it or not, my son had a temper. I knew how to handle it, but every time it came out in full force like that it reminded me how much he was like his father.

Declan

Knowing Amelia was here in the same building as me was driving me fucking crazy. I tried to focus on my clients, but I couldn't shake the constant urge to go find her and talk to her, to apologize and try to initiate the presumably long and difficult process of repairing our fractured friendship. So far, I'd managed to resist. It was better to stay away. After how things had gone down years ago, and how she'd cut out all connections to me, I figured being forced to see or speak to me was the last thing she'd want. And I couldn't blame her. She deserved to be able to settle back in without having to deal with me.

On Tuesday, Colleen forwarded me an email with some pricing for Merrill and Hogan. They still hadn't signed the contract, asking for cost tweaks on every damn little thing each time I was sure they were ready to commit. Josh had been handling the cost/benefit breakdowns for me, but when I opened the message, I immediately spotted a different name at the top: Amelia York.

I read though the numbers she'd provided a few times, but something wasn't quite right. It seemed to me she'd missed a factor that could potentially lower the price a bit more, so I hit the Reply button and typed a message asking her to relook at one thing to see if it made a difference. I didn't add any friendly comments or personal questions, just kept it simple, professional, and to the point. I figured she'd prefer it that way.

As I hit Send, it crossed my mind that this was the first time we'd been in contact since that day in the park when she'd told me...what she'd told me. Just sending that email was opening a communication back up between us, for better or for worse. Hopefully for better.

I'm not sure what I expected, but what I did not was for Amelia to send her reply to Colleen instead of to me. Her choice to not deal with me directly surprised me, and if I'm being honest, hurt a little. Our working relationship had once been so great, but now it felt like we were back to being strangers.

The figures looked better this time, so I decided to just forget about it. She had good reason to not want to talk to me. But now that she was back, at some point we'd have to interact whether she wanted to or not.

I had client meetings the following two days, but on Friday afternoon I was in the office going over a contract. Two quick knocks interrupted my concentration, and I looked up to see Nicole.

"Got a sec?" she asked with a smile.

"C'mon in."

She took a seat in one of my guest chairs. The same one Amelia used to always sit in. I shoved that thought away and looked back down at the page I'd been triple-checking to make sure nothing had been missed.

"I've been totally slammed this week. And I've got plans tonight, so I'll have to come into the office for a few hours tomorrow. Do you want me to come by after?"

"Sure," I said. I raised my eyes back to hers and flashed her a grin. "Want me to make you dinner?"

"It might have to be a late one. I'll have to let you know." She sighed, pushing a chunk of hair behind her ear.

I studied her face. She didn't look happy, and I didn't think it was because she was swamped with work. "What's wrong?"

Nicole shrugged. "Nothing, really. I just wish we could go out dancing. Or go see a play. Or a band. Or something. Lately we just seem to spend all our time at your place."

Smirking, I bounced my eyebrows at her. "Oh, I don't know. You always seem to enjoy yourself."

Her cheeks went pink as her eyes shot to mine. "I do," she said. She was cute when I managed to embarrass her. "But you know what I mean."

"Do you wanna go out tomorrow night? Because we can do that, if there's something you have in mind."

"How about we make a date for next Saturday? I might not get over until later tomorrow, so there's probably no point in going out. But I think Darren O'Connor is playing at The Hitching Post next weekend. I'll check into it."

I had no idea who Darren O'Connor was, but I nodded my agreement. "Sounds good."

"Great. I gotta bounce." She got to her feet, shaking her head. "Three new hires, a massive stack of performance reviews, and two Christmas parties to plan when it's still sweltering and the holidays are the furthest thing from anyone's mind. I just keep repeating: I love my job, I love my job, I love my job."

"How's that working out for ya?" I chuckled.

Nicole snorted. "Ask me tomorrow." She waggled her fingers at me as she left.

I'd just returned to my desk after a quick workout downstairs in our 'corporate gym.' It wasn't much: just a treadmill, an elliptical and a stationary bike, with a pile of free weights in one corner. There were no windows, although one wall had floor to ceiling mirrors at least, making the small space feel larger. A few years back, the partners had acknowledged the need for staff health initiatives, thrown some money at the idea of a gym, and promptly forgotten all about it. I knew Nicole used it sometimes, and I went down when I could squeeze in a few spare minutes, but mostly the room stayed empty.

The clock above my desk said it was almost five. Time to go pick up Alexis. I quickly checked my emails, then packed up my laptop and headed for the parking lot.

As I came around the corner by the back door, I suddenly found myself face to face with the very person who, though I was trying to give her space, never strayed far from my mind. We both stopped in our tracks. Amelia's eyes shot wide. I think mine did, too.

"Hey," I said, grinning. And it was no forced grin; my lips couldn't help betraying how happy I was to see her face after so long. She wore a white short-sleeved top and dark skirt, both of which showed off her tan. Her hair hung straight around her face, still dark as the last time I saw her. She looked wary, which was understandable. She also looked fucking gorgeous.

"Hey," she muttered, flashing the barest hint of a half-smile before moving past me to the door. Maybe I should have just let her go. It was clearly what she wanted.

But I couldn't. "Wait."

She turned back to me, her brow now furrowed. She looked at me expectantly. Impatiently.

"I don't mean to delay you if you're in a rush," I started, unsure what to say but needing to say something. "I just…how are you?"

Amelia frowned. "I am, actually. In a rush. I'm fine." Though her hand remained on the door handle, for a second her eyes softened. "You?"

"I'm okay. I was glad to hear you were coming back." What an inane thing to say. But it was the truth.

"Oh yeah?"

"And pretty surprised. I thought this would be the last place you'd ever want to work again."

With a small shrug, she said, "It was a bit of a surprise to me, too. But here I am." She edged a few inches closer to the door.

I cringed inside. This was even more awkward than I'd expected. She couldn't wait to get away from me. But I just couldn't let her walk away yet. "Look, Mel?"

She flinched at the sound of the pet name, and I instantly regretted the slip. *Dammit. Think, Kavanaugh!* But my ability to formulate proper sentences seemed to have vanished.

Instead of replying, she just stared at me.

"I'm sorry." Massive understatement. But there it was: the first of many apologies I was sure. "I know you have to go. I just wanted to say welcome back." *Lame, lame, lame.* There were so many things I needed to say to her, but welcome back was not one of them.

"Uh, thanks." Her rich brown eyes were guarded again. She didn't trust me. And why would she? If I were her, I wouldn't trust me either. She turned away then and walked out the door. Instead of following behind her to my own car, I waited for a few minutes to give her time to leave without having to see me again.

Shit. Fixing this was going to be a hell of lot harder than I'd hoped. If it was even fixable.

But I wouldn't be able to live with myself if I didn't at least try.

Chapter 20

Amelia

Saturday morning I awoke to a bright patch of sun across my bed, putting me instantly in a good mood. I was thankful it was the weekend, because it'd been kind of a strange week. Well, most of it had been okay. For the first time since my return, I'd had to do a pricing request for one of Declan's potential new clients. And to no particular surprise, he'd responded asking for me to relook at my numbers. Which shouldn't have annoyed me, yet it did. There was no *hey, long time no see*, no *how've you been all these years,* no nothing. Just cold and practical. Just that typical demanding expectation. As if we didn't even know each other. I had no interest in getting into a long back and forth with him over a minor pricing issue, which had sometimes happened in the past, so I'd just sent the revised figures to Colleen. I knew I had no real reason to be irritated by it, but the fact that he could still get under my skin with little effort only increased my annoyance. To my relief, he hadn't messaged me again.

The rest of the week had gone pretty smoothly and I'd thought I'd managed to pass another entire week without running into him face to face. But on my way to the parking lot on Friday afternoon, my luck had run out. I'd nearly bumped right into him in the back hallway.

As was to be expected, Declan looked older: deeper lines, more silver at his temples. But he still looked good. Too good. Better than any forty-one year-old guy should, honestly. Why couldn't his looks fade with age like the rest of us? It really wasn't fair. Just seeing him again had caused a rush of warmth to spread over me. And I kind of hated myself for it.

But all that aside, our run-in had been just what I'd been dreading. Awkward. Weird. Weirdly awkward. We seemed to have no idea what to say to each other now. Seeing him and not being able to be who we used to be to each other hurt. Probably more than I was willing to admit even to myself. So I'd made an excuse and gotten away from him as fast as I could.

It was sad that we could no longer even have a casual conversation, that we'd turned into such utter strangers. I knew I needed to get over it, though. Declan was no longer my concern, and the less I had to do with him now, the better.

I found Liam already up, working on a puzzle on the big dining room table and chatting happily about school with my mother as she made breakfast. After we ate, I was wiping down the kitchen counter when I heard him calling me from the next room.

"Mommy? Come see what I found!"

I tossed the cloth in the sink and came around the corner. He was sitting on the floor in the corner of the living room beside the bookcase. A bunch of compact discs were spread out in front of him. Gramma had gone upstairs to have a shower, and left to his own devices he'd started exploring the shelves. When he saw me, he held up a CD. "What's this?"

"Those are Grandpa's CDs. They have music on them." The one in his hand was David Bowie's *Hunky Dory*, one of my favorite albums since I'd been nearly as young as Liam.

"What kind of music? Can we play it?"

"Sure. I think you'll like this one. Grandpa always loved it." I took the CD from him, opened the case and popped out the disc, sliding it into Gramma's seldom used stereo up on the top shelf.

As the first notes of *Changes* came from the speakers, Liam began to smile. I couldn't resist singing along and soon we were dancing around the living room couch as I sang and Liam laughed. I still remembered every word.

We were still dancing when my mom came back down and she sat and enjoyed the rest of the album with us. It had been a long time since I'd listened to David Bowie. After my dad passed away, I'd always turned off the radio when old Bowie songs came on. They had been just another painful reminder of him, and I hadn't needed any more reasons to feel sad. But now, as I sang and danced with my son, I was happy to share a part of his grandfather—and his mother—with him. It felt like Dad was in the room with us, too, watching and smiling right beside my mom.

I helped my mother run a bunch of errands in the afternoon, and once we got home, neither of us felt much like cooking. Instead I called Pizza Palace and Liam and I went to pick up our order. We got there a bit early so I handed my phone to him to play a game on while we waited. I was staring out the big front window at the street when I noticed a familiar red truck pull up. My eyes shot wide as an even more familiar tall man with cropped blonde hair climbed out of it and headed our way.

Scott broke into a smile as soon he spotted me. "Amelia! Holy cow. Long time no see!" He came straight over and for a second it seemed like he was about to hug me. But, apparently thinking better of it, his arms fell back to his sides.

Jesus. First Declan, and now Scott. Someone's punishing me for something. But at least this time I didn't have to fake being polite. I was glad to see him. "Hey Scott, I know, way too long. I'm just picking up dinner to take back to Mom's."

He nodded. "Yeah. Me, too. I mean, not to take back to your mom's. Just…y'know."

"Yeah." The guy working was busy making someone else's pizza, so I knew it would still be another few minutes. "Doesn't look like our orders are ready yet, so I guess you're stuck waiting with me." I hoped he didn't mind. I could think of a few reasons why he might not be too thrilled to have to make small talk with his ex-wife.

Scott laughed, and I was relieved to hear the familiar sound. Though it had been years ago, I knew I'd hurt him pretty bad. I wouldn't have blamed him if he still wanted nothing to do with me. But it seemed I had nothing to worry about. From the look on his face, he was happy to have ran into me.

His attention turned to Liam and he looked down at him with a smile. "Who's this little guy?"

Before I could answer, Liam looked up, jutted out his chin, and declared, "I'm Liam."

"Why hello, Liam." Scott stuck out a hand and shook my son's smaller one. "Pleased to meet you." His eyes shot to mine and I could see the question written in them.

"Uh, yeah. So this is kinda awkward, telling you this at Pizza Palace, but…this is my son." I set my hand on Liam's shoulder. Liam was no longer listening, his attention focused back on the small screen.

Scott's bright smile faltered, his brows flying nearly to his hairline. "Whoa. You have a son? Holy crap, Ames! How…why…why don't we know this?" He stopped, words failing him.

"I know. I know, and I'm sorry about not telling you, but—"

"It's been, like, forever, since we've heard *anything* about you. We knew you were living in Richmond, but that's about it." I couldn't help noting all those 'we's' instead of 'I's.' I had to keep reminding myself he and Liv were partners. God, they'd already been married nearly as long as Scott and I had been. I'd been in hiding for so long that big chunks of other people's lives had entirely passed me by. Scott glanced at Liam again. "So how old is he?"

"He's four." I stepped a few feet away from Liam. He was so engrossed in the game I doubted he was listening, but I still wanted to put some space between him and this conversation.

"Why didn't you or Dee tell Liv? Why did you keep him a secret?"

I sighed. "It's complicated. I don't expect you to understand right now, but I hope you can trust me when I say I had very good reasons. And someday I'll explain them to you guys." I darted my eyes toward Liam and lowered my voice. "But not now."

Following my lead, Scott also spoke softer. "Fine. Okay. Am I allowed to ask you this? Who's the father? I know it's none of my business anymore, but I just…is it anyone I know?"

I got why he was asking, but I had no intention of telling him. In fact, I hoped he'd never find out the truth. "No." I shook my head. "And it doesn't matter. We're not together. Haven't been since conception. Even then, not really."

Scott frowned. "Does he know you got pregnant?"

I nodded.

Exhaling a derisive snort, he shook his head in disbelief. "And he bailed on you? What a dick."

"It wasn't like that." Well, it had sort of been like that, but not in the way Scott assumed. "This was my choice, not his."

"Still. That must've sucked." My ex looked at me with sympathy.

"You mean being a single mom?"

He nodded.

The last thing I wanted was his pity. I'd made a tough decision, but it had been the right one. So I tried to brush it off. "Sometimes. But mostly not. I had Dee and Terri. And Mom. It's honestly better this way. And before you ask, yes, I thought it all through. It was not a rash decision, no matter what my mom may've thought."

Scott chuckled. "I bet she was just *thrilled*. How's she now? Better, I hope?"

"Yeah, she's good. We're actually staying with her for a bit until I can find an apartment or whatever for us. I'm back working in Lynchburg again."

"Cool. Cool. I assume Dee told you we also have a son?"

I smiled. "Of course. Sorry for making this all about me. What's his name again?"

"Marco." He grinned. It was a shy little grin, but I knew exactly what it meant. That grin said what I'd always assumed, that Scott was just over the moon to be a dad.

In that moment, I was happier for him than I think I'd ever been. I threw caution to the wind and flung my arms around his neck. "I'm so, *so* happy for you. Really I am."

Giving me a quick squeeze, he stepped back. "Thanks." He was still smiling.

I was smiling right back. My Scotty was finally happy in all the ways he deserved to be, all the ways I'd never been able to make him happy. And I knew he wasn't *my* Scotty anymore, but after spending so many years together, a part of us would always belong to each other. "Wow. I can't believe you're a dad now."

Bobbing his chin toward Liam, who was still tapping away at my phone, he said, "And you're a mom. Who would've thought this is how we'd end up, both of us parents, but..."

"But separately? I know. Our lives took some unexpected turns, that's for sure. But it seems to have all worked out for the best." I looked up at him, my face now serious. "*God*. Is this too weird? It is, isn't it? It's weird."

Laughing, he replied, "It's a bit weird, yeah. But I guess that's to be expected."

I shrugged. "Maybe someday it won't be."

"Hopefully." Scott examined his fingernails. I could tell he wasn't sure that was possible. And for that, I couldn't blame him one bit.

Just then, the pizza guy slapped the bell on the counter and called out: "Extra-large for York?"

"That'd be me." I went up and paid for our pizza. As I turned back to Scott, I said, "It was great running into you. I'm glad you got to meet Liam."

"Me, too. Catch ya later, kiddo," he said to my son.

Liam looked up for a second and said, "Bye." As I saw those big blue eyes, I thought of something else.

"Hey Scott?"

"Yeah?"

"Could you please not tell anyone about...you know? I'd rather the, uh, guy I mentioned before not find out."

Another deep frown marred my ex's forehead. "Why not? Is there a problem? Because if there is, the local sheriff's a buddy of mine."

"No. No problem. No restraining order or anything like that. I just don't want info to get back to him, and I don't know who all he knows."

Scott sighed softly. I knew by asking him to keep this a secret it had made him far more concerned about my well-being than I wanted him to be. It was a nice feeling to know he still cared, but I would have honestly preferred he forget he ever ran into us tonight. No chance of that, though. "Okay. If that's what you want."

"Thanks. I mean it. Have a great night." I was well aware that next time I ran into him or Liv I'd have a lot more explaining to do.

On my way home I found myself wondering if I'd be able to mend my damaged friendships with Scott and Liv. I missed them, especially Liv. She hadn't deserved to be cut off, not the first time, and definitely not the second. She probably never wanted to speak to me again. If she'd done to me what I'd done to her, would I be able to forgive her? Maybe. If she explained why. But maybe not. Maybe I'd be too hurt to ever trust her again. And if after hearing my reasons she still wanted nothing to do with me, would I even be able to blame her?

No, I realized. I'd understand all too well.

Declan

Since our run-in last week, it had become next to impossible to keep my mind off thoughts of Amelia. As I drove Alexis to Laura's parents' place on Saturday, I found myself scanning the people out my window, hoping to spot her. I had no clue where she was living now, but I knew her mom lived somewhere in Swann's Landing. At least she used to. After so long, what the hell did I really know anymore? Not much.

On the way home, I stopped at the Food Lion just outside the city to pick up some stuff for dinner. As I pulled into the parking lot, I blew out a sigh, my fingers squeezing the wheel. What was I thinking? I usually avoided this store. Most of the time I shopped at the Wholefoods near the office, but it wasn't just inconvenience that kept me away. There were too many memories. Amelia and I had used this parking lot as a meetup and make out spot for months, back when things had been good. For years I'd gotten good at suppressing that stuff, but over the past few weeks, it'd all come flooding back, each and every wonderful and agonizing flashback. Maybe some part of me had turned into this Food Lion on purpose? Maybe I was a sucker for punishment?

Probably the second one.

Nicole didn't show up until nearly seven, and the moment she arrived she opened her laptop on the breakfast bar and pulled out a stack of files. "Sorry about this," she said with an apologetic shrug, "but I still have to finish up some stuff for the Children's Christmas Party. I figured I could just do it here."

BWK hosted a special holiday party every year for the kids of staff. I'd been taking Alexis to it since her very first Christmas. They always hired a Santa to give a gift to each child, one the parent had chosen from a catalogue months before.

"No prob. I'll heat up dinner while you work." I'd prepared and pre-cooked a lasagna a couple hours ago, so it was just a matter of reheating it and getting the cheese all gooey again. I heard a sigh behind me as I shut the oven door. "What's up?" I asked as I set the timer.

"Nothing, really. It's just that there's four people who still haven't said if their kids will be coming and I need to submit the gift order on Monday. I'll have to e-mail them again and remind them. And it's Saturday, so they probably won't even read it until Monday, let alone reply."

I turned back to her. "People suck. But that's their problem. If they miss it, they miss it."

"Yeah," she said, but she shook her head. "But then their kids miss out, and I don't wanna have to deal with pissed off parents."

I had a sudden thought. "The catalogue's online, right?"

"Of course."

"Well, who hasn't replied? If I know them, I'll text them right now and tell them you need to know ASAP or their kiddos won't get a gift."

She smiled at me over the top of her laptop. "Thanks for the offer, but you know I can't share that with you. I'll just have to hope they check their work email over the weekend."

I took down a couple of glasses from the cupboard and opened the bottle of wine I'd already selected, pouring one half full and setting it in front of her. "Sounds like you could use this."

With a grateful smile, Nicole took a sip. "Thanks, D." She got up and came around the counter, standing on her toes to kiss me. "You're the best."

"Yes I am," I smirked, grabbing her ass with both hands. "And just so you don't forget, I'll prove it to you later."

She laughed as she extricated herself from my grip. "I'm sure you will. Back in a minute." She headed down the hall to the washroom.

Grabbing two placements, I laid them on the counter beside her laptop. As I went around the end to set out knives and forks, I happened to glance down at the stack of papers she'd brought. The top one was a list of names. Four of them were highlighted in pink, presumably the staff who still hadn't replied about the Christmas party. They were:

Anna Duchesne
Michael Handler
Gisella Mendoza
Amelia York

With a frown, I leaned closer to see if I'd misread. Amelia shouldn't have been on this list. She didn't have children. There must've been a mistake.

But her name was right there in bright pink near the bottom. There was a number one to the right of it. I scanned up to find my own. It also had a one beside it. Brittany Kemperman from the Art Department's name was below mine. There was a two next to it. And I knew Brit had two kids.

"Hey! No snooping!" Nicole scolded with a laugh as she came back in.

I jerked back as if I'd just been caught looking at porn. I probably looked guilty as hell. Quickly I tried to mask it. "There's an error on your list. But it's a good one. You actually only have three people you still need replies from."

She came around the counter to see what I was looking at. "What d'you mean?"

I pointed at Amelia's name. "Amelia York. She doesn't have any kids."

"You're not supposed to be reading that stuff." Nicole moved the stack of papers back inside the folder.

"I wasn't snooping. I was setting our places for dinner and those highlighted names just jumped out at me. Neon pink is not exactly subtle. Thought you'd wanna know one was wrong."

One of Nicole's eyebrows arched as she studied me. "Have you talked to her since she came back?"

"A little," I said. "I bumped into her the other day and said hello. That's about it."

"Well, things can change in people's lives, you know. She may not have years ago, but she definitely has a kid now. A son, I think, if I'm remembering correctly. Maybe you should say more than just hi next time you see her?"

My eyes flared. I even felt my jaw drop and hurriedly covered my mouth so Nicole wouldn't notice. The last conversation I'd had with Amelia before she'd vanished popped into my mind. I'd been a total mess that day, the day she'd told me she was pregnant, but I clearly recalled how angry she'd been. She'd wanted nothing more to do with me. And I'd thought she was planning to get rid of it. I'd been sure she didn't want it. Could she have changed her mind somehow? Or could I have been wrong?

No. No way in hell that pregnancy was this child. Though I'd been under the impression she had no interest in being a mom, she must have met someone else and had a baby over the intervening years. That was the only explanation that made any sense. Maybe she'd even remarried. My gut clenched at the thought. I had no idea what had gone down in her life, but I hoped she was happy now. She certainly hadn't been able to find happiness with me.

Not gonna lie; I seriously considered asking Nicole to leave again so I could muddle through my thoughts alone. But that wouldn't have gone over very well and I decided not to push my luck so soon after last time. Instead, I tried to put it out of my head and enjoy my evening with my hot girlfriend. And I did try, I really did, but no matter how I attempted to distract myself, I couldn't quite succeed. I couldn't let it go. Later that night after Nic was asleep, I went downstairs and checked Facebook. Still no sign of Amelia, although she'd probably blocked me a long time ago. I didn't use social media much, but I even downloaded Instagram and Twitter onto my phone and searched. Nada. Google only brought up an article from the Swann's Landing local paper about some fundraiser she'd worked on years ago. No accompanying photo, unfortunately.

I opened a text to ask Josh what he knew. I had most of the message typed before I deleted it and set my phone down. Even if he did know about her kid, chances were good he wouldn't tell me anything. Because it was none of my damn business.

Probably.

But I had to find out for sure.

I couldn't sleep for shit. When I did doze off, fucked up dreams woke me right back up again, my body rigid and sweaty, my heart racing. All I could recall of them was that I was desperately searching for something—or someone—that for the life of me I could not find. But whatever it was, I needed it. Needed it like my life depended on it.

I woke late, bleary and dragging my ass. If my head had been pounding, I'd swear I had a hangover, but the single glass of wine I'd had last night sure as hell hadn't done it. Though my body begged for rest, going back to sleep was not an option. I needed some answers and I needed them now. It was time to make like Sherlock and do a little sleuthing.

Jumping into the shower, I turned the water cold to try to wake the hell up. Not pleasant, but it seemed to do the trick. Over breakfast I told Nicole my in-laws needed me to pick Alexis up early, so she kissed me goodbye and took off shortly after. It was a lie, but not a major one. Guilt didn't even occur to me. I had shit to do.

Once she was gone, I got in my car and headed to work. I went in the rear door, walking straight past my own office and through two cubicle farms until I got to Accounting. I stopped in front of the office next to Josh's. A small plaque on the door, still shiny and new, read *Amelia York,* and I couldn't help smiling. She finally had her own office, with a door she could shut if she wanted some peace and quiet. Knowing Amelia, I figured she was probably pretty happy about that particular upgrade. Much around here had improved since her previous tour of duty, but even more remained exactly the same.

Though I knew no one else was around, I still darted a guilty glance around me before stepping inside her darkened office. Pulling the door closed, I switched on the overhead light.

A low bookshelf sat along one wall. A few thick manuals were piled on the lower shelf, but otherwise it was empty. On top, there was only a potted plant and a stack of case files. Nothing of interest there. I went around her desk and examined the windowsill. Also empty. Turning back, I scanned the small room again. A framed picture of mountains hung on one wall. It looked pretty generic and I assumed it had already been there when she moved in.

Beyond the nameplate on the door, nothing about this office said it was Amelia's. Not even a cardigan hanging over the back of the chair, and I knew the A/C always made her cold. I was just about to give up and leave when I spotted a small picture frame tucked into the shadow of her monitor. Frowning, I reached for it.

The black and white photo showed Amelia with two women and a small boy. The child stood between her and a taller, light-haired woman. He wore a baseball cap, but bits of dark hair stuck out from beneath the edges. Was this her son? Or did he belong to one of the others? Both Amelia and the woman on his other side had their arms around him. I lifted the picture closer, examining the boy's face. Everyone in the photo was smiling. Was his smile like Amelia's? Maybe? A little? It was hard to tell. Something about the shape of his face did seem familiar, but I couldn't pinpoint why. But how old was he? My best guess was maybe about three, but I had no clue when the shot had been taken.

I took a picture of it with my phone and, with a sigh, set the frame back where I'd found it. If anything, my gnawing suspicions had deepened. I couldn't be sure, but it was definitely possible.

Opening the Internet app, I searched for *York* in Swann's Landing. If Josh could find out where her mom lived, so could I. This time I lucked out: there was only one, on Jefferson Avenue. I found it easily on the map, but that's no great achievement. The town wasn't exactly sprawling. Checking the time, I saw I still had an hour before I had to pick up Lex. It would only take me thirty minutes to get there. Less, if I let the Mustang gallop a little on the highway.

I made it in twenty.

Jefferson Avenue was in an older neighborhood not far from downtown. Dozens of mature oaks lined the streets. They even had old-timey ball streetlamps on each corner. It didn't take me long to find the right house as Amelia's old Honda sat in the driveway. Though tempted, I didn't slow. Her car might've been nondescript, but mine was bright blue and very noticeable. I didn't dare linger lest she peek out a window. I turned at the next street and parked further down so my car couldn't be seen from her mother's place.

Swiveling in my seat, I dug around for an old baseball cap I was sure I'd seen in the back. After a moment of searching, I found it beneath a pile of Alexis' books. I pulled it low over my eyes, got out and walked back to Jefferson, stopping in the shade of one of the big trees just around the corner. I couldn't be easily spotted, but I had a clear view of the front of the house.

I had no real plan. I figured I'd just pretend to fiddle with my phone for fifteen minutes or so and then go pick up my daughter. I didn't even really know what I was looking for, but something told me I was in the right place to find it.

Amelia's childhood home was a two-storey white colonial with dark shutters and trim. A covered veranda ran the entire width of the front. It looked like there was a porch swing at the far end. It was obvious the house used to be impressive, but now it could use a bit of sprucing up, or at least a fresh coat of paint. I knew her dad had passed away years ago. If her mom had lived here alone since, that would explain the minor signs of neglect.

I scrutinized each window. There were no signs of life, but the Honda implied Amelia might be inside. I checked the time again, then took another glance around. Hopefully no nosy neighbors would spot me skulking and call the cops.

Usually Lady Luck thwarted me every damn chance she got, but today I must've gotten into her rare good graces. Just as I was about to call it quits, the front door opened and a woman and small boy came out.

Amelia.

She held his hand as they walked to her car, the top of his head just a bit higher than her waist. He looked about the right age. My fingers dug into the rough bark of the tree as I watched Amelia open the rear door and help him into his car seat. She leaned in to buckle him up and I caught a glimpse of his small face over her shoulder. He had messy dark hair and bright red spots on both cheeks. All too familiar red spots. They meant he was upset, although angry or just over-tired, I didn't know. He began rubbing his eyes and, though I couldn't make out the words, I knew the whiny tone of complaint when I heard it. She smoothed his hair back as she whispered something to him, then kissed him on the forehead.

And I knew.

In that moment, I knew. Though she'd never said a word to me about him, I knew. Though I couldn't even see him all that closely, I knew. I had not one single motherfucking doubt.

That boy was my son.

Chapter 21

Declan

I had all of about five minutes to try to process this giant fucking curveball before I had to get my shit together and go pick up Alexis.

My first reaction was pure, utter joy. I had a son. A beautiful son who was part me and part her—the woman who stopped my breath even now, all these years later, every single time I thought of her. It was a goddamn miracle. Without even having met the boy, I knew I loved him just as fiercely.

But.

But I was also furious. I had a son, yes, and that was incredible, but he didn't even know me. Probably didn't even know I existed. Or worse, thought I wanted nothing to do with him. My hand clenched into a fist against the tree bark, and I had to grip my wrist with my other hand to restrain the urge to punch it. The last thing I needed was a trip to Emerg with broken knuckles. I sucked in a deep breath and forced myself to calm down. It was unlikely Amelia had told him his father didn't want him. She probably hadn't said anything about me at all. The boy was only four, after all. But she had made a choice to not tell me about him, to hide him away from me. Four years gone that I could have had with my son. And with her! Four years that we could have had to fix this colossal mess we'd made and maybe even been happy!

Four. Fucking. Years.

Just gone.

I began walking back to my car before I got another urge to slam my fist into an immobile object. Jesus Christ, *why*, though? Why wouldn't she have told me? But at that thought, a familiar voice piped up in my head: *You know damn well why. Because the both of them are better off far, far away from you. Because you end up destroying those you love.*

It was true. That actually explained it all. She knew I ruined everything I touched. Hell, she'd wanted so badly to keep him from me that she'd even sacrificed some of her closest friends. A deluge of sadness drowned my rage. I couldn't be angry at her. How could I? I got it. This was no one's fault but my own. I'd been a useless mess. She'd been right to assume they were better off without me.

I got into my car, but I didn't turn on the engine. I gripped the steering wheel in both hands as something else struck me.

She'd made a choice based on the man she'd perceived me as back then. But that had been almost five years ago. I was beyond fucked up five years ago. I wouldn't have wanted to raise a child with me either, back then. Though far from un-fucked, I was in a significantly better place now. She just didn't know it yet.

But maybe, if I played my cards right, I could show her.

I didn't say a word to Alexis, or Josh, or anyone else about what I'd discovered. I knew I needed to be extra careful about everything from now on or I'd end up fucking things up even further. It wasn't easy—I was impulsive as hell and had a deep desire to get to work fixing things as soon as possible. But this was far too important to risk screwing up. I had to plan my actions carefully.

On Wednesday I was out for most of the day at meetings. When I got back to the office about four, I saw that Amelia's car was still in the parking lot. Grabbing a client file from my desk, I headed for her office. She had recently quoted me costs for some bus shelter ads, so it would make the perfect cover.

When she glanced up and saw me standing in her doorway she looked irritated. No surprise there; I knew she wouldn't be exactly overjoyed to see me.

"Hey," I said, flashing her my most winning smile. "Got a minute?"

Amelia's lips pressed tight, but she nodded. "Sure."

I came in and took a seat. Opening the file, I made up a bullshit question about the pricing she'd provided, which she easily explained. The whole thing took all of two minutes.

When I didn't immediately get up to leave, she frowned. "Is there something else?"

"Actually, yes. The last time we spoke—well, not the last time, but the last time years ago—I, uh..." I stopped with a sigh. "I was pretty messed up that day. My head was elsewhere. I know I reacted badly to what you told me and I need to apologize for that."

Her brows drew in. "Whatever," she said, shrugging. "Water way under the bridge at this point."

"I know, but I want to explain. I'd just found out that my dad, James, well you remember he had a brain tumor?"

She nodded.

"I'd just gotten back from taking him to an appointment with his specialist when you called. We'd found out his tumor was growing again. Everything all went pretty fast after that. He only had five more months."

Amelia's eyes softened and I caught a glimpse of the woman I'd once been so close to. "I'm so sorry, Declan. I know how much he meant to you."

"Yeah. It sucked. But it doesn't excuse my behavior. You deserved better, and if I'd had time to get my head on straight, you would've gotten a way different reaction."

"Well, like I said, it was a long time ago."

"I would've been happy, you know. If I hadn't been mired so deep in my own shit, I would've been overjoyed. So I'm sorry. Really."

She stared at me for a few long seconds. "Apology accepted," she said at last. For a second her eyes darted to the picture by her monitor and my heart jumped a little, hoping she'd say something. It was stupid of me. Of course she wouldn't. Not yet anyway.

"I know it doesn't change anything, but I needed you to know that." I got to my feet. I didn't want to push my luck further. That was enough for now.

Amelia was still looking at me, but now her expression was unreadable. Deliberately, I suspected. "Thanks for explaining. I appreciate the honesty. And again, my deepest condolences about your dad. I know all too well how hard that must've been."

I tried to smile, but it faltered. "I know you do. Have a good night."

There was something else I had to do, but I wasn't looking forward to this one. I decided to put it off until Friday so there would be a few days buffer before we might run into each other again.

I'd asked Nicole earlier to go for a drink with me after work. We took our own cars and met at a bar downtown called Lazy Eye Louie's. It was a favorite hangout for her and her friends, and at just past five in the afternoon, it was already jumping. One look around told me I was nearly the oldest guy in the joint. When the hell had that happened?

I went up to the bar and came back with a mug of craft beer for myself and a glass of wine for Nicole. Before she'd arrived, I'd secured a table in the back corner so we'd have what I hoped would be a modicum of privacy.

She smiled as I handed her the wine. "Exactly what I needed, thanks."

"Cheers." I clinked my glass against hers. "To the weekend.

"To the weekend." She took a sip. "So are you still up for going clubbing with me tomorrow night?"

It was really too loud in there for the conversation I needed to have, but although I didn't relish hurting her, I dove in anyway. "Yeah, so, I wanted to talk to you about that. I, uh, I don't think it's gonna work out."

She frowned. "Why not? Did something come up with your daughter?"

"No, I..." I stopped with a sigh. "Not just tomorrow night. I've been thinking that maybe this..." I motioned between us. "Has run its course."

Her frown grew deeper. She leaned in closer to me. "I can't hear you super well, but it sounded like you're breaking up with me. Are you seriously dumping me right now?"

"I'm sorry." I tried to put my hand on hers, but she pulled it away, her face rigid. "I just don't think this has any real staying power, and you deserve to be with a man who sees a future with you. Someone closer to your own age."

She glared at me for a few seconds, then lifted her glass and took a long drink. When she set it back down, the muscles in her jaw had relaxed. "You're probably right," she said.

Had I heard her correctly? "I am?"

"Yeah. I mean, it was fun and all but—"

"Hell yeah it was fun." I grinned, unable to help myself.

She shook her head, but she was smiling back at me now. That was a surprising, but very good sign. "I mean, it's not like I was picturing us growing old together or anything. It was great while it lasted, but just being friends is fine, too."

"You're really okay with it?"

"Well, truthfully I was getting kinda sick of staying in every Saturday night anyway. I think it's for the best."

I reached for her hand again and this time she let me hold it. "I know you were. And I'm sorry about this. Really I am."

"No worries, D. We're all good. But you know what? I see my friend Tish over there with her new guy, so I think I'm gonna go say hi. You mind?"

"Go ahead. I'm gonna take off once I finish this." I held up my mug. "So I'll talk to you later, okay?"

She leaned in and kissed me on the cheek. "Have a good weekend." Then she picked up her wine glass and began to work her way through the crowd.

I watched her go with a slight feeling of melancholy, but no real sadness. She was right. This was for the best. It was high time I began building the life for myself and Alexis that we both deserved, and to do that I needed to focus on what was most important. I cared about Nicole and wished her nothing but the best, but it was time to let her go.

I stared at my bedroom ceiling most of Friday night, my brain on overload as it ricocheted between thoughts of my past fuckups and trying to figure out what steps I should take to fix my future. Nothing felt right though. What could I possibly do that would convince Amelia that she should tell me about our son and let me be a part of his—and her—life? How could I show her I was still the man she'd once loved? That I was a good dad? That I'd never hurt her again?

Yeah, right.

She'd never buy any of it. Not now. To even hope she might was completely fucking ludicrous after all our history. But still. Ludicrous or not, I couldn't not try. There *had* to be a way.

I finally dozed off into a fitful few hours' sleep just before dawn, waking only when I heard Alexis come into my room.

"Morning, sweetie." I squinted against the sunlight peaking around the blinds. "Is it time for breakfast?"

"Not yet," she whispered. "Can I get into bed with you for a bit?"

"Of course." I threw back the covers and she snuggled in beside me, something she used to do all the time, but lately had only been coming in for cuddles maybe once a week, most often on Saturday mornings when neither of us had to rush off anywhere. Knowing they wouldn't last forever now that she was getting older, I cherished each and every soft moment together.

I wrapped an arm around her and pulled her against me so her head rested on my chest. A few loose curls tickled my chin.

"Daddy?"

"Yeah?"

"Becky's dad is getting married. She has to be the flower girl."

I knew Becky was one Lex's friends from school. She'd been over once or twice, but I couldn't recall ever meeting her parents. "Oh yeah?"

"She doesn't wanna, though."

"No? Why not?"

"She doesn't like her new step-mom. She said her dad never spends any time with her now."

"That's too bad. Maybe Becky should talk to her dad about that?"

"I guess." Alexis was quiet for a minute or two, but I knew by her breathing she wasn't dozing off, just deep in thought. Then: "Dad?"

"Yes?"

She shifted her head so she was looking up at me. "Would *you* ever get married again?"

I frowned. "I don't know. Maybe someday. If it was right."

"Right how?"

"Right for me, right for whomever I was thinking of marrying, but also right for you. I wouldn't do anything that wasn't right for you. You and me, we're a team. Can't have one without the other." I gave her a smile, squeezing her close as she laughed.

"To invite someone else to join our little team would mean it has to be okay with all of us. Including you. You know that?"

"I know." She nestled her head back against my chest, apparently happy with my answer.

I thought again about Amelia and the boy whose name I didn't even know. How long would it be before Alexis would meet them—assuming she ever would? After all the tragedy we'd gone through, how would my sweet girl react to suddenly having a younger brother? The thought of Amelia and I marrying someday and creating a happy family together was always in the back of my mind, but right now I couldn't let myself fantasize about something that might never happen. I had more immediate concerns to focus on.

Even if I did somehow manage to convince Amelia to let me get to know our son, I didn't want Alexis to meet him and potentially get attached to him while there was still a chance that his mother might take him away again. And yes, I realized this train of thought was similar to how Laura had felt back when I'd told her about meeting my birth father and that he was dying. She hadn't wanted Alexis to get attached just to lose him. She'd wanted to protect our daughter from that pain. But it had happened anyway, and I didn't regret it for a second. Lex and Grandpa James had completely adored each other and now she would always remember him.

So would I really keep her from meeting her brother? I sighed softly. No. I couldn't do that to her. And if things went the way I hoped, she'd get to meet him soon.

After dropping Alexis off to her grandparents that afternoon, I gave in to my burning curiosity and swung by Jefferson Avenue again. And again, there sat Amelia's little blue car in the driveway. Was she living with her mother these days? I'd bet having a built-in babysitter would come in handy. And the boy had probably recently started school.

I blew out a long sigh. His first day of school. Another milestone missed. So many important moments already gone. And every day that passed I missed out on more.

Exhaling a sigh, I slowed to a crawl and stared at the windows. My son was right inside that house. Right now. He was so close, yet we lived in completely different worlds.

I'd promised myself I wouldn't give in to my impulses. I'd sworn I'd be careful with every choice going forward. The last

199

thing I wanted was to fuck this up. But I was weak. And in the end, I just couldn't help myself.

I couldn't wait a second longer.

Sliding alongside the curb, I cut the engine, got out and hurried up the path to the door, punching the doorbell before I could change my mind. Inside I could hear voices, including a child's laughter. At the door chime, they went silent. My heart throbbed in my ears as footsteps approach the door.

Shit. What the hell am I doing?

I had a sudden urge to flee. But before I could move a muscle, the door was pulled open and Amelia stood there. Her eyes shot wide when she saw me.

"Who is it?" an older woman called from within. Her mother.

"Nobody," she replied loudly, tilting her chin toward her shoulder, but not breaking eye contact with me. "Just a salesman. I'll take care of it."

The *nobody* hurt. Is that all I was to her now? Just some nobody? My gut twisted. I was an idiot. This had been a terrible, terrible mistake.

I had to force my wooden body to move aside as she stepped onto the porch, closing the door firmly behind her. She looked pissed. And I didn't blame her. "What are you doing here?" Before I could formulate an answer, she added, "How'd you even know where to find me? Did Josh tell you?"

I shook my head. "Of course not. He wouldn't…" I stopped as movement from the window to the right of the door caught my eye. The curtain pulled aside and a small face looked out at me curiously. He had very familiar blue eyes. Just like Alexis' eyes. Just like James.

Just like me.

At the sight of him, the tension gripping me let up and an insuppressible smile stretched my face.

Amelia turned to see what I was staring at. When she realized, her face fell.

There was no going back now. "Who's that?"

She looked back at me, her expression now guarded. I swear I saw fear beneath that steely surface. "None of your business." She pointed toward the street. "I don't know why you're here, but I think you should go."

"Isn't he?" I asked her in a soft voice.

"Isn't he what?"

"My business?"

Now she was full on glaring at me. "*Seriously*? She told you? I can't believe she told you! That's completely unethical. I could get her fired!"

I couldn't help it; my own temper began to rise. Gritting my teeth, I tried to stay calm. "She who? Not you, the one who *should've* told me, that's for damn sure."

Amelia's brows narrowed sharply. "Your little hookup in HR. Nicole? She just *happened* to blab my private details to you in the throes of passion? Is that what happened? Because I maintain: this isn't your business!"

I frowned, shaking my head. "Of course not. She'd never do that." I hadn't even realized Amelia knew I was dating Nicole. I debated informing her that we broke up, but decided it wasn't important right now. She would find out soon enough.

"If not her or Josh, then how? " She turned to the side and ran her fingers over her hair. When she looked back up at me, her eyes were fiercer than ever. "Why are you here, Declan?"

A quick glance toward the window showed the curtain back in place. The boy had apparently lost interest. "I think you know exactly why. And I think you also know we need to talk about this."

She sighed. Not a sigh of defeat though. Not by half. Grabbing my arm, she dragged me toward the porch swing where we couldn't be seen from the windows.

"What do you know about Liam?" she asked bluntly the second we sat down.

I smiled. "His name is Liam?"

"William James York. After my dad. Liam for short. Answer the question."

There was no point in hiding anything. I told her how I'd seen the piece of paper noting she had a child, and how I'd driven by the house last weekend and spotted her outside with him. After that, my curiosity was piqued. "Please. I just wanna know the truth. I think I have a right to."

Amelia's lips pressed into a tight line as she regarded me. Seconds ticked by as I waited for her answer. Birds called each other from the treetops. Cars passed on neighboring streets. The world around us was calm and peaceful, but in our little porch-swing bubble an invisible storm raged. Finally she blew out a long puff of air. "Fine. I suppose there's no point denying it."

"He's my son?"

She nodded, resigned, her gaze now on her twisting fingers.

This should have been one of the most joyous moments of my life, confirmation that we had a child together—and it was, in so many ways it was, but...it was clear Amelia was far from happy about me knowing. And there were still so many unanswered questions. I tried to keep my tone as gentle as possible as I asked, "Why didn't you tell me?"

Her eyes shot to mine for a second, just long enough for me to see the anger once more flaring within them. "You even have to ask? No matter what you said the other day, to me it seemed pretty clear you didn't want him. Or me. I had to make a decision and I decided we were better off on our own. Can you really blame me?"

"I did want you," I protested, but I kept my voice soft. "I would've wanted both of you, if I'd known, but I just...I thought you hated me. Hell, I would've hated me, too, after everything. I was a total basket case back then. I thought you didn't want kids, and God knows you wouldn't want one that had half my genes." She still wouldn't look at me. "I'm sorry for being an ass. And for jumping to the wrong conclusion."

"Yeah, well. What happened back then no longer matters. What *does* matter is what you want now."

"What do I want? I have no idea. It wasn't like I planned on coming here today. It just kinda happened. I know what I don't want is to make your life difficult. You've had more than your share of that and I don't wanna add to it." I paused, a sudden smile curving my lips. "Well...I guess there *is* one thing."

At last she looked over at me, "What's that?" But I could tell by her expression that she knew—hell, that she'd even been expecting it.

"I know it might be asking too much too soon, but...would it be okay if I met him? Just for a minute?"

Amelia still looked worried, but a little of the frost had melted. Pursing her lips, she got to her feet. "All right," she sighed. "Hold on."

I followed her to the door, waiting outside while she went in. My palms were sweaty, and I wiped them on the thighs of my jeans. My gut clenched anxiously. I couldn't remember the last time I'd felt this nervous. Oh wait. Yes, actually, I could. That day so long ago in the hotel room, waiting for Amelia to arrive. Waiting to fall off the edge with her.

A minute later, the door swung open again and she ushered Liam onto the porch. "I want you to meet Declan," she said to him. "He's a friend from work."

It felt good to hear her call me a friend, even though I knew she didn't mean it.

Liam had crumbs at one corner of his mouth, remains of the snack she'd interrupted. His eyes were bright and curious as he looked up at me. "Hi."

"This is my son, Liam."

I got down on one knee so my face was level with his. He looked so much like childhood photos of me it was almost eerie. "Hey buddy. It's awesome to meet you." I stuck out my hand. Liam took it immediately, pumping it up and down with a flourish he must have seen on TV or in a movie. I couldn't help laughing, and in response he giggled, too. It was nearly the sweetest sound I'd ever heard, reminding me more than a little of Alexis when she was that age.

My throat began to tighten. I had to clear it before I said, "So how old are you, Liam?" The words came out a little rough.

"Four. I'm in kindergarten. My old best friend was Quentin and my new best friend is Marco. His hair is white."

"Blond, little man. His hair is blond," Amelia corrected gently.

"Looks white to me."

From the corner of my eyes, I could see her looking at me, but I couldn't tear my gaze away from Liam. The lump in my throat grew larger.

When I didn't say anything else, she must have decided this was over. "Hey, I think PAW Patrol is about to start. Why don't you run back inside and watch it with Gramma?"

"PAW Patrol!" he yelled happily, spinning on his heels and dashing in before I could even say goodbye.

"Be right back." Amelia disappeared into the house after him.

I got to my feet, turning away from the door and bracing a hand on one of the support pillars bracketing the steps. My heart was racing again. With my other hand I covered my eyes, trying to hold back the waterworks. But I had zero chance. I was in no state for further conversation. Ugly tears were imminent and I didn't want Amelia or anyone else to witness me losing my shit.

As I trotted down the steps to the path, I heard the door creak open behind me and knew she was standing there watching me stride to my car. Leaving, just as I'm sure she thought I always did. She probably thought I would always leave her, that I was completely incapable of being there when she or Liam needed me. And I didn't have the composure right now to show her she was wrong.

She didn't call out and I didn't turn around. But we both knew this wasn't over. It was just the beginning. All the things that needed to be discussed, figured out, etcetera, we could deal with later. Though I felt bad about it, it was probably for the best. Emotions were running crazy high right now. We probably both needed some time to process.

Stupid, spontaneous, reckless, whatever you want to call how I'd blindsided her today, it was worth it. Amelia and I might be broken—for now anyway—but nothing could ever change the fact that our love had created a miracle.

I got in my car and closed the door, leaning back in my seat with my eyes squeezed shut. And I made another promise to myself, one I intended to keep as if my life depended on it. Though it might take the rest of that life to prove it to her, I would never leave either of them ever again.

Chapter 22

Amelia

Three thoughts kept running through my head on repeat. In no particular order, they were:

Did that really just happen?

Oh my God. Crap crap crap. Dammit.

Now what?

I tried to act calm, but inside I was panicking. One of my worst fears had just come true, yet I had to hide all my worry away and pretend things were normal around Liam and my mother. I did the best I could, but once Liam was finally tucked in bed, I told Mom I had some work I had to do and excused myself to my room. I could tell by her expression that she knew something was wrong, but she didn't push me to tell her for which I was grateful. She'd know soon enough, but not until I figured out what changes were coming.

My hands were trembling as I sat on the edge of my bed, phone in hand. I wanted to call Josh, wanted to ask his advice, but once again worried it would put him in an awkward position. So instead I texted Dee: *If you have 5 min can you call?*

Proving once again why she was my best friend in the world, my phone rang ten seconds later.

"Hey."

"What's up?"

I sighed, tears welling up as soon as I heard her voice. "He knows. About Liam. He found out and showed up here today." I punctuated that last sentence with a sob.

"Shit. Really? Man, I *knew* you going back there was a huge risk. Tell me what happened."

Once I filled her in, voice cracking every few words, I added, "Now what?" Gasp. "I've no idea what I should do." Sniff.

I heard her blow out a puff of air. "Oh honey. I'm so sorry. I know this isn't what you wanted at all."

Swiping away my tears, I tried to swallow the thick lump in my throat. "I'm just...I'm really scared. I'm shaking like a leaf right now."

"Okay, Ames, I want you to set the phone down and take three deep breaths, full inhales and full exhales. Count to ten on each one. Then come back to me."

I did as I was told. I also went into the bathroom, blew my nose and splashed cold water on my face. I think it worked. My head felt a little clearer, anyway. "Okay, I'm back."

"Better?"

"I think so. Thanks."

"So why are you scared? D'you think he's going to try for custody? Did he say that?"

"No," I admitted, wiping at my eyes again. "He didn't say anything like that. He only asked to meet him. But what if he does? I can't lose Liam. I just can't!"

Declan's voice popped into my head: *I won't lose my kids.* That's what he'd said to me after Laura threatened to take Alexis and leave if he didn't break off all contact with me. If anyone would understand my fears, he would. Wouldn't he? Was I worrying for nothing?

"You won't. There's no way. You're a great mom and no one could ever take your kid from you. You hear me? It's not gonna happen."

"Am I being ridiculous?"

"No, you're being a protective momma-bear. I'd expect nothing else. And I know the idea of Declan being a regular part of your life scares you, too, even if you don't want to admit it. What you need to do is talk to him about how all this is gonna work."

"I know. I just don't know what to say."

"Start by asking him what he wants. And then tell him what you want. And then you two work it out."

206

"Yeah, I guess, but—"

"No buts. Just do it. You need to figure this stuff out ASAP to ease your own mind. And then call me and tell me how it went."

I snorted, finally relaxing a little. "Yes, ma'am."

Dee laughed. "Don't ma'am me. Just figure this shit out. I promise you it won't be as bad as you've worked it up in your head for all these years. Just don't let him walk all over you. You call the shots when it comes to Liam. You and you alone."

"Thanks, Dee. Love you."

"Love you right back."

I ended the call and lay back on my bed. She was right, of course. I'd played out the scene of Declan confronting me in my head a million times since the day I decided I was going to raise our child on my own. Not one of those overwrought fantasies had looked anything like this afternoon. I knew logically talking about custody with him probably wouldn't be as horrible as I imagined, either. Hopefully he'd understand that I wasn't going to give up full custody. But I wouldn't prevent him from getting to know his son. Not anymore. As much as I wanted to protect Liam from anything that might ever hurt him, I realized I couldn't. Not with this. It wouldn't be fair to him to keep him from forming a relationship with his father.

I had no idea what the future was going to bring, but I knew I could no longer hide from it.

On Monday, I made a point to walk with Sam back to her desk after lunch so I could pass Declan's office. The blinds were still drawn and his laptop wasn't there. Which meant he was out for the day so I'd have to wait until another day to talk to him. That was fine. Putting it off for another day was a bit of a relief.

Tuesday afternoon, I deliberately used the washroom over on the other side of the Sales department. This time his office door was closed. Presumably that meant he was in, but I kept on walking, not wanting to interrupt whatever he needed privacy for.

Around four o'clock I called my mom and told her I'd be a bit late getting home, then grabbed my bag and headed back to Sales. The door was still shut, but I could faintly hear his voice inside. On the phone, I assumed. I decided to go down to the little gym in the basement for a quick workout, and then check again on my way out. If he was still busy, I'd try again tomorrow.

After changing into shorts and a t-shirt in the washroom, I went downstairs and got on the stair stepper. I set my program for a ten minute hilly climb. BWK hadn't done much in the way of decorating. All I had to look at was my own reflection in the mirror. As I got going up the first incline, I couldn't help appraising my body. Bad idea. Since Liam, I had curves and bulges in places that had once been flat. I frowned at the dimples of cellulite marring the backs and sides of my thighs. Though not precisely overweight, I could definitely use some toning. Maybe I should start coming down here after work on a regular basis? Scowling at my old running shorts, I wondered if I should also buy some new workout clothing. My hair was beginning to frizz from exertion. Blowing out a long puff of air, I dragged my eyes away from the mirror. Staring at myself was too depressing. Instead I glanced around the room, looking for anything else to focus on, but other than the few other pieces of equipment there was nothing. I sighed, wishing I'd brought my ear buds so I could at least listen to music on my phone.

Just as I started up the next hill, having now worked up a damp layer of sweat, the door to the hallway swung open. I looked up with surprise to see Nicole enter the room. She wore a tight fitting purple tank top and matching black and purple spandex shorts. Because of course she did.

"Oh, hey Amelia," she said with a bright smile. "Hope I'm not interrupting."

"Oh no," I said, trying and failing to not sound short of breath. "I won't be much longer."

"You're good. I'm gonna use the recumbent." She tossed a small towel and her phone onto the rack below the display screen of the machine next to me. "You just surprised me. Usually it's just me down here. There's maybe three of us in the whole building who ever seem to use this room. But I'm not complaining; it's nice to have company."

I looked at my time. Still another six minutes to go. I'd planned to do some stretches afterward to cool down, but now decided against it. Nice as Nicole seemed, I no longer wanted to linger.

"How're things in Accounting?" she asked as she straddled the bike.

Great. She wanted to chat. What could we chat about? Her boyfriend? Maybe we could compare notes on his bedroom skills?

Ugh.

Instead I said, "Good, good." I wondered if Declan had told Nicole about our history. Unlikely, based on how cheerful and relaxed she seemed around me. Which meant she probably didn't know about Liam. Yet. But she would. He'd have to tell her soon enough, and then I predicted her demeanor would become a lot frostier.

"So how was your weekend?"

Still with the questions. She wasn't taking the hint from my short replies. Why couldn't she just put on her headphones and shut up? I kept on climbing. "It was...it was okay. Nothing too interesting." A massive lie, but it's not like I was going to tell her what had really gone down. "How 'bout you?" I glanced over at her as I asked and noticed her smile falter.

"To be honest, it could've been better."

Kind of a leading reply. I didn't really want to know, but I was too nice to just leave her hanging. "Why? What happened?" I kept my focus on my progress instead of looking back at her.

I heard a small sigh. Then: "It's not a huge deal, really. We were always pretty casual, but...the guy I've been seeing broke things off."

My natural inclination was to stop stepping and turn to her. As it was, I had to conceal my surprise and keep going. He'd ended things with her? Before or after he'd confronted me about Liam? And did the timing even matter? "That's, uh..," I stopped to catch my breath. Sweat dripped down my temple and I swiped it away with the back of my hand. "That sucks. You okay?"

She blew out a laugh, pedaling faster. "I'm fine. We're still friends, so it's all good. It was the right decision. Just took me kinda by surprise is all."

You and me both, I thought. Out loud I said, "Still not fun."

"Yeah. But it's for the best. We're very different people. He's older, and mostly likes to just stay at home instead of going out and actually *doing* stuff. You know?"

"Sure," I agreed, but I was surprised by her words. The Declan I used to know loved going out and doing stuff, especially seeing live music. "So you're not upset by it?"

"Honestly? I was. For a hot minute. Then I realized he was right."

"You're already over it?"

"Well, I still care about him, but yeah. I guess I am."

Though our situations were very far from the same, I did feel a bit of sympathy for her. Apparently the two of us could now start the Dumped by Declan Kavanaugh Club. Not that she knew that. And I had no intention of telling her.

After washing my face, reapplying deodorant, and changing back into my work clothes, I returned upstairs to see if the man in question was still around. As I rounded the corner into Sales, he was just coming out of his office, clearly on his way out.

A tight smile surfaced when he saw me. It didn't linger. "Hey." Something about him was different from how he'd been on Saturday. Better. His eyes were brighter, his back straighter. He seemed more like his old self.

"Hey. Can you spare a few minutes? We should probably talk."

"You're right. We should." He reopened his office door and gesturing for me to enter ahead of him.

I took the same guest chair I'd always sat in. It felt familiar and right, like it had been waiting all these years for me to return. Unfortunately I was too keyed up about what I needed to say to be able to relax and remember any of the good chats we'd had. I could only focus on the here and now.

"So?" he asked as he sat down behind his desk, folding his hands together on the glossy wooden surface as he looked at me. His desk was always neat and clear when he left for the day, a tendency we both shared.

"So, it's been a few days. You've had some time to think about all this, and what it means."

He snorted softly, shaking his head. "All I've done is think about..." He paused to make finger quotes. "All this."

"Me, too. I'm worried about how it's going to impact Liam. I have to think about what's best for him. So I need to know what you want."

"What I want?"

I sighed. Was it really so complicated that I had to spell it out? "Going forward. What you want with regard to Liam."

Declan sat back in his chair, his eyes fixed on mine. "Well...I didn't want to push you or anything, not until you were ready, but—of course—I'd like to have the chance to get to know him, and he, me. If and when you're cool with that."

With a nod, I replied, "Yeah. Well, that's what we need to discuss. I don't want to make any huge changes in his life yet, like if you suddenly wanted to take him out on his own or back to your place or something. He's had enough change lately and is only now starting to adjust to his new home and school. But I think…I think it'd be okay for you to come over and spend a little time with him. Just for short visits for now."

"Short visits are perfect. That way he can get used to me. Is he shy?"

I shrugged. "He can be sometimes. Other times, it seems like he'll talk to anyone. It depends on his mood."

Declan smiled. "Sounds a bit like his mother."

I bristled. "Like you'd know?" He flinched at that, and I regretted the outburst.

"I guess I wouldn't. Not anymore." Now he just looked sad. Sighing, he leaned forward again. "What do *you* want, Amelia? Now that the cat's outta the bag, how would *you* like to see this play out? Barring giving me some kind of memory wipe, that is." Joking or not, his face remained serious as he waited for my answer.

Tempting as the idea was, making him forget Liam existed unfortunately wasn't an option. I nibbled my lower lip for a moment, debating. Then, slowly, deliberately, I said, "What I want is for you to make me a promise." His mouth opened to respond, but I sped up before he could cut in. "Promise me you'll never take him from me."

A deep frown creased his forehead. "I'd never do that."

Though I had no right to ask it of him, for my own piece of mind I had to anyway. I took a deep breath. "You need to promise. If you ever loved me, if I ever meant anything to you once, you need to swear you'll never try to take Liam. You'll never even ask for fifty-fifty custody. I can't lose him, Declan. Not even for a week every other week. I know you have rights, and I know one of those rights is time with your son, but I can't stress enough that, for me, this is non-negotiable."

His eyes were wide as he got to his feet and came around the desk. Sitting down in the empty chair beside me, he reached for my hand and held it in both of his. I almost yanked it back, but for reasons I can't explain, I didn't. He was looking at me so seriously and it reminded me of other serious conversations we'd had years ago, conversations that ultimately ended up meaning nothing, in the end.

His intense blue eyes drilled into mine. "I swear I'll never take Liam from you. Not even joint custody. You have my word. I hope you'll let me be a part of his life going forward—and Alexis, too, at some point—but I promise I'll defer to your decisions. If you need me for anything, or want my advice or input, I will gladly help. But I won't ask to take him, not even overnight or for the weekend, until you're both ready for that. If you ever are."

"I appreciate you understanding," I said softly. My hand in his had gone sweaty and I pulled it away at last.

"Of course. Whatever you need."

"Thank you."

Declan leaned forward and braced his elbows on his knees, his head turned so he still looked right at me. His face was very solemn. "But I need a promise from you in return. I need *you* to swear you'll never up and vanish with him again."

I nodded. "That's fair. I promise from now on you'll always know where to find us."

"Good." One corner of his mouth curved up into a half-grin. "That's all I need."

Now that we'd gotten through all the tricky bits, some of my tension ebbed. Maybe I shouldn't have trusted him—it's not like he'd hadn't broken promises to me before. Yet I did. I recalled all too well how Laura had gotten him to cut me out of his life. She'd threatened to take their daughter and unborn child away from him. His fear of losing his kids was why he hadn't been able to leave her. So I believed him when he said he'd never try to take Liam from me, and I'd meant it when I'd sworn I'd never keep Liam from him again either. He was a good dad, a devoted dad, and no matter what hell he'd once put me through, I knew he'd never abandon our son.

I mirrored his grin. "So…would you like to come over on Sunday? After lunch maybe? Saturday won't work; we're visiting friends."

Declan's face lit up with a wide smile and I had to look away. God, that *damn* smile—it did strange things to my insides when he looked at me and smiled like that. I wished he didn't still affect me that way, but I couldn't seem to squash it.

"I'd love that," he said.

"Great." I gave him my number and he put it into his phone. "Just text and let me know when."

As I started to rise he stopped me. "There's one more thing we should probably discuss."

212

"What's that?"

"Money."

I frowned, but I sat back down. "I'm not asking you for support if that's what you mean."

"I know you're not, but I want to give it anyway."

Shaking my head, I said, "That's not necessary. I didn't even tell you about him, so I don't think it'd be right to turn around now and ask for child support."

"Kids are expensive. Let me help pay for some stuff. It's the least I can do. I was thinking five hundred a month might be reasonable. Is that okay with you?"

I stared at him, my mouth dropping open a little.

"Just text me your email and I'll e-Transfer it over."

Finally I found my voice. "You really don't—"

He cut me off firmly. "I want to. And that's also non-negotiable. Unless it's not enough, then feel free to negotiate all you like."

I swallowed, nodding. "If you insist."

"I do."

Child support had been the last thing on my mind. But he wasn't wrong. An extra five hundred a month would help pay for food and clothing and taking Liam to the movies, plus some left over to put into his bank account for the future. I still didn't feel comfortable taking money from Declan, but for Liam's sake, I relented. "Okay," I said. "Well, thank you again. You've been more than fair about all this."

He waved this off. "I was a complete ass to you and I hurt you. There's nothing I can do now to change that, but going forward I just want to make all this as easy on you as possible."

I didn't know how to respond without getting into things I didn't really want to talk about, so I just nodded and headed for the door.

"Have a good night. I'll look forward to Sunday."

"Good night."

As I strode to the car as fast as my legs could carry me, I wondered how things would be now that we were forced into each other's lives because of the child we shared. Would it be sheer torture having to spend regular time with him? Or would we somehow be able to become friends again?

And did I even want that?

Declan

Though work was extra busy, the rest of the week seemed to crawl by. All I could think about was visiting Amelia and Liam on Sunday. And Sunday felt so damn far away.

After I dropped Alexis off in Swann's Landing on Saturday, I decided to call Ryan. He'd mentioned earlier that Diana was going out of town for the weekend to visit her mother so I invited him to come over. We hadn't hung out just the two of us in a long time, and I figured we could both use the company.

He agreed, although it took some coaxing. Just before six, he showed up at my door with two steaks and a six-pack. I was pretty sure he wasn't supposed to drink, what with having addiction issues and all, but I took them from him with a smile anyway.

We put the steaks on the grill and cracked open a couple of beers. As I handed him his, I said, "Should you be drinking?"

"Eh. It's only one."

"I mean with the whole NA recovery thing. Thought booze was off limits, too?"

My brother smiled. "It's been years. I'm fine."

I clinked my bottle against his and took a swig. "If you say so. You still going to meetings?"

With a small shrug, he said, "Sometimes. When I have time." He took a drink. "Heard you landed Merrill and Hogan. That oughta pad your commission nicely."

I thought of the five hundred that would be going to Amelia each month from now on and I nodded. "It sure doesn't suck."

"I bet. Got a couple irons in the fire right now, myself."

I arched a brow. "Do tell."

Ryan upended the bottle to his lips again and shook his head. "Don't wanna jinx it. You'll know soon enough if anything good comes of it." He took a seat in one of the lawn chairs. It was a little chilly today for sitting outside, but the sun was out and its warmth felt good. "So what else's new with you these days?"

I looked over at him, considering. "A lot, actually. I have some big news. But it's still on the down low, so you can't say anything to anyone. Not even Diana. Or Dad. I'll tell them once things are all figured out."

He raised his eye to mine, showing a bit of interest. "Well now you've got me curious."

"It's complicated," I said. "I know you're gonna have a lot of questions."

"Whatever. Just spill, brother."

This wasn't going to be easy to explain, so I just jumped in. "So you know Amelia York?"

Ryan nodded. "Sure. Why?"

"She, uh, so she has a little boy."

"Okay. Good for her. So?"

"I only just found out. But see, the thing is, it turns out he's kind of your nephew."

He looked confused. "*Kind of?* What the hell are you talking about?" Then his brows flew up as the pieces clicked into place. "*Oh.* You've gotta be kidding." He shot me a knowing look. "A married chick somehow managed to fall into your bed? Why does *that* not surprise me?"

I exhaled a long sigh. Though things had been a lot better between us over the past few years, my brother clearly still jumped to negative conclusions about me. And this time he wasn't even wrong. Amelia and I *had* first gotten together back when we were both still married, although Ryan knew nothing about it. "It wasn't like that. She split with her ex a long time ago. I ran into her again at Josh's wedding."

"Of course you did. Let me guess. You two couldn't keep your hands off each other?"

"Not exactly. Dude, shut the fuck up with the commentary and let me explain."

He mimed closing a zipper across his lips, but his expression couldn't hide what he was thinking. I didn't want to drag this out. I just needed him to know. So I told him how I'd gotten shitfaced at the reception, how Amelia had tried to help me up to my room, and what had happened after.

Ryan was now grinning.

"What?" I asked.

"I'm just amazed it took ya so long."

"Why? Because of that bullshit rumor that was making the rounds at work before she quit?"

Laughing softly, he said, "No, because I have eyes. And I know you. I may've been pretty fucked up a lot of the time back when she worked with us the first time around, but I saw you guys together plenty. I noticed the way you looked at each other. Believe me when I say you two hooking up is *not* a surprise. What *is* a surprise is that you're only just telling me now. And you have a secret baby? What the actual fuck, Declan?"

"We only spent that one night together. Like I said before, I just found out. Our son—Liam—he's four."

Ryan's jaw dropped damn near to his chest. "*What*? You're shitting me?"

I couldn't help it; I laughed out loud. The expression on his face was priceless. "All true."

"She never told you she got pregnant? Or, wait, I bet I know exactly how it went down. She *did* tell you and you were a total dick to her about it? Am I right?"

Heat rushed to my face. I sighed again, taking the chair beside him. "Something like that," I muttered. "I assumed she wanted an abortion. I'm not proud of my actions. Not that it's any excuse, but I'd just found out James only had a few months to live. I wasn't in a good place. I've apologized to her and explained, but…I think it's too late for forgiveness."

"Jesus Christ. You really screwed the pooch with that one. How'd you find out about the kid then, if she didn't tell you?"

I told him what had happened, and that Amelia had agreed to let me visit Liam tomorrow. "I'm hoping to try to fix things, rebuild our friendship. If she'll let me. Which she may have zero interest in, but I have to try."

"Are you bringing Lex?"

"No, I haven't told her yet. I wanted to wait until things were more…I don't know…settled I guess. You can't say anything to anyone about this, okay? You swear?"

He nodded. "I swear. I guess I should say congratulations. You have a secret four-year old." Getting to his feet, he smiled and clapped me on the shoulder. "I'm thrilled for ya, bro. After everything you've been through, this is great news. You deserve some happiness."

I wasn't so sure about that, but I didn't comment. He had the gist of it, but I had no intention of filling him in on all the ugly details of Amelia's and my history. It was nobody's business but ours. And if we were ever to be repaired—which was probably unlikely—I had a shitload of work ahead of me.

Chapter 23

Amelia

After a big pancake breakfast on Sunday, I made Liam say goodbye to Auntie Dee and Auntie Terri and we got on the road back to Swann's Landing. Liam had had a great night of popcorn, movies, and sleeping in his old bedroom, which still looked pretty much exactly like he'd left it a few months ago. It seemed like he was finally starting to think of his bedroom at Gramma's as his, but I also knew he missed the old house with his aunties as much as I did.

Liam didn't understand why I'd been in a rush to leave this morning. I hadn't said anything to him about Declan visiting yet, but maybe it would be a good idea to try to prepare him a bit.

"Hey, little man." I glanced back at him in the rearview mirror. "D'you remember my friend you met on Gramma's porch last weekend? The guy with the dark hair?"

"He shook my hand?"

"Yes, him. He's actually coming over this afternoon. What do you think about that?"

"Okay. Does he have a kid?"

"He has a daughter, but I don't think he's bringing her." Not this time, anyway.

"Why not? How old is she?"

"She's, uh, nine or ten. I think she's at her grandparent's house today."

"Oh. Can I play on your phone?" He'd already lost interest in some adult coming over, assuming they were coming to visit me and not him. Adults were boring, especially when they weren't bringing any kids he could play with.

With one hand, I reached into my bag and passed my phone back to him. Once I heard the beeps of his game starting, I turned up the music.

A few minutes later, he said, "Mommy? You got a message."

Liam knew his alphabet and had been learning to read basic words over the past few months. "Oh yeah? Can you read any of it to me?"

"Be. Ov...er. At. Then there's a one. And a dot. Then there's a red heart and a D. What does it mean?"

Heat flooded my cheeks. Stupid, I know, but another thing I had no control over.

"That's from my friend. He's saying he'll come at one o'clock to visit us."

Liam didn't reply, distracted once more by his game.

Why did Declan have to include a heart? *Why?* It was completely unnecessary. I told myself it was because he was excited to spend time with Liam. Our personal past was in the past and I intended it to stay that way.

The problem was, going forward Declan would never again be just a part of my past. He was in my life forever now. Whether I liked it or not.

Right on the dot of one o'clock the doorbell rang. My mom was out visiting a friend, so it was just Liam and me, which worked out well as I hadn't told my mom about Declan yet. I took a deep calming breath and went to answer it.

"Good afternoon," he said, smiling. He had a brightly wrapped box under one arm.

"Hey." I pointed to it. "Whatcha got there?"

He dropped me a wink. "Shh. It's a surprise."

I frowned. "You know his birthday was back in June, right? And Christmas is still months off."

"I know." He just stood there grinning at me. It was obvious how excited he was. He was fairly glowing and it made him look nearly ten years younger. It kind of unnerved me.

218

"C'mon in. Leave your shoes on. We're sitting out back." It was a beautiful autumn afternoon, and I wanted Liam to play outside in the fresh air as much as possible before the colder weather arrived. Winters in Virginia didn't bring much snow, but were often chilly. Which reminded me, I still needed to buy Liam a warm coat and a new pair of boots. The money Declan had sent me last week would come in handy.

When we went out onto the deck, I saw Liam playing with his trucks in the green plastic turtle sandbox my mom had picked up for him from a yard sale last month. Once we moved into an apartment, I knew Liam would be upset to leave that sandbox behind. He didn't know how good he had it at Gramma's.

"Liam?" I called. He looked up at me but didn't move. I could hear him making rrrr-ing sounds as he pushed a red truck through a hill of dirt. I tried again. "C'mere please."

"It's okay. He's fine," Declan said to me.

"He should at least come over and say hi." I raised my voice louder. "Liam!" This time he dropped the truck and got to his feet, brushing off his hands on his jeans before stepping out of the sand box and coming up onto the deck.

"You remember my friend? You met him last weekend?"

With an easy grin, Declan said, "Hey bud."

"Hi." Liam wasn't even looking at him. His eyes were fixed on the gift in Declan's hands. "What's that?"

"This?" Declan held it out, "It's a birthday present."

"S'not my birthday." Liam looked doubtful, but I knew he was itching to open it.

"I know. I'm a few months late, but better late than never, right?"

My son's eyes sought mine, silently begging me to let him accept it. "Go ahead," I nodded. He grinned, grabbing the package and dropping onto his bum on the deck. Within seconds he'd torn the wrapping off to reveal a bright yellow box with a photo of a big toy digger on the side. The words *Mega Digger 3000* were emblazed above it.

"Whoa!" he exclaimed.

"Very whoa," I said, shooting Declan a pointed look. "That's some gift."

Flashing an apologetic smile, he just shrugged. "I saw it at the store yesterday and couldn't resist."

I turned back to my son. "Liam, what do you say?"

Liam had been trying unsuccessfully to pull open the side flap. He looked up at his father again, blue eyes wide. "Thank you! It's super awesome!"

"You're welcome. Here, let me help you with that." Declan got down on his knees and carefully opened the box, then started unwinding the many twist ties holding the toy in place on the cardboard. Once it was free, he handed it to Liam. "It *is* super awesome, isn't it? I think you better try it out."

Liam carried it with pride down the steps to the sand box and set it among his cars and trucks. He began piling up another mountain of dirt, presumably to give the new arrival some work to do.

I went inside and came back with iced tea to drink as we sat in the shade of the overhang while Liam played. It felt kind of weird sitting with Declan watching our son make happy motoring sounds on the lawn. I got a strange sense of déjà vu, like maybe I'd dreamt this very scene before.

"You didn't have to give him a big, fancy gift, you know." I said quietly.

"I know. I wanted to."

"There are better ways to get him to like you."

Declan snorted. "Go ahead. Judge away. You have every right to. But I wasn't lying. I bought it on a whim. Figured he'd love it. And it looks like I was right." He indicated toward the sand box. The digger was covered in dirt. It already looked like it had been part of Liam's toy collection for ages.

And Liam? He was lost in his own little world, barely even aware of our existence. Playing outside in the dirt on a beautiful day like today was much better than sitting inside staring at the TV or a game on my phone. Sure, he'd need a bath before dinner, but that was okay. My son was a big fan of bubble baths.

"So is this the house you grew up in?" Declan asked, turning back to me.

"Yep." I pointed to the far end of the yard at the wooden swing hanging from the oak tree "See that swing? My dad put it up for me when I was little."

"That's cool. We never had a backyard swing. Or a sandbox. Patrick was always way too busy to build us stuff like that. We did have a plastic slide my aunt gave us, but I was too big for it, although I do recall Ryan playing on it."

I frowned. "That's a shame."

"It was okay. We used to go to a neighbor's place after school, at least until I was old enough to watch my brother myself, and she'd take us to the park sometimes. So it wasn't all bad. Dad put in a lot of hours, but he was trying to provide for two kids on his own. He did the best he could. I don't resent him for not being around that much. At least not anymore."

"Yeah. I guess your life ended up going down a similar path, didn't it? Is your relationship with him better these days?"

Declan nodded. "Definitely. We'll never be super tight, but we can spend time together now without friction. So that's something. And he's good to Lex." He paused to take a sip of iced tea. "We were both widowed with small children, but I wouldn't say it was exactly similar." He looked like he was about to say more, but instead he went quiet.

I debated asking him to elaborate, but decided against it. I had no interest in talking about Laura, or the accident. It had been a terrible tragedy, and maybe one day we'd be in a place with each other where he'd feel comfortable discussing it and I'd be fine with listening, but today was not that day.

Declan swept an arm in front of him. "This is a pretty nice place. I bet your mom's glad to have you two here for company."

I shrugged. "You know, as it turns out she is. She really seems to love having Liam around. I wasn't too sure if she would. I honestly never even thought she liked little kids that much. But after he was born, she came right around. She totally surprised me."

Just then Liam got to his feet and came back up the steps. "I'm thirsty!" he announced, staring at my glass.

"How thirsty? Drink of my iced tea thirsty or get you your own glass thirsty?"

"Drink from yours." He moved in close beside me.

I noticed a piece of oak leaf stuck in his hair. Plucking it out, I said, "Okay, but first what do you need to say?"

"Please?"

"That's better." I held it out to him and he began to gulp it down. My glass was nearly empty when he set it back on the table.

"Hey Liam, how 'bout I push you on that swing back there?" Declan said.

Liam turned to him, frowning. "I'm a big boy now. I don't need pushing."

"Liam!" I scolded. "That's not very polite!"

He stuck out his lower lip, but before he could protest further, Declan added, "What if I just give you one big push to get you started? Would that be okay?"

My son's grumpy face relaxed. He looked up at Declan, considering. Then he smiled. "Okay." He started running back to the swing and Declan followed after. Although I'd always known he was a great dad, this was a side of him I'd never seen before.

I watched Liam settle himself on the seat and then Declan pulled the swing back nearly as high as his head. "Ready?" he asked Liam. Liam clearly said yes, because a second later, Declan let go and a loud squeal of glee burst from my son as he shot forward, his little legs pumping frantically.

Declan stepped back and watched him from a few feet away. Not for long though. Liam soon shouted, "More!" I felt my heart clench in my chest as Declan moved back into position and began to push him. Liam kept pumping, swinging higher and higher and making whooping sounds. It was beyond adorable.

I was about to call to them to slow down or Liam would end up vomiting the iced tea everywhere, but I changed my mind. They were both enjoying themselves. If Liam threw up, I'd change his clothes and they could start right back up again. A few dirty clothes were a small price to pay for making his first memories with his father.

His father. *God.* Liam had no idea who Declan even was yet. With chagrin I realized the disservice I was doing to my son by not telling him. He was going to find out soon enough, so why delay it? Was I just being selfish? Wanting to keep my child just mine for a little bit longer now that a relationship with his dad was inevitable?

And Declan himself had lost a child, a horror I couldn't even conceive of. Had he dreamed of playing with a son the way he was now playing with Liam? It wasn't right for me to stand in the way anymore. They needed each other far more than I needed to stay away from Declan.

I sighed, reaching for the pitcher and refilling my glass. It was time to do the right thing. For Liam's sake.

Several minutes later, two laughing, red-cheeked guys rejoined me on the deck. Declan was grinning that grin again, barely able to take his eyes off his son. Liam grabbed my iced tea and drained half of it without asking this time. I didn't scold him for it, though.

He looked up at Declan. "Wanna play with my new digger?"

222

"Very much," Declan said.

Liam took one step toward the grass, then stopped and turned back to him. "Hey, what's your name?" he asked.

Declan opened his mouth, but before he could reply, I cut in. "Hey Liam, sweetie, come here a minute." When he approached me, I pulled him onto my lap. "There's something I need to tell you."

He looked at me with a bright quizzical expression. When I didn't immediately continue, he said, "What?"

I darted a glance at Declan. We hadn't discussed this in advance, and I knew I was making a sudden decision that would impact all three of us. But I also knew it was the right one. "His name is Declan Kavanaugh. And the thing is...what I need to tell you is...he's your father."

Liam twisted so he could look at Declan, his little brows draw in. "He is?"

"Yes. And I'm sorry. I know it's a lot to lay on you all at once." I gave him a squeeze. "So you can call him Declan. Or, if you want, you can call him Dad. It's up to you. Whatever you feel comfortable with."

At first Liam didn't say anything. He just stared at Declan. They stared at each other. Then my son turned back to me. He put his hands on my cheeks like he always did when he wanted to tell me something he considered very serious. "Mommy?"

"Yes, little man?"

"You said you couldn't find my Daddy."

I covered both his hands with mine. "I know I did. But you know what? He found us anyway." My throat had gone hot and tight. I knew my voice would crack if I tried to say more, so I just leaned in and kissed him on the cheek.

Liam stared at me for a few more seconds, then pulled his hands from under mine and slid off me. He went over to Declan and grabbed his fingers. "Come play?"

Declan smiled and there was clear relief in that smile. "Of course." Hand in hand, they went down to the sandbox.

I watched them play, sitting in the shade and sipping tea, for nearly another hour before my mom poked her head out the back door.

"I brought Chinese food for dinner. Will your friend be joining us?"

I shook my head. "Not this time."

Mom gave me a knowing smile and I could tell what she was thinking. She was hoping this man playing with her grandson was my new boyfriend. Whether she recognized him or not, I couldn't tell. Later, after Liam was in bed, I'd tell her the truth about what was going on, at least the important parts. I assumed she'd be happily surprised and try to convince me that Declan and I should get back together, and I was already preparing arguments against it in my head.

"Liam, time to go wash up for dinner," I called. If we ate out here, I could delay his bath until after.

They both came up the steps. "Are you having dinner with us?" he asked Declan.

"Sorry, buddy. Not this time. I have to go pick up my daughter."

Liam didn't seem to register that Declan having a daughter meant he had a sister, but I figured I'd tell him about Alexis some other time. "Okay." To both our surprises, he held his arms up to Declan. As I watched, Declan, still smiling, got down on one knee and folded Liam into a hug. That clenching feeling in my chest came again. Again, I told myself I was doing the right thing. No matter how much having Declan around might hurt, it was the best thing for both of them.

"See you soon," Declan said to Liam.

"Bye!" Liam ran inside.

I got to my feet and looked up at Declan and I swore I saw tears shining in the corners of his eyes. "I'm sorry I kept him from you," I said softly. "I shouldn't have."

He swiped at his face. "You did what you thought was right," he said, his voice rough. "I was pretty upset when I found out, but now I get it."

"Do you?"

"I think so."

I sighed, my eyes going to the swing my dad had hung for me all those years ago, when I was around Liam's age. My dad had pushed me on that swing many, many times, making memories with me that I'd have forever. "Today was…it was good. He really likes you."

"I'm glad. I like him, too." Declan paused for a moment, then said, "So, you surprised me earlier. When did you decide to tell him I was his dad?"

"Sorry for not giving you the head's up on that. I just didn't see any reason not to. He asked who you were and it felt right to tell him the truth. Hope you don't mind?"

Declan smiled. "Not at all. I'm glad." Before I could say more, he added, "Guess I'd better run. Talk to you later." With that, he went around the side of the house and disappeared.

When I went inside, my mother turned to me with wide eyes. Liam was sitting on one of the kitchen stools drinking from a blue plastic cup. She walked up to me and took me by the arm, "Your son just told me that man is his father," she whispered, although none too softly. "Is that true?"

I bit my lip. "It's true. But I'll explain later, okay?" I darted my eyes toward Liam so she would get the hint.

"Yes. You will."

After we polished off the Chinese food, I took Liam upstairs and started running his bath.

"Did you have a good day today?" I asked him as I stripped off his dirty clothes and tossed them into the hamper.

"Yep."

"What did you think of Declan?"

"He's nice."

"Do you have any questions about anything?"

Liam braced a hand on my shoulder for support as he stepped into the tub and sat down among the bubbles. "No."

"Would you like to see him again?"

This time he turned to me, smiling wide enough to show lots of small white teeth. "Can he come play with me tomorrow?"

I laughed. "No, not tomorrow. He has to work, same as I do. But maybe next weekend?"

"Yay." Liam reached for one of his toy boats, immediately burying it in a mound of bubbles. Pushing it around his knees with one hand, his eyes fixed on its path, he said, "Is he really my Daddy?"

"Yes. How do you feel about that?"

Still not looking up at me, he said, "I like Daddy."

I ruffled his hair and reached for the shampoo. "Good. I was hoping you would. Now time to lean back and get your hair wet."

I no longer had any doubts that the two of them would love each other like crazy. No doubts at all. The only doubts remaining were all about how I'd be able to handle it. And they were big ones.

Declan

I'd been in such a great mood the past few days that a few of my co-workers had even commented on it. I probably should've been annoyed that they thought a happier me was out of character, but I honestly didn't give the slightest fuck about their opinion of me. I *was* happy. I had a son. And along with him came a unique opportunity I totally didn't deserve, but intended to grab anyway—the chance of fixing things with Amelia. I was filled with a hope I hadn't had in a very long time, and it felt great.

And they weren't the only ones who'd noticed my improved mood.

After dinner on Wednesday, Alexis and I were lounging on the living room couch watching a rerun of *America's Funniest Home Videos*. As per usual, my kid was laughing her ass off at the crazy antics caught on film. Often I sat with my laptop in front of me, working while she watched television, but tonight both computer and phone had been set aside.

"Dad, did you see that guy? Face first right into the wedding cake! Totally destroyed it! That was *so* awesome!"

"What a mess, though. I bet his new bride didn't think it was so awesome."

"Yes, she did! There she is, right behind him! She's laughing!"

I chuckled. "He's lucky to have such an understanding wife. Your mom would've killed me if I'd wrecked *our* cake."

Alexis turned to me. She was trying to look serious, but the twinkle in her eyes gave her away. "She really would have."

"Yep. I'd be dead," I said, nodding. "You'd have no dad."

Her eyes narrowed. "What's up with you?"

"What d'you mean?" But I know what she meant. I just wanted to see what she would say.

She considered me for a few seconds. "You're all smiley."

"Am I?" I laughed.

"See? You're all laughing and stuff. I mean, you do, sometimes, but it's, like, *way* more."

I reached over and grabbed her around the waist, pulling her closer and lightly tickling her sides. She squealed, trying to escape, so I stopped tickling and instead hugged her to me, kissing the top of her head. I wanted to tell her all about Liam, but I couldn't. It was too soon. I needed to develop a relationship with him myself before adding a brand new sister into the mix and risking overwhelming him. "Guess I'm just happy," I said.

"Good," she replied, hugging me back and then extracting herself from my arms. The commercials were over and another wacky video was about to start.

I couldn't help wondering what she'd think of Liam. Would she be jealous, after having me all to herself her whole life? And what would she think of Amelia? There were so many potential minefields, but I couldn't tackle any of them until Alexis knew the truth. I hoped she'd go with the flow, but I was a little worried. The important thing I needed to always remember was to make sure she didn't feel left out or second best. She had no experience with siblings, so it would be a learning curve for both of us.

Later, once Alexis was in bed, I started thinking about my afternoon with Liam. I could still recall the sound of his laughter as I'd pushed him on the swing. Damned if I wasn't missing that kid already. My son. I was missing my son. It was going to take a bit of time to get used to the fact that Amelia and I had a son. And I couldn't wait to see him again.

So I texted her: *Hey. How're you guys?*

It took about half an hour to get a response. *We're good. You?*

Great. It's really hard not to tell Lex, but I know it's too soon.

That earned me a one word reply: *Yeah.* She clearly wasn't feeling too chatty.

I decided to get right to the point. *Would it be ok if I visited on Sat?*

This time I waited for fifteen minutes. Maybe I was bugging her at a bad time. Maybe she just didn't feel like talking to me. Finally my phone pinged. *We're going with Mom to the Multicultural Festival at Franklin Park.*

After a quick Google search, I found out she was referring to an afternoon of food, displays and live world music. Franklin Park was near Swann's Landing's small downtown, if you could even call it that, and it was about a five minute drive from Alexis' grandparent's house. I hoped the weather on Saturday would be nice. Pretty much anything could happen at this time of year, and a rainy, cool day would not make for a particularly fun afternoon at the park.

I can come find you guys there after I drop off Lex. That okay?

I thought maybe Amelia wouldn't answer at all, and I'd have to pop by her office sometime this week and ask again, but my phone pinged a final time not long after. It was another one word reply, but I didn't take it personally. She'd texted: *Sure*.

And that smile everyone had been noticing was back on my face again.

Chapter 24

Amelia

We woke up to a gloomy drizzle, but by late morning the sun had come out and dried up all the damp. Which was good, because we were looking forward to a fun day at the Multicultural Festival. Mom must've been feeling maternal, because she had a picnic basket all ready to go by noon. I loaded my car with lawn chairs and we headed over to Franklin Park.

It was busier at the park than I'd anticipated and the closest lot to the festival was already full. I dropped Liam and Mom off with the basket and went to look for a spot in the parking lot on the far side. Luckily I found one, and as I was walking back to find them, I spotted Liv with her mom and a little boy about fifty feet in front of me. I knew the right thing to do was to go over and say hello, but I'm ashamed to admit I didn't. I actually hung back a bit, widening the space between us and shifting behind another group of people to conceal myself. Stupid, I know. There was no good reason to avoid my former best friend, other than the guilt I felt at having cut her out of my life. I knew at some point we'd have to talk, but it could wait a little longer. I had enough on my mind knowing Declan would soon be joining us.

When I reached the area where all the booths were set up, I craned my head, looking around for my mom. Two seconds later I spotted her; she was standing on her tiptoes by a picnic table waving frantically at me, clearly thrilled to have found a free one. I hurried toward them, the now unneeded folded chairs I carried banging against my hip with every step.

By the time we got settled and pulled out our sandwiches, an African quartet had begun playing on the stage. It was kind of nice to sit and listen to the drums as I ate. Liam wasn't too interested in relaxing, especially once lunch was gone. I'd just settled into a lawn chair so I could tilt my head back and close my eyes to the sunshine when he poked me in the arm.

"Mommy, there's Marco. Can I go over?"

I sat forward, shielding my eyes against the glare so I could see where he was pointing. "Where?"

"Right there!" He indicted again toward a child with snow white hair. The little boy was sitting on a blanket with two women. Liv and her mother. *Oh God.* Marco was Liv and Scott's son. Who, of course, went to the same school as Liam and, of course, was close enough to the same age to be in his class. Why had I never pieced that together before?

Well, I thought. *This oughta be interesting.*

With a sigh, I told Mom I'd be right back as Liam grabbed hold of my hand and dragged me in Marco's direction.

As we approached, Liv's mother spotted me and smiled. "Oh, hello Amelia! Look Olivia, it's Amelia York."

Liv turned to me just as Liam reached Marco. Her eyes then shot to Liam, then back to me, then to her own son. From the curious expression she wore, I knew Scott had kept my secret. She had no idea about Liam. But now I'd have to tell her.

She got to her feet beside the boys. "Hey monkey," she said to Marco. "Who's your friend?"

Marco didn't look up at his mother. "Liam," he said. His voice was high and clear.

Pasting on a smile, I said, "Hey Liv. I didn't realize the Marco Liam talks about was your boy."

Liv snorted, but she didn't look too annoyed. More perplexed. "And I clearly had no idea about..." She paused, waving her hand toward Liam. "So Liam is *your* son?"

I nodded, feeling sheepish. "Sorry. It's kind of a long story."

"Yeah, I'm sure. I'm sure there're plenty of long stories you haven't told me."

My face grew hotter. I glanced at the boys, but they were now sitting on one corner of the blanket taking turns looking at the phone in Marco's hands. I decided to see if I could avoid a big confrontation, at least for now. "Is it okay if Liam sits with you guys for a bit and plays with Marco? We're right over there." I indicated over my shoulder towards where my mom sat watching the musicians.

One of Liv's eyebrows arched. She turned to her mother. "Mom, can you keep an eye on the boys for a minute? I'll be right back." Grabbing me by the elbow, she led me between groups of people on blankets until we were at the side in the shade of some tall pines.

"What the actual hell, Ames?"

I sighed. "I know."

"I doubt that. What are you even doing here? I thought you lived in Richmond?"

"I do. I mean, I did. I got a new job, so I'm—we're—staying with my mom right now until I can find a place."

She nodded. "Okay, fine. But tell me this: how the hell do you have a kid the same age as Marco and I didn't know anything about it? Why didn't Dee tell me? Why didn't *you*?" Her face had turned as red as I knew mine was, but her color was from a very different emotion.

I looked down. "It's…it's super complicated. Believe me, I had good reasons for staying away. Important reasons, although nothing to do with you, I swear. But things have changed recently. We're not hiding anymore." Liv still looked at me skeptically. She probably would never forgive me for cutting her out of such a major chunk of my life and keeping so many secrets. But I had to at least try. "I've actually been meaning to message you, but…"

"But? But I don't rate anymore? You think I don't know that? You've made it abundantly clear I have no place in your life now. And if it's because of Scott, I guess I sort of get it, although it still sucks because you never even talked to me about it. Not once, over all these years. *God*, you were my *best friend,* Ames! And you just ditched me. Twice! I mean you went and had a kid and didn't even tell me!" Her voice caught and it made tears rise in my own eyes.

"I know. And I'm *so* sorry, Liv."

Her eyes flared as she shook her head. "Sorry just doesn't cut it. Whatever reason you had, you never trusted me enough to share it with me. Which tells me a hell of a lot about our so-called friendship." She put her hands on her hips, still glaring at me. "Look, you know what? I'm fine with Marco playing with your boy, but I think that's gonna have to be the limit of our interactions from now on."

"I understand," I mumbled, swallowing hard.

"I really don't think you do." With that, she spun on her heel and headed back to her family.

I couldn't blame her, not one bit. I deserved it. But it still stung.

I'd been dozing beside my mother, listening to the music with my eyes shut when my phone beeped. Reaching for my bag to grab it, I opened the text without much curiosity. I already knew who it was from.

Just parked. Where are you?

It was crowded now and I wasn't sure Declan would be able to find us very easily. Assuming he'd parked in the far lot like I had, I texted back: *I'll come to you. Walk toward the sound of drums.* After telling my mom I'd be back in a few minutes, I began winding my way toward the path leading to the parking lot.

It didn't take long to spot him. He wore jeans and a baby blue golf shirt that I knew from a distance matched his eyes. I sighed to myself. It wasn't fair in the slightest. Why did he have to look so damn good all the time, even after all these years? Most people's looks faded with age, but Declan Kavanaugh seemed to age much like the fine whiskey he enjoyed. From what I could tell so far, it seemed like Liam had inherited his father's genes, making me wonder what kind of trouble he'd get into with the ladies when he got older.

When I got closer, I stopped and waved. His face lit up as soon as he saw me. The sight of that smile still made warmth spread over me. Maybe it always would.

He jogged over. "Hi."

"Hey." I pointed back towards the crowd. "We're this way."

He fell into step beside me. "Turned into a great day, didn't it?"

"Uh huh."

"This is your hometown, right? D'you know lots of these people?"

I slowed my pace. "A few. Why?"

232

He chuckled. "Much like at work, I know gossip tends to travel fast in small towns. Just wondered if you were hesitant to be seen with me?"

How ironic, I thought. Years ago we had to hide our relationship from prying eyes. Now we could be together out in the open, something I'd long thought I'd wanted, yet here we were, only spending time with each other because we had to for the sake of our son. Now it didn't matter who here saw us, because I didn't much care what they thought about me. Well, except for Liv. And Scott, but thankfully he wasn't here. Scott and Declan meeting was a scenario I very much wanted to avoid. However badly Liv thought of me now, if she knew the whole truth, it would be much worse.

"I doubt anyone cares who I talk to."

We walked a few more paces. Then he said, "So what have you told your friends about Liam's father?"

This was a question I wasn't expecting, although perhaps I should've been. I came to a halt and turned to him. "Well, Dee knows the truth. And Josh, now, too. That's it."

"What do the rest of them think? That you had a one night stand with a stranger?"

I shrugged. "Probably. I don't really..." I trailed off with a sigh.

Now he was looking at me curiously. "Don't what?"

"It's just that I don't have that many friends these days. Just Dee and her girlfriend. And Josh and Holly. All the rest kind of faded out of the picture when I moved to Richmond. Which I guess was on me. And now I sound totally pathetic, don't I?" I chuckled.

Declan frowned. "Didn't you used to be pretty social?"

"In case you haven't noticed, I've changed an awful lot." I started walking again and he hurried to keep up. "Speaking of old friends, I actually ran into my former best friend here earlier. Turns out her son is in Liam's class and they're buds. Who would've thought? She pretty much hates me now though, so *that* conversation was super fun."

"Why does she hate you?"

I sighed again. "Because I cut her out of my life. She's married to my ex now, and I admit that's been kinda weird, but it's not the whole reason. I just needed space after...well, after everything. I went all hermity for a long time."

"I noticed."

I glanced over at him. I had to stop myself from responding: *you did?*

My surprise must have shown on my face, because he flashed me a small smile. "Did you think I wouldn't?" he asked softly.

Once again, I deliberately didn't reply

We reached the table where my mom sat discussing the African drummers with one of her friends who had joined her in my absence.

"Hey Mom?" She looked up at me, at first with slight irritation at being disturbed. But she smiled when she saw who I was with. "This is Declan."

My mother got to her feet, still smiling widely. She reached for Declan's hand and gave it a pump. "Brenda York. So nice to see you again, Declan. I actually know your mother-in-law, at least a little. We did some volunteer work together several years back."

I didn't remember Mom telling me she knew Laura's mother. Not that it mattered.

"Oh yeah?" Declan said. "I just dropped my daughter Alexis off at their place."

"Of course. I'd forgotten you had a daughter. How old is she now?"

Before they could get too enmeshed in conversation, I said, "I'll just go grab Liam. Be right back."

Liam was not very happy to have to leave Marco, but when he saw Declan had arrived, he perked right up. Both Liv and her mother said goodbye to him, but only her mom wished me a great rest of my day.

"Hey, buddy," Declan said to Liam when we returned.

He stared solemnly at his father. "I made somethin' for you," he said shyly. Luckily the music had just stopped, or Declan wouldn't have heard him.

"You did? What is it?"

Liam tugged on my mother's sleeve. "Gramma, d'you have the picture I made?"

Mom smiled as she reached into her bag and pulled out a piece of sketch paper. It was a drawing of Liam's, one I hadn't seen before. I took it from her to have a closer look. It had two rough crayon stick figures, one sitting and one standing. Two lines went up from the one sitting to what might have been a tree, although it was purple, so I couldn't be sure.

"When did you draw this?" I asked Liam.

234

"After breakfast," he said, taking it out of my hands and presenting it to his father.

A huge smile crossed Declan's face as he stared at it. "Is that me pushing you on the swing, like we did last weekend?" he asked, raising his gaze back to Liam's.

Liam nodded.

"It's amazing. I love it."

Liam shuffled closer to Declan, both of them looking at his drawing together. "See that?" Liam pointed at a yellow, brown, and green squiggle in the corner.

"What is it? Wait, I know. Is it your sandbox with your new digger in it?"

"Yes!" Liam replied triumphantly. I had to give Declan credit; I would not have guessed that one.

Just then an accordion on stage sounded a few test notes. Another band, dressed in brightly colored Eastern European costumes, was about to start their set.

"Hey listen," Declan said to Liam, although his eyes shifted to mine. "I spotted a playground over by the parking lot. You wanna go over there? I'm sure I saw swings."

"Yes," Liam repeated. "Mommy, come," he said to me, reaching for my hand.

"Guess we're going for another walk," I told my mom. She seemed plenty occupied chatting with her friend, so I doubted she'd miss us.

Liam kept hold of my hand until we were away from the crowd. I deliberately fell a few steps behind the two of them and let them walk together. Once again, I was amazed by how much my son was a miniature version of his father.

When we got to the play area, Liam asked Declan to push him on the swings. I took a seat on a nearby bench and just watched them, much like I had in our backyard the week before. Once Liam grew bored with swinging, he ran to the play structure, climbing the steps to the top with Declan following as best as he could on the kid-sized bridges and platforms.

Liam, now in total show-off mode, grabbed onto the fireman's pole. Before he slid to the bottom, he called, "Daddy, watch this!"

I perked up, shading my eyes with one hand so I could see them better. That was the first time Liam had called Declan *Daddy*. I squinted, trying to see Declan's reaction, but, whether purposeful or not, his face was turned away from me. I couldn't help thinking that if things had been different this would have been a momentous moment for us both. Tears would've been shed. High fives would have been slapped. But if our lives had taken that path, this moment would have happened years ago, with us raising our son together as a family. The fact was that reality had been nothing like my fantasies of years past. Now I could only imagine how much hearing that word must mean to him.

They ran around for a while longer, but soon Declan ambled back over to me, a little short of breath, yet still smiling. He sat down beside me and we both watched Liam, who was taking turns on the tall slide with another boy about his age.

"He's a great kid," Declan said.

"I know."

"I mean, you've done a great job raising him. Single parenting isn't easy, I know."

I shrugged. "Thanks. I had plenty of help though. I had Dee and Terri. And now I have Mom. So at no point was I doing it on my own. Although I do need to start looking for a place for just us so my mom can have her house back."

"Oh yeah? Here? Or in Lynchburg?"

"Don't know yet. We'll see what I find."

Declan was quiet for a few seconds, his eyes fixed on Liam. "I'd be happy to help you find a place. That is, if you want my help."

I pushed a loose strand of hair behind my ear. "Maybe. I'll let you know."

"What's your timeframe?"

"Well, I told her we'd just stay for a few months until I could save up enough money. So maybe by Christmas. But I know she'll want us there over the holidays, so more likely it'll be later in the winter."

Liam came running up to us. "Mommy, can we get ice cream?" he asked, pointing to an ice cream truck parked along the edge of the trees.

Declan jumped right up. "Great idea, bud."

The three of us walked over and got in the line-up for cones. When we reached the front, I showed Liam the choices. "Chocolate dip," he said.

"Two chocolate dips," Declan told the teenage girl at the window. He turned back to me. "How 'bout you?"

"Doesn't matter," I replied. Then I quickly added, "Anything but strawberry."

236

His brows narrowed for a second, but he told the girl, "Make it three."

We got our ice cream and headed back to the playground. "Marco!" Liam shouted, taking off toward the play structure, ice cream already dripping down his hand. I predicted his cone's future would include a few more licks and then abandonment. Glancing around, I spotted Liv's mother standing beneath a tree talking to another woman while she watched her grandson.

Declan and I returned to the bench we'd vacated. We sat in silence, eating our ice cream as the boys played. I was just about to suggest we should head back to find my mom when he said, "This is just beyond surreal. Seven years ago, this was all I ever wanted. And now..." he trailed off.

My lips pressed into a hard line, but my eyes never left my son. "I've learned not to romanticize the past. The truth is, seven years ago I wanted to die. Now I have everything to live for."

Declan

Daylight was beginning to fade by the time I helped Amelia and her mom pack up their stuff. On the way to the parking lot, they invited me to come back to their place for dinner. I agreed on the condition that they let me pick up pizza, which earned me a "Yay" from Liam and a small smile from Amelia. She'd smiled several times over the course of the afternoon, which I knew I should have considered a win. Yet I was troubled.

Don't get me wrong—I was having an amazing day. Playing with Liam was a blast, and he'd even called me Daddy once, a moment I swear will be seared into my memory for the rest of my days. His mother, however, had spent most of the afternoon doing what she usually did when around other people: wearing her strong face and pretending she was happy for the sake of everyone else. I knew that face all too well, because I spent most of my time trying to do the same, although I admit I couldn't do it even remotely as well as she could. But try as she might to pretend she was cool with all of this, I could tell my presence still made her uncomfortable. And I got that, I really did.

When she'd admitted she'd wanted to die seven years ago, I'd understood that, too. It hurt like hell to hear it, but what I didn't think she realized was that the day she'd presumably been referring to was also one of the worst of my life. I'd been buried under a mountain of guilt and regret ever since, not just for what I'd done that day, but for so much more. Layers upon layers of it, and sometimes it got so heavy I could barely function.

We got to their house and Liam immediately ran to the bathroom. While he was gone, I asked Amelia if she'd mind if I took him with me to pick up the pizza.

Her lips pursed as she darted her eyes toward the closed bathroom door. Clearly, she was still hesitant to let him out of her sight. "You can come with, if you're worried I might run off with him," I said, punctuating the joke with a lopsided smile. It wasn't even slightly funny, but I wanted to diffuse the concern I could read in her eyes.

"No. It's fine." Amelia shook her head. "It's not that. He just sometimes stays in there a while. If you wait, the pizza'll be cold before you get back with it. But whatever, it's no big deal. We can always reheat it."

Nice cover, I thought, but didn't say. A minute later we heard a flush and the sound of hand washing. When Liam came into the hallway, I said, "Wanna come with me to get the pizza?"

Liam looked to his mother. With what I assumed was reluctance, she nodded, and when he got the okay, his whole face lit up. "Yes!" he yelled, running over to me and grabbing my hand. I tried to gauge Amelia's feelings. Much as I loved that Liam already seemed so taken with me, I knew our burgeoning relationship was causing her some trepidation.

"Back in ten," I assured her. "Don't call the cops if we're a few minutes late, okay?"

Her lips curved into a small smile, a fraction of the beatific smile I'd fallen hard for, but it still pleased me to see it. She dropped a kiss on Liam's cheek and we headed out the door. I'd put Alexis' old booster seat into the back of my car earlier. Although Liam was only four, he was big for his age, so I buckled him in.

"So which way to Pizza Palace?" I asked, catching his eye in the rearview mirror once I'd backed out onto the street.

Liam pointed forward. "That way."

When I got to the stop sign, I said, "Which way now? Left or right?" I'd driven past Pizza Palace dozens of times over the years and knew exactly where it was, but I thought Liam might get a kick out of directing me.

"Left." I looked in the mirror again. He was pointing right. Grinning, I turned right.

"How far should I go?

"Turn there, by the blue house."

I turned. We were coming into Swann's Landing's small downtown. "Is it on this street?" I asked.

"Over there. By that big white place. With the towers." He meant the pillars in front of the town hall. Pizza Palace was two doors down.

"Thank you," I said as I pulled into a parking space. "You give great directions."

"You're welcome." He sounded so pleased with himself I had to muffle my chuckle. Good on Amelia for teaching him manners. There were times Alexis still forgot to say please and thank you, and she was six years older.

Once I helped him unbuckle his seatbelt we went inside. A tall guy with a blonde buzz cut stood at the counter paying for his order. As he turned around, his eyes landed on Liam. Then they rose to me. I had a weird sense that I'd seen him somewhere before, so I smiled. He didn't smile back; he just brushed past us and left. Maybe I'd been mistaken.

"Two large 'zas for York," I told the guy at the cash register.

"Be right up," he replied.

I paid him and before long our pizzas were on the passenger seat filling my car with the tantalizing aroma of pepperoni and fresh baked bread as we headed back.

After dinner, Liam dragged out a board game and the four of us sat in the living room laughing and playing *Trouble*. At least until Amelia noticed him yawn.

"Okay, little man. I think it's time for your bath," she said.

Liam's lower lip jutted out, his expression going from happy to indignant in a split second. "No! Not yet! I wanna play s'more."

"You can play tomorrow. Right now you need to get ready for beddy." Amelia turned to me. "Thanks for hanging out today."

"No problem." I made no move to rise.

She frowned, just a little, but I caught it. "Sticking around for a bit?"

"You mind? Maybe I could tuck him in before I go?"

Instead of replying, Amelia shrugged. Taking firm hold of a reluctant Liam, she led him upstairs. A few minutes later I heard the sound of running water filling the bathtub.

I chatted with her mom for a bit while I waited. It was clear Brenda York approved of me. Over the course of our conversation, she questioned me about my job, Alexis, even my house. I could tell she thought Amelia should be dating me, not just allowing me to spend supervised time with Liam. That was a point we definitely agreed on, but Amelia had to make her own choices regardless of what her mother or anyone else thought.

It crossed my mind that at some point she might want to date, and that there would be absolutely nothing I could do about it except wish her well and offer to watch Liam when she went out. And that would pretty much suck. The very thought of her with another guy was like a knife to the gut. It'd been brutal when she'd still been married and I'd had to shove images of her with her ex out of my head on a daily basis.

At last Liam came bouncing down the steps in his blue and red shark pajamas, kissed his grandma goodnight, and grabbed my hand. "Mommy says you're reading me a story tonight," he said, tugging me up.

Grinning, I said, "Lead the way."

When we reached the top of the stairs, I glanced into the open door on the left and spotted Amelia's jacket draped over a chair. *Her childhood room*, I thought. *Must be weird as hell to be back after all these years.*

Liam pulled me down the hall to another open door. Inside, Amelia was sitting on a single bed with *Charlotte's Web* in her hands. She got to her feet and handed me the book. "We're on chapter eight."

I smiled as I took it. I'd read this to Alexis a few years back. She'd cried at the end when Charlotte died, and I'll begrudgingly admit the corners of my eyes might have been a little damp as well. Sad as it had made her, she'd loved it so much she'd asked me to read it again a few months later.

"You gonna stay and listen?" I asked Amelia as Liam threw back the covers and climbed into bed.

She looked surprised, as if the idea hadn't even occurred to her. "No, you go ahead. I'll come back and kiss him goodnight when you're done." Then she disappeared. I didn't hear the creak of footsteps on the stairs, so I assumed she'd gone to her room. To give us some privacy, but still remain nearby in case Liam needed her. Of course.

"So catch me up," I said to Liam as I sat on the edge of the bed. "What part are you at?" His eyes were bright and curious as he did his best to explain the story, but by the time I finished reading the chapter, his lids had begun to flutter. I closed the book and set it on the small table. "Night, buddy," I whispered, pulling the covers up around him. "I'll go get your mom."

"Night Daddy," he replied softly, his voice the lazy, hazy sound of one on the verge of sleep.

There it was again. *Daddy.* I smiled as I kissed his forehead, marveling once more at the simple fact of him. Of this. Of all of it. It was a goddamn miracle is what it was. One I didn't deserve, but was really fucking grateful for, you know?

My heart was full of warm fuzzies as I got up and went into the hall to let Amelia know Liam was almost out. She was sitting on her bed looking at her phone, her dark hair down and half-covering her face. I had a sudden urge to go to her and pull her into my arms, to tell her how happy I was and how much I loved them both. But I didn't. I knew better. And I was right. As soon as she saw me, she got to her feet and brushed past me on her way to Liam's room. I knew she wasn't deliberately being rude or cold, she just had more important things to do. But I still felt a pinch inside as it was hammered home once again what we no longer were to each other.

I headed downstairs but instead of rejoining Brenda in the living room, I went out onto the porch for some fresh air. Leaning against one of the posts, I checked my messages as I waited, assuming Amelia would want me gone as soon as possible, so would come looking for me to say goodnight once Liam was asleep.

And I wasn't wrong. A few minutes later, I heard the door open as she came outside. "There you are," she said. "I wondered if you'd left."

I straightened up as she approached. "Not yet. I should probably get on my way though."

She nodded. "Thanks again for today. Liam had a great time. He really likes you."

"That's good. Because I really like him, too."

"I know you do. I'm...I'm glad you two are bonding." My brows shot up and she noticed my reaction. "No, really, I am. I see now how wrong I was to keep him from you. You're good for him. And Liam's happiness is all that matters."

"What about your happiness?"

She drew back a little in surprise. "I'm happy if he's happy."

I frowned, recalling some of the things she'd said earlier. Although it cut me deep, I didn't dare ask about her wanting to die years ago. But the other thing didn't feel so risky. "Can I ask you something?"

"What's that?"

Bracing my forearm against the post, I said, "Why not strawberry?"

Amelia's eye's narrowed in confusion.

"Earlier. At the ice cream truck. You said anything but strawberry, but I could've sworn you used to like it."

"It's complicated." She shrugged.

Of course it is. Isn't everything? Shit, complicated is all we know.

From her closed off expression, I figured whatever it was it was something painful, and probably something to do with me. Deciding to push my luck a little, I said, "Why?"

Amelia looked down at her fingers. "I don't really wanna talk about it."

Okay, maybe pushing wasn't such a great idea. "It's okay" I told her. "You don't have to—"

"Fine," she sighed. "It was a long time ago, but…fine. I'll tell you."

I stared at her, willing her to look at me, but her eyes remained downcast.

"That day—the day you…ended things—I went for a walk. To clear my head or whatever. And some kid had dropped their strawberry ice cream on the sidewalk. It was really hot that day and it was all melting into a pink puddle." She stopped. A few seconds went by and I wasn't sure if she'd even continue. At last she blew out a puff of air. "And it just hit me: *I* was like that ice cream. Discarded and forgotten and…and just…worthless. Slowly melting away until there's nothing left. Like it was never even there. I haven't been able to stomach it since."

Fuck.

A bolt of guilt stabbed me and I had to grip the post tighter to keep myself upright. Shit, I'd hurt her *so* much. I hated myself for it. I didn't—couldn't—reply at first. And she still wouldn't look at me.

"What if…" I started, but I had to stop to clear the lump from my throat. "What if that kid never forgot that ice cream? What if he missed it so much it killed him inside, and nothing could ever replace it? What if he regretted having dropped it *every single day*?" My voice became a whisper. "What if it was the worst mistake he ever made?"

Amelia finally raised her gaze back to mine, her brown eyes huge, but still guarded. I could tell my words had gotten through, though: her lower lip trembled. Not much, but a little. Enough. Enough to know my unplanned admission hadn't been a mistake. She might not have wanted to know that our split hurt me, too. Maybe it was easier for her to assume I'd been callous and cruel and tossed her aside like trash. It probably was. But that wasn't even remotely true and—perhaps selfishly—I needed her to know it.

Whatever her thoughts were on the matter, Amelia still couldn't look at me for long. After a few seconds, she averted her eyes back down at her hands, now knotted and twisting together.

She didn't reply.

Chapter 25

Amelia

My stomach rumbled and I glanced at the time. It was nearly eleven-thirty, close enough to lunchtime that I wasn't going to bother opening another email. I grabbed my wallet from my bag and went next door to Kaitlyn's office.

"Time to eat," I announced.

She looked up at me, a frown line forming between her brows. "I think I'm gonna skip the caf today. I'm swamped."

"If you need some help, I'm happy to take some requests when we get back. C'mon." From her expression, I knew she was about to offer more protests, so I added, "I'm not taking no for an answer today. I have to tell you guys something, and I'd rather not have to say it twice."

Kaitlyn perked right up at that. "What is it?"

I smiled, knowing dangling a carrot would work. "Come along and you'll find out."

She shook her head in mock-annoyance, but she also stood and reached for her bag.

After we got our food, we headed for our usual table. Sam was already there. Before I could even get a spoonful of soup to my lips, Kaitlyn told her, "Amelia has some news." Both sets of eyes turned to me expectantly. "Well?"

"I, uh…" My cheeks grew hot. "There's something I need to tell you. I should've told you when I first came back, but then I didn't, and the days went by, and it all just felt weirder and more awkward that I hadn't said anything in the first place."

"Well whatever it is, time to spill it already," Sam said with a smile. I wasn't so sure she'd be smiling once she found out what I was hiding.

On impulse, I took my phone from my pocket and pulled up a photo of Liam I'd taken a few days before. Before I could show it to them, Sam said, "Wait, don't tell me—you've got a secret boy toy, don't you?"

"Not likely!" I snorted, although her comment was kind of ironic considering the secret relationship with Liam's father that I'd had to hide from them for months during my first stint here. I turned the phone so they could both see the picture. "But I do have a boy in my life. My son, Liam."

Sam squinted at my screen, then looked back at me with confusion. "*What*? You have a kid and you didn't tell us?"

"Shhh," I cautioned. "I'd still kinda like to keep my private life private."

"But not from us," Kaitlyn said. She took my phone from my hand so she could see the photo better. "He's totally adorable. How old?"

"Four. He just started Kindergarten."

"So what's the deal with his father?" Sam asked, picking up her sandwich. "When and how did you meet? If I recall right, you were single at Josh's wedding, weren't you?"

I bit my lip. "Actually…it's funny you mention it, because that was the night I got pregnant."

I heard Kaitlyn suck in her breath beside me, but it was Sam whose reaction I watched. She narrowed her brows. "Are you serious? Who'd you hook up with at the wedding? Last time I saw you, you were talking to…" Her eyes shot wide. "Hold on. I remember there was a fight over at the bar and you..."

"You were trying to help him," Kaitlyn continued, her own eyes also huge. "He was really drunk and you were trying to help. You left with him. I assumed you were taking him up to his room."

"I was," I cut in. "Josh was busy, and for his sake I was trying to avoid an embarrassing scene."

"Wait. *What?*" Sam grabbed my phone again and studied Liam's photo. Her other hand shot out and took hold of my wrist as she looked back up at me. "Are you seriously telling me right now that your baby daddy is frickin' *Voldemort*?"

"Shhh," I said again, glancing around nervously. My face felt like it was on fire. I think heat was radiating off my skin. Nodding, I lowered my voice to a whisper. "*Please* don't make this into a big thing. It happened. It was totally consensual. And in the morning we went our separate ways. Everything's good. There's nothing to freak out about."

Sam snorted. "I beg to differ! Jesus, girl, you had his kid? That's a pretty huge *thing*." She was doing her best to keep her voice down but she was still several decibels louder than I would've preferred. I couldn't help scanning the room again, but no one seemed to be paying us any attention.

"And he knows?" Kaitlyn asked me. "You told him, right?"

Turning back to her, I nodded again. "Oh yeah. Of course. We're not together or anything, but we're…we're fine. I mean, sometimes it's a little awkward, kinda, but the two of them, they pretty much adore each other. So I deal. He only sees him on weekends. Like I said before, it's all good." I saw no need to tell them that Declan had only recently found out. That would just mean a whole lot more explaining. And explaining our history was the last thing I wanted to do.

"Okay," Kaitlyn smiled. "I mean, if you're cool with it, then we're cool with it." She nudged Sam with her elbow. "Right, Sam?"

Sam still stared at me in shock, her sandwich untouched on its plate. "Ryan's never said a word to me about this. Does he know?"

I shrugged. "I have no idea."

"So he's never met…what's your kid's name again?"

"Liam."

"Right. So Ryan hasn't even met his own nephew?"

"Not yet, no. I'm sure he will at some point. The holidays will be here before long. Maybe then."

"That's a bit weird, isn't it? You don't even know if Volde—" Kaitlyn nudged Sam with her elbow. "If *he's* even told his family about your son? After four years? Why the big secret?"

I sighed. "Maybe he's told them. Maybe he hasn't. I haven't asked and he hasn't said. The truth is we're still figuring things out. Don't forget I only moved back a few months ago. Before that, things were…more complicated."

Kaitlyn put an arm around my shoulders. "It's clear this isn't your favorite subject. Maybe we should stop barraging you with questions."

"Fine," Sam agreed with a frown. It was obvious she still had loads more to say. "For now, anyway."

"Thanks," I said. "I know it's a huge bomb to drop, but I couldn't keep this from you guys forever."

"Well, we're glad you told us. Now you'll just have to invite us over to meet him sometime soon."

"I can definitely do that," I agreed, at last picking up my spoon and starting to eat my now lukewarm soup.

Declan

"Ready?" Colleen asked, her head popping around the edge of my open office door. I glanced at the clock and sighed. It was time to go. Patrick had scheduled a company meeting this afternoon to announce some new clients, a few new hires, and to pump everyone up about the Christmas party next month. I'd have skipped it, but I knew my absence would be noticed and questioned if I didn't at least show my face. So I got up and joined my assistant and a few others on their way to the cafeteria.

The room was already crowded when we arrived. Colleen went to join a friend of hers who'd saved her a seat and I found a place to stand along the side. The long tables had been folded flat and now leaned against the back wall. All the chairs were lined up in rows. The far end of the cafeteria had been set up with spotlights, speakers, and a microphone. I scanned the room until I spotted Amelia sitting beside Kaitlyn in the second row from the back. Josh was on the other side of Kaitlyn. He leaned in to speak to her and while they chatted, Amelia glanced around until her eyes locked with mine. I fluttered my fingers at her and she give me a small smile.

Had she been searching for my face in the crowd? I covered my mouth to hide the grin that surfaced. Funny how this place sometimes felt like high school, looking for your crush among the masses. Not that I thought she had a crush on me. But she used to, way back when. Was it so inconceivable that we might rediscover what we'd once had?

Before I could think more on it, the lights dimmed and two spotlights came on as Patrick, all suited and booted for the occasion, approached the microphone. He began to speak. "I

want to thank you all for taking time out of your busy day..."
That was about the point where I tuned out. I already knew his
entire speech, as he'd run it by Ryan, myself, and a few others
in an executive meeting a few days ago.

Again my eyes wandered, picking out faces I knew in the
crowd. Strangely, my brother was nowhere to be seen. That
was odd. Ryan knew full well today's meeting was mandatory.
Had he had a client meeting he couldn't get out of? My gaze
landed once more on Amelia. Her attention was fixed on my
step-father, good little employee that she was. I spotted her
phone clutched in her fingers on her lap. Shuffling a step to the
right so Marilyn Silver blocked any view of my hands, I pulled
out my own phone and with a smirk texted her: *That monotone
will put us all in a coma. But better than working, right?*

When her phone vibrated, I saw her frown. It morphed to a
small smile when she looked down and read my message. Her
eyes shot to mine and she nodded.

I flashed her a grin and, assuming she'd go back to listening
to Patrick, began reading a poster Nicole had put up about the
Christmas party. Before I got halfway down, my own phone
vibrated.

You look bored.

Yep, I responded. Once more I glanced around the room.
Then I wrote: *Lady in row in front of you and 3 seats left?
Nearly asleep.* The woman in question—I think her name was
Jessica—had bobbed her chin up sharply at least twice now as
she tried to keep herself from dozing off. Patrick's speeches
weren't exactly known for rousing excitement, as most of the
employees of BWK were well aware.

I watched Amelia glance over at Jessica. She pressed the
palm of her hand to her nose and mouth, presumably to
smother a snort of laughter. A minute later, my phone buzzed
again.

Marilyn's trying to hide her yawn.

Half this room will be out by the time he's done, I typed back.
This time she didn't respond. I think she was trying to pay
attention to what was being said about the new hires. By the
time he got to the third one, I'd lost interest again.

*To your left, against the wall by the side door. Those 2 are
def hooking up. Check out their body language.*

Amelia glanced their way, then back at me. One side of her
mouth curled up into a half-smile. As Patrick started in on
information about the Christmas party, we continued to text

back and forth in the dark of the room. Once I saw Kaitlyn lean in and whisper something, likely asking who she was texting. I wondered if Amelia told her the truth. Probably she'd made something up to derail further questions. It was doubtful she'd want to admit she was still friends with me.

But I knew my messages had amused her this afternoon, which not only made me happy, to tell the truth it also made me pretty damn proud of myself. I still had it. My charm, or whatever the hell it was about me that made her like me in the first place. She wasn't completely immune, even now. Try as she might to resist; I'd still found a way in. I could still make her smile.

And I intended to keep on making her smile for as long as she was willing to keep on letting me.

On Saturday, I set two steaming bowls of pasta on the breakfast bar and turned around to call Alexis for lunch. Before I could even open my mouth, she bounced into the kitchen with a big smile.

"Do I smell mac 'n cheese?" she asked hopefully.

"Good nose on ya," I replied, sliding onto my favorite stool. She jumped up beside me and dug in. I took a bite, chewing thoughtfully as I watched her eat. It was about time she knew she had a little brother. It was also about time she got to meet said little brother. I just couldn't think of a good way to broach the subject delicately. Blurting out 'Hey, guess what? You've got a secret brother!' didn't seem like the most sensitive way to go about it, especially knowing how excited she'd been back when she found out Laura was pregnant. Losing her mother and unborn sister had—of course—scarred her deeply. I couldn't help worrying how she'd react when she found out about Liam. But she needed to know and putting it off was only delaying the inevitable.

Then I remembered Josh saying a few days ago that Amelia and Liam were coming to visit them today. I wondered if any of them would mind if we just happened to drop by. I knew Liam would be happy to see me, and I was supposed to spend time with him tomorrow anyway. The grown-ups, however, might be a different story. I could always text Josh and ask, but that would risk a no. Sometimes it was better to ask for forgiveness than permission.

"Hey Lex?" She looked up at me, chewing a mouthful of macaroni. Before she could attempt an answer and end up spitting bits of food everywhere, I kept talking. "Didn't you say you wanted to give Emily one of your stuffies? Wanna go visit Uncle Josh and Aunt Holly this afternoon?"

She swallowed, grabbed a napkin to swipe her lips, and replied. "I'm gonna give her Professor Pink Bear. Remember how she wouldn't put him down last time they were here?"

"I do. And I think that's super nice of you. You'd make a great big sister."

"I know," she replied solemnly, her spoon already back in her mouth. And she would be, given time. She just didn't know it yet.

After I cleared the lunch dishes away, she packed her knapsack for Gramma's and we got in the car. I'd take her to Swann's Landing after we popped into Josh and Holly's. As I came around the corner on their street, I spotted Amelia's Honda in the driveway. Hopefully my surprise visit wouldn't irritate her. I didn't think it would, but it was definitely a chance.

I rang the doorbell. We waited on the front step, and when no one answered after a couple of minutes, I rang it again.

"Maybe they're not home?" Alexis said doubtfully, tugging on my sleeve.

"Give it another minute. They might be out back." I poked the bell a third time. If they still didn't hear it, I'd go around the side of the house and check the backyard. It was a beautiful sunny day, so sitting outside made sense. The third time was the proverbial charm, though. About thirty seconds later, I noticed the curtain flutter as someone looked out. The door was subsequently pulled open and we found ourselves face to face with a confused Holly.

"Oh hi," she said, smiling at Alexis. "Hope you weren't waiting long. We're sitting out back and I thought I heard the bell." Her eyes flashed to mine. "I didn't realize Josh invited you guys over."

"No worries," I said, not bothering to explain that he hadn't as we followed her through the kitchen and out the back door. Josh and Amelia were sitting at the patio table with drinks in their hands watching the kids play. Amelia wore a deep red shirt that looked absolutely incredible on her. But then again, I was extremely biased. When they looked up and saw me, their eyes shot to each other with matching 'what the fuck' expressions.

Josh got to his feet. "Hey kiddo. Nice bear." He ruffled Alexis' hair with a smile.

"It's for Emily," she told him.

"Go say hi if you want," I said to her, pointing to the rear of the yard. Liam and Emily sat on the grass near the hedge playing with what looked from this distance to be Woody and Buzz Lightyear. Alexis trotted over to them, the pink teddy clutched in her arms.

Josh's cheerful expression slipped away as he turned to me. "So what brings you by?"

"Sorry man, I know I should've texted, but we were on our way to her grandma's and she asked about giving the teddy to Em and I just decided to swing by." My gaze shifted to Amelia as I added, "Hope you don't mind."

Holly and Josh also turned their attention to Amelia. She smiled, maybe a bit uncomfortably, or maybe that was just my imagination, and said, "Not at all."

"Great!" I dropped into the empty seat beside her.

"Would you like a beer, Declan?" Holly asked me.

"Just a Coke if you have it. I have to drive again soon."

Amelia's gaze returned to the kids. She leaned toward me and dropped her voice. "Does Alexis know about Liam yet?"

"Not yet."

Josh frowned. "Don't you think you probably should've told her *before* bringing her over? Especially since you knew Amelia and Liam would be here?"

"You knew we were here?" Amelia asked, arching a brow.

I shrugged. "Josh might've mentioned it."

She gave me a look like she was trying to figure out what I was up to. Either I wasn't very difficult to read or—more likely—she just knew me too well. "Let me guess," she said. "You thought maybe if you just showed up and they met, you'd have a good excuse to break the news to her?"

"Maybe," I said with another shrug.

"Declan! That's a huge thing to drop on an unsuspecting kid. You can't just sideswipe her and then force her to immediately have to deal with it! Especially after…" She trailed off, but I knew what she'd been about to say. Her expression morphed from irritation to sympathy. She'd just understood exactly why I hadn't told my daughter yet.

"She's right," Josh agreed, still sounding disapproving. He still didn't get it, and I didn't feel much like explaining.

251

Holly returned with my Coke and joined us at the table. Josh filled her in on our conversation. Instead of mirroring her husband's judgy face, she asked, "So how do you want to tell her?"

"Don't know yet. I hoped maybe the chance might present itself naturally. Or I'll tell her after we leave. I'll figure it out."

Amelia shook her head. "You do realize once Liam sees you, Alexis is going to notice how familiar he is with you. And what if he calls you Daddy?"

"I didn't think of that," I admitted. I hadn't thought any of this through very well at all. I was just running on instinct.

Her chin lifted in the direction of the kids and I saw Liam looking our way. "Well you'd better think about it fast."

Holly glanced over her shoulder at them as well. "Oh geez. Em has chocolate milk all over her shirt." She got to her feet and called her daughter over. Then she put a hand on Josh's shoulder. "C'mon inside and help me get her changed."

As Emily started running toward her parents, Liam recognized me and broke into a huge smile. I couldn't help smiling right back as he got up and trotted over. "Hey buddy!" I called rising to greet him as he flung himself into my waiting arms.

Josh, Holly, and Emily went into the house. Alexis had also come back and as I met her eyes over Liam's shoulder, I noticed her frown. "You know my dad?" she said to Liam. He turned and looked up at her in confusion.

This needed to be nipped in the bud pronto. I sat back down. "Lex, I want you to meet a couple of people very important to me." I gestured toward Amelia. "This is Amelia York. She also works at BWK, and we've known each other a long time." Then I looked back at Liam. "And this is her son, Liam."

"Hi," she said, a little shyly, a little impatiently. I still hadn't explained why this boy had hugged her father. Or why his hand was still on my arm.

Liam just stared at her.

"Come closer, hun." She shuffled forward and stood beside Liam. Her eyes darted accusingly to where he was touching me. "So. The thing is. Amelia and I have something super important we need to tell you both. It's gonna sound crazy, but it's true. You and Liam are, well…you're brother and sister."

Alexis looked at me as if I'd gone completely batshit crazy. "I'm not his sister!" she said indignantly.

"You are. Well, technically you're his half-sister. But the half part doesn't matter." I turned to Liam, but he'd slid behind the back of my chair and climbed into his mother's lap. "Liam, what do you think? Isn't it cool to have a big sister?"

Liam's eyes shifted from Alexis to me and back again. He didn't reply. Amelia pulled him against her chest in a sideways hug. "I don't think he knows what to think yet. It's a lot to absorb. He's going to need time to get used to it. They both will. All of us will."

"I'm not his sister," Alexis repeated. "Don't tell him I'm his sister when I'm not!"

I turned my attention back to her. Her fiery expression reminded me uncannily of her mother. "I'm sorry Lex, I should've told you this sooner. But now you know. And it's okay to be confused and upset. It's also okay to be angry with me. You're completely entitled to feel whatever you're feeling right now. But I hope you'll be able to get used to the idea, because you're likely gonna be seeing a lot of Liam going forward." *And hopefully his mother, too.*

Her forehead furrowed. "How old is he?" she asked, pointing at Liam as if I wouldn't know who she was talking about. Liam's thumb was now lodged firmly in his mouth, his eyes fixed on Alexis.

"He's four," Amelia answered for me. "Don't be too mad at your dad. He just found out himself not that long ago. Liam and I only moved to Swann's Landing recently. So I know this is all pretty weird. For all of us."

Alexis' face softened a little. She shrugged her small shoulders. "It *is* weird. *Super* weird." To me, she asked, "So he's really my brother? Like, for really real?"

"Really, really. And he's pretty awesome. I think you're gonna love him." I indicated an empty chair. "Why don't you sit? Ask us any questions you have. We'll try our best to answer."

She sat in Holly's vacated chair. After looking hard at Liam and Amelia for a few seconds, she turned back to me. "I have one question."

"What's that?" I replied, hoping it wasn't about how Liam came to be conceived.

"Can I have a drink of your Coke?"

I laughed, pushing my glass across the table. "Help yourself." And just like that, the entire mood lightened.

Liam pulled his thumb from his mouth. "What's her name?" he whispered to his mother.

"Alexis," she whispered back with a smile. "You could just ask her yourself, you know."

His gaze shifted to me. "Why d'you call her Lex?" he said at a normal volume.

"It's short for Alexis," my daughter told him before I could answer. "My mom and dad called me that when I was little. But no one else really does. Just Dad. And sometimes Uncle Ryan."

Liam looked thoughtful. "Like Superman's enemy, Lex Luthor?"

I chuckled. "Yeah, kinda. But she's not a super villain." I flashed Alexis a grin. "At least not that I know of." She giggled and the sound made my heart feel lighter.

"Can I call you Lex?" Liam asked her.

She bit her lower lip. "I guess. If you want."

"Okay." Liam smiled at her. In that moment I knew he'd be fine with having a big sister. Alexis would take a bit longer to adjust to the new normal, but that was okay. She could take as long as she needed.

The screen door banged open as Emily ran outside ahead of her parents. "C'mon 'Lexis, c'mon Liam," she called. They got up and ran off to play with her again. I knew Alexis was probably still reeling from the massive bomb she'd just gotten dropped on her, but outwardly you wouldn't have known it. She raced ahead of the younger kids to grab Buzz Lightyear up first, before they could reach the abandoned toys.

"Well, that wasn't so bad," I said.

"Could've been worse," Amelia agreed. "Liam seems fascinated by her. Not too sure what Alexis thinks, but that's pretty understandable."

I looked back at my daughter. She was laughing as she made Buzz fly over Liam's head. "I think she'll be fine. Kids are remarkably resilient to change."

"I hope so," Amelia said. "Liam's had enough change for a lifetime crammed into the past few months. But yeah, so far he seems to be adjusting well to it all."

"That's great. Especially since you're going to have another move coming up," Holly said.

I glanced at Amelia. "You already found a place?"

"I haven't even started looking. But I need to. Soon."

"I've been trying to talk her into moving to Lynchburg," Josh said. "But she's being resistant."

"Liam just started school a few months ago. I don't want to make him change schools now that he's made some new friends. Moving from Richmond was pretty hard on him and he's finally getting used to things. So I might look for an apartment in Swann's Landing. That way my mom can still watch him after school, too."

"Makes sense," I agreed. She shot me a little half smile.

Alexis dashed over to the table again, seizing my Coke in both hands and chugging several big gulps. Before I could reprimand her for not asking first, she'd put it down and ran back to the smaller kids. "You're welcome!" I called after her. She looked over at me and I scrunched up my face, tilting it to one side and crossing my eyes. It looked like she giggled, but I couldn't tell for sure because both Amelia and Holly burst out laughing at my antics.

I turned to Amelia with a grin and she was grinning right back at me. And I swore I felt even more weight lift.

Before I got on the road to Swann's Landing the next day, I made a pit stop at my brother's. I wanted to borrow his leaf blower and it was on my way out of town, so I figured why the hell not.

Diana answered the door of their white bungalow. Her hair hung loose around her face and she wore a long, thick sweater, though the day was warm. As usual, she looked irritated. "Ryan's not here," she told me tersely.

Although vaguely disappointed my brother wasn't around, I didn't much give a fuck about her pissy mood. "That's fine. I just wanna borrow his leaf blower. Is it in the garage? I'll go grab it and have it back tomorrow before he even misses it."

She shrugged, stepping aside and opening the front door wider. The other door into the garage was down a short flight of stairs from the entryway. I could've just gone in from the driveway, but maybe they kept the overhead door locked these days. As I headed for the steps, she said, "Wait. Can I speak to you for a moment?"

I turned back, peering at her more closely. Her forehead was shiny. She had dark circles under her eyes. A cluster of pimples marred her chin. That wasn't normal. I mean, I knew she could cover these things with makeup, but still. Something was off. Usually Diana looked like she'd just stepped off the pages of a fashion magazine. Even at home. But today she seemed tired, like trying to pull herself together was simply too much work to bother.

"You look like shit."

She rolled her eyes. "Thanks a lot. Such a charmer. It's no wonder you're single."

"Well you do. Are you sick?" I took a step backward. "Because I don't wanna catch it."

"I'm not sick. I'm…" She stopped with a sigh. "Have you noticed anything unusual about your brother's behavior lately?"

I thought back. "I haven't seen him around work all that much. And he missed a meeting on Wednesday he was supposed to be at. But I assumed he was just tied up with clients. Why?"

"I'm worried about him." She exhaled a low sigh.

"Why?" I repeated, frowning.

"I think he might be using again."

My eyes narrowed. Not this again. No way. After nearly offing himself last time, Ryan couldn't possibly be so fucking stupid. "What makes you think that?"

"He's been acting strange lately. And he's been out a lot. Multiple times a week. Sometimes he says it's work, sometimes friends." Diana eyed me closely. "A few times he said he was with you."

I hadn't hung out with my brother since the day I'd told him about Liam. "How long ago did he tell you that?"

"I don't know. I think last week."

Shit. "It's been at *least* two weeks. Maybe three."

"So he's been lying to me. Which means either he's screwing some slut on the side, or he's using again."

"Or it could be something way less exciting. Like maybe he's been planning some cool surprise for you? Maybe it's not that big a deal?"

"Maybe. But he hasn't been himself. I know him. I can tell. He barely spends time with me anymore. Something's off, and I don't think it's just…" She trailed off, breaking eye contact.

"What? What were you about to say?"

"Stress. I don't think it's just stress."

I arched a brow. "Oh come on. What were you *really* gonna say? Ryan deals with stress all the time. It's part of the job."

Diana's eyes shifted back to mine. She sat on the steps leading up to the living room and dragged a hand through her dark hair. It fell limply back into place around her shoulders. "I'm pregnant," she said quietly.

"Are you serious?"

She nodded. "We haven't told anyone yet. Ryan isn't ready to."

"Congratulations," I said, breaking into a smile. I really meant it, too. My brother would make an awesome dad. Well, as long as he stayed firmly on the wagon. "Ry must be over the moon. Maybe he's been out secretly stocking up on onesies and diapers?"

"Not likely," she muttered. "He's been pretty freaked out by the whole idea, actually. It came as a bit of a surprise, and I don't think he's taking it too well. He claims he's fine, but the frantic look in his eyes whenever he's reminded of it says otherwise."

"And you suspect it might've driven him to relapse?"

She shrugged helplessly. *Helpless.* Now there's a word I never thought I'd use to describe Diana Sharpe. She was one of the strongest, most confident women I knew. A total bitch sometimes, but I tried not to hold it against her. She loved my brother and she was good for him, so I just did my best to get under her skin whenever I saw her. But now was no time for ribbing.

"Look, try not to worry. I'll see what I can find out. Have you searched the house? I know all his little hidey-holes."

"Of course," she snorted. "That was the first thing I did. I've gone over the place end to end. Multiple times. I haven't found anything, but I assume he'd be a lot more careful now."

"You mind if I have a look?"

She waved past herself up the steps. "Be my guest."

So I searched. I searched every nook and every cranny of every room in the place, including the garage. Diana padded after me in her fuzzy slippers, but she didn't try to help. She just leaned against the door jamb and watched. When I finally emerged from the garage with only the leaf blower in my hands, we regarded each other with matching frowns. "Well, either he's being a hell of a lot smarter about it than he used to be, or there's nothing to find. But better safe than sorry. I'll check his office tomorrow."

"Thanks, Declan."

"No need to thank me. He's my brother. Don't worry, we'll get to the bottom of whatever's up with him. I promise."

"I'll hold you to that." Her hand slid to her stomach, fingers splayed protectively.

"Hey, so congrats again. Can't believe I'm finally gonna be an uncle."

"Don't forget you know nothing about this. Not a peep, okay?" She smiled wanly, but it didn't reach her eyes.

I ran my fingers across my mouth mimicking closing a zipper. "Go rest. Take care of the both of you. I'm sure Ryan will be back soon."

"He'd better be," she said, and at last I heard a hint of that old familiar fire in her voice.

Chapter 26

Amelia

"Daddy has a brother. D'you know that, Mommy?" Liam told me.

"I do," I replied, tucking the blankets up around his shoulders. He wriggled beneath them. "He works at the same place as we do, so I know him."

"Daddy has a sister, too. But she lives far away."

I nodded. "I think she lives in Buffalo."

"Where's that?"

"Up north. By the border to Canada."

"Oh." His eyes were big. "That's far."

"It's not that far, really. I think she visits him and Alexis on holidays."

Liam smiled. "Like Christmas?"

"Maybe," I said. "Are you excited for Christmas already?"

"Yes! Will Daddy and Lex come here for Christmas?"

I shrugged. "I don't know. We haven't talked about it yet."

"Hope so." He settled back into his pillow and I hoped that was a sign he was ready for sleep. But no. "Did you know Daddy lives near Emily?"

Liam had been peppering me with questions and comments about Declan ever since his dad had left to go pick up Alexis hours ago. This afternoon he'd taken Liam to the park to feed the ducks, and clearly between tossing chunks of bread they'd talked a lot about Declan's life. I'd decided to stay behind this time so they could do some one on one bonding. I knew Liam was perfectly safe with Declan, and that I'd need to get used to them spending time together without me, but I'd still gotten a little twinge inside when they'd walked out the door. Though I was fully aware I had nothing to worry about, I couldn't seem to help it. It was nothing like the swell of panic I'd felt the first time I'd watched them leave, so I took comfort in knowing things were becoming easier. Slowly.

I indulged Liam for a few more rapid fire facts about his father, then I kissed him goodnight and shut off the lamp.

"Love you, little man," I whispered as I got up to go.

I heard a yawn, then, "Love you, Mommy."

No matter how often I heard those words, they always gave me a deep rush of pleasure. Every single time.

I went down the hall into my own room, picking up my phone from the nightstand as I sat on the bed. There was a text from Dee.

Hey girly. Just checking in. How r u & L? How's it going with D?

It had been a few weeks since I'd last chatted with her. *FaceTime?* I typed back, getting up to close my door so my voice wouldn't carry down the hall and through the crack of Liam's not-quite-closed door.

My phone beeped and I opened the app. Dee's concerned face stared back at me. "Something wrong?" she asked.

"No, no. I'm fine. Just hadn't talked to you in a while."

"I hear ya on that. Life just keeps getting in the way. The salon's been insane! Christmas parties seem to be earlier and earlier every year."

I smiled. "That's good, though. Keeps your bills paid."

"True, true." Dee nodded. "So, more importantly, how're things with *you*. How's it been, having to spend time with *him*?"

I didn't need to ask who she meant. Exhaling a small sigh, I said, "Weird."

"Yeah."

"But it's getting easier," I added. "Like, it's still kind of awkward, and maybe it always will be, but...it's not as bad as I'd worried it'd be. He's...I don't know."

She looked dubious. "You don't know? Please. You do *so* know. He's trouble. A heap of it."

I chewed my lower lip. "He's okay."

"You sure about that?"

"Liam absolutely adores him. You should see the two of them together, Dee. It would melt even your cold heart."

She snorted. "What about your own heart? That's the one that needs to stay frozen. Never forget that."

And she wasn't wrong. But nothing about our situation was ever quite that simple. "I know. But he's…he still makes me laugh. I think we can be friends. For Liam's sake, it's important that we try."

"He makes you laugh?" She sounded skeptical. "Not sure I like the sounds of that. Be careful, baby girl. Be very, very careful."

"I am. You don't need to worry."

Dee rolled her eyes. "Of course I do. So when can Terri and I come visit again? I think I'd like to finally meet this guy, size him up in person."

"Well, he usually visits on weekend afternoons. And you're at the salon at those times."

"I could clear a Sunday. Just tell me when."

I was quiet for a few moments. Then I said, "I'd love to see you, honest I would, and so would Liam. But I don't know if it's a great idea for you to meet Declan right now. Considering how you feel about him, I'm pretty sure you wouldn't be able to hide it. I just don't want things to get heated with Liam around."

"Ames, you know I would never start shit with him or anyone else in front of Liam. Give me some credit."

"Fine," I sighed. "Maybe next Sunday?"

"Cool. Let me look at my schedule and talk to Terri, and I'll text you later to confirm. Speaking of my better half, I should run. I promised I'd make cookies tonight."

I stifled a laugh. "Is that code for something? Cause if so, I don't really wanna know."

Dee laughed. "No comment. Namaste, girly." With a beep, her face blinked away.

Crap, I thought. I'd forgotten to tell her I'd run into Liv, and the tense conversation we'd had. Dee clearly hadn't heard about it from her, or I would have gotten a message right after. I really did miss Liv. I hated that I'd hurt her so bad that she didn't even want to try to fix things anymore. I opened a new text, but after staring at the screen for a several seconds I closed it again. Liv was going to need more time before she'd be ready to speak to me again, and I really didn't want to risk antagonizing her further. I needed to focus on much more pressing concerns.

Concerns such as planning something for next Sunday that included not just Mom, Liam, and myself, but Declan, Dee, and Terri as well. The whole thing made me uneasy. I definitely didn't look forward to my best friend and…whatever the heck Declan was to me now…being in the same room together. Though Dee had promised she'd be on her best behavior, I knew all too well her opinion of him. And I wasn't confident she'd be able to hold back from telling him exactly what she thought.

Monday was gray and wet. BWK building management had finally turned on the heat and the radiators were blasting. Though it was pretty warm in the office, it definitely felt like November outside.

I was kneeling on the floor in the file room looking through the bottom row of SM-SP, when I heard someone come in behind me. Glancing over my shoulder, I was shocked to find Declan standing there. He wore a black button-up that fit him like it was custom made. That shirt was familiar. Had I seen it before? Sudden flashes of memory hit me. Him pushing me against the stacks, edges of files poking into my back as he kissed me. His hands roaming my body. The back of my ankle wrapping around his calf as I pulled him closer. His body pressing hard into mine. And me finally forcing us to stop in case we got caught, barely able to speak, my breath escaping in short, hard gasps.

Heat flooded me and I scrambled to my feet, hoping he wouldn't notice.

"Hey," he said. He looked surprised to see me, so I assumed he hadn't come to the file room looking for me. His face tilted slightly as he examined me more closely. "You okay?"

"I'm fine," I said, trying to keep my voice steady.

"Then why do you look so nervous?" He flashed that wicked smile I loved more than I was willing to admit. "Promise I won't bite."

My face got even hotter. I couldn't deal with this right now. I didn't know what he had in mind, but I needed to not be here, with him. Frowning, I pulled the case file I was holding against my chest and started around him. Instead of searching for

262

whatever he'd come back here for, he decided to walk with me back to my office.

Once I had my desk between us, I turned to him quizzically, confidence returning now that we were away from a place that held emotional memories. "Is there something you need?"

He took a seat without being asked, so I sat down as well. "You hear about the Rock on the River music festival?"

I shook my head.

"It's at Riverside Park this weekend. Seven or eight different acts. I was thinking of going, and wondered if you might want to come?" He pushed a lock of dark hair off his forehead, an act that made him appear bashful. Something I knew he was anything but.

My eyes followed the movement. I didn't want him to notice, so I glanced over my shoulder out the window at the rain streaming down the glass. When I looked back at him, I said, "It's outdoors? At this time of year?"

"They have several big tents, and they'll have patio heaters scattered around if needed, but yeah, outdoors. It's supposed to be really nice on Saturday though, warm and sunny. I could bring a blanket and we could sit on the grass. I took Alexis last year. I think you'd really enjoy it."

"Maybe." I replied. It might be something Liam would also enjoy, so why not? "Text me the details and I'll let you know." I opened the file I'd just retrieved to let him know I had work to do.

He got the hint, getting to his feet. "Sorry if I surprised you back there. Didn't mean to."

I lifted my eyes back to him and flashed a small smile. "No problem. Talk to you later." From the look on his face, I suspected he wasn't sorry in the slightest.

After he left, I got lost in the problem I was trying to figure out and didn't even hear my phone beep until it was almost time for lunch. The first text was Declan sending me the website link for more info about the music festival. His second message said: *What if we didn't bring the kids this time? Might be more fun just us?*

I frowned down at my phone, my brows nearly touching over the bridge of my nose. Was he seriously asking me on a date? Was *that* what this was about? My traitor brain decided now would be a perfect time to flash again on the memory of us making out in the file room, and once again I felt my temperature rise. Clicking through the link he'd provided, I scanned the lineup for Saturday. When I saw who was playing second to last, it suddenly all made sense.

Jim Coltrane.

On my way back from lunch, I saw Josh was in his office. He smiled when I stepped into the doorway, waving me toward a chair. Shutting the door behind me, I sat down. Open file folders were strewn across his desk, and more stacks of them lined the floor along the side wall.

"What's up?" he asked with a curious glance at the closed door.

"Sorry to bug you, but I wanted to ask you something. Do you know anything about the Rock on the River festival this weekend?"

"I know Declan usually goes. I've never been myself. Why?" He reached for his mug and took a sip.

"He, uh, he asked me to go with him." I felt my cheeks getting warm again. *Just like the old days,* I thought.

"Oh yeah? You mean all of you, with the kids?"

"That's the thing. Just us."

His brows bounced. The frown that surfaced just as quickly vanished. "And how do you feel about that?"

I snorted. "You sound like my therapist!" I said, and Josh laughed. "It does seem like it could be fun."

He studied my face for a moment, eyes narrowing. "But you're hesitant?"

"Can you blame me?" I exhaled a sigh. "Although, honestly, things are getting easier between us. What do you think? You think I should go?"

"Does he mean for it to be a date?" Josh's eyes peered into mine. I knew his second, unspoken question was: *Do you want it to be?*

I shrugged. "I have no idea."

Josh folded his hands together as he considered me. "Well...think about it this way: the better you two get along, the better it will be for Liam. If you think there's a chance you could be friends again, maybe you should consider going so you can work on that? Just make it clear to him that you're just going as friends, and it's not a date."

Sitting back in my chair, I thought about it. "That's a good point. I do miss our friendship. And of course, it would be better for all three of us if things were more comfortable between us.

264

We're going to be in each other's lives pretty much forever now. Might as well try to make the best of it."

Josh nodded. "I think it's wise to at least make an effort. Even if it's hard for you at first, maybe doing things like this will make it easier." Then his expression hardened. "But just so you know, if he hurts you—either of you—ever again, I might just have to kill him."

I laughed and he couldn't maintain his stern face. "You're like the big brother I never had. But I'd hate for you to end up in prison for first degree murder on my account. Holly would never forgive me. Or you."

"Fine," he said, grinning. "I won't actually kill him. But he'll wish I had. That's a promise."

I got to my feet and pulled open the door. "Well, let's hope it won't come to that."

Declan

I was humming to myself as I closed my laptop and got ready to leave for the day. I hadn't even known I was doing it until I stopped and suddenly realized how quiet it was.

Recalling Diana's concerns, I poked my head out of my office. It looked like everyone had already gone home. She was probably overreacting and had gotten herself all worked up for nothing, but I'd promised her I'd do some more snooping. If it turned out she was right and I'd blown her off, and something awful happened to my brother, I'd never be able to forgive myself.

I glanced up the hall toward Ryan's open door. I knew he wasn't around. He'd been out visiting clients all day. At least that's what his schedule said. He'd lied to Diana about hanging out with me, so who knew what else he was lying about? Something was definitely up with him, but that didn't necessarily mean he'd fallen off the wagon. Hell, it could be pretty much anything. Knowing Diana the way I did, though, I sure hoped he had a goddamn good reason for lying to her. Whatever it was, I'd rather my brother had a piece on the side than find out he was back on pills. Not that I thought he'd do that. He wouldn't. He knew as well as I did that Diana might actually murder him if she found out. And then there was the rather important little fact that they were expecting a baby. Why wasn't he over the moon about it? I wished he'd just tell me about the pregnancy so I could ask him myself. But that would require us to spend time together, which we hadn't in weeks. Was it just life being busy, or had he been avoiding me on purpose? I made a mental note to text him and invite him over for a beer.

I went back to my desk and grabbed my jacket and case. Before anyone could come along, I strode down the hallway and ducked into my brother's office, pulling the door shut behind me. If someone happened to spot me coming out after, I'd just say I was looking for a piece of information. It wasn't even a lie.

As I'd done so many times over the years, I began pulling out drawers and opening cupboards. I went through the pockets of the jacket hanging on the back of the door. I even checked behind every file in the file cabinet. After a meticulous search, I was left empty-handed.

I stood back with a sigh, surveying the small room. He knew I'd found his cache of pills in here before, because last time he'd caught me red-handed. And beat the shit out of me for my trouble, a memory I'd rather forget. If Diana's suspicions were right and he *was* off the wagon again, he'd finally smartened the fuck up and wasn't stockpiling at home or work. So either he had a secret stash somewhere in his Porsche, which would be stupid as hell if he ever got pulled over, or he was hiding them somewhere else. Or option C, none of the above, and something completely different was going on.

With a small sigh, I left his office. As I got into my car, I wondered if there was some way I could jimmy my way into his and search it, too. Shocking to some I'm sure, I didn't have a juvenile delinquent past, so I doubted I could pull it off without leaving obvious damage to the lock.

I'd let Diana know I didn't find anything, though, and maybe ask her if she could find a way to search his Porsche without him knowing. And I'd invite him out and see if I couldn't get him to spill anything. But honestly? After nearly dying seven years ago and being forced to spend a few months in rehab, I had a hard time believing he'd be so stupid as to start up again. It had scared the living shit out of not only all of us, but of him as well. Now that he was happily reunited with his One True Love, his life should be just the way he wanted it. Something else had to be up, because he'd never be so idiotic as to fall back on old bad habits and ruin everything.

Would he?

Chapter 27

Amelia

I stared at myself in the full length mirror on the inside of my closet door, the same mirror I'd checked my outfit out in hundreds, possibly thousands of times in my teens. Just the process of holding a shirt against my chest and scrutinizing it, then tossing it aside and grabbing another one brought back the insecure yet nervously excited feelings of teenager-hood.

But what did I even have to get insecure or nervous about? Nothing. This wasn't a date. This was just two not-quite-but–almost-kinda friends going to see some live music together. That's all. Nothing more. So I had no reason to feel anxious.

You sure about that? a familiar voice piped up in my head. My dad's voice. And if I was being honest with myself, then no, I wasn't totally sure about anything between Declan and me now. It all felt sort of wobbly, like I couldn't quite find my footing. Unstable. And I was not a fan of unstable.

Maybe by the end of the day I'd feel more confident about where we now stood with each other. Maybe things would be easier, less uncertain. That was the main reason I was going after all: to work on making our relationship—our friendship—smoother. For Liam's sake.

Declan and Alexis had come by about half an hour ago and taken Liam for lunch at Finnegan's while I got ready. I figured

Declan wanted to hang out with him a little before stealing his mother for the day. For once I was too preoccupied by the idea of spending so many hours with Declan to feel weird about Liam going off with him without me. Or maybe this whole situation was just getting easier.

I wished I had someone to talk to, but the only one who might understand the trepidation I felt was Josh, and he was busy with his own family. I didn't want to bug him with my worries. My mother would drop rather unsubtle hints that I should throw myself at Declan so the four of us could spend the rest of our lives together. And Dee would just tell me not to go at all. So, though my anxiety was thrumming, I had no choice but to keep it to myself.

Finally I chose a blue shirt and jeans. I'd throw a hoodie in my bag for when the sun went down, but Declan had been right, it was a glorious day. You'd never know it was only a month until Christmas as it felt more like September. It was the perfect day for a concert in the park.

Standing back, I rolled my shoulders, then stretched out my arms. My neck and upper back ached, probably from tossing and turning most of the night, and then finally falling asleep in an awkward position. My overactive mind was the enemy of sleep, but I'd never once been able to stop it once it got unleashed. I touched my toes and swept my body upward, reaching to the ceiling as high as I could. It seemed to help, although the tension across my shoulder blades remained.

By the time I'd run a brush through my hair and put on a bit of light makeup, I heard the door open and the kids come in. It was time to say goodbye to Liam and get going.

"Mommy, Lex stuck French fries up her nose!" Liam told me excitedly, laughing like it was the funniest thing he'd ever seen in his life.

"You did?" I turned to Alexis. "Did you eat them after?"

She wrinkled up her face. "Ew! No."

Declan smiled, putting a hand on her shoulder. "She was just showing off for her little brother. But it's not something she makes a habit of. Right, Lex?"

Alexis glanced up at him. "Whatever." She sounded more like sixteen than ten, and I suspected he'd just gotten a glimpse of what he was in for in a few years.

Mom came into the foyer as the kids ran past her to the living room. She gave me a quick once-over, nodded in what I assumed was approval, and said, "Shouldn't you two be heading out?"

"We should," Declan agreed. "Thanks again for watching Alexis for an hour, Mrs. York—"

"Call me Brenda."

"Okay, Brenda. Mr. Logan will be by to pick her up about two. We appreciate it."

"It's no problem. She and Liam are easy."

I looked at her in surprise. Easy was not a descriptor I ever thought I'd hear my mother say about children. Any children. I mean, I knew she loved Liam and had been great watching him for me over the past few months, but she still seemed mostly uninterested in other people's children. So was she just trying to suck up to Declan, or did she really enjoy being around Alexis? I hoped for the latter, but with her I couldn't be sure.

"Well thanks anyway, Mom." I went past her into the living room, kissed my son on the cheek and then walked out the door with Declan. For our not-date. That felt an awful lot like an actual date.

When I stepped outside, I looked to the driveway and frowned. Instead of the sky blue Mustang Boss I was expecting, there was a black SUV parked beside my Honda. I turned back to Declan. "Where's your car?"

He grinned. "You're looking at it."

My eyes flared, darting to the SUV again, then back to him. "*What*? What happened to your Mustang?" I hadn't actually seen Declan's car since last weekend. An image of him getting into an accident with it popped into my head, and I had to repress a shudder.

"I traded it in," he said with a small shrug. "Figured it was time for something a little more family-friendly."

"But...you loved that car!" I couldn't believe it.

A wistful expression crossed his face. "Yeah. I did. But it was just a car, and it was time to say goodbye. And believe it or not, I kinda like the new one. Wait 'til you see the inside. You're gonna love it!"

I frowned. He'd traded in his beloved Mustang for a family-oriented, 'safe' SUV, one that had ample room for kids and all their stuff. Was this some sort of grand gesture to prove to me that he was serious about wanting to be part Liam's life? Part of my life?

"I'm just surprised. You don't seem like an SUV kind of guy."

"I admit it's a big change," he said, hitting the remote button to unlock the doors, "but it drives really nice. It's cool sitting up high after all these years being down so low."

"Okay. As long as you're happy. Let's go."

The new car's soft leather seats were super comfortable. The drive into Lynchburg, however, was not, at least not for me. While I'll give Declan credit for trying to initiate conversation several times, we always fell back into silence. And not the easy kind. As I stared out the window at the passing scenery, I wondered how on earth we were going to get through the rest of the day if I couldn't let go of this tension. I flexed my shoulder blades back and forth, trying to ease the stiffness.

"You okay?" Declan asked, glancing my way.

"Yeah. Just slept weird last night." I raised my shoulders up to my ears and held them tight for a second before releasing them.

A flash of concern crossed his face. His eyes back on the road, he said, "I have Advil in the glove compartment if you need some." He reached across and popped it open.

The bottle was tucked to the left of some folded papers, so I grabbed it, shook out a couple of pills, and swallowed them down. "Thanks." Hopefully they'd do the trick.

By the time we got to Riverside Park, the lot right across the road was packed. I had my window down a few inches and I could hear the sound of drums and guitar, but couldn't make out the singing. It sounded like folk music, which wasn't my favorite, but I could get into it. Declan found a spot at another lot a few blocks away and, along with loads of other festival goers, we made our way over the hill to the big clearing in the middle of the trees.

We wound through clusters of people until we got to the line up to enter the fenced off 'over 21' section. Once we showed our IDs and were allowed inside, Declan found us a spot along the side and spread out the plaid blanket he'd brought.

I made myself comfortable. Realizing he was still standing, I looked up at him, shading my eyes from the sun. "Be right back," he said. I watched him work back through the crowd until he reached the bar. Assuming he was grabbing himself a beer, I turned my attention to the stage. A group of three women were singing a country song about cheating husbands. Their voices harmonized beautifully together, but though I recognized their talent, country music just wasn't my thing.

Behind the stage was forest, so many trees I couldn't even see the James River through the branches, although I knew it was back there somewhere. I spotted a trailhead into the bush. Maybe I'd bring Liam here sometime and we could go for a walk along the river.

By the time the band launched into their third song, an anthem to sisterhood, Declan returned and sat down beside me. He had two bottles in his hands and he handed me one. It was a peach vodka cooler, and for a few long seconds I just stared at it. I hadn't had a drink in years, but he didn't know that. I thought about the ache in my upper back. And I thought about spending the rest of the day with him, trying to figure out what to say, how to act, and finally I just mumbled, "Thanks." Raising it to my lips, I took a tentative sip. It was smooth and fruity and it tasted divine. I had a second swallow before setting the bottle down beside me, not wanting to drink too fast and give myself a head rush.

"I didn't know what you liked, so I took a guess. Is it good?"

"It's perfect."

"Great." He took a sip of his beer and made a face. "Tastes like shit, but I guess it'll have to do." He lay back, bracing himself on his elbows. "Who's this?"

I looked at the pamphlet I'd picked up when we came in. "Chantilly Lace. Meh. Up next is William Watterson. You know him?"

Declan nodded. "I've heard of him, but don't really know his stuff. " After a second, a small grin appeared and he added, "I do like his name."

I smiled back. "Me, too."

"Remind me again, what's Liam's middle name?"

Shifting onto my side to face him, I said, "James."

His grin grew wider. "Perfect. Why'd you pick James?"

My mind flashed back to the day I'd found out I was having a baby boy.

"Hey Preggo!" Terri greeted me cheerfully as Dee and I came in the door of her apartment. "How'd the ultrasound go?"

"Good," I said as I shrugged off my coat. "The baby's fine. Developing normally." Dee had come with me to the clinic for moral support. She'd spent a lot of effort trying, although mostly failing, to lighten my mood. I'd been feeling sad and grumpy for days, my thoughts continually drifting to a particular missed life path, one that had never really been mine to walk in the first place.

Terri pushed out a chair for me with her foot. "Did y'all find out if it's a boy or girl?"

"It's a boy," I said as we joined her at the table. Unzipping my bag, I pulled out the black and white photos the technician had printed off and handed them to her.

"Is that him?" She pointed to the blob in the middle that was vaguely baby-shaped.

I nodded.

"Cool. So a boy, huh? Have you thought about names yet?"

I shook my head. "Not at all. But I guess now that I know the sex, it's probably time to start." I got up and opened the fridge, pulling out the milk carton and pouring myself a glass. I forced myself to drink milk every day as recommended by my doctor to get more calcium to the baby, but I'd never been a huge fan. Sitting back down, I took a big swallow, grimaced, and said, "I might name him William. After my dad."

Dee nodded. "William's a good name. Ancient, traditional, strong. And lots of ways to shorten it. You could call him Willie, or Billy, or Liam."

"Liam's cute," I agreed. "Or Will. I don't love Willie. My dad got called Bill, but I can't see myself calling my kid that."

"Bill kinda sounds like an old man," Terri agreed.

Dee picked up her phone and started tapping away. "Variations of the name William: Bill, Will, Wilber, Wilfred, Willem—oh, I like Willem!—Liam, Wilhelm, Wiley. Wiley's kind of cute, and not super common."

"I guess I should make a list."

"You could always use William for his middle name, if you come up with something else you like better."

"That's true."

Later that night I lay curled up on my side in bed thinking about possible names. Though he had no say in any of this and never would, I couldn't help wondering what names Declan would like. I recalled that weird dream I'd had after I'd found out I was pregnant, the one where he'd told me it was a girl and insisted we had to name her Laura. Although I knew he'd never want that, I was glad I wasn't having a girl. As I thought more about what he might want, I came to a decision. The baby's middle name would be James. If I found a first name I liked better than William, he'd have two middle names.

William James. I liked it. It sounded like the name of a king. My little king.

"William James. What do you think of that?" I whispered, rubbing my belly. Just as I did, I felt a flickering sensation.

A broad smile stretched my cheeks. This time I was positive it wasn't just gas. That had been the baby. He approved.

"Are you serious?" Declan said. "You named him after a man you'd never met, just because you thought it'd be what I'd want?" He looked absolutely incredulous.

I exhaled a small laugh. "Doesn't make a lick of sense, does it? But yeah. I don't know how to explain it. It just felt right."

"Even though you never intended for me to even know he existed?"

My face grew warm. I reached for my bottle and took another drink. "I'm so sorry about that. If I hadn't made that choice, James would've known about his grandson." I couldn't meet Declan's eyes.

After a few seconds, he said, "I understand and you've already apologized. We're past it. What's done is done and all we can do now is try to make a better future. I'll tell Liam all about James someday. He'll know about him."

"Good. I talk to him about my dad all the time. He knows who his grandpa was. Although I'd give anything for Dad to have known him, it still means a lot to be able to tell Liam stories and show him pictures and stuff. It's still a legacy, just not the ideal kind. Can't believe the poor kid doesn't have any grandpas." I sighed, leaning back onto my elbows.

"There's always Patrick," Declan said, speaking louder so I could hear him over the swell of the music. "I haven't told him about Liam yet, but I guess I should soon. I know he'll want to meet him."

I didn't want to admit that the thought of Liam being swept up into Declan's entire family still made me uncomfortable. It was inevitable it would happen at some point and there was no good reason to continue to delay things. Maybe it was because I didn't feel like I had my own place among his family. But that was silly. Liam did, and that was all that mattered. So I just said, "Yeah."

Chantilly Lace finished their set and roadies started setting the stage up for William Watterson. I sipped my drink, but we didn't chat much during the intermission. The couple cuddling on the blanket behind us was discussing where they wanted to go on their next vacation. Listening to them plan a romantic getaway felt awkward, and it was almost a relief when I spotted a tall dark-skinned man in a white fedora walk to the center of the stage. A matching white acoustic guitar was slung over one shoulder. Four men followed behind him and I realized William was more than just William; he actually fronted a band. After introducing the other members, he began by strumming his guitar for us, showing off his skills before breaking into an upbeat pop song about a girl on a yellow bicycle. It was a bit twee, but I liked it. I sat up straight so I could see the band better, and I noticed Declan did the same.

Around the middle of the set, I leaned closer to him and said, "I've heard this song before. Did it get radio play around here?"

Declan nodded. "Josh and Holly like him. I think they might've even played this song at their wedding." He chuckled. "Not that I recall much of it."

I snorted. "No, I bet not."

Something flickered in his eyes. I wasn't sure if it was something good or bad, but he returned his attention to the stage. For a few more seconds I examined his profile. He looked very focused, but whether that meant he was deep in thought or just enjoying the show, I wasn't sure. We didn't talk much for the next few songs. The band was pretty good, so good I even made a note in my phone to check out more of their stuff later.

Toward the end of William Watterson's set, Declan excused himself to go find the washroom. By the time he returned, the band had wrapped up. He sat back down and without a word handed me another vodka cooler. I was already feeling pretty chill, so I told myself I'd go slower with this one.

Declan's gaze was trained on his hands hanging clasped between his knees. "So, I need to ask you something."

"What's that?"

"That night after Josh's wedding. The night we…" He stopped to rake his fingers through his hair. "I didn't, you know, take advantage of you, did I? I mean I sort of remember, but

274

it's all a bit fuzzy. I *really* hope I didn't do anything you didn't want me to."

I reached out to touch his arm, but dropped my hand before I made contact. "No. You didn't."

He exhaled a long sigh. "That's a relief. I'd hate to think I…" He stopped, unable to voice his fear.

I couldn't help it; my mind shot back to what he'd said to me that night. For a moment I was tempted to ask if he remembered it, and if, in his drunken state, he'd really believed I was Laura. But I kept my mouth shut. He'd certainly high-tailed it out of my room in the morning when he'd realized he was in bed with me. I recalled the whole thing all too well, but there was no point in rehashing what it had really meant now, all these years later, so I just said, "You have nothing to worry about."

He shook his head. "I couldn't live with myself if I'd done that."

"You didn't," I repeated. Before I even realized I was going to say it, I added, "You just snuck out the next morning and pretended it never happened."

Declan's eyes flared, almost as if I'd struck him. "I definitely owe you a shitload of apologies. For so many things. But doing the walk of shame that morning is not one of them. I didn't sneak out on you, although I get how you'd think that."

I frowned. "Yes. You did. I woke up and you were gone. I never heard a peep from you after and I basically had to trick you into talking to me when I found out I was pregnant. So don't pretend you didn't regret it. It was pretty obvious you did."

He picked up his bottle and drained the last of it before turning back to me, his clear blue eyes boring into my own. "You're wrong. I woke up and I saw you there and…I was happy. Really happy. But I also felt and smelled like crap. I didn't want you to see me like that, so I went up to my room to grab a shower and brush my teeth. And Lex called and by the time I got back down, you'd already gone." The side of his jaw clenched. "I was upset, for a moment. But then I realized it was for the best. I was a complete mess. You were better off staying far away from me. I think maybe I even wanted you to hate me. God knows I hated myself back then."

My mouth fell open, but no words came out. He'd been happy? And then he'd talked himself out of it? Poor guy. Sometimes I forgot how much hell he must've been in.

Rubbing the back of my neck, I sighed. "I wanted to," I admitted. "I tried to. But I never quite could."

One corner of his lips twitched up. "Could've fooled me."

I didn't reply.

He was still looking at me. I could tell there was something more he wanted to get off his chest. Instead of prompting, I waited him out, taking another drink of peach goodness. At last he said, "I'm really sorry for all the stupid shit I did and how much I hurt you, sorrier than you'll ever know." That little half-grin reappeared, then widened. "But you know what? I'm not sorry we created an amazing little boy together. Planned or accident, happy parents or estranged, I think…I think maybe Liam is a sign."

"A sign of what?"

"That we're meant to be in each other's lives. I mean, what're the chances that you'd end up pregnant the same…" he stopped, breaking eye contact.

I got a sudden ache in my chest at the memory evoked by the words he didn't say. But much as that particular topic would probably always be a sore point, I forced that resurrected stab of betrayal away. We were having a nice day. Getting upset at something that happened long ago and had already been buried wasn't going to help.

"The same way Laura did? Astronomical, I'd bet. I was even on the Pill, too." Declan hadn't shared that particular detail, but Josh had told me. At the time, it'd made me suspect Laura had lied about being on birth control, that maybe she'd gotten pregnant on purpose knowing it would keep him with her. But after what happened to me, I wasn't so sure.

His eyes bugged. "You're kidding me?"

"It's true." I paused, unsure about explaining the real reason why my birth control hadn't worked. I'd made a stupid mistake, and I didn't know if wanted to admit it. But I was feeling braver, whether from the vodka or just because for the first time in forever I was starting to feel a connection with Declan again. And really what did it matter if I shared another low point? He'd survived far lower. And he'd never know my very lowest point. "It was my own fault. I didn't remember that my St John's Wort pills made my birth control less effective. It wasn't like I expected to be having sex at all. I'm sure I read the label when I first started taking them, but I forgot. One time and I ended up knocked up. Go figure."

"See what I mean? He was meant to be." Declan smiled again and I wished he'd stop. Every time he smiled it did crazy things to my insides. Things I knew full well I should be trying to avoid. "So why were you taking St. John's Wort?"

I bit my lower lip, but the question didn't bother me the way it would have before. "I couldn't afford my anti-depressants anymore. It's an herbal supplement you can get over the counter."

"Ah." He got quiet. Maybe he was thinking that my depression had been because of him. If so, he was mostly right, although there were several other contributing factors.

The sun had started to dip toward the horizon and the next act was already set up on stage. Somehow we hadn't even noticed. A few guitar notes twanged and Declan perked right up. As soon as I heard the familiar melodic voice of Jim Coltrane, I straightened up, too. He was the main reason we were here, after all.

From what I could tell from our vantage point, Jim looked pretty much the same as the last time we'd seen him. He was older, and he had longer, shaggier hair and an even longer, shaggier beard, but he still resembled a down on his luck crooner, the kind you might see playing beside an open guitar case on a street corner: faded plaid unbuttoned shirt over a white tee, jeans with frayed hems, a gray newsboy cap pulled low on his forehead.

I hadn't listened to his music since Declan and I split up. It had been just too painful to hear Jim's voice. So I didn't know the song he was singing, yet it still seemed familiar. It was about getting his heart broken, as so many of his songs were. The poor guy obviously hadn't had good luck with women.

As Jim started into the second song, I rolled my shoulders back. The ache in my muscles still hadn't abated much, and now that I was sitting up with my back straighter, it flared right up again. I stretched my arms over my head and then behind me, trying to alleviate the tension.

"Still sore?"

I nodded.

"Can I help with that?"

I looked at him. "How?"

"Let me rub your shoulders and upper back. I can try to work out those kinks."

I tried to suppress a grin. "Promise those are the only kinks you'll work on?"

His eyes narrowed, creases forming around them as the biggest smile I'd seen all day bloomed. As if by instinct I mirrored it. "If you insist," he said.

I shifted forward and he moved behind me and, though I knew Dee would have a total conniption if she found out, I pulled my hair aside and let him massage me while we enjoyed the show.

Declan's hands felt good. Too good. *Not as good as they'd feel on my naked skin*, I thought. *No! Impure thoughts!* I silently reprimanded myself, chuckling softly as I picked up my bottle. It was almost empty so I finished it off.

"You want another?" I heard him murmur, his lips far too close to the exposed skin on the nape of my neck.

I shivered. "No, I'm good." I was already buzzed enough. Didn't need to make it worse.

"Cold? Wanna put on your sweater?"

"Maybe later."

His thumbs pushed into the hard knots at the edges of my shoulder blades, moving in circles as his fingers rubbed the inside of my shoulders close to my neck. I titled my head left and then right, giving him better access. It felt heavenly. Arching my spine under his hands, I gave into the pleasure. I swore I was relaxing more every minute.

He'd worked his way down to my lower back when Jim began to play "Heaven in You," a song with which we were both very familiar. I got a whiff of Declan's cologne, something fresh and ocean-y, and that tightness coiled again deep in my gut. He smelled incredible. His touch felt amazing. And then he started to sing, soft and sort of under his breath, but I could hear, and I remembered when he'd sung this song before, and the wall I'd carefully constructed crumbled further.

Without letting myself think about it, I leaned back into him. For a second he stopped singing. Just for a second. Then his arms came up around me, gentle, not forceful. His warmth radiated from his chest to my back and I was no longer even slightly cold. A moment later he began to sing again.

We didn't speak. We just stayed like that for the rest of Jim's set.

And Declan still knew every word.

Declan

I didn't want to say or do anything that might spoil the moment. I was well aware how fragile this was, how easily it could break. And God knows I was prone to doing stupid shit and fucking up the good things in my life.

So I just let Amelia lean against me and I held her loosely, giving her the option to escape if she wanted, and I enjoyed Coltrane.

Feeling her warmth against me, smelling the soft scent of her shampoo where her hair brushed the side of my face, watching my favorite artist perform, I felt like I'd died and gone to Heaven. Not that I believed in Heaven—and if it did exist, I sure as shit wouldn't be going there—but this was everything I'd been wanting for so damn long. I didn't want to ruin it.

Even after Coltrane said his thanks and left the stage, she lingered in my embrace for another minute. I still couldn't believe this was even happening, couldn't fucking believe she was letting this happen. One could possibly argue that we were just two friends enjoying each other's company, I suppose, but anyone who argued that clearly didn't know us or our history. Nothing was without meaning for Amelia and me. Every little touch contained a great volume of unspoken emotion.

At last she sat up and reached for her bag to pull out her phone. When she looked at the screen, I noticed a small frown mar her forehead.

"What's up?" I asked. "Message from your mom?"

"No, just surprised at the time." She looked back at me. "Are you into the last act?"

I shrugged. "Not really. I already saw who I came for. Why? You wanna cut this short and head home?"

"Would you mind? I know you had this whole thing planned…" She trailed off, looking apologetic.

"It's fine. I didn't have any concrete plans really, just to hang out and enjoy the show, which we have. You want to get back to Liam in time to tuck him into bed, right?"

"I was kinda hoping, yeah." She smiled and I felt a little flip in my chest. Was that where that old cliché *my heart skipped a beat* came from? Shit, I didn't need my body parts to tell me how I felt about this woman—although they did, on the regular. I already knew. I had for a very long time.

I stood up and offered her my hand. To my surprise, she slipped her fingers into mine without her usual hesitation and let me help her to her feet. I folded up the blanket, tucked it under my arm and we made our way out of the park as I tried and failed to suppress my grin.

On the drive home, Amelia seemed a lot more relaxed. I'd half expected her to clam up with regret after our little cuddle during the show, but to my happy surprise she didn't seem bothered. We kept the topics light, chatting about work and Liam and her Mom. When I pulled into the driveway, she didn't invite me to come in, but that was okay. I would see Liam tomorrow, and I figured she was probably ready to escape my company after so many hours together.

But she didn't jump right out of the car. Clearly she wasn't in that much of a hurry to get away. "I had a great time today," she said, turning to face me.

"I'm glad. Me, too."

She didn't reply, but she didn't move to leave either. Her eyes stayed on mine. We regarded each other silently. It was driving me crazy wondering what she was thinking. Whatever it was, the next move was hers. I tried to stay still, but it wasn't easy, knowing she was watching me so closely. Maybe she knew how much of an effort it was for me. Maybe she didn't care.

The leather of her seat gave a soft squeak as she shifted closer. What was she doing? I wanted to ask, but I forced myself to shut up.

It took everything in me not to reach for her when she raised her hand and brushed the tips of her fingers over my cheek. I swear I stopped breathing for a few seconds. If she noticed, she didn't retreat.

Oh-so-gently she traced the line of my jaw, scraping lightly against the stubble. Though I was mostly succeeding at not moving under her touch, a certain other part of my body had its own agenda. I was now at full attention—a soldier ready to salute the goddamn Queen. But I couldn't stop that any more than I could slow the pounding of my heart. Even her gentlest, most innocent touch turned me right the fuck on. If these were different circumstances, this would not be a problem. But right now it was not helpful.

I wasn't sure how much longer I could keep still while she reacquainted herself. Soon I was going to break and crush her to me and kiss her soundly. And I couldn't risk that. It might ruin everything.

But then the most amazing thing happened. I had no clue what was going through her head, but at that moment I ceased caring. She leaned forward and pressed her lips to mine.

Though I didn't think it possible, I got even harder. And I couldn't not kiss her back. I just couldn't. It wasn't even a fucking option.

So I did.

I hadn't once tried to make a move on her over the past while as things had slowly been improving between us. Don't get me wrong; I'd wanted to. So much. But I respected that if anything were to change between us, it would have to be her call. So I'd been careful. I'd given her space. Well, mostly. She'd let me put my arms around her earlier. And that would have been enough, you know? Just that was enough to send my heart soaring indefinitely. I'd been missing her touch—missing *her*—more than I could put into words.

And now, finally, thank fucking God, she'd willingly kissed me. We were kissing each other. For the first time in what felt like a lifetime. And though we both knew our problems were still far from solved, for the moment we surrendered.

We didn't stop to ask questions. We just gently, carefully, kissed. After a minute or two, I pulled her closer and ran my fingers up her back. Though I was sorely tempted, I resisted the urge to drop my hand to the curve of her ass.

I didn't even use my tongue. It was the closest thing to a chaste kiss Amelia and I had ever shared. Usually passion won over pretty much immediately with us. But not this time. We were both cautious. Usually the mark of a bland, forgettable kiss, but somehow—I can't even explain it, but somehow this sweet, nervous kiss was the best kiss I'd ever had in my entire life.

When she pulled away at last, it felt like she'd taken some important part of me with her. Which sounds stupid, I know, but that's how it felt. I didn't mind, though. She could have it if she wanted it. She could have all of me, or none of me, or anything in between.

I looked into those wide brown eyes and ached to tell her I loved her. My mouth even dropped open to let the words fall out.

But I stopped myself. She wasn't anywhere near ready to hear those words. During that fateful phone call all those years ago, she'd told me I wasn't allowed to say that to her anymore. And she was right. I'd given up all rights to tell her how I felt.

"Sorry," she whispered, looking kind of flustered.

Damn it. I couldn't help it; a soft sigh slipped out "For what?" I could sense our newfound closeness perched on a precipice, wavering on the verge of toppling over and vanishing once more.

She blinked, surprised by the edge in my voice. "I just...I wanted to remember what it was like."

"And?" I breathed, almost afraid to hear the answer.

Amelia gave me a soft smile. "I remember now." Then she grabbed her bag and opened the door. I watched her until she disappeared inside the house. She didn't look back.

Chapter 28

Declan

I woke up in a fan-fucking-tabulous mood. I swear I hadn't felt this happy in years. *Years*. Alexis even commented on my cheerfulness on the car ride home. We sang along to the radio the whole way.

Though neither of us mentioned the kiss, Amelia seemed happy to see me when I dropped by to play with Liam for an hour. Her cheeks went a little pink when she opened the door and found herself face to face with me, but that was the only hint that anything was different. Whatever she thought about what happened Saturday, she didn't say. But she smiled that sweet, shy smile I adored and that was all I needed. She didn't stick around, heading out to get groceries, but I didn't mind. Liam and I had fun and I was just glad to be there.

On Monday, for the first time since before my life went to shit, I was actually excited to go to work. The last thing Amelia had said to me Saturday was *I remember now*. And this nearly alien sense of excitement and hope brought back some memories of my own. It reminded me of how I'd felt back when she and I were happy. After so many years of darkness, the whole world seemed bright and full of possibilities again.

It was a little overwhelming, honestly. In the best way possible.

As if Mother Nature was in tune with my mood, it was a gorgeous sunny morning, although there was a chill in the air that had me zipping up my jacket and fumbling on the top shelf of the front closet for Alexis' mitts and my leather gloves. After dropping her off at school, I made a pit-stop at a drive-through to pick up two coffees. And instead of going to my own office when I got to work, I walked right through Marketing and headed straight for Amelia's.

When she glanced up from her computer and saw me standing there, she smiled, and I swear I fell in love with her all over again. "Brought you coffee," I said, coming in and setting the cup on her desk.

Laughing, she raised her travel mug. "Got one. But thanks."

"Well, now you have a refill. It's from Buddy's, so it's the good stuff."

"Noted. How was the rest of your weekend?" she asked. She didn't look like she wished I'd spontaneously combust, or at the very least go away. That was a definite improvement.

"Amazing," I replied with a knowing smile. "Best weekend in ages. You?"

I think she blushed. She took a sip of from her mug to cover it, grimaced and set it back down. "Pretty great, actually." I hoped she meant it.

Glancing at my watch, I got to my feet. "Guess I should go be productive or something. Don't wanna bug you when you're working."

"That's okay." She reached for the cup I'd brought her and took a sip from that one. The result was yet another amazing smile. "You're right. This is way better than cafeteria coffee."

"Say that again."

She titled her head. "Say what again?"

I tried to keep a straight face, but I know the corner of my lips twitched. "That I was right."

Laughing, she threw an eraser at me. I dodged and it hit the wall and bounced to the floor.

"Told ya. Buddy makes the best java in town." I picked up the eraser and tossed it onto her desk. "Hey, so I was thinking…how's your Friday look? Wanna go for lunch? I mean, if it wouldn't be weird or anything?"

She arched a brow and for a second she reminded me so much of Diana I had to do a double take. Then her smile resurfaced and I relaxed. Amelia was nothing like Diana; she was thoughtful and kind and not remotely bitchy. Yet I had to admit the self-confidence she'd gained over those long, lost years had made her even more attractive. I had a sudden urge to close the door, pin her up against it, and kiss her thoroughly. And maybe I would have, if I was even the slightest bit confident it wouldn't set us back twenty steps for the two we'd just taken forward. Good thing I still had a modicum of self-control.

"Lunch would be nice. Add it to my calendar," she replied, dismissing me, but in a far kinder, less irritated manner than usual. I didn't mind. We both had shit to do.

With a smartass salute, I left her office, still smiling, still not giving a fuck what anyone else but her thought.

As I passed Ryan's office, I saw he was actually in for once. Not that he didn't come to work anymore—I'm sure he did—but I hadn't seen him much lately, and when I had, he'd always been with others.

I knocked on the edge of his doorframe and he looked up from his monitor, eyes narrowed, lips thin. His annoyance at the sight of me was pretty much the polar opposite of Amelia's earlier reaction. My world seemed to have turned a little upside down recently. But I wasn't complaining.

"Sorry to interrupt," I said, dropping into an empty chair. The other one was stacked with files.

"I've gotta get this proposal out, Declan. Can whatever it is wait 'til later?"

His office was dim, blinds drawn against the sunlight, but I examined his face, trying to see beyond the irritation. Were his pupils contracted? Were those dark circles below his eyes darker than usual? Did he look haggard, run down, pale? Possibly. But I couldn't be sure.

"Just wanted to know what you were up to after work on Friday. I was thinking we could go grab a beer, catch up a little." I tried to keep my tone light.

Ryan's attention was back on his monitor. "I'll have to let you know. Pretty swamped this week."

"Oh yeah? How's Diana doing?"

His eyes darted back to mine, a frown creasing the skin between his brows. "She's fine."

So he still wasn't going to tell me about the pregnancy. Interesting. "And you? Are you fine, too?"

My brother's annoyance deepened. "Is that why you popped in? To ask me how I am? I'm busy, that's how I am. Look, I'll talk to you later, okay?"

"Friday night after work?"

He sighed. "Fine."

"Great. Say about five?" He didn't reply, so I stood to go. Just as I turned to the door, I saw him reach for his phone. His fingers were trembling.

Shit. Diana was right. Something was definitely off. I just hoped it was anxiety over the prospect of becoming a dad and not because he'd chosen to self-medicate and in the process taken a swan dive off his favorite wagon.

As soon as I left my brother's office, I pulled my own phone from inside my jacket and texted Diana: *Have you searched his car yet?* I wasn't looking where I was going, eyes fixed on the screen, and nearly bumped right into Nicole.

"Oops," I said. "Distracted walking. My bad."

"I heard there's a big fine for that if you get caught." She smiled at me as she said it. We hadn't talked in weeks, not much more than a hello in passing since I'd broken things off with her. To my relief, she didn't seem like she wanted to high-tail it away, though. That was two for three today—I had to be on some kind of roll.

"Good thing I wasn't caught then." I arched a brow. "Unless you plan on reporting me?"

"Nah. You get a free pass for the first offence." Falling into step beside me, she said, "So, how've you been?"

There were so many different ways I could answer that, and not so long ago I would have told her all, well, most of them. But I just said, "Great. You?"

Her smile faltered a little, but it reappeared so quickly I might have imagined it. "I'm good. How's Alexis doing?"

"She's fine." This was awkward. And it really didn't need to be. I wracked my brain for something interesting to add that wouldn't betray Amelia's wish for privacy. "Still bugging me to sign her up for guitar lessons."

We'd just reached my office door. Nicole turned to face me as we stopped. "Oh yeah? Are you gonna?"

"I think for Christmas, yeah. She can use my guitar. And if she takes to it, I'll get her one of her own for her birthday."

Nicole nodded. "My friend Lila works at The Music Emporium downtown. Go in and see her and tell her you're a friend of mine. Not only does she teach lessons, she can also help you and Alexis pick out the right guitar once you're ready."

"Thanks. I might just take you up on that. Text me the info?"

She smiled again, not as wide as before, but definitely genuine. "On it," she said, waggling her fingers at me as she walked away.

I hadn't been sure until that moment, but I realized the two of us could actually stay friends without our past getting in the way if we chose to. And I was pretty sure we'd just chosen to. So other than the perplexing matter of Ryan acting sketchier than usual, my life felt like it was finally on the right track.

On Sunday I showed up at Amelia's just after one o'clock. She had mentioned that a couple of her friends might drop by, but I didn't think much of it. I was cool with meeting her friends. In fact, I took it as a very good sign that she even wanted me to.

Our lunch on Friday had gone well and the great mood I'd been in all week had, if anything, soared higher. She hadn't seemed tense or withdrawn, easily chatting and laughing with me the whole time. It was a massive relief to have at last worked our way past all that excruciating awkwardness. I didn't try to kiss her again—no idea how, but I somehow managed to resist the urge to even touch her—but I had every hope things were moving in the right direction. Forgiveness was probably still a long way off, but at least it no longer felt impossible.

Ryan had bailed on me on Friday night, claiming he was stuck in a meeting that was running long. But he'd offered to rebook for the following week, so I wasn't super concerned. I had some pretty important other things on my mind.

Brenda York answered the door. "Oh Declan, c'mon in. The girls are sitting in the living room." She used the word *girls* as if they weren't all in their thirties.

As I stepped into the foyer, Amelia came down the hall toward me, flashing me a cute little smile I couldn't help mirroring. That smile had always meant she was pleased to see me, and I'd despaired for too long that I'd never be on the receiving end of it again.

She grabbed my forearm and led me down the hallway to the living room. Liam was on the couch snuggled up to a woman with glasses and straight black hair twisted into fanned pigtails on either side of her head. On the other side of him was a pale blonde, slightly heavier woman. "This is my BFF Dee and her girlfriend Terri," Amelia said. "Guys, this is Declan."

Terri got to her feet and stuck out a hand. As I shook it, she said, "Pleased to meetcha. I've heard a lot about you."

I chuckled. "I just bet you have. Nice to meet you, too."

Dee just frowned and said hello. It didn't take stellar intuition to tell she didn't like me much. But why should she? Dee had taken Amelia in after she left her ex, which I understood was right after Amelia and I had split. So I assumed she knew the whole sordid story. She'd been there for Amelia when I wasn't able to be, supported her during her pregnancy, and helped raise Liam for the first four years of his life. Even if she hated me, I could only be grateful to her.

Liam, on the other hand, jumped up and threw his arms around me. I picked him up and positioned him on my hip. "Hey buddy. How was school this week?"

"Good. Marco and I made up a new game."

"Oh yeah? How's it go?"

He told us how they'd set up a store and were 'selling' stones they found on the playground to the other kids, who apparently used sticks of varying lengths for currency. It was actually pretty clever. The whole time I saw Dee glaring daggers at me from the corner of my eye.

Amelia must've noticed, because she sat down in Liam's vacated spot and started asking about Dee's brother, which led them down a conversation path I had no hope of following.

Liam took me up to his room to show me his latest Lego creation, and after I oohed and awed over how awesome it was, he convinced me to read to him from his big book of the history of Lego. By the time we went back downstairs, Brenda was offering everyone coffee.

"Can I have chocolate milk?" Liam asked.

"Of course. Why don't you come help me get the drinks ready?"

Liam followed his grandma into the kitchen and I sat in an empty chair with the others. All conversation ceased immediately.

After a second or two, Amelia said, "I was just telling them about the music festival last weekend."

288

"I love Chantilly Lace," Terri piped up. "Those girls sing one helluva harmony."

I smiled. "The whole thing was pretty awesome. And the sun stayed out all day, so we really lucked out."

"Oh no!" I heard Liam cry from the kitchen.

Then Brenda: "Oh Liam. You need to be more careful. Here, let me wipe that up."

Amelia got up from the couch and went to see what had happened. I heard a sort of dismayed laugh. "You're completely covered in chocolate milk, little man," she said. "Let's go upstairs and get you changed."

I suddenly remembered I had a treat for Liam in the backseat of my car. He'd told me how much he loved Swiss Rolls, but that his mom only bought them on special occasions. Though it wasn't a special occasion—although this entire week since the concert felt like a special occasion to me—I'd spotted the snack at the grocery store this morning and picked it up for him. "Back in a minute," I said to Amelia as they headed up the steps. "Just have to run out to my car."

As I reached for the doorknob, I heard Dee say to Terri, "Be right back."

She appeared behind me. "Mind if I walk out with you?" she asked in a low voice. Like she didn't want Amelia to hear. Which piqued my Spidey senses that something unpleasant was about to go down.

"Sure."

Pulling open the front door, I followed her out onto the porch with growing trepidation, figuring I was about to get a lecture for some, or possibly all, past failings. But no matter what Dee said to me, I could handle it. Hell, I knew I deserved it. I wasn't too worried, because I was confident that Amelia and I were at last on the path to fixing things. I thought nothing she, or anyone else, said could make a difference now.

But, as per usual, I was wrong.

Dee followed me to my car and then turned to face me, bracing one elbow on the edge of the roof above the driver's door. "So…straight talk?"

I nodded.

"I don't like you much."

"Kinda figured," I said with a lopsided grin and a half-shrug. "And I totally get that. Pretty sure there's even a We Hate Declan Kavanaugh Facebook group you can join."

She shook her head, ignoring my attempt at levity. "I don't think you do. I don't think you *get* what you did at all."

My grin fell away. "Believe me, I do. I hate that I hurt her. If I could take it all back, I would. But I can't, so I'm just trying my best to make it up to her."

Dee took a deep breath, her head tilting up to the sky before leveling her eyes back to mine. "Like I said, I don't like you. But I love my girl in there. And she lo—" She stopped herself with a sigh. "Well, let's just say she has a blind spot when it comes to you."

Amelia still loved me? Was that what she'd been about to say? "Me, too," I said. When Dee frowned, I clarified, "I mean, I love her, too. Always have." Where was she going with this?

"Good for you. But as I know you're fully aware, sometimes love just isn't enough. And I'm worried right now, Declan. I'm very worried. Love makes us do stupid things sometimes. Love blinds us. I suspect she's considering taking you back. And she shouldn't. You're not good for her."

"I'm trying to be," I sighed. "I'd do anything for her and Liam. Whatever she wants."

Dee's expression was stern. "Would you really? Anything?"

"Yes. Anything." My tone was firm.

There was a pause. Then, softer, she said, "She never told you what happened that day, did she?"

My brows drew in tight. "What day?" But I knew. Deep down, I knew exactly which day she meant.

"The day you destroyed her. The day she nearly died."

Seven years ago I wanted to die. The words Amelia had said that day at the park while we watched Liam play. I'd wanted to ask what she was meant but hadn't quite dared. A pit fell open in my gut. "What. The hell. Are you talking about?" I sounded the dictionary definition of terse. Because I knew. Suddenly I knew just what Dee meant. And it shattered me to the core.

She didn't break eye contact. "Ames is gonna murder me for telling you this. But you need to know. She tried to kill herself." Dee's voice thickened. "Because of you. I nearly lost my best friend because of *you*."

Fuck. Fuckity fucking fuck. I clutched my forehead, raked my fingers through my hair. I could barely wrap my head around it. *Jesus H. Christ. What the fuck had I done? What the fuck had she done?*

"I.."

Dee held her hand up to stop me. "Let me finish. Between you leaving her, and her dad dying, and then her leaving Scott—it was all too much. She just lost it. She hasn't been herself since, although after Liam came along she got a lot better. For so long she'd been so depressed." An accusing finger jabbed my way. "You haven't been around. You don't know! She wouldn't tell me every dirty detail, but I could read between the lines. She felt worthless. She *needed* you, and you dumped her. Like she meant nothing!"

Clearly some part of my brain was still working, because I heard myself say, "I know, but I swear I'll never leave her again." Immediately, I regretted it. It sounded feeble as hell.

Dee exhaled a heavy sigh. "You just don't get it, do you? Becoming a mom has changed her, gave her something to live for, stabilized and strengthened her. She's come so far and I'm so proud of my girl. But having you back in her life? You make her vulnerable. Volatile. What happens when things go to shit again? She may not have succeeded that time, but…" She stopped, unable to finish that sentence. It didn't matter. We both knew what she meant. "You have the power to *end* her. Don't you see that?"

I was silent. My throat had gone dry. "Duly noted," I finally said. It came out in a rasp.

When I didn't add anything more, Dee gave me a curt nod and went back inside. I guess she figured she'd accomplished her goal.

I stood there for a minute, just staring into space. At some point I must've started walking back toward the house. I got as far as the porch steps, but then I just turned and sat down— well, *fell* down might be more accurate. My legs no longer wanted to support me. I clapped both hands over my face to shield it from the light. It was better in the dark. I didn't deserve light. I didn't deserve anything.

My mind was reeling. My chest ached. My gut felt like I'd been stabbed.

My fault. All my fault. I'd nearly lost Amelia. *Amelia! Jesus.* What would I have done if she'd died? All the worst shit happened because of me.

Laura's death.

My unborn daughter's death.

The love of my life had tried to kill herself.

All because of me.

I was the fucking kiss of death.

Amelia

When I came downstairs with a clean Liam and returned to the living room, I was surprised to see Declan wasn't with the others. I went to the front door and looked outside just in time to see his new SUV reverse out of the driveway and head off down the street.

That's weird, I thought, frowning. He'd left without saying goodbye? But then I realized that Alexis must've called and asked him to come get her right away. I sent him a quick text asking if everything was okay and tried to put it out of my mind.

"Where'd Declan go?" my mom asked when I sat back down with them. She'd set out steaming mugs of coffee for us all.

"He had to take off. Something must've come up with Alexis."

Dee glanced at Terri, jumping to the conclusion he'd bailed on us for some selfish reason, I was sure.

"Daddy left?" Liam asked, his lower lip jutting.

"Yes, but don't worry. You'll see him again soon. Maybe you can FaceTime with him later before bed?"

"Okay," he said, mollified for the moment. I picked up Declan's untouched mug and took it to the kitchen. As I dumped the coffee back into the pot, I heard Liam squeal and Terri laugh. No doubt they were horsing around and no doubt my mom was shooting them a completely unnoticed frown. Turning around, I was startled to find Dee standing behind me.

"Oh, hey," I said. "Didn't hear you come in."

"So he just left?" Her eyebrow was cocked dramatically, an expression Terri and I sometimes referred to as Dee's Judgy Face.

I shrugged. "I assume his daughter called and he had to rush off and get her. Hopefully nothing's wrong." Rinsing out the mug, I set it in the sink.

"He didn't even text you?

I pulled my phone from my pocket and checked. Nothing. I shook my head. "Not yet."

"How considerate."

"Dee."

"Well, it *is* kinda rude. But I'm sure you'll hear from him soon enough with a perfectly reasonable excuse."

"Seriously. Drop it, okay?"

"Consider it dropped." She flashed me a smile and wrapped an arm around my shoulders. "Now here's a sweeter subject. How 'bout we slice up that coffee cake we brought?"

Dee and Terri said their goodbyes after dinner, with big hugs and promises we'd get together again soon. They invited us to spend a couple of days with them while Liam was off for Christmas Break next month, and I told them I thought that was a great idea.

After they left, I went back into the kitchen to load the dishwasher. Mom came up from the basement with some clean tea towels and as she was refilling the drawer by the sink, said, "It was nice to visit with everyone today. Shame Declan had to rush off."

"Yeah." I still hadn't gotten a reply to my text, and I admit, I was growing a little concerned. My mom looked tired, although not at all unhappy. Grabbing the dishrag, I began to wipe the countertop. "I'll finish cleaning up in here. Go rest your feet."

"Thank you." But instead of leaving the kitchen, she braced a hand on a chair and regarded me with a look I knew meant she had something she wanted to say. "Do you remember me telling you back in the summer that a new condo development was being built over on Lincoln Street?"

"No." It actually did ring a slight bell, but not enough that I recalled any detail. Although come to think of it, I had noticed a large building going up on the far side of the river.

"Well I did. I swear you tune me right out sometimes. Anyway, it turns out they're marketing it to seniors. My friend Jodi and I went over to the Open House on Friday to check the place out. It's really nice and modern, with an indoor pool, and a gym, and walking paths along the river."

"Sounds great." Dropping the dishrag into the sink, I turned to face her as all this really sunk in. "Wait. Don't tell me you're actually finally thinking of selling this place and moving somewhere a bit more manageable?"

She clicked her tongue against her teeth, a habit she had when she was agitated. "I don't know," she sighed. "I've lived here most of my life. This house is full of so many memories. It's difficult to imagine it not being home anymore."

"Mom, Liam and I won't be here forever, and, like I keep telling you, it's way too much work for you. Even with me coming and helping out, this place is too big for just one person."

Pulling out the chair, she sat down in the same place she'd taken most of her meals for her entire adult life. "I guess what I'm saying is that I'm ready to at least think about it." Her face lit up again. "You should have seen the condos, Amelia. Such a beautiful view! Maybe sometime you could come look at one of the units with me, give me your opinion?"

My mother actually wanted my opinion? I was surprised. But pleased. "Of course. I'd be happy to. And don't get me wrong— I know just what you mean about this house. Selling it would be sad for me, too. But I think it's time. I need to find my own place and so do you. It's time to start fresh with the next phase of our lives."

"You may be right," she agreed. Her eyes were no longer on me and I knew she was again thinking of all the happy times she'd spent here with my dad.

I was, too. There was no denying it. Letting go of this house would hurt. Though I fully supported my mother selling it, it was hard to wrap my head around the thought of never again walking inside the front door, never again being hit with that comfortable, safe, sort of leathery smell that I'd always associate with home. She was right when she'd said it was full of so many memories, and with the exception of the horrible night my father died, all of mine were good ones. How would I be able to say goodbye to this house forever?

But I would. Because like I'd just said, we both needed to move on with our lives, and clinging to the past now that we'd outgrown it would only hold us back.

Right on the dot of four on Monday, I powered down my laptop and headed to my car. I couldn't linger today, as I had a therapy appointment at four-thirty.

I hadn't seen Declan, but his car wasn't in the lot so I figured he'd been out at client meetings. And it wasn't like we were at a point where we told each other our schedules or anything. He had texted me back last night, apologizing for leaving without a goodbye and saying he'd had to go get Alexis, just as I'd assumed. He'd also FaceTimed with Liam before bed for about ten minutes, but didn't stick around to talk to me once they'd said goodnight. A tiny thread of concern still pinged in my brain, but I told myself I had no reason to worry. With a smile, I recalled the way his eyes had crinkled yesterday when he'd walked in and saw me approaching. He'd been happy, excited even, to spend time with us. Whatever might be going on with him, I was sure it had nothing to do with me.

Traffic was heavy along the road to Swann's Landing and I ended up pulling into the parking lot a few minutes past four-thirty. I hurried inside and the receptionist waved me right in.

"Sorry, sorry," I said to Debbie Westwood as I took a seat. "Traffic was crazy today."

"Was there an accident?" she asked.

My mind immediately shot to Laura's fatal crash along that very road six years ago. It had been right around this time of year, too. Could that be why Declan had been acting a bit distant the past couple of days? Those memories probably hit him hard every November. "No, just busy," I said.

"So how've you been, Amelia?"

I'd decided since I only had thirty minutes, I wasn't going to waste it. What was weighing on me was too important, and I needed some impartial advice from someone who wasn't already predisposed to tell me to either run far away or jump straight into his arms. "I'm good," I replied. "But I'm feeling a little unsure about something that's been on my mind lately."

She smiled encouragingly. "What's that?"

"Well, it's about Declan, actually. Surprise, surprise, I know. But the thing is, we've been growing a lot closer recently. We even went out on a…a kind of a date thing last weekend. We went to see some bands play at a music festival. Just the two of us. For the entire afternoon. I'd told him it wasn't a date when I said I'd go with him, but looking back, I guess it kind of was."

"Why do you say that?"

I sighed. "I'm not upset, let me just make that clear. He didn't do anything wrong. I just don't know if…" I waved my hand around vaguely. "If all this is such a good idea."

Debbie jotted a short note. "Can you tell me about your day at the music festival?"

"I was worried it'd be weird. And it was, at first. But before long it wasn't. At all. We actually got along really well. We had a few drinks. And a few laughs. My neck and shoulders were all sore from sleeping twisted or something, and he offered to give me a back rub, and for some reason I said yes." I stopped, my cheeks warming.

"Okay. What else happened?"

"The one singer was a guy we'd seen before, back when we were together. Declan's a huge fan, and his music was always kind of a point of connection between us. So yeah. We were enjoying the show, and he was rubbing my shoulders and it felt really amazing and I...I ended up leaning back against him. He put his arms around me. And I let him. We kind of cuddled for the rest of the set. And it was really nice. Everything was relaxed and easy and...I was happy. We both were."

She nodded as she made another note.

Before she could ask me another question, I blurted, "I kissed him. At the end of the night, before I went into the house. I think I surprised us both, but...yeah. We kissed."

"How did that make you feel?"

I knew my face was very red at this point. I could never help blushing when it came to all things Declan. "It...it brought back a lot of memories. Good ones. But I worry. I have my son to think about now. I can't just jump back into something with Declan and risk it all ending horribly again. Liam loves his dad. He'd be devastated if we... if I...if that happened." I finished lamely.

"So you're worried about the ramifications of a romantic relationship ending that hasn't even really begun yet? That's what's holding you back? Have I got this right?"

I nodded. "We have so much history. It's not the same as starting to date someone new. He's not just some guy I'm into, he's Liam's father. And he's...he was the love of my life."

She raised her eyes to mine. "He was the love of your life? Or he still is?"

I released a slow sigh. "I tried to let him go. For years I tried. I really did. But maybe I was just lying to myself. Because the truth is that I've never stopped loving him, no matter how much I wanted to. And I know he still has feelings for me, too. But how can I ever trust him with my heart now, after how many times he's let me down?"

With a sympathetic smile, Debbie said, "I know you're struggling with that. And there's no easy answer. But consider this: is your life, and your son's, better without him in it?"

I didn't hesitate. "No. Liam completely adores Declan. I know now how wrong I was to keep them from knowing each other."

"And what about you? Are you happier with him around?"

At first I didn't reply. I stared down at my fingers twisting in my lap. Instead of answering her question, I softly asked the most important one of my own: "What if things go wrong again?"

She wrote something else on her pad, taking a few long seconds before looking back up at me. Folding her fingers in front of her, she said, "What if things go wrong? Let's think about that. What would happen if you two got back together and then somewhere down the road realized that you're not meant to be in a relationship after all? Other than you no longer being a couple, what would change? He'd still see his son, I assume?"

"Definitely. I'd never try to keep them apart. Never."

"Okay. Do you think you'd still be able to be friends?"

I snorted. "I guess we'd have to try. For Liam."

"So maybe it wouldn't be quite so catastrophic? You're both older now. Presumably wiser. And you have your child's best interests to think about."

"That's true." I nodded. "Maybe I'm just over-thinking things. But it's hard not to, after so much hurt in our past."

"I understand that. And I think it's natural for you to have reservations. Let me also ask you this: what if, by some miracle, things actually go right? What then?"

I bit my lower lip. That scenario was the fantasy that I'd been harboring since I'd first realized I'd fallen in love with Declan so long ago. But it had seemed so ridiculous and foolhardy to even let myself fantasize about such things that I'd buried it away. Only in my dreams did we ever actually live out our happily ever after. And most of the time not even in those. "It could be the life I've always wanted," I mumbled.

"Pardon me? Can you please repeat that?"

"It could be everything I've always wanted." I said, louder. "But in order for us to have that, I'd need to be able to fully trust him again. And I don't know if I can. I think a part of me would always worry that he'd leave me again."

Debbie glanced up over my head at the clock on the wall. "Unfortunately our time is almost up. But what I'd like you to consider, *really* consider, right now is this: would the chance at getting everything you've always wanted be worth the risk?"

I didn't answer; I just thanked her and stood to go.

But I thought about it. I thought about it a lot. And after Liam was asleep and I was nearly ready for bed myself, I dug around in the bottom section of my jewelry box until I found the little blue box Declan had given me for my thirtieth birthday. Opening it, I stared for a long moment at the silver Möbius ring on a chain nestled inside. What if we could have the life we'd always wished for after all? What if it was at last within reach? Could I live with myself if I pushed it away, not just from me but from our son as well?

I didn't know if I could.

With trembling fingers, I fastened the chain around my neck and let the ring fall down beneath my pajama top, cool metal against warm skin.

And absurd as it sounds, it felt like, after so long away, it had finally come home.

Chapter 29

Amelia

Declan was definitely avoiding me.

At first I'd thought it was just my imagination, but now it had been several days of not seeing him. And not even a text since Sunday evening. After how comfortable we'd been with each other last week, I was sure something had to be wrong.

Why, especially after the sweet kiss we'd shared after the festival, would he avoid me? I hadn't felt this close to him since...since before. Before Las Vegas. And I was pretty sure he'd been feeling the same way. Was he regretting us reconnecting? Did he maybe want to stay just friends after all? Those sure weren't the signals I'd gotten from him before Sunday, but maybe he'd changed his mind? But why?

Wait.

Before Sunday.

Dee.

She'd gone outside with Declan when he went out to his car. I'd overheard her ask if she could walk out with him. *Crap.* Had she said something to him that upset him so much he took off? Was that it? But what could she have said that would make him leave without even saying goodbye to me? Or to Liam?

Wait.

Oh no! She wouldn't dare.

Would she?

My heart began to race. Grabbing my phone, I called her. It went straight to voicemail.

"It's me. Call me back ASAP." I threw my phone on my desk and stared at it for the next minute, willing it to ring. It didn't.

I tried to distract myself by reading some emails, but I couldn't focus. My fingers went to the ring around my neck and clutched it, twisting and spinning it.

Twenty minutes passed. I picked up my phone again and texted: *Call me. Important.*

After another unproductive half hour, I gave up trying to work. Was Dee avoiding me now, too? She'd only do that if she felt guilty about something. So what did she have to feel guilty about? On the other hand, maybe she was just busy. I couldn't wait any longer. I called her again. This time she answered with a sheepish, "Hey Ames. Sorry, but I'm just—"

"*What* did you say to him?"

"What?" I could hear other voices and a roaring that sounded like a hairdryer; she was at the salon.

Getting up, I shut my office door. Then I repeated louder: "What? Did you say? To Declan? On Sunday?"

"I…" She paused. "Hold on. Let me go in the back." In a few seconds, the background noises muffled. "Okay. Fine. I talked to him. I'm sorry, but he needed to know."

The knot in the pit of my stomach tightened. "Needed to know *what*? He's barely spoken two words to me since then. Tell me what you said."

Dee went uncharacteristically quiet. Then she sighed. "You weren't gonna tell him, were you? I know you, and I know you'd just pretend like it never happened. But it did. And he deserves to know."

Panic surged through me. "No. *Please* tell me you didn't? You told him about…?" I stopped to suck in a breath. "That was not your secret to spill!"

She fell back on the same defense. "He needed to know. If you're thinking of reconciling, he needed to know."

I pulled the phone away from my ear and took a few more deep inhalations, forcing myself to calm. "You are literally the only person I ever told about that. I trusted you. You had *no right* to tell him. It was *not* your call!"

"I had to say something. I couldn't just let you fall into the same destructive pattern again. He messes you up, Ames! You *know* that. Remember what he put you through? Think about it!"

"I *have* thought about it. It's nearly *all* I've been thinking about. I've been wracking my brain for so long trying to decide what's best for Liam and me. And now that I finally think I know what I want, you've gone and probably screwed the whole thing up!"

"Ames..."

I kept talking. It was important she hear this. "For all his flaws, for all he's hurt me, I know Declan is a good person. He's just trying to do his best for everyone he cares about. And he cares about *us*. You need to understand—you can't just drop something like this on him. He'll blame himself. He'll think I'm better off without him."

"Maybe you are! *You've* gotta understand how much I worry about you. I just want what's best for you. And that man is *not* what's best for you."

My hands were shaking. "That's not your choice to make. This is *my* life."

"Exactly. And I want you to still have one."

That stung. How could she ever think I'd do something so stupid ever again? I'd never in a million years do that to my son. Fuming, I didn't respond.

Silence spun out between us. Finally she said, "I'm sorry. I shouldn't have said that. Look, I know you're mad right now, but—"

"I'm not mad, I'm *furious*. You betrayed my trust. You threw a massive wrench into something that could maybe turn out to be the best thing that's ever happened to us. Don't you see that?"

Dee's voice dropped to a whisper. "Maybe I did fuck up. But I did it for you. I know you don't see that right now, but it's true. I'm so sorry. I hope you can forgive me."

I blew out a puff of air, sending a tendril of hair flying off my cheek. "That will depend on if I can fix this." Before she could reply, I hit End and tossed my phone on the desk.

Dammit! I leaned back into my chair, threw back my head and groaned at the ceiling.

A lot of complex emotions were cascading through me. Strongest at the moment was anger. Right behind that was fear, over the conversation I now needed to have with Declan, and how he might react. But the current flowing around these, carrying them along, was shame. Deep shame over what I'd almost done.

I didn't like thinking about it. I'd wrapped it up and buried it away and pretended it hadn't happened for so long it had become easy to forget. But now Dee had forced me to exhume my darkest moment. And it really had been my darkest moment, worse even than the night my father died. It all came back with such aching clarity. I remembered how desperate I'd felt. How lost. How alone. I no longer had my dad, Declan had abandoned me, and perhaps worst of all, somewhere along the line I'd managed to lose myself, too. I'd looked in the mirror that day and hated the stranger looking back. I didn't even know her, but I'd hated her so much. I'd wanted her to die.

But that was a long time ago. My life was vastly better now and I had so much to live for. But I worried, sometimes. Because I never wanted to end up in that horrible, dark place again.

I got up and went to the washroom. Thankfully it was empty. After locking myself into a stall, I tried to go over in my head what, thanks to my overprotective best friend, I now had to say to Declan. I knew him well enough to know he'd have taken all the blame. He carried so much guilt for so many things, but this particular thing didn't need to be one of them. What I'd done that day was no one's fault but my own.

Though I was tempted, I didn't walk over to his office, or text saying we needed to talk. I didn't want to have this conversation at work, and from past experience, I knew he either wouldn't reply to my text or would make up some excuse to delay it. But he was coming to visit Liam on Saturday and I also knew he wouldn't miss that for anything. So I'd find a way to talk to him then. It was only two days away. Two days for him to stew. Two days for me to dread the exact conversation I'd hoped to never have with him, but now could no longer avoid.

Luckily for me, a particularly complex pricing request came in not long after I returned to my desk and working through it took my mind off agonizing over things. An hour later, just as I was about to head to Kaitlyn's office to go over some other numbers, my cell phone rang. Picking it up, I saw a number I didn't recognize.

"Hello?" I said, cradling it against my shoulder as I stood to grab some files.

"Amelia?"

"Mom? Whose phone is this?"

"I was so worried I wouldn't remember your number properly. You've got to come home right away. There's been an accident."

"*What*?" An icy spike pierced my ribcage as I braced a hand on the edge of my desk. "Is it Liam? Is he okay?"

"He's…oh Amelia. There was a car…it just came out of nowhere!"

"Mom! Tell me he's all right!" My insides felt like they'd flash frozen.

"He was on his bike and…"

"Mom!"

"Yes, he's…I think he'll be fine." I exhaled a sigh of relief as she kept talking. "He hit his head pretty hard. And he was cradling his arm. I think it might be broken. We're at Emerg at SLG. The doctor's with him now."

"Be there soon," I said, hitting the End key and reaching for my bag.

My mind had one focus and one focus only: get to my son. I didn't stop to tell Kaitlyn or Josh or anyone else where I was going or why. I don't remember traffic lights or stop signs or anything much about the drive. But I do know I walked into the Emergency room craning my head for my mother just over twenty minutes later.

SLG was Swann's Landing General, our small local hospital. If anything major happened patients were transferred to Lynchburg or Richmond or—God forbid—all the way to DC. I took some small measure of relief in the fact that they were keeping him here, at least for now.

My heart was racing as I looked around, at last spotting Mom in a chair by the reception desk. She turned and saw me, waving me over. "Amelia, good. It looks like he has a concussion, and they're putting a cast on his arm. We can go in, I think." She turned to the nurse behind the desk. "Liam York's mother is here. Is it okay if we go back?"

The nurse picked up the phone and made a short call, then nodded at us. Mom immediately went through the gray double doors to the left and into the examination area behind. I followed her past two drawn curtains before she pulled the third one aside.

My poor little boy lay on a raised bed with his left arm extended over a towel as a nurse in purple scrubs fitted a cast over his wrist and forearm. He had some bandaged scrapes and the beginnings of a large bruise on the left side of his face, but, typical Liam, he seemed fascinated as he watched her tend to him. As soon as he saw me, he broke into a broad smile.

"Mommy! Guess what?" Before I could respond, he said, "I fell off my bike! Broke my arm, just like Brooke at school. She has a pink cast. Can I have a pink cast?" he asked, turning back to the nurse.

"Well, for now you're getting what I have, which is plain ole' white. But you can ask your friends to color it pink if you want." As she spoke, I came around the other side of the bed and took Liam's good hand in mine. The nurse looked at me and smiled. "Hello Liam's mom. I'm Sandra."

Although my son was clearly not too upset right now, I was upset enough for both of us, far too upset to waste time on introductions or pleasantries. "How bad is he hurt?"

"The doctor should be back in to talk to you in a few minutes, but the gist of it is that he's got a hairline fracture, some minor abrasions, and a concussion. Not great, but sounds like it could've been a lot worse from what Liam's grandma told me about what happened." To Liam, she added. "You are a very lucky little boy."

I released a sigh of equal parts relief and frustration and pulled the chair behind me closer to the side of the bed, not letting go of Liam's hand. My mother settled into the second chair against the wall. "Mom, please tell me exactly how this happened," I said, my eyes fixed on my son.

I heard her draw in a breath preparing herself to tell me, and I couldn't help it; I immediately wondered if she was somehow at fault. Or, more likely, she blamed herself.

"He wanted to ride his bike home from school today, like we sometimes do on nice days. I brought it with me and he rode beside me while I walked. We were on that stretch of Pine Street where they've ripped up the sidewalks—you remember they're replacing the pipes over there?"

"Sure. You said a car was involved?" I turned to face her.

"We were on the edge of the road, but close to the curb, and I was keeping an eye on him, I swear, but he likes to speed up a bit then stop and wait for me to catch up. He thinks it's funny."

"Gramma walks slow," Liam said solemnly.

"Just as we got past the intersection at Forbes, a car turned onto Pine. It was going way too fast, didn't hardly even slow for the stop sign. I don't know why they think they can drive like that in residential neighborhoods!" Noting my look of frustration, she got back on topic. "Liam hit the brakes to wait for me just as it came around the corner, but he lost control and his bike skidded sideways into the road."

"It went right out from under me!" Liam said. "Then kaboom!"

Eyes narrowed, I asked him, "Did the car hit you?"

"No, thank Heavens," my mother replied. "It hit his bike tire and sent the whole thing flying. But Liam's leg was still over the crossbar, so he went flying right along with it. He hit his head on the pavement and landed on his arm. I just thank the Lord it wasn't worse." She crossed herself, and I realized just how shaken she really was. My mother hadn't gone to church in years.

"And the driver? Did they stop to see if he was okay?"

Mom nodded. "Yes. It was old Wilbur Sage. You remember him? He used to run the gas station out by the highway when you were a teenager. He's retired now."

"Was he drunk?"

"I don't think so. I think his eyes are just going. The man really shouldn't be driving anymore. I borrowed his phone to call 911 and the police arrived just after the ambulance. They said an officer would be in touch to get my statement."

I shook my head, anger surging through me. "He should get more than losing his license! He should be charged with endangerment. Liam could've been killed!"

My mother pursed her lips, glancing over at Liam, then back at me. "Perhaps we should discuss this later?"

Reluctantly, I nodded. She was right. I needed to put a lid on my rage at that stupid old man for now. For Liam's sake.

"That's about it," the nurse said as she finished with the cast. "You're all patched up, buddy. I'm sure Dr. Fielding will be back shortly." With that, she pulled aside the curtain and disappeared.

Buddy. Oh crap.

As if she read my mind, Mom asked, "Have you called Declan?"

"No, not yet. I rushed straight here as fast as I could. I'll go do it now." I got up and went back out to the waiting area. No answer. It didn't go straight to voicemail like he'd hit Ignore; it rang six times before the message kicked in. When the beep sounded, I said. "It's me. Amelia. You need to call me right away. Liam was in an accident. Don't freak out though. He's hurt but it looks like he'll be okay. We're at the Swann's Landing hospital. I'll explain the whole thing when I see you."

As soon as I got back and sat down, my mother said, "Is he coming?"

"I…" Before I could finish, an older man with graying hair and deep lines around his mouth pulled back the curtain and came in. He held a clipboard in one hand.

"Dr. Fielding?" I asked.

"Last time I looked," he replied with a grin. Glancing down at the chart, he said, "You must be Mrs. York. And this young man I've already met. How're you feeling now, Liam?" He went over and sat on the edge of the bed.

My son looked at him with wide eyes. "My face hurts," he said, rubbing one of the bandages with his good hand.

Dr. Fielding nodded. "I just bet it does. I'm sorry to have to tell you that your head might hurt for a few more days. And that arm is going to hurt even longer."

Liam's bottom lip protruded, a sure sign of displeasure, but he didn't say anything.

The doctor swiveled his upper body to face my mother and me.

"His arm will take four to six weeks to heal completely. As for the concussion, has he ever had one before?"

"Nope, never," I said. "First broken bone, too. First accident, really. Guess he decided to get it all out of the way at once."

Dr. Fielding jotted something on the chart. "I'd like him to stay here for observation tonight, but he should be able to go home in the morning." Turning back to my son, he said, "Liam, do you know what a concussion is?"

He shook his head. His eyelids were starting to get heavy.

"Well, a concussion is a brain injury. Luckily yours is a mild one. It's caused when you fall hard on your head and your brain gets jolted against the inside of your skull. I know you're tired, but I'm sorry to say you probably won't get a very good sleep tonight. A nurse will be waking you up every three hours to check on you."

"Why do you need to do that?" my mother asked.

"She'll be making sure he wakes up fine, and that he's not experiencing confusion, nausea, slurred speech, vision problems, severe headache, or numbness. I'll get him transferred up to a room as soon as possible, and I'll pop back in to see him again later before I leave. I'll be back in the morning, and if everything looks good, I'll release him then."

"Thank you, Dr. Fielding," I said.

"You're welcome." To Liam, he said, "All in all young man, I'd say you were pretty lucky. See you later." He smiled at us encouragingly and then left the room.

I reached for my phone. No missed calls or texts. Declan must be in a client meeting, I thought, because as soon as he got my message, I knew he'd rush here much like I did.

Not ten minutes later, the curtain was pulled all the way aside and Sandra the nurse reappeared. "Time to go upstairs," she told Liam cheerfully. His eyelids fluttered open, but he just looked at her, confused. She moved around behind his bed, unlocked the wheel locks, and began to push the bed, with Liam in it, out into the hall. We followed her into a large elevator and rode up to the third floor. Once we disembarked, we went around a corner and down a long hallway. At last she stopped in front of room 310.

"Right in here," she said to us as she expertly maneuvered the bed into place against a wall. Mom and I arranged two of the chairs closer to his bedside and sat down just as Sandra asked Liam if he'd like a drink.

He nodded, so she brought him a cup of ice water with a bendy straw. Once he'd had a sip, she set it on the side table within easy reach. "Are you hungry?"

Liam blinked, then shrugged.

"Well, one of the stripers will be in with dinner shortly," she told him. He didn't respond, his eyes once again losing focus. I figured he'd be completely out in a minute or two.

I slid my phone from my pocket again. "Holy cow, it's nearly six!" I said to my mom.

"Is Declan on his way?"

"I haven't heard back from him yet, but he'll probably be here soon."

"Is Daddy coming?" Liam asked softly. Was he just exhausted from all the excitement, or did I need to worry about the potential side effects from the concussion? Both Dr. Fielding and Nurse Sandra had just seen him, so I decided it had to be the former.

I reached for his hand and gave it a squeeze. "I'm sure he'll get here as soon as he can."

A small sob slipped out. My son had had a truly horrible day. It was amazing to me that he hadn't cried the entire time I'd been with him, although I knew without asking that there had been plenty of tears earlier. "I want Daddy." His voice was wobbly as fat drops welled up in the corners of his eyes.

"I know, little man." Turning to my mom, I said, "I'll go try him again. Be right back."

After kissing Liam on the forehead, I left the room and closed the door behind me. I headed down the hall until I found a small waiting area and called Declan again. Still no answer. I texted him this time: *Liam's been in an accident. We're at SL hospital. Please call ASAP.*

I was starting to get angry. Where the hell was he? How could so much time have passed without checking his messages? Had he let his battery die? Did he not own a charger? How could someone on the road as much as Declan not have a remote charger?

Scrolling through my contacts, I called Josh.

He answered on the second ring. "Hey Amelia. What's up?"

"Josh, hey. Sorry to bother you, but I really need to reach Declan. It's kind of an emergency and he's not answering his cell. Do you have any idea where he is?"

"Not a clue. I didn't see him today. What's going on?"

I told him what had happened and Josh promised he'd also keep trying to reach Declan until one of us succeeded. When I disconnected, I was full on furious.

Was he avoiding my calls or listening to my message because of what Dee had said to him? Was that it? I thought of Liam, all tearful, telling me *I want Daddy,* and my fury raged higher. This was playing out just as I'd always feared, always worried might happen if I let Declan into our lives. His son needed him, really needed him, and he was nowhere to be found.

He'd bailed on us—on me—when we needed him most, just like Dee said he would.

With a deep sigh, I slipped my phone back into my bag and tried to calm myself before I returned to Liam's room.

I hated to admit it, but maybe Dee was right after all. Maybe we *were* better off without him.

Declan

I was in a foul mood. Colleen was no stranger to my bad moods, and for the most part she'd been leaving me alone. I'd taken to hiding in my office with the door closed and attempting to distract myself by responding to client concerns. But it wasn't helping. Nothing I did was going my way. I'd been working my ass off to convince a certain big name drug chain to sign with us, but it looked like we were going to lose out to one of the Madison Avenue agencies. Since we'd already offered competitive pricing and above-and-beyond service, I figured it had to be for prestige reasons. And that was one thing I couldn't compete with. So basically my week so far had been an utter shitshow.

And it was about to get a lot worse before it got better.

After how idiotically happy I'd been the week before, falling back to my old hopeless, miserable self hit me harder than usual. I couldn't even remember the last time my mood had been this rotten. No, that was a lie. I totally could. After James had passed. And after losing Amelia the second time. And after Laura and the baby had died. And losing Amelia the first time. Granted, not all of those were my fault. But most of them were. The list of fallout from my fuckups just went on and on. And now there was one more, one I'd never even known about.

I'd been right all along—she was better off without me. But things were different now. I could no longer avoid her for long. Not only were we back to working in the same building, but, more importantly, there was also no way in hell I'd give up time with my son. My kids were pretty much the only things I still had going for me. Yet, much as I looked forward to seeing Liam, I was glad there was still a bit of time before the weekend. I needed more time to wrap my brain around what Amelia's friend had told me. Though I'd kept my distance the last few days, it had never been my intention to stay away for long.

Even this much time was too much. Hell, I was already missing her so bad I'd nearly got up and walked over to her office a dozen times. But I didn't. I just wasn't ready to face her yet. So I'd dove into work behind closed doors. Until just after two on Wednesday anyway. Because at 2:02 on Wednesday, my cell phone rang.

And everything changed yet again.

It was my brother's home number on the screen. "Ryan?" I said, stupidly. Because why the hell would he be home at two in the afternoon on a workday?

"It's me." She didn't sound like herself. Her voice was hoarse, almost as if she'd been...crying? *Diana*?

Oh fuck. "What's up?"

"He didn't come home last night. And I can't reach him. Declan, what if...?" She didn't need to finish that sentence.

"Don't. Don't say it. I'll be right over. Then we'll go find him and bring him home."

I heard what might have been a sniffle.

When she didn't reply, I said, "Okay?"

"Okay."

"See you in a few minutes."

Grabbing my jacket, I walked out, not pausing to power down my laptop or tell Colleen I was leaving. I just made a bee-line for my car and sped to my brother's house. I was damn lucky I didn't get pulled over.

I pulled into the driveway beside her Audi and slammed the gearshift into Park. Diana was already standing in the front doorway waiting for me.

"I figured out why he's not answering his phone," she said as I approached. She held up a cell phone. "Found this on top of his dresser. The sound was off."

"Now that's proof right there of weird behavior. He's been gone an entire day with no phone?" I shook my head. "Is it locked? Give it here, maybe I can find something helpful."

She laughed, a dry sound that didn't contain an ounce of humor. "You think I didn't already go through it? Every email? Every text and DM?"

"And? What'd you find?"

"His dealer. At least I think so. C'mon." She stepped outside and locked the door behind her. "I know where he might be." Her hair had been brushed smooth and she was wearing makeup, but I knew that had-it-up-to-here look all too well. My brother was going to get one hell of an earful once we found him. If we found him.

"Where're we going?"

"Bubba's. It's a crappy little hole in the wall over on the far side of the river. Know it?"

I shook my head. "Nope. But we'll find it." Before I could make a move toward my SUV, Diana pulled out her key fob and unlocked her Audi. "I can drive," I told her, mindful of her agitation.

"Fine. You drive." She walked around and got in on the passenger side. Of her own car. Shrugging, I got behind the wheel.

Twenty minutes later, we pulled into a cracked and garbage-strewn parking lot behind a rundown block of buildings. At one time there would have been a row of storefronts, but now most had boarded up windows. At one end a grimy convenience store still seemed to be in business. At the other was Bubba's.

Dust motes hung in the patch of sunlight revealed when I hauled open the door. As we walked into the dimly lit room, we were immediately assaulted by the combined scents of cigarette smoke, spilled beer, and rancid grease. The grizzled patrons on the stools along the bar had not come to Bubba's for a drink; they were here for the sole purpose of eliminating sobriety. Not one of them looked up to check out the new arrivals. I figured, much like vampires, the sudden bright light would hurt their eyes.

"Any clue what he looks like?" I muttered to Diana.

She didn't answer, instead strolling over to an empty space at the bar between an old woman who appeared to be asleep on the bar top and a wild haired guy who, by the looks of him, was more than likely homeless.

There was no need for her to call for the bartender's attention. He stepped right up and appraised her. "Help ya?" he said, his gaze darting between her face and her tits. I'd bet he didn't get women who looked like Diana in here often.

"I'm looking for a guy named Frank," she said, replacing her usual demanding tone with a softer, flirtier one.

The bartender was a heavy set guy, with a round beer belly, yet heavily muscled biceps. I assumed they got a good workout tossing out drunks. And he was not immune to her considerable charms. "Lotsa people come in an' outta here," he shrugged, trying to play it cool. "You got a pic?"

"No. But I have a photo of another man who might have been with him a few times. Possibly recently." She held up her phone and showed him a picture of Ryan. I glanced at the patrons again, including the ones at tables along the side and in the back. My brother, with his L.L. Bean clean cut good looks, would stand out like a goddamn beacon in this place. If he'd been here, the bartender would remember him. The question was: would he admit it?

He took Diana's phone and brought it closer to his face, then looked at her over the top of it. "Who's he to ya? Husband?"

I noticed the barest perceptible flinch, but she hid it just as quickly as it appeared. "Brother. So was he here? He was probably with Frank."

She said the name just a little louder this time and I heard movement from a booth against the side wall. Quickly I shot over there, catching a skinny man by the forearm as he was making a dash for the rear door.

"Frank I presume?" I said, hauling him backward. He was so thin a good breeze could've knocked him down. It took very little effort to drag him back to his seat, even with his attempts to resist.

Diana came to meet us as I shoved the guy back into the booth he'd vacated. A naked bulb on a cord hung above a table that hadn't been wiped down in a very long time. It was covered in sticky circular stains and I made a point not to rest my arms on it.

She showed Frank the photo on her phone. "You know this man?"

He glared at us, refusing to reply.

I grabbed him by the loose fabric at the shoulder of his shirt and lifted him up an inch, trying to play bad cop to Diana's good cop. For the life of me, I couldn't quite decide if that was a role reversal or not. "Look again," I snarled.

"Get your hands the fuck off me," he said gruffly, struggling to get loose.

I released him but stayed right beside him, hovering and trying to look intimidating. As I was wearing an expensive leather jacket over a button-up dress shirt, I highly doubted I was succeeding, but I figured it was worth a shot.

Diana tried again. "Look, this doesn't have to be a problem. I already know you know my husband. I just need to know the last time you saw him. It's important."

Frank's eyes widened. "You're RK's wife?"

RK? I rolled my eyes. My brother was *such* an idiot sometimes.

She nodded. "Did you see him today? Or yesterday? Can you recall?"

The man frowned, swabbing a palm over his face and pausing at his forehead to press his thumb and forefinger against his temples. "Jesus-fucking-Christ. What did he do?

312

Did he go see Sammy? Sammy's a fuckin' menace. Tell me he didn't go see Sammy?"

I sat down on the bench beside him, forcing him to shuffle over a few inches. "Frank? I want you to listen closely. It's very important. We're not cops and we have no intention of getting them involved. But we really need to find…uh, RK. Now think hard. *When* did you last see him?"

"He was in here yest'day. I dunno when. Daytime. I didn't have what he needed this time. I was all out. He got pissed. Then he demanded another connection. Threw a coupla Benjamins at me, said he didn't care what it cost."

Diana smiled at him. And if I didn't know her as well as I did, I might even have thought it was genuine. "And what did you tell him? How do we find this Sammy?"

Frank barked out a laugh, shaking his head like we were both idiots. "I'll tell ya the same thing I said to RK. You don't find Sammy. Sammy finds you." His voice dropped lower as he held Diana's gaze. "Believe me, sweet thang, you do *not* want Sammy to find you."

Her Good Cop mask vanished, replaced with pure ice as she leaned across the table until she was only a few inches from Frank's face. "If RK went to find Sammy, then *we* need to find Sammy. And you're gonna tell us how to do that. Aren't you, *sweet thang*?"

I had to give her credit. Frank's Adam's apple bobbed in his throat. He fumbled in the breast pocket of his flannel shirt and pulled out a matchbook. Inside was scrawled a phone number. "You didn't get this from me," he said, shaking his head as he tossed it at her. "And you ain't never seen me neither."

I stood up to let him pass and he went straight out the rear door without looking back.

"Classy," I muttered to Diana as we headed for the front. "Ry's really hangin' with the cool kids these days."

Diana didn't reply. The moment she got back in her car, she pulled out her phone and called the number on the matchbook.

"Is this Sammy?" she said a minute later. Then, "Didn't catch his name. What does it matter? I need to procure some…supplies." Another pause. "Richmond? Fine. Where?" She jotted something below the phone number. When she ended the call, she turned to me. "We're going to Richmond."

I glanced at the time on the dashboard. "I need to make a call first." I reached inside my jacket, but my phone wasn't in its usual spot. Nor was it in either side pocket, or my pants.

Shit. It must've fallen out somewhere. Or maybe I left it on my desk? I did pretty much run out of my office like my ass was on fine.

"Can I use your phone?" I said. She seemed deep in thought, simply handing it over without looking up. After I called Patrick and asked him to pick up Alexis at the sitter's and take her back to his place, we headed for the highway that would take us to Richmond. And hopefully Ryan.

Chapter 30

Declan

It was just past five when I pulled in behind a decrepit Feed 'n Fuel in what was quite possibly the sketchiest part of Richmond. This Sammy guy was supposed to be meeting us here. He hadn't said what he looked like or what kind of car he drove, but I figured, like Frank had said, he would find us.

No one seemed to be around but a few stray cats investigating the overflowing dumpster. I killed the engine and turned to Diana. "So now what?"

"Now we wait."

I eyed my surroundings. "Don't recommend we wait for long."

"Someone will be here. And then we follow that someone to Ryan."

"Great plan," I snorted. "But what if that someone wants to rob us? Or kill us? Then what?"

She just looked at me. Then she opened the glove compartment to reveal the handle of a revolver.

The fuck?

In one quick movement I reached over and slammed it shut, staring at Diana incredulously. "Are you fucking kidding me right now? We're not in a goddamn Liam Neeson movie! *Jesus*. Where'd you even get that thing?"

She shrugged. "I've had it for years. Tucked it in there yesterday, just in case."

"Is it loaded? Do you even know how to use it?"

She shot me an irritated look. "Of course."

"Wow." I shook my head. "Well keep it hidden. The last thing we want is trouble." Nothing about this situation felt right, but if Sammy did show up and saw the gun, I didn't see finding Ryan in our future. Maybe a jail cell. Maybe a morgue. But not my brother.

But we did need to find him, and I was willing to risk a lot to make sure he was safe. So I dropped the subject, hoping the gun wouldn't be needed.

After ten minutes of staring out the window in uncomfortable silence, I turned back to her. "Maybe you should call him again?"

"No need," she replied indicating behind me.

I turned to see a scruffy girl of possibly twenty approaching. Though there was a decided chill in the air, she wore only ripped out jeans and a gray tee. "Is Sammy a chick?" I asked under my breath.

"Nope." Diana opened her door and stepped out.

Reluctantly I did the same.

"Where's Sammy?" Diana asked with a touch of irritation.

The young woman's bloodshot eyes were ringed in messy black eyeliner and she had a wild head of dirty bleach-job hair. She scowled at us with clear distrust. Ignoring Diana's question, in a rough voice she said, "You got the dosh?"

"*Dosh*? Really?" I said. "What decade *is* this?"

They both ignored me. "Wouldn't be here if I didn't," Diana replied. "Now where's Sammy?"

The girl snorted. "Who d'ya think sent me?"

"Is he with RK?"

Her eye's narrowed. "Shoulda guessed you were friends of RK's," she said with a derisive snort. "No cash, no stash. Sammy's rules." Shrugging, she turned to leave.

Diana stepped forward and grabbed her by the arm. As she twisted back to us, I spotted red track marks on the inside of one pale elbow just above Diana's fingers. "Take us to RK. I'll make it worth your while."

The girl appraised us both again, then held out a hand, palm up, to Diana. The implication was clear. Diana reached into her pocket and slapped down a fifty.

The bill was tucked inside the girl's bra so fast I barely saw it vanish. "Block down on yer right. Shit-green door. Go downstairs." Then she ran off, faster than I would have thought a strung-out junkie could move.

Diana took three steps forward before I stopped her. "No way. Get back in the car. We are absolutely not walking. Not around here."

This time she didn't argue.

It was a block and half down, on the left. Not the right. It took us nearly fifteen minutes to locate the green door that I could have found in five if I'd had enough details. I parked on the street out front of a run-down duplex with a sagging roof. There was a skinny dog on a chain in the front yard of the other side, the side with the brown door hanging half off its hinges. The mutt was asleep in the dirt. If we'd had any food in the car, I would have tossed it to the poor thing.

Before we got out, Diana retrieved the gun from the glove compartment and tucked it inside her jacket. I sighed audibly, but didn't comment. Maybe she was right; maybe we were better off with some sort of backup. Even if I didn't like the idea one fucking bit.

We went up a broken cement walkway to a door painted many decades ago in a color that truly could only be described as Shit Green. Diana knocked a few times, but when no one answered after a minute, she tried the handle and found it unlocked. The hinges squeaked as she pushed it open and we stepped inside. I headed straight down the darkened stairs with Diana on my heels.

"Ryan?" I called in a loud whisper. No answer. I could hear music playing somewhere above us, but the junkie girl had told us to go down to the basement. An open door was on our left, and I peeked inside. It reeked of stale sweat and beer. Piles of dirty clothes littered the floor, and a heavyset guy with a graying beard lay passed out on the bed. Wrinkling my nose in disgust, I stepped back into the hall.

Across the way was a longer room with a bar along one wall. Bongs, bowls, pipes, and other drug paraphernalia were scattered on its surface and on the floor. Two stained couches bracketed a table covered in beer cans and cigarette butts.

Which reminded me. "Hey, has Ry been smoking again? Have you smelled it on him?"

She stood in the doorway surveying the detritus. Now she looked at me oddly. "Not a whiff. Not in years. Why?"

317

"He tends to fall back on old habits when he…well, falls back on old habits." I couldn't decide if her not noticing any cigarette stink was a good sign or not.

Diana disappeared back into the hallway. Before I could rejoin her, I heard her suck in a sharp breath. "Ryan? Baby?" Then more muffled: "Oh God, Ryan. Wake up!"

I rushed over and found her in the next room down. My brother lay on a mattress on the floor, one arm flung across his eyes and what looked to be dried puke caked down the front of his shirt. He wasn't moving. Diana knelt beside him, her fingers on his neck pulse.

"*Shit*. Is he breathing?" I asked. "Should I call 911?"

"He's breathing, but it's too slow. C'mon Ry. Come back to me." She pushed aside his arm and slapped his cheeks. Relief coursed through me as I saw his eyelids flutter. A moment later they cracked open.

He squinted against the overhead light, brows draw tight. "What?" He stopped to cough and Diana gripped his shoulder and pulled him onto his side. When his coughing fit subsided, he croaked, "Where am I?"

"You're okay. You're gonna be just fine," she said, stroking his arm. To me, she said, "There's a bottle of water in my car. Can you go grab it?"

"Maybe I should help y—"

"Just go. He needs a drink."

Don't we all? I thought, but I went. When I returned with the half-full bottle, Diana had my brother propped up into a sitting position against the wall. He was way too pale, and had dark hollows below each eye. His lips looked sort of bluish-purple, like he'd put on lipstick. She tilted the water bottle to his mouth and he drank gratefully. About fifteen seconds later, he pushed it away, turned to one side and vomited the water back up.

"Sorry," Ryan mumbled. He wasn't meeting either of our eyes.

"Jesus, bro. How many did you take? Do you even remember?"

He just shrugged. It seemed like it took a lot of effort.

"You're dehydrated. You need to drink more," Diana told him softly. She gripped one of his hands in hers. I noticed his fingernails were grimy. Why I was surprised by that, I couldn't say. Everything about this entire situation was grimy. Why would his fingernails be any different?

He drank a few more swallows and we waited to see if the water would stay down. Though I had plenty I wanted to say to him, I kept my trap shut. He knew full well he deserved a shitload of lectures from both of us and he was likely dreading every one. But right now his stupidity was a lot less important than his health. So my opinion on the matter could wait.

"So?" I said to Diana after a few minutes had passed with no further puking. "Should we take him to Emerg?"

She checked his pulse again. "His heartbeat's not erratic. Thankfully, this is not an OD situation, it's just a partied way too hard situation." Patting his sweaty cheek, she said, "You're definitely an idiot, but not one that needs his stomach pumped this time." With a disgusted glance at his shirt, she added, "You seem to have taken care of that all on your own."

Was that relief I saw on his pallid face? He was damn lucky to be alive and he probably knew it. "So who's this Sammy guy?" I asked.

Now Ryan's eyes flew all the way open. "Is he here?" He went still, his gaze darting up to the ceiling and I wondered if Sammy was the source of the music I'd heard. "We hafta..." He stopped to stifle another cough. "We should get out of here before he comes back."

Diana turned to me "Think between the two of us we can get him to the car?"

I nodded. "C'mon, Ry," I said as I wound a hand below his armpit and around his back. "Can you stand?"

Though he tried his best, he was weak, staggering under his own weight. But with our combined efforts—well, mostly mine, let's be honest—we managed to get him up the stairs and down the walk to Diana's car. She pulled open the rear passenger door and I helped him onto the backseat, leaning across him to do up the seatbelt, although I figured he'd spend the drive lying rather than sitting.

The trip home was a mostly quiet one. The sun set as Ryan's snores emanated from the backseat, but Diana and I didn't talk much. When we were approaching Lynchburg, I said, "Should I go straight to that rehab place he was at before?"

She shook her head. "Not tonight. But we'll definitely be having a serious conversation about that tomorrow. For tonight, just take us home please."

So I took them home. To my relief, my brother woke up as we pulled into the driveway, and seemed a little steadier on his feet. I helped him inside and down the hall to his bed. Diana pulled off his shoes and began unbuttoning his filthy shirt.

"Wait. Before you go, can you help me help him shower? He can't go to bed like this."

I sighed, but of course she was right. It took us another thirty minutes to get him clean and back into bed. Tomorrow I'd take him to the rehab center myself if I had to.

"Okay, well, I'm gonna go pick up Alexis," I said.

Diana was sitting on the edge of their bed beside Ryan, who had already fallen back asleep. She turned to look at me and I swear to God I've never seen such gratitude in her eyes. "Thank you, Declan. I mean it."

"Call me tomorrow if you need anything at all. Hell, even if you don't."

She nodded. With another quick glance at my brother's pasty, but very much alive face, I headed for the door. No matter how fucked up his addiction demons were, how many setbacks he had, and how long it might take to overcome them, I'd be there with him every step. Even though he might hate me for it much of the time.

I needed my brother alive. And so would his child.

When I got behind the wheel of my car, I reached for my phone to call Patrick and tell him I was on my way. Then I remembered I'd left it somewhere. I turned on the interior light and checked the few places in my car I sometimes stashed it, but it wasn't in any of them. On impulse, I leaned down and felt underneath my seat. And there it was. It must have slipped out of my pocket as I got out earlier. Smiling, I fished it out and unlocked the screen. And then my smile faded.

Twelve missed calls. Six voice mails. Three texts. The first one, from Amelia, sent my stressed out brain into another round of panic: *Liam's been in an accident. We're at SL hospital. Please call ASAP*

Adrenaline surged through me. I didn't call; I didn't even pause to listen to the voice mail messages. I just threw my phone in the cup holder, put the car in drive, and sped to Swann's Landing as fast as I could.

Amelia

"Mom, please. Take my car. I'll be fine, I swear." She'd been looking tired for a while now. I was sure I did, too, but I simply couldn't bring myself to leave Liam.

"I can stay," she said, shifting in her chair. Although my mother still had a valid Virginia driver's license, she hadn't driven in years. It was only a few short blocks to home, though. I was confident she'd be fine.

I dug in my purse for my keys and unwound the car key and fob from the rest. "Here," I said as I handed them over. "Please go home. You should get some sleep."

"So should you. Come with me. You can come back first thing in the morning."

"I'm staying."

She looked at me and sighed and I knew she was done arguing. Slipping her coat on, she took a few steps toward the door, but turned back before she opened it. "Still no word from him?"

I shook my head.

"That seems very strange. Hope everything is alright."

If she knew our history, she'd know him bailing on me really wasn't that strange. But I was still furious that he'd do it to Liam. "I'm sure it's fine," I said. "Goodnight, Mom."

She gave me a wan smile and left.

Yawning, I leaned back in my chair. She wasn't wrong about one thing. I *was* exhausted, both mentally and physically. Examining her recently emptied chair, I debated pulling it close to mine. Could I lie across both of them? I could see no possible position that would be even remotely comfortable, so I stayed where I was.

I dug out my phone again. Still nothing. I texted Josh to check in. He replied a few minutes later saying he hadn't been able to reach Declan yet, either. Angry as I was, suspicious as I was that he might be avoiding me on purpose—which I realized was completely irrational, but I couldn't help it—now I also worried that something could be seriously wrong.

But what? What would keep him from getting to Liam? From even responding? If his battery had run down, he would have recharged it by now. Unless he lost or broke his phone?

I watched Liam as he slept, his sweet little face marred by bruises and bandages and my anger rose up again. Tired, irrational anger, but all I could think was: *where the hell are you?*

321

As if in answer to my thoughts, the door opened and Declan came striding into the room. Clumps of hair stuck out in all directions and there were high spots of red on his cheekbones. He went straight to Liam's side, gently stroking the unblemished part of his face as his other hand clutched his son's fingers. Liam shuffled position a little but didn't wake.

"Let him sleep," I said quietly.

Declan startled, his head whipping around as he noticed me sitting there. His eyes were wide and worried. "How is he?" he asked.

"Concussion and a broken arm." I replied tersely. "Not great, but he'll recover."

He slumped into the chair beside me. "So what happened?"

"He had an accident on his bike on the way home from school." My brain silently added: *And it was a good thing Mom could reach me, because no one would've been able to reach you.*

"Shit."

"Yeah." We were quiet for a bit. At last I couldn't hold back any longer. "I called you several times. Where *were* you? Was your phone off?"

He winced. As he started to reply, the door swung open and the nurse came in. I'd been expecting her any minute to check on Liam, so it was no surprise.

"You're still here?" she said to me with a smile.

"Yeah. But we'll get out of your hair for a few minutes so you can do what you need to do," I replied.

Declan followed me into the hallway, Instead of standing outside Liam's room, I went down to the waiting room near the elevators.

"So?" I said as we sat down.

He leaned forward in the hard plastic chair, his hands clasped between his knees. "I didn't know. My phone must've fallen out of my jacket pocket and slid under the seat of my car. I didn't find it until many hours later."

I arched a skeptical brow. "You couldn't hear it? Was the battery dead?"

"It wasn't that. I was in Diana's car by the time I realized it was gone."

My eyes shot wide. "You've gotta be kidding! You were with Diana of all people for hours and never noticed your phone was missing?" I stood up and turned away from him, covering my eyes with one hand. Then another thought hit me and it

322

stopped me dead. "Wait. Don't tell me you two…" I trailed off, unable to even say it. How could this day possibly get any worse? I felt sick to my stomach.

I heard Declan heave a deep sigh. "Ryan was missing," he started, his voice deadpan. "He didn't come home last night. Diana called me in a panic to help her find him. She was terrified he might have OD'd again. We both were."

Suddenly I understood. I remembered how shaken he'd been when Ryan had nearly died years ago. Declan had gotten him to the hospital in time, but it had been close, and he'd nearly lost his brother. Much as I felt sympathetic to whatever ordeal he'd gone through tonight, I also felt a wash of relief that the conclusion I'd jumped to had been way off base.

"Did you find him?" I asked, sitting back down and looked over at him. I wanted to touch him, to close this distance between us. But I didn't.

He nodded He was staring down at his hands. "After a shitload of running around to various sketchy places, we finally did. He was passed out in a basement of some dump in Richmond. I still can't believe he fell off the wagon again. He's been clean for so long! Or so I'd thought, anyway. Maybe I've been so wrapped up in my own crap that I failed to even notice. Diana did though. She always does. And I should've listened to her."

Declan and Diana had talked about Ryan being back on drugs before tonight? He'd never mentioned it. Which meant he still didn't feel comfortable enough to share important parts of his life with me. If this had any hope of working, we needed to figure out how to be honest and open with each other again. And I knew deep down that whether I wanted to or not, it had to start with me.

"It's not your fault. You did everything you could," I said as kindly as I could.

He shook his head again. "It doesn't matter now. What matters is that he needs to get his ass back into rehab. I'm gonna take him there myself tomorrow, but Diana wanted to keep him home tonight. I found my phone when I got back to my car after everything. Got your message and drove straight here."

I attempted a small smile. It was important he understand I wasn't upset anymore. "It's been a hell of a day, hasn't it?"

Declan raised his eyes to mine. "Understatement of the year." He didn't smile back as he said it. Instead, he blew out another sigh. "Did you *really* think I was off screwing my sister-in-law? Do you really think so little of me, even now?"

"I...no. Of course not. I was just angry. Stressed out and upset and Liam needed you—*I* needed you—and you were nowhere to be found and I lost my temper. I'm sorry." I was tempted to reach for his hand, but still I stopped myself.

"I would've been right here beside you both if I could have. I hope you know that."

"I do," I nodded. "C'mon, let's go back to his room. He might still be awake and you can talk to him for a minute or two."

When we walked back in, the nurse was just finishing up. "Okay, Liam. You're right as rain. Back to dreamland you go." As she passed us on her way to the door, she said to me, "If you want my advice, you should really go home. Having you here is a distraction, and he needs all the sleep he can get. Come back first thing tomorrow. He may not even notice you're gone."

"I'll take that under advisement," I replied. Much as I wanted to stay, I was starting to think she may be right.

Declan went over and sat on the edge of Liam's bed. "Hey buddy. How ya doing?"

"Hi Daddy." Liam's voice was soft and sleepy, but I could hear how pleased he was to see Declan.

"You really did a number on yourself, didn't you?"

A big yawn. Then: "Fell off my bike."

Declan gently pushed Liam's hair off his forehead, scrutinizing the scrapes and bruises on the side of his face. "Did your bike survive?" he asked.

Liam shook his head. "It got smooshed by a car. I nearly did, too."

"Oh honey," I said, coming around the other side of the bed. "You must've been *so* scared."

"Only a little. Gramma said I was a brave boy." His eyelids were fluttering.

"You are the bravest boy I know," said Declan. He leaned over and kissed Liam on the forehead. "And I'll bet Santa will bring you a new bike if you ask him."

We sat back down as Liam dozed off. Declan pulled out his phone. "I need to call Patrick. He picked up Lex for me. Damn, I should've called earlier. She's probably asleep in his spare room by now." He went out into the hall.

When he reappeared, I asked, "Everything okay?"

"Yeah, she's staying there tonight."

"Did you tell him about Ryan?" Before the words were even out of my mouth, I realized how dumb the question was. He'd only been gone a couple of minutes. If he'd had to explain Ryan's ordeal, it would have taken much longer.

"No, I think that can wait 'til tomorrow. Ry has enough to deal with right now. Diana'll probably threaten him with imminent death if he doesn't agree to go back to rehab."

"Understood." We'd been talking softly, but just then Liam snorted in his sleep and rolled over away from us. Maybe the nurse had been right; maybe we were disturbing his rest. I turned to Declan. "Do you mind giving me a lift home?"

"Of course."

I got up and went to my son, dropping a gentle kiss on his cheek. "Goodnight, little man," I whispered. "I'll see you in the morning."

It was raining as we walked out to Declan's car. We drove the short way in silence, the only music the rain drumming on the roof. As we pulled into my mom's driveway, I turned to him and at last reached for his hand. "Come inside," I said.

I thought I saw a frown in the dim light from the dashboard. "I should probably get home," he replied after a moment. "It's been a very long day."

"Stay with me tonight."

He looked over at me, already shaking his head as he pulled his fingers free.

"Please. I want you to. And we can go back to see Liam together in the morning."

I could tell he was debating arguing. But after a moment, he relented, turning off the engine and reaching for his door.

When we got inside, he toed off his boots and headed for the living room. And it was tempting. It was so tempting to just let him sleep on the couch and put off the conversation we still needed to have. But though we were both exhausted, this couldn't wait any longer.

"No," I said.

He turned back to me. "No what?"

"Come upstairs. With me."

Declan frowned. "I don't think—"

"Please just come. I don't want to be alone." I held out my hand. He stared at it for a several very long seconds. At last he took it and let me lead him to my bedroom. Once we stepped inside, I shut the door firmly behind me.

"Just," I waved my arm around the room, "make yourself at home. Back in a minute." Grabbing my pajamas, I went into the bathroom to change and brush my teeth. When I came out, he was still standing in the same spot I'd left him. He looked uncomfortable, although he'd taken off his jacket and folded it over the arm of my overstuffed chair. I pulled back the blankets and sat on the bed, leaning against my pillows.

"Maybe this is a bad idea," he said abruptly, taking a step toward the door.

"It's not," I sighed. "Can you sit down, please?" I patted the mattress beside me. "I know it's been a long, crazy stressful day, and I know we're both about ready to pass out, but I really need to talk to you about something. It can't wait."

His expression was unreadable as he took a seat in the chair. Out of reach. Which hurt. And he wouldn't look at me. Which also hurt.

Okay. You can do this. Just talk. I took a deep breath. "So, the thing is, I, uh, found out what Dee told you on Sunday."

His shoulders tensed, his gaze darting to mine. For a second. Then he looked away again.

"I assume that's why you've been avoiding me?"

A soft sigh slipped out through his nose. His jaw was clenched tight. After a moment, he whispered, "Is it true?"

My cheeks grew warm. "She shouldn't have told you. She was out of line."

"Would you've told me yourself?" His face was drawn, pained. I could feel it; it radiated off him like a heat wave.

I shrugged, biting my lower lip.

We were both quiet for a long beat. The thrumming of raindrops on the windowpane filled my ears like white noise in my brain. Finally, in a softer voice, I said, "It was a long time ago. I was drunk. And I was devastated. And…and I felt like I had nothing left. I know that doesn't excuse it, but...yeah. I did something stupid. I've regretted it ever since."

"I should've been there," he forced out, eyes cast down. It sounded like it hurt him to talk. "With you. In person. I should've excused myself from that damn meeting and answered my phone when you called. I should've told Laura to go fuck herself and figured out another way." His voice had grown rough. "It was my fault."

I sat up straighter, leaning toward him. He still wasn't looking at me. "No. It wasn't. My actions. My fault. I was the idiot. It was by far the dumbest thing I've ever done. And I really need you to understand that you have *nothing* to worry about. Nothing like that will ever happen again."

He raked his fingers through his hair. "I'm not good for you, Mel. Us? Together?" He gestured back and forth between us. "It's a mistake. Taking me back would be a huge mistake."

With a long sigh, I moved to the end of the bed and reached out for his hand. "Tell me something?"

"What?" He stared down at our joined hands. His fingers trembled ever so slightly in mine.

"Do you still love me?" I knew he did. But knowing wasn't enough. I needed to hear it from his lips.

At last his eyes lifted back to mine, and I was relieved to see his face had softened. "Yes, of course. So much."

"Well, I love you, too. I always have. Even when I wanted to hate you, I couldn't. And now? Now we're parents of this amazing little boy. And I'm not just being impulsive. I've given this a lot of thought, and I want to make it...us...work."

There was still so much pain in those intense blue eyes. "What if loving each other isn't enough?" he said, the words strangled, like he had to force each one from his throat. "If being with me makes you less instead of more, then you shouldn't be with me. You should be with someone who brings out the best version of you."

"Do you really believe that? That us being together makes me weak?" I shook my head vehemently. "No. You make me stronger. Being apart is what makes me weak."

He didn't reply, but his thumb began to trace circles on the back of my hand—a good sign that I was finally getting through. Looking closer, I saw tears in his eyes. My own throat was aching and tight. I tugged on his fingers as I shifted backward, pulling him with me until he lay beside me on the bed, at last looking at me. Really looking at me. Open, instead of closed. Relief rushed through me and I realized I was no longer quite so sleepy.

"Are you sure?" he whispered.

I nodded, moving a little closer. "I'm sure. I can't promise things will always be easy—knowing us, they probably won't be—but, yeah. I wanna be with you. I want us to be a family."

"That's all I've ever wanted," he whispered, his lips now barely two inches from mine.

Joy welled up inside me and I was tempted to surrender right there and then. But that logical voice in my head piped up, reminding me I still needed to protect my heart, not just for my sake, but for Liam's. I braced a hand on his chest, pulling my head back a little so I could see him better.

"There's just one more thing." My voice was firm, my expression solemn. "I need to make something very clear. There won't be any third chance. If you screw this up, if you walk away again, we're done for good. I mean it, Declan. I can't go through that again."

He nodded. "I know. But it's a non-issue. Leaving you was the worst choice I ever made. I promise on my life I will never leave you again. I'm yours for the rest of ever."

I'm yours for the rest of ever. Until there's nothing left of me. It was a Jim Coltrane lyric, and hearing him say the words made my heart feel like it was too large for my chest. "That's a pretty big promise," I said. "The rest of ever is an awfully long time. For today, how 'bout we just think about right now?"

Declan smiled, the widest, most relieved smile I'd ever seen. It was the most beautiful thing and I swear I fell in love with him even more at the sight of it. Then that joyful smile morphed into the wicked grin I knew so well. "Now is good. But I have to admit, I'm thinking quite a bit about the very near future. And the delectable things I'm going to do to you." He leaned in and nibbled my earlobe, sending a shudder through me.

I snorted, smacking him playfully on the shoulder. "Seriously? I finally agree to get back with you and sex is all you can think about? You do know my mom's asleep in the next room, right?"

He chuckled, shaking his head in bemusement. "Way to dampen the mood. And this is all your fault. Just being around you turns me on. I have no choice in the matter." Tilting his head forward, he kissed me. A real kiss. The kind of kiss I'd been aching for. The kind of kiss that made me wish we had the house all to ourselves.

When we broke apart, his face was serious once more. "I love you so damn much. I've been waiting ages to be able to tell you that whenever I wanted. You're gonna get sick of hearing it."

I pulled his body tight to mine, marveling at how amazing it felt to be back in his arms. "You know, I don't think I ever will."

328

Chapter 31

Declan

My first thought when I woke was, much like my brother's first words last night, *where am I?* All in a rush I remembered and a grin stretched across my face. Yesterday might've been hell on wheels in most respects, but the end of the night was worth every excruciating second that preceded it.

Only one thing could have made it better.

Though Amelia and I had slept in the same bed, we were not naked. I'd pulled off my shirt and pants last night, but still wore my boxer briefs. I'd assured her we could be very quiet, but she wasn't comfortable messing around with her mom in the next room. And to be fair, we were both pretty fucking exhausted anyway. Not to say I was too exhausted for fucking, but...yeah. Sleep came pretty easy last night. Especially with her in my arms.

Although if we were going to eventually become a family of four, as we'd admitted we both wanted, she'd probably have to get used to having sex with other people in the house. Was it possible she'd never done that before? The only times we'd made love in the past, we'd been in hotels. But a future together that included two kids would make for a very different type of relationship. I'd had experience with such things, but it was clearly going to be an adjustment for her—an adjustment I was looking quite forward to helping her with.

I propped myself up on one elbow so I could see over her shoulder to the clock on her nightstand. It was just past seven. And I really had to piss. Carefully, I slipped out of bed and went into the bathroom connecting Amelia's bedroom to Liam's. When I returned, she was rubbing her eyes.

"Guess I should get up so we can head to the hospital," she said, yawning.

"Hold that thought." I slipped back beneath the sheets and slid over until my chest was right against her back. Pushing her hair off her cheek, I dropped a kiss behind her ear. "Good morning," I whispered.

She laughed softly. "Good morning to you, too." Rolling over, she slid her arms around my waist and kissed me.

If only we were naked.

If only her mother wasn't here.

If only.

She leaned back so she could look into my face. Her eyes were bright and happy, an expression I hadn't seen in far too long. She smiled a soft, happy, just-for-me smile and I swear I stopped breathing for a second. "This is nice," she said softly. "I wish we had more time."

That, too. But maybe we could spare just a few minutes? I tugged her body back against mine, pressing into her, making sure she knew exactly how turned on I was. "Ditto," I murmured, recapturing her lips.

She kissed me back, letting me run my hands from the side of her face down the curves of her body—and what fabulous curves they were, maybe a bit more pronounced than in years past but every bit as delectable. It only lasted for a minute or two, just long enough for me to want desperately to throw caution to the wind. I no longer gave a single fuck if her mom heard us. But Amelia did. And that was what mattered.

"We'd better not," she said as she pulled away, biting her lower lip, looking guilty, looking frustrated, let's be honest, looking cute as hell. I did not want to let her out of this bed. But I knew she needed to get back to Liam. We both did.

"Fine. But first dibs on the shower," I said, squeezing her ass and then jumping up and heading to the bathroom again. I had to cool down, stat.

After a quick and chilly shower, I came back into her room feeling much more myself, although clean clothes to put on would have improved things. Once we got Liam back here and settled, I definitely had to go home. And call Diana. And pick up Alexis from school. And talk to Patrick. And at some point Amelia and I needed to discuss how we both wanted to proceed going forward. But that last one could wait, at least for now.

When we got to the hospital, Liam's doctor was in the room with him. They both looked up when we walked in.

"I'm Dr. Fielding," the doctor said, extending a hand to me. "You must be?"

"Hi Daddy," Liam said before I could reply.

"I'm Declan," I said to the doctor. Reaching over to ruffle Liam's hair, I added, "How ya doin' this morning?"

"Sleepy." Liam's volume dropped. "My head hurts."

"I'll bet. You really did a number on yourself."

Amelia came over and gave him a kiss on the forehead. "Poor sweet boy. Tough night?"

"A lady kept waking me up," he pouted.

"I know, hon. You can crawl into bed and have a nap as soon as we get home." She turned to Dr. Fielding. "Is he okay to go?"

"I don't see why not." He pulled a card from his breast pocket and handed it to her. "Call my office and make an appointment for Liam next week. I want to check his arm and make sure he has no lasting effects from that concussion."

"Will do," she said as she tucked the card into her bag. "Does he need a prescription?"

"I don't think so. You can give him a Children's Tylenol if you think he needs one. If the pain gets bad, and the Tylenol doesn't seem to be cutting it, call that number and I'll fax a prescription for a mild painkiller to Deetmiller's Pharmacy downtown." With that, the doctor said goodbye to us all and left.

Amelia had brought Liam a change of clothes, and once she helped him get dressed and signed a few papers at the nurse's station, we were allowed to take him home.

Liam yawned most of the drive and didn't argue when we took him upstairs. Amelia gave him half a Children's Tylenol with some water and tucked him into bed. After she kissed him, I said goodbye and gave him a hug, happiness bursting inside me at the idea of all of us living under one roof at some point so I could hug him every day and no longer have to miss him in between visits. But of course I couldn't tell him that yet. Not until his mother was ready for him to know.

Amelia walked with me out to my car. "So you're taking Ryan to rehab?"

"I need to call Diana. But yeah, I assume so. It's the best place for him right now. He needs to get his shit together before the baby comes."

Her eye flared. "Baby? You're kidding me? Diana's *pregnant*?"

I nodded. "She swore me to secrecy though, so not a word until the news breaks. Especially around Sam."

"My lips are sealed." She wiped away her smile, although the corners of her mouth still curved up. "I can't even imagine her with a big baby belly, trying to walk around in short skirts and spike heels. She'll fall right over! And how will she deal with spit up on her clothes? God, I *cannot* wait to see this."

"It's gonna be a learning curve, that's for sure. But you can't say anything. I'm serious. Diana knows people. She'd probably have me murdered in my sleep just for telling you." I couldn't maintain a straight face though; an insuppressible grin broke through.

Amelia put her hands on the sides of my neck, stood on her tiptoes and kissed me. "Then I guess I'd better say goodbye now, in case you're dead soon."

"You wouldn't have time to miss me. I'd come haunt you, especially when you're alone in bed. You'd never get another full night's sleep." Winking, I leaned in to kiss her again. "But then again, I don't have to be a ghost to keep you up at night."

She blushed and it made her look at least ten years younger. Stepping back from me, she said, "Call me later then? Tell me how it goes with Ryan?"

"Absolutely." I got into my car and powered down the side window. "Love you."

As I started to back out the driveway, I heard her say, "Love you, too." And because of that simple fact, I knew no matter what shit the rest of the day threw my way, it wouldn't faze me. I could deal with anything now.

When I got home, I went inside to change and call Diana. Before I could even tap Ryan's name on my contact list, my phone went off in my hands. I know I've called her a witch a few times, and a word that rhymes with it innumerable others, but today she seemed spookily prescient.

"How's he doing?" I asked without preamble.

"He's…okay. Still pasty. Still grumpy. He's only eaten half a piece of toast."

"Did you talk to him about rehab?"

I heard a small sigh. "Of course. But I didn't exactly give him much choice. He's going. I already called them and told them to expect us."

"Did he fight you on it?"

"Not once I told him he'd lose me and our child forever if he didn't get himself clean. I mean it, too. It was a royal pain in the ass before, but it's a deal breaker now."

Jesus. That brought a sudden flashback to Laura's threats, but of course those were for very different reasons. Diana was one hundred percent in the right with this. She needed to be able to count on my brother if they were going to raise a kid. Although I knew addiction wasn't as simple as just deciding to stop, and I'd always be there to help him if he relapsed, he had to try his best to get his shit together for his family's sake.

"I'll drive," I told her. "Be there in ten."

"Fine." She ended the call.

They were both sitting on the front steps waiting for me. Diana looked up as I pulled into the driveway, but my brother's eyes remained on his gloved hands. She tugged on his arm and he startled a little, like he was lost in thought. Moving carefully, he reached for the black duffle bag beside him, got to his feet and followed her to my car. He was a bit pale, but mostly looked back to his regular self. I wasn't sure which of them would sit in the back, but it turned out I was playing Uber driver, because Diana urged Ryan to slide over so she could climb in beside him.

"You remember where to go?" she asked me.

"Yep." I looked back at them in my rearview mirror. "How ya doing, Ry? Other than feeling like you were run over by a truck, that is."

He snorted, at last raising his eyes to mine in the mirror. "More like a tank. Every bone hurts. My head is killing me. But it'll pass." He stifled a cough. "Whose car is this? Where's your Mustang?"

Right. Because we hadn't really talked in weeks. I had so much to tell him, but most of it would have to wait. "Traded it in," I said, putting the SUV in reverse and backing onto the street. "You like?" I knew full well he didn't.

Ryan shrugged. "Whatever turns your crank."

That brought another thought to mind. "Hey, where's your Jag? Did you drive it to Richmond?" If he had, it was probably long gone by now, never to be seen again.

"At work."

"Really?" Diana asked, incredulous. "How'd you get there then? Did that Sammy dude come get you?" I was surprised she hadn't thought about his car before now either, but she'd obviously had a lot on her mind.

"Took the bus," Ryan said. "I was too strung out to drive."

Wow. He'd had the presence of mind to take the fucking bus, knowing how wasted he intended to get? That was...I hated to say an improvement as the entire situation was completely FUBAR, but, well, it kind of was. Thank fuck he hadn't been stupid enough to drive.

The rehabilitation center Ryan had stayed at eight years ago was aptly called A Fresh View. It was hidden away out in the countryside south of Lynchburg. When we walked into the lobby, I was surprised to see it was already decorated for Christmas. How was it December already? The past few months seemed like they'd whipped by, changes coming faster than I could keep up.

Diana went to speak to the woman at the front desk while my brother and I took a seat in the waiting area. He was avoiding eye contact again. I knew that meant he was feeling guilty about his recent terrible life choices, but it still unnerved me when he acted all shifty.

"You tell Dad?" he asked suddenly.

"Not yet. But you know one of us has to. I assume you'd prefer it was me?"

He sighed. "I wish he didn't have to find out at all."

"He needs to know. He'd want to know. You know he only wants what's best for you."

"He'll be so disappointed. I can just picture his face. I don't want to see that face, Declan. I hate that face."

I snorted. "You hate that face? I've had to deal with Patrick's disappointed-in-you face pretty much my entire life. You only see it rarely. And frankly, you kinda earned it this time."

Ryan braced his elbows on his knees and covered his face with his hands, heaving another deep sigh. "I know," he said, the words muffled.

"But think of it this way, once you tell him your bigger, much more important news, that face will go away, and he'll be all happy, supportive dad and grandpa again."

My brother turned his head to stare at me finally, brows arched. "She told you?"

"Yep. And before you ask, no I haven't told anyone else." Except Amelia, but he didn't really need to know that. I wished I could share my happy news that Amelia and I were back together, but that would have to wait. Today, and probably for the next little while, this needed to be all about him. "I'm really happy for ya," I added, clapping him on the shoulder. "You're gonna be a natural. Once you get your shit together, that is."

"Which is why we're here," Diana said, joining us. "Ry, an attendant will be out in a minute to show us to your room."

I walked back with them to see where Ryan would be bunking for the next two weeks. He wasn't doing partial rehab this time. Diana had requested he go into a full rehab program for the first two weeks and then they would reassess to see if he could drop down to evenings and weekends after that. I know her goal was to have him home for Christmas Day, even if he had to go back the day after.

But for the next two weeks, he'd be off work. So Patrick definitely needed to know what was up as soon as possible.

"I'll let you guys get settled," I said to Diana. "I'll wait for you out front whenever you're ready."

"You can go," she said. "I'm going to stay here with him for a while. I'll call a cab once I'm ready to go home. You've done enough for us the past couple days, and I know you need to go pick up Alexis soon."

"You sure?"

"I am."

I turned to Ryan, who had already stretched out on the single bed. He looked tired, but that was no surprise. Withdrawal was a painful, often unpleasant process, and needing as much sleep as possible was part of it. "I'll come see you tomorrow, okay? If you need anything, just call or text me a list and I'll bring it."

Ryan snorted. "What I'll be needing, you won't be bringing. But thanks for the offer."

I shrugged. "Anytime. Now I have to go make a call. And after I do, I predict you'll have another visitor to expect."

Diana reached for my arm as I turned to leave. "Ask him to come tomorrow, not tonight, okay? Let's give Ry one more night of relative peace."

"I'll try, but no guarantees he'll listen. Talk to you later."

My conversation with Patrick went pretty much as I'd imagined it would go. He was upset, but once I explained that Diana and I had everything under control now, he calmed down. Convincing him to not drive immediately out to A Fresh View took another few minutes of cajoling, but eventually he agreed to visit tomorrow. Once I hung up, I realized I felt better about the whole thing. They would take good care of Ryan here, and once Patrick found out about the baby, he'd be over the moon and that would ease things between father and son.

I didn't want to jinx it, but suddenly everything in my life finally felt like it was on the right track.

I pulled up to Amelia's place just after four on Saturday, later than usual but I'd gone to visit Ryan for an hour or so after lunch while Alexis hung out at Josh and Holly's. Though she wanted to see her uncle, it was only day two of his withdrawal and I knew he'd still be feeling like utter shit. So I didn't think bringing her along was a good idea. I'd told her she might be able to come with me next Saturday, but we'd have to play it by ear.

Before I even stepped up onto the porch, Amelia came outside and slipped her arms around my waist to greet me with a kiss.

"I could get used to this," I murmured.

"Me, too." She took my hand and led me inside, her eyes sparkling. It made my heart soar to see her so happy to see me. I probably didn't deserve it, but damned if I didn't love it.

The whole rest of the day, playing with Liam, during dinner at Finnegan's, which I treated them all to, watching a movie on the couch after we got back, Amelia kept sliding me glances and smiling that cute little knowing smile. And since I noticed all, or at least most, of these, I assumed I was doing the same right back at her. I could not wait to get her alone. Shit, I felt like a teenager again, waiting all night for the chance of a kiss, or if I played my cards right, more.

So, once Liam was in bed and asleep, I pulled her into her bedroom, shut the door and backed her up against it. Pressing the length of my body against hers, I leaned in until our lips were barely an inch apart. Her heartbeat throbbed against my chest. "D'you want me to stay?" I whispered.

"Of course I do. But I don't know if it's a great idea. My mom—"

"Is right downstairs. I'm well aware. And later she'll be sound asleep one room over. And so will Liam. "

Her cheeks colored. "You can stay. I'd love you to stay, but..." She trailed off, breaking eye contact.

I arched a brow. "You wanna keep things strictly PG? Is that what you're trying to say?"

"I don't *want* to." She bit her lip. "I just...I want our first time together after so much...after everything...to be special. Not all sneaky and worried we might be heard."

I stepped back from her and took a seat in the chair, beckoning to her to join me. After a second, she came and sat on my lap, curling up against my chest. "I get that," I said to her. "I do. It's just that being around you drives me completely insane. I want you so bad, Mel. Is that so wrong? What if we snuck down to the basement later, after everyone's asleep? That's two floors below any snoring family members. Is that private enough for you?"

She chuckled. "You'd think so, wouldn't you? But the vents make it so you can hear everything from my mom's room. I learned that the hard way when I was a kid. My parents could hear every word that was said down there if the furnace wasn't running."

"Why Amelia, I thought you were a perfect child! What could they possibly have overheard?"

Laughing, she said, "Liv and I were planning revenge on a boy who always pulled our hair. We were gonna dump our Jello on his head the next day at lunch. And he totally deserved it, too. Until we both got to school and found neither of us had any Jello in our lunchboxes. We had no dessert at all! Mom told me what they'd heard when I got home and I was grounded from seeing Liv for a week." She paused for a second, frowning. "I wonder if Liv even remembers that."

"Have you talked to her since that day at the park?"

She shook her head. "She needs time. Probably lots of time. Maybe forever."

I hugged her closer. "She'll get over it. Someday."

Amelia sighed softly. "You don't know her the way I do. She never spoke to Darren Rayburn again."

"Who's Darren Rayburn?"

"The little boy who used to pull our hair. And he went all through high school with us. That's twelve years of school with her not once ever speaking to him. She can hold a mean grudge. And what I did to her is a lot worse than hair pulling."

I kissed the top of her head and decided to change the subject. "Speaking of people whom I suspect can hold a grudge, have you told Dee about us yet?"

"Dee is still in my bad books right now. But I'll tell her. I should tell her about Liam's accident, anyway. Maybe I'll just text her." Sitting up from me, she got to her feet. "C'mon, let's go down and watch TV with Mom for a bit."

On Monday morning, I popped over to Amelia's office. Making sure no one was watching, I slipped inside and shut the door. I didn't mind that she wanted to wait until things were just right, but that didn't mean I had to make it easy for her. Plus, I had an idea.

A pleased smile appeared when she looked up and saw me. "G'morning. You just come to say hi, or is there something you need?"

"Definitely the latter." I held out my hand, and as she took it I pulled her up into my arms and kissed her. Not just a good morning peck either. A real kiss. With tongue. When we finally broke apart to catch our breath, I flashed her my wickedest grin. "What I *need* is for you to have lunch with me today."

"After a greeting like that, how can I refuse?"

"You can't," I agreed. "So what if by *lunch*, I actually mean come back to my place for an hour?"

She blinked, her smile faltering. Then she turned and sat back down. "I don't think that's such a good idea."

My brows narrowed. I took a seat across from her, pulling the chair up to her desk so I could lean in close. "It's *not* a good idea; it's a completely fabulous idea." Pausing, I scrutinized her expression. "But you don't agree. What am I missing?"

Her face had flushed. "I just don't think I'd be comfortable there."

I was confused. It seemed like the perfect solution to grab a bit of privacy from our busy lives. "Why not?"

Amelia sighed. "For a smart guy, you're pretty dense sometimes. Your house? Was *her* house. Her home. With you. The home you guys built a life in, created a family in. I'm sorry,

338

but the idea of…of being with you there totally weirds me out." She stopped to push a piece of hair off her forehead. "I just…I can't take her place. I don't even want to."

Shit. I was a complete idiot for not considering that. Of course she wouldn't want to have sex at my place. *Of course* it would be weird for her. I leaned closer and grabbed both her hands in mine. "I don't want that, either." My words got more earnest, tumbling out of my mouth. "I don't *want* you to be her. Hell no. Not even a little. I hope you know that. I want *you*, Mel. Just you. Only you."

Biting her lower lip, she said, "I do know. It's just awkward, thinking of her, and what we did, and what ended up happening. I still feel guilty."

"Not half as much as I do." I paused, debating. But it was important I be completely honest with her, so with a small sigh I said, "Can I tell you something? Since we're sharing all our secrets now?"

"Of course."

"The accident was my fault."

She frowned. Whatever she'd been expecting, this sure wasn't it. "How could it've been your fault? There was a snowstorm. And a trucker veered out of his lane or something. There's no way you could've prevented any of that. It was a total accident!"

"It was my fault she was on that highway rushing back here in the first place. I had a big meeting that day that got pushed back an hour. Our babysitter had plans and needed Lex picked up by 5:30. So I called Laura at work and asked her to come get Lex and take her back to the station with her so I wouldn't miss the meeting. She had her own deadlines, her own career, and asking her to do that was selfish of me. I put my needs before hers and she paid the price for it."

"Oh Declan," Amelia sighed as she laced her fingers through mine and squeezed. "I get why you feel guilty, but I really think you're being too hard on yourself. There's no way you could've known. It was a normal request between parents to solve a problem. You—"

"I was daydreaming about you." I blurted.

"What?"

"Right before the meeting. Right about when Laura was speeding down that icy road to do me a favor, I was lost in thoughts of the woman I missed more than anything, the woman I wished I was with instead of her. She may've been a total bitch sometimes, but she didn't deserve that. I was a terrible husband."

Amelia stared at me with deep compassion in those big brown eyes. "You weren't. You did the best you could, like we all did. I was a terrible wife to Scott for similar reasons and I beat myself up about it for a long time. But then at some point I just decided it was time to move on, to forgive myself and just try to do better. And you need to do the same. Forgive yourself."

I nodded. "I'm definitely going to do better. I intend to spend the rest of my life trying to do better by you. If you'll let me."

She got up and came around to me. I stood as well and let her pull me back into her arms. After another sweet kiss, I leaned close to her ear and whispered, "What about we just go for a drive until we find somewhere secluded?"

Laughing, she said, "I'm not having sex in your car!"

"Well, what if I get us a hotel room again? I'm serious." I was at the point where any plausible idea was going to be suggested, even right here on her desk. Or floor.

"Last time was in a hotel and it was pretty much the opposite of romantic. Or sweet. Or special."

"Oh I don't know," I smirked. "We made Liam. I'd call that pretty special."

Rolling her eyes, she said, "You know what I mean."

"So what then? We just abstain until you get your own place? Because that could take months." I smiled as I said it, not annoyed with her at all and wanting her to understand it. I knew she was just overthinking things and that she wanted everything to be perfect.

"I know, I know. Just…give me a little time. We waited so long the first time and it was worth it. We can do it again."

"Of course. Take all the time you need. We'll figure all this out, I promise." I gave her one last kiss and then headed for the door. Waiting was going to pretty much kill me, but I'd wait as long as she wanted. Because I wasn't going anywhere.

Never again.

Chapter 32

Amelia

After kissing Liam goodnight, I went to my room and picked up my phone. For a long time I just contemplated it. It was time I called Dee and told her. She wouldn't like it one bit, but I needed to tell her anyway, because it was important we get past this. She was like a sister to me, and she and Terri were like other moms to Liam. There couldn't be friction between us for long. It was almost nine, so she should be home. I had no good excuse to delay this.

I opened a text and typed: *ok if I call?*

Setting the phone on my night table, I changed into pajamas and went to brush my teeth. When I returned, she'd replied with three letters: *ofc*—short for *of course*.

Still I hesitated. She wasn't going to understand. She was going to think I was a complete idiot for giving Declan another chance. I didn't want to feel judged for my choices by my best friend. I didn't want to feel judged by anyone, but especially not by her.

Apparently Dee was eager to speak to me, though. Before I could call, the phone buzzed in my hand.

"Hey," I answered. "You beat me to it."

"Hey yourself. I was glad to get your message."

Because you want to hear that I've forgiven you, I thought. But first things first. "I need to tell you something."

"What's up?"

"Don't freak out, because he's basically okay, but Liam was in an accident last week."

"*What*? What happened?" I heard Terri in the background asking what was up.

Filling her in took longer than expected because Dee had to relay everything I said to Terri and I had to answer questions from both of them. When I finished, Dee said, "Would it be alright if we came to visit our lil' broken boy on Sunday?"

"Sure. He'd love to see you guys."

There was a brief pause. "Would *you* love it?"

I sighed. It was time to clear the air. "I'd be happy to see you both. But I should warn you, there's a good chance Declan'll be here."

A slightly longer pause. "I take it you two worked things out?"

"We did. The night Liam spent in the hospital, he came back here with me and we discussed a lot of stuff. Painful stuff, but it needed to be shared. Everything's good between us now. Great, actually. And I need to know that you're gonna be okay with that. Because he's a part of our lives and if you're going to spend time with us, you're going to be spending time with him, too."

She released a breath. "I just want you to be happy."

"I am. Does this mean you can be happy for me?"

"Of course. But I reserve the right to kill him slowly and painfully if he ever hurts you again. Just so long as that's clear."

I snorted. "You might have to get in line."

"I can wait my turn." I heard her whisper to Terri that Declan and I were back together. Then, to me, she said, "This is it for you, isn't it?"

"What?"

"It. The life you've dreamed of for what feels like forever. I can tell from your voice. This, right now, with him, with Liam, this is your happily ever after, isn't it?"

A wide smile spread across my face. "I don't know. But...I think so. I hope so." I took a big breath, and before she could say more, I added, "No. No more waffling. I've spent way too long hesitating. You're right. This is it."

On Friday after work, Declan came with me to look at a couple of places for rent. After our talk in my office, I'd gone online to see what I could find in my price range. Because he was right, it could be a while before I had my own home where we could occasionally be alone, when the kids were at school or being babysat, anyway.

I knew I was being a bit ridiculous. I knew it, but I couldn't help it. I didn't want to just blow money on a hotel room every time we wanted to make love. I understood that, as parents, we'd have to figure out quiet, secret ways to do it once the kids were asleep. But for our first time together after so much hurt and separation, I wanted there to be no restrictions. I wanted us to be free to do and say whatever we felt like, without all the worry and shame we'd carried before. I wanted us to be able to focus on just each other. And I didn't think wanting that was wrong.

I didn't find anything viable in Swann's Landing, but I did spot two rental possibilities in Lynchburg, so I'd made appointments to see both. My mom had agreed to make Liam dinner tonight and Alexis was sleeping over at a friend's place after school, which freed up Declan to come along.

When I got into his car, he flashed me a smile. As I fastened my seatbelt, he reached over and ran his hand along the top of my thigh. Nothing overtly sexual—just a light brush of contact and only for a few seconds, but at his touch warm tingles shot from the pit of my stomach up my spine. He didn't even drop a typical flirty comment; he just put the car in reverse and backed out. I looked over at him, but his eyes were on the road. My gaze shifted to his hands, both now on the wheel and I found myself hoping he'd touch me again.

I tried to focus on the task at hand. Being near him was as distracting as ever, but we had things to do. I needed to find a place to live.

We headed to Montana Crescent to check out the first apartment. The ad had described it as quaint and cozy, but in reality it needed of a lot of updating and was far too tiny. It might have been okay for just one, but there was no way it would've been comfortable for Liam and me. Both bedrooms barely had room for our beds, let alone dressers, and the living room would've been a tight squeeze for our furniture. Hard pass.

Next we had an appointment to see a small house over in the west end. It was a bit more than I wanted to spend, but the photos looked cute, and I knew from the listed dimensions that the bedrooms were larger. It also had a backyard, which was a huge plus.

"I approve of the location," Declan said as we made our way there. "It's only a few minutes from my house."

"That'd be convenient." Being only minutes away from him instead of thirty or more would be great. Though we saw each other almost every day now, at least for short periods, I would definitely appreciate him being around even more.

He touched the small of my back as we walked up the path to the door, and again I felt that rush of heat.

Pull yourself together, woman! Being around Declan still made me feel like a schoolgirl with a crush, even after all these years.

The first thing that hit me when the owner led us inside was the smell. The place reeked of what I suspected was cat urine. And every room was fully carpeted but the kitchen and bathroom. Sure, the aging carpets could be shampooed, but I was doubtful any amount of cleaning would completely rid the place of that stench.

When the lady took us back to look at the bedrooms, I glanced out the window and immediately knew Liam and I could not live there. The backyard wasn't even really a yard; it was a collection of weeds and bare patches of dirt. There were no trees, no fence, and a vacant lot dotted with garbage right behind. With a busy road on the far side. No way would I feel comfortable letting Liam play back there.

So that was another no. And I hadn't seen any other listings that might work.

"There's always next month," I said hopefully as we drove away. "Something good'll turn up soon."

"I know," he said, but he looked a little dejected. "Where to now? Wanna get something to eat?"

"I could use a washroom, actually." I admitted.

He glanced over at me. "My place is three streets from here. Is that okay? Or would you prefer we find a restaurant?"

I thought about it for all of two seconds as I uncrossed and re-crossed my legs. Would it kill me to pee at his house? It would not. Refusing to even see the inside of his place was silly. "Yours is fine."

Two minutes later, he pulled into the double wide driveway of a nice two-storey, gray brick home. It had a wide front yard with mature trees, and a row of spruce shrubs ran from the front stoop all the way to the side of the house.

As we walked up the steps I could feel anxiety tugging at me, but I resolutely ignored it. *It's just a house*, I told myself. *Just bricks and mortar and shingles. Nothing more.*

Declan unlocked the door, then slid an arm around my waist to lead me inside. I could feel the warmth and pressure of each fingertip. Nerves forgotten, heat flooded my face. Then, as before, it dove lower.

He'd been doing stuff like that all week: small touches, little things like brushing his hand against mine as we walked. Or surreptitiously running a finger along my forearm as we stood chatting. Or touching my thigh in the car, or the small of my back, or my elbow. He hadn't kissed me since our talk in my office on Monday, but all those little touches—God, was he doing it on purpose just to drive me crazy? Cause it was working.

"The washroom's down the hall to your right," he told me as I toed off my boots.

"Okay. Be right back."

After taking care of business and washing up, I splashed cool water on my face. I was having trouble focusing. Every time I tried to think about practical stuff, my thoughts were invaded by images of Declan kissing me. And dragging off that black shirt he wore. And unzipping those dark wash jeans. And...and I needed to stop this. Jumping on him was *not* part of the plan. At least not right now. And not here.

Wait, why was that again?

Oh yeah. Because that was what I'd decided. My choice. Not his.

"Coffee?" he asked as I came into the kitchen."

"Coffee'd be great." Was my voice a little shaky? Or was that just my imagination? I sighed as I slid onto a stool at the breakfast bar. "I was really hoping one of those places would be perfect for us. But it's fine. I'll find something soon. Once the holidays are over, I'll start a more intense search."

He turned away from the kettle to look at me. "It's really important to you for things to be perfect, isn't it?"

"Some things, yes." I said, shrugging. Was he referring to finding a place to live or...?

"You just hate not being in control." One corner of his mouth quirked up. "For so many years so much has gone down in your life that you had no control over, so now you need to rigidly plan everything out or it makes you crazy."

I snorted. "Are you seriously Freuding me right now?"

"Just making an observation. Am I wrong?"

No. Truthfully, he was not. Not in most ways. There was one way, however that I was more than happy to relinquish it.

The coffee maker burbled in the corner, but the pounding of my heart seemed to drown it out as I got to my feet and came around to him. "*Sometimes* I like giving up control," I said softly. "Maybe you remember?"

Declan's eyes widened and two spots of red appeared high on his cheeks. I'd shocked him. I couldn't help smiling, proud of myself.

"Oh, I definitely remember," he chuckled.

I wanted to reach for him and drag him to me, but I paused. Just for a moment, I stopped and glanced around us. We were in a white and stainless steel modern kitchen. It looked utilitarian. Not feminine. No sign of her here. There'd been no sign in the washroom, either. I'm sure there *were* still memories of her around, after all her daughter lived here, but none that I'd spotted. And so what if there were? Why should such things even matter to me? After everything Declan and I had been through? After all these years? He loved me. We loved each other. Laura was his past, and I understood he'd never forget her, but I was his future. Never mind that, I was his now. And right now, I wanted this. We both did.

So screw it. A house was just walls and windows and doors. A house was just a house. It wasn't a person. It held memories of her for her loved ones, but memories were fine. Memories were sort of like ghosts. I wasn't threatened by a ghost. If her ghost was still hanging around here, she could just leave. Or watch, if she was into that.

At that last thought, a giggle slipped out. Declan looked at me quizzically. "What?"

"Doesn't matter," I smiled, trying to look seductive and probably failing, but that didn't matter either. Sliding my hands up his chest to the sides of his neck, I drew him close. Just before I kissed him, I murmured, "Maybe the coffee can wait."

And then our lips met and it reminded me so much of the first time we kissed years ago in his office not long after my dad died that I got a bit overwhelmed. Moisture rose to the corners of my eyes. This time they weren't tears of sadness, though. This time they were the exact opposite.

346

I pulled back for a breath and saw he was staring at me in wonder. "You sure?" he asked softly. Just like he had before the first time we'd made love. So careful to make sure it was what I really wanted, that he wasn't pressuring me into doing something I'd regret. But just like back then, all my doubts had been vanquished.

So I smiled. And I nodded. And then I just held his gaze. Waiting.

I didn't have to wait long. His cautious expression morphed into delight. Just for a moment. Then it was replaced with a seductive grin. Even more heat blossomed down below. *God, that grin.* It was quite possibly my favorite of all his various grins. Before I could move, he picked me up bridal-style and kissed me. The next thing I knew, he had carried me down the hall and into the first door on the right. Our lips only broke apart when he laid me on the bed within.

This was definitely not the master bedroom. One glance told me no one slept in here regularly, so it must be a spare room. No ghosts here.

Declan pulled off his shirt and sat beside me on the bed. Sitting up, I dragged my own top over my head and beckoned him to me again, anxious for skin on skin contact, needing to feel his warmth against mine and know that this time what we were doing wasn't wrong, that finally it was right. And it always would be.

He kissed me aggressively, like at any moment I'd come to my senses and stop him. Or, just as likely, because he was as desperate for this as I was. I gave back to him as good as he gave, opening my mouth and my arms and my heart to him. Fully.

At last he pulled away a few inches, his breath a bit ragged. "I wanna touch you all over."

"That's the plan," I smiled.

"No, really. I've missed every last inch of you. And I'd like to reacquaint myself."

I unzipped my jeans and pushed them off, taking my panties and socks right along with them. Reaching behind my back, I unhooked my bra and dropping it over the side of the bed. "Go ahead," I said, smiling.

Declan

Amelia lay back on the pillow, naked before me for the first time since... No. not going there. I couldn't allow myself to think about how I'd wrecked it all before. The years had changed her a little; her curves were a bit fuller, her stomach maybe a little softer. But these small differences only added to my attraction. She was absolutely still the most gorgeous woman I'd ever laid eyes upon.

At first all I could do was stare, my gaze roaming over her smooth skin, her plump lower lip, the creamy slope of her chest, the soft swell of her hips. She was absolutely perfect. I had to be the luckiest guy on the planet.

I tried to shake off this lovelorn trance. This wasn't an end; it was a beginning. I didn't need to memorize her every detail. Hopefully I'd have the rest of our lives to do that. I needed to focus on right here right now. Focus on pleasing her.

First things first: the rest of my clothes had to go. Once they'd joined hers on the floor, I placed my hands on either side of her shoulders so our chests were only inches apart. Leaning down, I kissed those luscious lips, already swollen and rosy from our make-out session. Next I pressed my lips to the middle of her forehead, and as I did, my nose nestled into her hair. It smelled sweet and rich, almost like chocolate, and I paused for a minute to savor it. I began my journey, kissing each temple, trailing my way down her cheekbone to her chin, then back up to the sensitive spot behind her earlobe. When I made contact there, she sucked in a gasp and I smiled. Exactly the reaction I was going for. I lingered a moment nibbling and sucking her earlobe until I realized she was holding her breathe. Chuckling softly, I began to kiss a path down her neck to her collar bone as she exhaled long and low. I could tell this was going to drive her crazy. Would she really let me control it all? Or would she eventually grab me by the hair and insist I get down to business?

And if she did lose patience and demand I fuck her right the hell now? I was one million percent good with that.

I worked my way along her arm before deliberately, slowly kissing and sucking each fingertip. I'd been hard as a rock for several minutes already but listening to her erratic breath, knowing she was watching me as I worshipped her body, made me possibly more turned on than I'd ever been in my entire life. And that was saying something, because she

348

always turned me on. Even when we were fighting. Oh hell, let's be honest. Especially then.

Next, I kissed a trail back up the inside of Amelia's arm to one of my favorite spots: her chest. The moment my mouth made contact with one hard nipple, her fingers threaded into my hair, not rough exactly, but insistent enough that I knew what she wanted.

Her pleasure was my goal. Smiling against her skin, I licked one pebbled peak before capturing it in my mouth, sucking lightly, loving the soft sigh from above. I took my time, savoring the taste of her, the feel of her body below mine, not shifting my attention to the neglected breast until I felt a slight wiggle of impatience from her. Her impatient wiggle was different from her shudder of desire and, though it had been far too long since I'd been in this particular position, I remembered well.

By the time I finished with her beautiful chest and had started down toward her belly button, I suspected her idea to let me control our lovemaking would soon be tossed out the window. That was okay though. I intended to just keep on worshipping her body. I had a plan in mind that she would most definitely enjoy. If she could be patient. As I ran my tongue in a circle around her belly button, I let my fingers brush over the wetness between her legs. Just once. Just light enough to tickle. As I did, she shuddered again, more insistently this time.

With a quick glance up to her face, I realized my chances of succeeding at kissing her all over were pretty damn low. Her patience was fast running out. But I wanted to see just how far I could go before she broke.

Amelia

It had been way too long. Though I hadn't admitted it, I hadn't had sex since Liam's conception. That was more than five years ago. Most of the time I'd been able to put it out of my mind, or satisfy my own needs. But since Declan came back into my life, it seemed like I thought about sex all the time. Being around him did crazy things to my libido. It always had.

And now that we were finally making love again, he'd decided to take things slow. Like really, *really* slow. Was he trying to torture me?

If so, it was definitely working.

We were in bed. We were naked. He was kissing and licking and touching me—*oh, the touching!* Both of us were incredibly turned on. Both of us wanted this. And yet he'd decided that, instead of just getting to it and saving the slow, careful exploration for later, he wanted to kiss me all over first. Like *all* over. Every inch. And sweet as it was, it was taking *forever*.

I'd told him I wanted him to take charge. And he had. But maybe I'd made a mistake. Because right now all I wanted was for him to just…just…

Argh

To just do me already! But I didn't want to ask for it, I just wanted him to do it.

I released a long sigh as he began to kiss the top of my thigh. He was *so* close to where I wanted him. But for some reason he'd decided to avoid heading straight there, and instead was working his way toward my feet. With one hand, he lifted up my knee and traced the outside of it with his tongue before starting down the curve of my calf. When he got to my foot, he took my baby toe in his mouth and sucked it, much like he had my breasts.

God, that had felt good. This just felt…wet. Nice, but not particularly sexy. Until his tongue tickled the sensitive spot on the arch of my foot and I shuddered.

Was that another chuckle? Yep, he was definitely trying to torture me.

As he picked up my other foot and started kissing it, I gave up trying to be patient.

"Declan?" It came out like a sigh.

"Uh huh?" He was looking at me with that cheeky grin. Like he knew exactly what I was about to say. Which he probably did. Had that been his plan all along? To drive me crazy until I begged him? Maybe, but at this point, I didn't really care.

"Please?" I whispered.

"Please what?" The grin spread even wider.

"You know. Just…please."

"Say it." There it was. Demanding, controlling Declan, the part of his personality that often got on my last nerve at work but that I loved in bed. Actually, maybe this was still going the way I wanted after all.

I jutted my lower lip out into what I hoped was a sexy pout. "Don't make me wait any longer. I need you. Right now. *Please* baby?"

Without responding, he got up off the bed, found a condom from who knows where, put it on and then crawled up my body until his face was right above mine. I spread my thighs apart and he settled between them. "Anything for you," he murmured. "Anything."

Our lips and tongues met like it hadn't been only minutes since we'd last kissed, like we hadn't kissed in weeks, years even, and as we did, he reached down between us and ran himself along my wetness.

At long last he slipped inside and we were finally joined as one again.

Declan

As I began to move inside her, I felt my throat constrict. I dragged my mouth from Amelia's and buried my face into the crook of her neck, one hand tangled in her hair. Tears sprung to my eyes and with my free hand I tried to wipe them away before she could notice. I don't know why; it wasn't that I was ashamed of feeling such intense emotions. It's just that the only time this had ever happened before was after Josh's wedding when we'd made drunken love in the middle of the night. I didn't remember much, but I remembered I'd cried. And it wasn't because I was drunk; it was because I was with *her.* Making love to Amelia was something I'd never expected to ever happen again. It had been like a dream come true. A hazy, booze-induced dream, but still. Much like a dream, it had barely seemed real.

The sentiment overwhelming me now was the same one I'd felt that night. Like I was finally home after being away for years. Sappy, right? But that's exactly how I felt. Being with Amelia was like coming home. And I intended to stay. Forever, if she'd let me.

Regaining control of myself, I started kissing her neck as I worked my hips against her. Her hands rubbed gently up and down my back as she began to arch her pelvis up to meet me. Rolling to the side, I shifted her on top so she could control our rhythm. This position was always one of my favorites as it gave me easy access to her breasts.

She gazed down at me, her huge brown eyes expressive. Curtains of dark hair swung back and forth on each side of her face with every movement. Her expression was solemn as she concentrated. Then she paused, pushing a loose chunk of hair behind one ear and that soft, sweet smile emerged. Bending forward, she kissed me and my hands slid around to her back and pulled her against my chest.

"I love you," she whispered when we broke apart for a breath.

"I love you, too," I replied.

We stared at each other for a few seconds. But, as always, I had to be the one to break the sweet moment. With a smirk, I said, "Enough with the serious. This is about having some fun." I rolled us back over and changed position so her hips were near the edge of the bed and I was standing on the floor, giving me the leverage I needed to adjust my angle for her pleasure. I began to move faster. From the sound of our breathing, I knew we were both getting close. There was no way this was going to go on for twenty minutes or more like it had years ago. We'd been apart too long. Next time could last longer. Right now, all we both wanted was release in each other's arms. And I'd be damned if I wasn't going to give her what she wanted.

I gripped her thighs as her fingers dug into the sheets and her hips rolled forward to meet my every stroke. Her face had gone red and I knew my own matched. I could feel my breath coming quicker as I grew closer. But even though the grand finale was fast approaching, I tried my damndest to hold it off. I wanted her to finish first. I tried to think about boring things like football scores and hockey stats, but it wasn't working. How could I possibly think about sports when I was finally making love to Amelia?

There was no chance.

Or so I thought. Just before I finished, she shuddered and gasped and stiffened below me and at that moment I was so goddamned happy I just let go.

I couldn't help it; I collapsed in a pile of deliriously ecstatic man-child on top of her naked, gorgeous, glorious body.

This was it. This was my moment. If I never was this happy ever again, it was all worth it. Whether she knew it or not, whether she wanted me or not, I was hers.

Always and forever.

Amelia

"You okay?" Declan asked. Wiping the sweat from his brow with a forearm, we shifted over so he lay beside me on the pillows, one arm still holding me against him despite how overheated we both were.

352

"Mmhmm…very extremely okay," I murmured, fighting to catch my breath. That was intense. Possibly more intense than it'd ever been before, and that was saying something. "You?"

"Perfect." He turned to face me and kissed my temple.

We cuddled close for a while, just holding each other as our bodies relaxed. I could feel exhaustion weighing heavy on my eyelids, but I resisted. I didn't want to fall asleep. Sleep could come later. I didn't want to waste what little time we had together sleeping. To distract myself, I let my eyes scan the room, examining the bookshelf at the end of the bed and the dresser with the television on top.

"Was this James' room when he stayed here?" I asked.

Declan's nose was against my jaw and I felt him nod. "Uh huh," he replied sleepily.

"I wish I could've met him."

I felt him exhale a puff of air. Nudging me affectionately, he said, "I wish you had, too. He'd have loved you."

"You think so?"

"I know so." Then he added. "I told him about you."

I frowned, turning my head to face him directly. "All of it?"

"Yep. The whole thing, from amazing to awful. He knew about the crazy difficult decision I made when I…" A deep sigh. "When I walked away from you. He worried I was making the biggest mistake of my life. And he was right. It was." Then a small smile surfaced. "He'd be thrilled to know we found our way back to each other. What I wouldn't give to still have him here so he could know you and Liam."

"I get that. All too well."

The expression he wore was of complete understanding, and I realized he might be the only one who really got how I felt about this stuff. "Of course you do. I know how much you miss your dad. What d'you think he would have thought of me? Would you have told him the truth about how we met?"

I snorted. "It wasn't our meeting that was the problem. It was what came after. As for what I would've told him, I don't know. I would've left out some stuff, obviously."

One side of his mouth curved up. "Obviously."

"He would've been disappointed in some of my choices, but I know overall he would have supported me. He *always* supported me. Sometimes, when I'm faced with a particularly difficult decision, I lie in bed and imagine telling him about my problem, and what advice he'd give."

"And what would he have advised you about giving me another shot?" Though he still grinned, the intense look in Declan's eyes betrayed the seriousness of the question.

"He would've told me to follow my heart. And that's exactly what I did."

He pulled me against him. "I'll never leave you again," he said softly. "Neither of you. You can count on it. I know it might take a while to fully earn back your trust, but I swear I'm in this for the long haul."

"Me too," I murmured. I rested my cheek on his chest, listening to the sound of his heartbeat as I savored the feeling. For the first time in a very long time, I felt truly safe. I was exactly where I was supposed to be. And though I'd told myself I wouldn't fall asleep, in the warm comfort of Declan's embrace, I did anyway.

Chapter 33

Declan

Amelia dozed off curled into my side, her head on my chest, her breathing deep and even and content. And I just...well let's just say it was the best goddamn thing in the entire world. I lay there awake, as still as I could, inhaling the sweet scent of her hair and loving the warmth of her breath on my skin. After all the shit that had gone down in the past, I didn't think I'd ever feel this way again. Yet here we were. Together.

Finally, *finally* together.

And me? I was finally content, a feeling I'd nearly forgotten existed. Hell, I felt almost delirious. She was, too. Not just blissed the fuck out from amazing sex, but really, truly happy. Of that I had zero doubt.

Which was why I was caught off guard when, after she woke and made a trip to the washroom, she started pulling on her clothes.

I rose up on my elbows, confused. "What're you doing?"

"Getting dressed," she replied matter-of-factly. Like it was an idiotic question. Which I guess maybe it was.

"Yeah, but why?"

"Because it's way too cold out to go home naked." She smiled as she said it. Making light of the question. I should've given her the response she expected and grinned back. But I didn't. I still didn't understand.

"Why d'you have to go home? Can't you call your mom and tell her you're staying here tonight? She won't mind, will she?"

Amelia sat on the edge of the bed and regarded me, her smile no longer toothy, but still intact. "*She* might not mind, but I would." Obviously noting my reaction, she added, "I'd love to spend the night with you, you know I would, but I want to be home when Liam gets up. He's never woken up without me there. And if we head out now, I might get back in time to kiss him goodnight."

I pushed the covers down and leaned forward to kiss her. "Got it. Just give me a minute." I was disappointed, but I understood. And I didn't want her to feel like she was letting me down. So I dressed and drove her back to Swann's Landing.

Although everything had been perfect only thirty minutes ago, now things felt kind of weird again. We didn't chat much on the drive. She fiddled with the ring pendant I'd given her years back—and I was pleased to see she'd started wearing it again—and I kept changing the radio station, never finding a song that I liked enough to let it play all the way through.

We chatted a bit about Ryan's recovery, and a new policy Patrick had put in place at the office, but it was all just small talk, with long gaps of awkward silence between. I fucking hated awkward silence, especially after the amazing sex we'd just had. There wasn't any good reason for it. Unless that actually was the reason? Maybe she regretted it? I knew she didn't feel comfortable at my house. Did she wish we'd resisted temptation? Could that be it?

Once I pulled into her driveway and killed the engine, I swiveled toward her. "Everything okay?"

"Yep. I'll look at some more rental listings tomorrow. I'll find something soon, I know it.

I brushed this off. "Not about that. About, y'know, us. We okay?"

Her brows drew in. "Of course!" She moved closer and put her palm on my cheek, kissing me, then pulling back so she could look into my eyes. "We're great. Why d'you ask?"

"Just making sure. I mean, clearly we're great in the sack. We just proved that again."

She blew an amused puff of air out her nose and rolled her eyes. "So modest."

"Who needs modesty? You and me? We're a fucking inferno. But I wanna make sure you're feeling all right. You know, emotionally? Tonight was kind of huge. And then you immediately wanted to head straight home. So I'm just checking in to make sure you're cool. Are you cool?"

She kissed me again, lingering a little longer this time, her hand sliding around to the nape of my neck and up into my hair. When we separated for air, she smiled and whispered, "As a cucumber. And I love cucumbers. But mostly I love you. I love us."

"I love us too. So much. You have no idea. And I wish you didn't have to go." I ran a hand up her jeans-clad thigh. "You sure I can't come in?"

Amelia sighed, but she still looked happy. I don't know why I'd thought she wasn't. Must've been my usual insecurities at work. The little buggers had plagued me so much the past few years, and I swear they never used to exist before I met her.

"Maybe next weekend, okay?" she said. "I need to ease Liam into our change of status. He's never had to deal with his mom being in a romantic relationship before. Even though he adores you, it might be a bit of an adjustment for him."

"I get that. I haven't told Lex yet either. Both kids may take some time to get used to the idea. But they'll come around. I promise you."

"Goodnight, Declan." Her hand dropped to her knee and squeezed my fingers resting there. Then she added, "I'll call you later, once I'm in bed."

Bouncing my eyebrows at her suggestively, I grinned. "I'll look forward to that."

I'd just gotten off a client call a few days later when I heard a tap on my office door. Swiveling my chair, I found Josh, his phone in one hand and a massive grin plastered across his face. Before he even said a word I understood the reason for that grin: he knew. Either Amelia had said something to him or she'd told Holly. Either way, the news was out.

"Hey."

"Hey." Josh dropped into a chair, extending an arm as he did to push the door closed. "What's up?"

I snorted. "From the look on your face, I'm pretty sure you already know what's up."

The wattage of his mega-smile dimmed a little, but didn't vanish. "So it's true? You guys finally kissed and made up? For real?"

I couldn't dampen my own grin as I nodded. "Not to jinx it, but yeah. So far, my charm seems to be working. I don't think all the damage has been repaired—I'm honestly not sure it ever can be—but, fingers crossed, she seems willing to give me another chance. Obviously she's lost all common sense." I stopped and dragged my fingers through my hair. "I don't deserve it, but I'll sure as hell take it."

"Well I'm thrilled for ya, buddy. Really. And no matter what you think, you *both* deserve some happiness. Just don't fuck it up this time."

I shook my head. "Nope. I've learned my lesson the extremely hard way. I'm never letting her go again."

"Just make her happy. And keep making her happy. That's the only life advice I've got."

"What are you, her big brother or something?" I chucked.

The grin reappeared. "Something like that I guess. What can I say? I care about both of you." Josh leaned back in his chair. "So, I know she's been looking for a place to live around here. You guys talking cohabitation yet? One big happy family?"

"It's still early days. But I won't say it hasn't crossed my mind."

He looked thoughtful. "You expect her to move into your place?"

I frowned. "I don't think she…" But then I stopped, remembering how she'd basically jumped my bones there a few days ago. "I don't know. I guess it could be a possibility. Maybe."

Josh opened his mouth and then shut it again. He looked skeptical.

"What?"

"I think you'd better talk to her about it. But try to look at it from her point of view. If your roles were reversed, would *you* want to move into that house?"

"Probably not," I admitted. I was trying not to let myself get too excited about our reconciliation or jump headlong into planning our future, but Josh was right. Living arrangements would need to be discussed at some point. Maybe it'd be best to sell my house and find a place we could start fresh and make new memories together. When she was ready. If she ever was.

"Just be honest. If you really wanna earn back her trust, tell her what you're thinking instead of holing it all up inside like usual."

I nodded. "I know. I'm trying. We both are."

Josh started to get to his feet, but I held up a hand to stop him.

"Hold on. Speaking of honesty, there's something else I need to say. I'm not sure I've ever thanked you for…" I paused, clearing my throat. Real talk with other men never came easy for me. "For, you know, just…always being there. All those times I sat at home getting shitfaced and you showed up and tried to distract me from the hellhole that was my life. I know you were just babysitting the drunk, making sure I didn't do anything stupid. But still. I, uh, I appreciate it."

"Holy shit. Wonders will never cease. Did Declan Kavanaugh just express gratitude? Without prompting?" Josh's face was utterly serious; his only tell was an arched brow. A second later, the corner of his lips curled twitched up into a smirk.

I threw my pen at him and he caught it deftly in mid-air. "Don't be a dick."

On Saturday afternoon I pulled up onto the gravel parking lot outside A Fresh View and turned to Alexis. "You ready?" This was the first time I'd brought her with me to visit Ryan and I wanted to prepare her.

She had been reading a book during the drive out here. Closing it, she looked up at me. "Ready."

"It'll be just like last time we visited Uncle Ryan here, except it's too cold to go for a walk on the back lawn now. You remember coming here when you were small?"

Lex frowned. "Not really."

"Well, as you know, Ryan is staying here for a few weeks until he gets better. But it's not like visiting someone in the hospital. He has his own room, but he's not confined to bed. He's wearing regular clothes. And he doesn't look very sick. He's a bit pale and could use to eat a few more burgers, but otherwise he's the same Uncle Ryan he's always been. He just needs to be taken care of here for a while and then he'll come home. You don't need to worry. Okay?"

With big, serious eyes, she said, "Okay."

As I opened my door, a gust of wind pushed it wide and I had to really pull to close it behind me. Both of us zipped up our coats against the chilly blast as we walked to the entrance.

When we got to Ryan's room, he was resting on his bed with his pillows propped up behind his shoulders and his eyes closed. His face seemed to have more color, but to me he still looked too thin.

The moment he heard us come in, his eyelids popped open. "Hey!" he smiled, sitting up. "If it isn't my favorite niece!" He threw open his arms and Lex ran to hug him. Over her shoulder, his eyes met mine. Dropping a wink, he added, "And my meh brother."

Snorting, I said, "After all we went through to get your ass into this place, I think I should at least rank higher than meh."

"Meh-plus? Is that a thing? Let's go with that."

I laughed as I took a seat. "You've called me a lot worse."

Alexis sat on the bed beside her uncle. Looking up at him curiously, she said, "Have you met my new brother Liam yet?"

Ryan shook his head. "Not yet. Maybe once I'm back home, you guys can bring him over to meet Aunt Diana and me."

She turned to me. "Can we, Dad?"

"Of course. Once Ryan's feeling up to it, we'll get them together with Amelia and Liam. For sure."

"At Christmas?"

I frowned. "I don't know, sweetie. Probably not by Christmas. But hopefully soon after."

"They're letting me go home for Christmas," Ryan said. "Just for the day, but still. It's something. Dad's coming over. Maybe you guys can drop by for a bit, too?"

My mind shot to Amelia. Would she want Alexis and me at her mom's with them on Christmas Day? Probably. At least for a few hours. Maybe, just maybe, she'd even be okay with us all waking up under the same roof on Christmas morning. I knew there was a good chance it was still too early in our reconciliation for her be comfortable with that, but having all four of us together at Christmas would be amazing.

"We'll see," I said. "I'll need to check with Amelia to see what their plans are. But I'll let you know. I'm sure I can work something out."

Ryan's eyes narrowed just a fraction. He dug out his wallet and removed several one dollar bills. "Hey Lex, did you see the snack machines out in the hallway when you came in? My stomach is growling like a bear. Could you maybe go get us all some chips? And chocolate bars? You can pick whatever kind you want."

"Really?"

"Sure. Would your favorite uncle lie to you? Grab me a Coke too, from the second machine. Thanks." He handed her the money and she left the room. Turning to me, he said, "So, you and Amelia? You fixed things?"

With a small shrug, I sat forward in the chair, bracing my elbows on my knees. "I'm trying." I could feel a smile stretching across my face as I looked at my brother. "Things are definitely better. We're working it out. How could you tell?"

Ryan returned my grin. "Cause you're happy. And you're normally pretty much the most miserable son of a bitch I know."

"I don't wanna jinx it yet. It's still really new. But yeah. I'm happy. I think this is it for us."

"Well I'm glad for ya." His voiced dropped. "And what does..." Pausing, he tilted his chin toward the open door. "Lex think about all this?"

"She adores Liam, and she seems to like Amelia, too. I haven't told her yet about Mel and I being coupled up. Re-coupled up? Whatever. But I have to soon. Because there'll probably be sleepovers in the near future. She's gonna notice we're together sooner or later, and I don't want her to get all bent out of shape about it. I don't *think* she will, but you never know. Having another woman in the picture is gonna be new for her. I never told her when I was seeing Nicole. To Lex it's been just the two us for so long."

He nodded. "That it has. Too long."

Just as he finished speaking, Alexis came back into the room with her arms full. She set Ryan's Coke on the side table along with an apple juice, two bags of chips, two chocolate bars, and a packet of peanuts. "I didn't know what you liked, so I got a bunch," she said to him.

"Excellent selections, Favorite Niece. Now let's go find something fun to do while you're here." Ryan got up and took Alexis to the games room. Soon they returned with the game of Trouble. The 'pop-o-matic' bubble-button in the center was broken, but there was a pair of dice in the box, so we used those. Alexis kicked our asses all three games. She was pretty pleased with herself, but after the third win I told her it was time for us to go.

"Can't we play just one more?" she said, her lower lip jutting out into a pout. I realized I'd seen Liam make that exact same facial expression last weekend. Clearly that pouty lower lip came from the Kavanaugh side. Well, the Miller side if we're being technical, but whatever.

"Sorry, hun. We can come back and visit again in a few days, though."

She gave Ryan another big hug and we said our goodbyes.

Snow had begun to fall while we'd been in visiting and I had to brush a thin layer of white off the car before I could drive. We didn't tend to get much snow in Virginia in December, but the weather forecasters were calling for a colder than usual winter this year. Maybe we'd get enough snow that Liam, Alexis, and I could build a snowman? I was already having visions of playing outside in the snow with the kids as I turned onto the road back to Lynchburg.

The light had dimmed enough that Alexis could no longer read her book. "When can we visit Liam again?" she asked as she stared out the window at the blowing flakes.

I glanced over at her. "How 'bout Sunday? I'll check with Amelia to see if it's okay." It was time to broach the subject. "So…what d'you think of her? Amelia?"

"She's nice." No hesitation. That was good.

"I agree. And, uh, you know she and I used to date, right?"

Alexis snorted. "Well duh! You're Liam's dad."

My eyebrows shot up, but I chuckled. I hadn't had the Sex Talk with her yet, but clearly she already had some clue where babies came from. From her friends at school? What had she heard and how accurate was any of it? I'd have to figure out a way to bring it up with her in the not too distant future. Then something else hit me: in a couple years she'd get her period. *Shit*. How was I going to deal with *that*? I mean, let's be honest. These were both subjects Laura probably would've been the one to talk her through. Alexis was getting older and she needed a strong, positive female role model in her life now more than ever. There were some things a woman was just better at, no matter how hard I tried to fill the gap.

"Good point," I replied. I was silent for a few moments as I tried to think of how to phrase it. Finally I asked, "What would you think about us dating again now?"

From the corner of my eye, I saw my daughter turn to look at me. She wasn't smiling, but she didn't look unhappy either.

She simply looked curious. "Sure." A small shrug accompanied this non-committal reply.

I waited. She didn't say anything else. "No other thoughts? Just sure?"

Alexis was still watching my face as I drove. "So are you?"

"Am I what?"

"Dating Amelia?"

I darted another glance at her. "Uh. Well. Yes, actually. We talked about it and decided we want to give dating another try. But we haven't really gone out on any dates yet. Any ideas where I could take her?"

Lex ignored my question. She had a more important one of her own. "Does that mean you guys'll, like, kiss and stuff?"

Laughing, I felt myself relax a bit. "Possibly. Would that bug you? Seeing us hug or kiss?"

"I don't know. Maybe." Well, at least she was being honest. I knew me showing affection to another woman would be strange for her. Of course it would. It was going to take time for her to get used to me having another woman in my life. But she would. After a moment, she added, "Would hugging and kissing Amelia make you happy?"

"Yes. Being around all three of you makes me happy."

"Do you love her? The way you used to love Mom?"

I glanced her way yet again. Her blue eyes were wide and she still wore the same serious, curious expression. "Yes," I admitted. "Very much."

"Then it's fine with me. I like when you're happy. And I like Liam and Amelia. We should invite them over to our house sometime. Maybe Liam would like to have some of my old toys."

Relief flooded me. "That's a great idea." I reached over and affectionately ruffled her curls, a gesture I knew she hated these days. I'd been doing it for so long that I often forget. Luckily, this time it elicited a laugh.

We both just wanted the other to be okay on this life path that no longer included her mother. And I think maybe we both realized that Amelia and Liam could be the way to it.

Amelia

I woke one morning to realize Christmas was a week away. And the thought of Christmas, perhaps magnified by waking in my childhood room, brought memories of my father. Grief was a funny thing. At first it was all-encompassing and overwhelming. Relentless. There was no escaping it. But over time it changed. It didn't become less intense, but it did become …less. Less always. Less everywhere. Easier to find manageable moments between the long horrible ones. After a while I learned to live in the new normal that became my life after the loss. But the loss never really went away. And when it did return, it still drowned me. Every time.

My chest began to ache as I thought of Christmases past with my dad. I could still hear his voice telling me I had to open the red box first, or to give Mom her gift before I tore into a second one. I could still see the way his eyes crinkled when he smiled. I could still recall the warmth of his hugs and the way he smelled, so familiar and comforting.

Grabbing a tissue from my nightstand, I dabbed at my tears. How was it nearly Christmas? How had autumn passed so quickly? How could it almost be the new year? A new year meant new beginnings, and this year even more so for Liam and me. I was excited about these particular changes though. And it was probably time to tell him the biggest one.

Before I could fold back the blankets and emerge from my cozy cocoon, my son pushed open the door and came into my room.

I'll have to teach him to knock before entering now, I thought suddenly. He'd never had to knock before, but if Declan was going to start sleeping over, I'd hate for Liam to walk in on us at an inopportune moment.

"Morning, little man," I said, sitting up against my pillow and patting the mattress beside me. He needed no further invitation, leaping onto the bed and wiggling beneath the covers. I wrapped an arm around him and snuggled him against me. "Sleep okay?"

"Uh huh." He rubbed an eye with his fist, clearly not fully awake yet. "Is Daddy coming today?"

I smiled. "Yes. I'm sure he's looking forward to seeing you."

"Will he be here soon?"

"Not until this afternoon." This seemed like as good an opening as any. "Speaking of your father, there's something I want to talk to you about."

"What?" Liam's head twisted so he could look up at me. His dark hair stuck out in all directions.

"Well…you may have noticed that Dad and I have been spending more time together lately."

He looked blank.

"We've grown a lot closer these past few weeks. Kind of like we used to be, a long time ago. And we're planning to spend even more time together going forward. Sometimes all four of us, sometimes just the three of us, but also sometimes just your dad and me."

"Okay." He still didn't get it, but he was only four.

I sighed. I didn't want to go into any details, but I needed him to understand. I decided to try a different tack. "You know how Aunt Dee and Aunt Terri are with each other?"

Liam nodded.

"They hold hands sometimes, and cuddle on the couch, and even kiss when they don't think we're looking. Right?"

He nodded again, his face scrunching up at the mention of kissing.

I kept going. "They love each other. And we're happy for them, because they're happy together. So what I'm trying to tell you is that your dad and me, we love each other, too. The same way Dee and Terri do. Do you understand?"

Liam's eyes lifted to mine again. His little brows were drawn in. "Are you and Daddy gonna *kiss*?"

Smiling, I struggled to hold back a laugh. "Sometimes, yes. Would you be okay with that?"

His eyes held mine for a few seconds longer. Then he shrugged and dropped his head to my chest again.

"I want you to understand that just because I love Daddy and we'll sometimes spend time alone together, it doesn't mean we love you any less. We love you bunches and always will." I gave him a squeeze and kissed the top of his head.

A soft yawn. Then: "Mommy?"

"Yes, honey?"

"Are we all gonna live together, like Marco's family?"

Now there was a question I had no good answer to. So I just went with my gut. "Maybe someday. But not right now, no. Daddy might sleep here on Saturday nights sometimes, though. What would you think about that?"

He sat up, his eyes sparkling with excitement. "Tonight? Can he sleep over tonight?"

"I don't know. Maybe. Do you want me to ask him?"

"Yes!" Liam pushed back the blankets, uncovering both of us in the process, and leapt out of bed, heading for the door.

"Where are you rushing off to?"

"To set out my Lego so we can work on the High Kingdom Castle when he gets here!"

Once he'd gone, I texted Declan and let him know I'd told Liam about us, and how he'd reacted. The last thing I typed was: *bring your toothbrush.*

After breakfast, Liam went back up to his room to play with his Lego. As I cleared off the table, I decided it was time we put up the Christmas tree. Glancing at Mom, I said, "I can't believe it's nearly Christmas. I was thinking I'd bring up the tree and we could decorate it with Liam. Is that okay?"

She was sipping her coffee and flipping through a magazine. Without raising her eyes to me, she nodded. "That's fine."

"I mean, it's not the same without Dad of course, but at least the three of us are together this year." I rinsed off our plates and put them in the dishwasher. I was still feeling a little melancholy and as I straightened up, a sigh slipped out. "I miss him even more at this time of year. But I'm sure you understand."

At that, she finally looked up. "Of course I do. And speaking of such things, there's something I need to discuss with you."

I put the glass I was holding in the sink and turned to fully face her, bracing my hands on the counter behind me. "What's up?"

Mom had a determined look in her eyes I knew all too well. "I've realized you're right. It's time to start the next stage of my life. So I've decided to buy one of those new condos I told you about. My agent and I are meeting in a few hours to start the paperwork. But please don't worry. My unit won't be ready until May, so you have plenty of time to find a place for you and Liam. If that's still what you want."

"Oh wow. That's *huge.*" I sat back down at the table across from her. Huge didn't even cover it. This was a major life change. "I can only imagine how difficult that decision must've been for you, but I agree. I think you're making the right choice. Guess we'll have to get this place ready to put on the market, huh?" I frowned. "That's gonna be strange, selling this house, won't it?"

Mom set down her mug and smiled at me. "This house is yours, too. Whatever money we get from it will be half yours. So you'll have a nice down payment for your own house once this one sells, if you decide to buy instead of rent."

My jaw dropped. "*What*? No. Don't be silly. It's your house and your money. I don't need it—I'll be fine."

She waved this off. "Your father and I discussed this a long time ago. If one of us passed and the other ever sold the house, half of the proceeds would go to you. You can do whatever you want with the money, but it will be yours."

My brows narrowed. I didn't know if I liked the idea, but I could tell from her expression that it would do no good to argue. So I nodded. "If you're sure. This is just…it's all pretty overwhelming. But thank you. I mean it. That will really help out." I went back to the sink and began rinsing off the rest of the dirty dishes. "So do you need a lift over there for your meeting?"

"Thank you, but no. She's picking me up." Mom glanced at the clock on the stove. "I should really head up and shower. Do you mind?"

"You go ahead. I've got this. And set your laundry basket out in the hall before you go and I'll throw in a load later."

Mom patted my shoulder as she walked past. "I'm going to miss having you and Liam around." And, proving just how far we'd come, I knew she actually meant it.

Once she'd gone and I'd finished cleaning up, I took a moment to sit back at the table. This was the kitchen we'd been eating breakfast in since I was a child. But soon we'd be eating in completely different kitchens. Never in this one again.

My head was spinning. My mom was going to move. We'd have to sell this house. I needed to find a new place to live. I'd woken up this morning thinking about all the changes to come, not even realizing there was one massive one I hadn't been considering.

The ghost of my father was everywhere in this house. To me that was a comfort. But to my mom, maybe it wasn't. Maybe it was an anchor tethering her to her past and preventing her from moving on with her life? I hadn't really thought of it like that before, but in many ways it made sense.

We all have tethers to important parts of our past. And sometimes we have to break them to keep from being strangled by them. To keep going.

I just knew that selling this house to strangers was going to be high on the list of hardest things I'd ever have to do.

Chapter 34

Declan

On Christmas Eve morning I woke to fat flakes of snow drifting past the windows and a thin white blanket over the roofs and tree branches. The snow we got last week had melted off, but since it was back so close to the holiday, I hoped the kids would get treated to a rare white Christmas.

Today's plans were simple. Alexis and I needed to head to the mall to pick up a few more gifts for Liam and Amelia, then home to wrap them and off to Swann's Landing sometime this afternoon until tomorrow. Much to my delight, Amelia had loved my suggestion that we all wake up together to open presents on Christmas morning. She grinned nearly from ear to ear at the idea, and I couldn't help wondering if this was something she'd wished for over the years, just like I had.

My phone buzzed against the dresser and I grabbed it, hoping it was Amelia. Instead I was surprised to see a message from Diana.

They're letting Ryan come home a day early. Can you come for dinner tonight instead of tomorrow? Show up after 3. Turkey at 5.

Ryan would be thrilled about the extra day at home. Figuring Amelia would understand if Alexis and I didn't show up until evening, I replied, *Sure.*

I got dressed and went down the hall to my daughter's room. To no surprise, she was sitting up in bed reading.

"Morning," she said when she saw me.

"Morning, sweetie. You'd better jump in the shower and get dressed soon. Turns out we're having turkey at Uncle Ryan and Aunt Diana's later, so we need to get to the mall to finish shopping ASAP."

A small frown creased her forehead. "Are we still sleeping over at Liam's tonight?"

"Definitely," I assured her. "We'll head out right after pumpkin pie. You don't want to miss your Aunt Diana's pumpkin pie, do you?" Well, the one Diana bought at the bakery, but Alexis didn't need to know that detail.

"No way!" she exclaimed. Two seconds later, she'd pushed past me and disappeared into the bathroom. Four seconds after that, I heard the shower come on. My girl loved her some dessert.

As I went down to the kitchen to pour us some cereal, I pulled out my phone to call Miriam. Unfortunately she wasn't coming down to visit us over Christmas this year, but I was already looking at flights to take Alexis up for a quick two day visit next week. As I went to click on my sister's name, the phone rang in my hand. The screen read B York, so I assumed it was Amelia calling from her mom's landline.

"Good morning," I answered cheerfully.

"Declan? It's Brenda York."

Last minute presents were bought. Gifts were wrapped— although Alexis' wrapping job was a bit sloppy, no one would ever notice but picky-pants me. Family was hugged. Other gifts were unwrapped. Turkey and fixings and pumpkin pie were eaten. And then we wished everyone Merry Christmas and got in the car to head to Swann's Landing.

More snow had fallen during the day, and the highway was a bit slick so I had to drive slowly. Unpleasant reminders of Laura's accident on that snowy night years ago kept popping into my head, making it less tempting to speed no matter how anxious I was to get to Amelia and Liam. But even those morbid thoughts couldn't dull my excitement. I was eager for our first full family sleepover, thrilled to spend my first Christmas with my new family.

So many amazing things to look forward to, and next year was going to bring even more.

I couldn't wait.

When I pulled up in front of Amelia's, a car was in my usual spot in the driveway beside her old Honda. I exhaled a frustrated sigh as I recognized it. *Shit.*

Some of my eagerness deflated. Amelia's best friend was here. And said best friend hated my guts. She despised the idea of us reuniting, sure it was the worst thing for Mel. But did Dee's opinion really matter? Mel and I were past all that now. We'd talked it out, kissed it out, fucked it out. We were happy now and working on building a future together. At least we had been. Who knows what might happen if Dee planted more doubts in Amelia's head?

"Dad? Are we going in?" Alexis asked. I'd just been sitting there staring at Dee's car.

"Of course," I replied. Lex picked up her backpack as I grabbed my duffle and the big box of presents from the back, and we headed for the door.

A few seconds after Alexis poked the bell, Amelia pulled open the door and greeted us with a big smile and a "Merry Christmas!" I could hear the clinking of forks against plates from the next room.

She leaned in to kiss me, but, conscious of Alexis watching, I stopped her before she made contact, brushing a crumb on her chin away with my thumb. "Did we interrupt dinner?"

"Terri brought over her homemade pumpkin pie. Do you guys have any room? Because it's to die for!"

I looked down at my daughter and she looked back up at me with a grin. "I'm pretty sure Lex *always* has room for pumpkin pie."

"Yes, please!" Alexis said to Amelia, unzipping and tossing her coat on the bench. Amelia put her arm around Alexis' shoulders and led her to the kitchen while I set down our bags and carried the box into the living room. As I looked for space to put our gifts under the tree, I heard Amelia introduce Alexis to Dee and Terri.

"Where's Declan at?" Terri asked after everyone said hello.

"In here," I called, as I finished arranging the presents. One box, however, stayed in my pocket. That particular item wasn't going to be given in front of others.

I came into the kitchen and found everyone seated around the table. Liam smiled a toothy smile when he saw me and said, "Hi Daddy!" He, too, had crumbs on his face.

"Hey buddy. Good pie?"

"*So* good!"

I forced a smile as I greeted Dee and Terri. No need to pretend as I said hello to Brenda, though. "Cup of tea, Declan?" Her eyes twinkled as she looked at me.

"No, thanks. I'm so full I couldn't even fit in tea," I said as I rubbed my stomach.

"Declan and Alexis were at his brother's for an early Christmas dinner," Amelia told Dee and Terri, obviously trying to explain my late arrival. I didn't think they deserved any explanations about where I was or what I was doing, but it seemed like Amelia was making an effort to patch things up with Dee. I knew how important these ladies were to her and Liam, and because of that, I had no intention of standing in the way of their friendship.

"How's your brother doing?" Brenda asked.

"Much better." I didn't know how much of Ryan's sordid tale Amelia had told them, so I kept my answer simple.

"Hello Declan," Dee said to me, her dark eyes holding mine. There was an unspoken message there, but I wasn't sure what it was. Don't fuck this up? I still hate you? Let's try to keep the peace for Amelia's sake? All three?

"Hi Dee," I replied evenly. "Good to see you again." A small lie, but sometimes small lies were necessary.

"Likewise." She smiled. It didn't quite reach her eyes, but I could tell she was trying, and I appreciated it. Maybe someday we'd look back at all this and laugh. But today was not that day.

Brenda, maybe sensing the slight tension, piped up. "Since the pie has been devoured, shall we return to the living room where it's more comfortable?"

"Liam, let's go upstairs and get your pajamas on," Amelia said.

In an instant, his smile turned into a scowl. "I don't wanna go to bed yet!"

"You can stay up with everyone for a while longer—although not too late, 'cause you know Santa won't come if you're still awake when he gets here. But jammies first, okay?"

"I'll take him," I said to Amelia. "You relax and we'll be back down in a jiff."

Liam turned to me excitedly. "Daddy, come, come! Come see the new Lego Auntie Dee and Auntie Terri got me." Grabbing my hand, he tugged me toward the stairs.

The moment we stepped into his room, he showed me his new Lego set. He'd placed the box on its edge on his windowsill so he could look at it like a work of colorful art until it was time to build it.

"Maybe tomorrow we can start work on it?" I said as he started changing clothes.

Liam turned to me with a frown. "No. First, we hafta finish the High Kingdom Castle."

I chuckled. "I thought we were done that one?"

"That tower's not right. See?" He pointed at the gray, black, and red castle on the floor in the corner. And he was right; one tower was slightly off-kilter as it narrowed toward the top. I couldn't believe I hadn't noticed when we'd built it last weekend. But Liam had. He had a sharp eye, my kid.

"You're absolutely right. I guess we need to fix that first before we start building the stable and horses."

"And the carriage. Don't forget the carriage."

"Right. And the carriage. And the little knights to ride the horses. We're going to have a busy afternoon tomorrow." I looked at him thoughtfully. "Since Lex will be here, d'you think we could invite her to help us?"

"Lex plays with Lego?" Liam looked surprised by the idea. I guess to him she was way older, too big to still play with toys. While Alexis had started to grow out of them for sure, she still wasn't completely done with her toys yet. It would be a sad day when I had to pack them all up for good.

"Sure she does. You should ask her if she wants to."

"Okay." He started toward the door, but then stopped and looked back up at me. "Where's she gonna sleep?"

"That's a good question. Your mom said she could make up the pull-out bed in the basement. Or the couch downstairs."

"Can I ask her if she'll sleep in here with me?"

My brows shot up. "Your bed's a little snug for two, buddy. It's a nice idea, but I don't think it'll work."

"Mommy can get blankets and pillows and we can sleep on the floor. I'll even move the High Kingdom Castle to my desk."

I glanced around at the available floor space. The bathroom door swung inward, so that shouldn't be a problem. Even if we moved the castle it might be a little tight, but it could work. And I kind of loved the idea that he wanted his big sister in his room with him on Christmas Eve. Getting down on one knee, I put an arm around his shoulders and gave him a squeeze. "I think that's an awesome idea. You ask her if she wants to, and if she's game, I'll help you move the castle and make a nice bed for her right there," I said, pointing to the floor. It wasn't a perfect solution, but it would do for now. If Lex didn't mind.

On the way downstairs to rejoin the others, I smiled to myself as I imagined what the four of us living together for real would look like. I wasn't sure what I'd done to deserve it, but at long last, my life was finally changing for the better. And I could not be happier about it.

Amelia

"Merry Christmas," a soft voice whispered by my ear, and though I was barely out of dreamland, I smiled. What an amazing way to wake up. Declan may have just awoken too, but he still sounded seductive. Or maybe I was just imagining it after last night. We'd finally managed don't-wake-the-household sex, and I'd fallen asleep exhausted but happy. Really, really happy.

Fingers brushed aside my hair and I felt a soft kiss on the side of my neck. Then on my shoulder. Heat bloomed down below and suddenly I wasn't sleepy anymore. I glanced at the clock on my nightstand. Six-thirty. It was still super early. But it was Christmas morning. So was it early enough?

Soft light came through my curtains as I rolled over in his arms and drew his face to mine. Morning breath be damned. Declan was the only Christmas gift I wanted. He pulled my body against his. We were both still naked and it was clear he'd woken up in the mood. One hand slid down my back to cup my butt and I shifted my knee up over his leg. Our kisses deepened as he pulled my thigh higher, opening me wider. Sucking in a sharp breath, I felt his hardness against me.

Then, like a splash of ice water, I heard the squeak of hinges as my door swung open. "Mommy? Daddy? Wake up! It's Christmas!"

Dammit. I hadn't reminded him last night about knocking first. But even if I had, he might have forgotten. It was Christmas morning after all.

"Liam, don't go in!" I heard Alexis call from the hallway.

Declan chuckled, rolling over and reaching to the floor for his clothes as Liam ignored his sister and bounced into the room.

"C'mon," my extremely excited son urged, coming right up to my bedside and grabbing my hand. "Let's go downstairs and see what Santa brought!"

"What makes you so sure Santa came?" I teased as I ruffled his already messy hair. I was smiling, but my mind was racing. How could I get him out of here without him noticing I had nothing on under the blankets?

Liam rolled his eyes at me. "Mommy, don't be silly. Of *course* he came. Get up! Get up!" He tugged on my hand again.

Declan came around the bed—tying the strings on his pajama bottoms as he walked, I might add—and scooped Liam into his arms, turning him sideways and flying him out of the room like a rocket. "Let's go see," he told both kids. The excitement in his voice made him sound like a kid himself.

Alexis hadn't even peeked around the edge of the doorway, perhaps worried about what she might see, but as soon as her father came into the hall I heard her say, "Merry Christmas, Dad!"

The second Declan pulled the door closed I slipped out of bed, rescued my nightgown from the floor, and went into the bathroom. So much for sneaking in some fun before the kids woke up. But that would probably become my regular life from now on, especially down the road once we moved in together.

Moving in together. The thought was both exciting and terrifying. All four of us living in the same house would have its challenges. Alexis was probably going to be the biggest of those, not only because she remembered her mother and I was not Laura, but because it had just been her and her father for so long. I had once again become the Other Woman, although in a completely different way than before. But, when the time came, Declan and I would work through any bumps in the road. I had faith it would all work out.

In the meantime, I needed to make more of an effort to bond with Alexis. Maybe I could take her out shopping for the after-holiday sales? I made a mental note to ask Declan what he thought about that as I headed down to join them.

Liam was right; Santa had definitely shown up while we were sleeping. Two jam-packed stockings hung from the fireplace mantle and, though it had seemed impossible last night, even more gifts were stacked around the base of the tree.

My son stood beside his stocking waiting impatiently for me. He knew he wasn't allowed to open gifts until everyone was in the room to watch. Mom sat in her favorite chair, a steaming mug already in hand. Declan also had a coffee. He patted the empty spot beside him on the couch and I spotted a third mug waiting for me on the table. Gratefully, I picked it up and took a sip.

"Merry Christmas morning, Amelia. Good of you to join us," my mother said.

Blushing, I replied, "Sorry to hold you guys up. I just had to use the bathroom. I didn't realize six-thirty was sleeping in today."

Liam had grown impatient. "Mommy, can I open my stocking? Please?"

I laughed. "Of course you can. You both can."

The kids dug in, pulling stuff out and spreading it in a circle around them on the floor. My mom and I had filled Alexis' stocking with plastic bracelets and hair clips and nail polish and other things I thought an almost-eleven year old girl would like. She seemed pleased, giving both of us hugs once she finished unpacking the contents.

"Maybe Alexis would like to hand out some of the presents?" I said to everyone. Liam couldn't read well yet, and I thought it would help her feel like part of our family.

I took another big swallow of coffee, and then got down on the floor to help her locate a box for each of us. Over the next fifteen minutes or so, a pile of torn wrapping paper grew and the packages under the tree diminished. We smiled, some of us even squealed, and there were plenty of thanks and hugs. When all that was left below the tree was a few gifts for Josh, Holly, and Emily, I started cleaning up the mess and my mom went to start breakfast.

Once our bellies were full, Liam promptly dragged Declan upstairs to build Lego. Declan shot me an apologetic look before he disappeared up the steps, but I didn't mind. We'd have time together later, as Alexis was going to her grandparents this afternoon and staying with them tonight.

I hadn't given him his gift yet. I'd decided I'd rather give it when we were alone, so it was hidden in my dresser waiting for tonight. I hadn't known what to get for him—he honestly seemed to have everything—but I'd finally decided on a silver watch I couldn't really afford, but splurged on anyway. I'd even had a D + A engraved on the back. Simple and elegant and I thought it was just his style. Hopefully he'd love it.

I'd noticed that he hadn't given me anything yet, either, and I couldn't help wondering if he'd had a similar plan about privacy. Which is why I was surprised when Declan came back downstairs, asked Alexis to go help Liam, and went into the living room.

"Hey Mel, could you come in here a minute?"

I was in the kitchen folding wrapping paper into the recycling bin. When I came and sat down beside him, both he and my mother were looking at me.

"What's up?"

He rested a hand on my thigh. "We have a surprise for you."

Was he giving me my Christmas gift in front of Mom? Wait, no. He'd said *we* not *I*. That seemed weird. "Okay," I replied cautiously.

They glanced at each other. When Declan shifted his eyes back to mine, he was grinning. Mom looked like she couldn't wait to see my reaction. What was going on? Had my mother and Declan been secretly conspiring? About my present?

"You know I was planning to put the house up for sale in the spring," Mom started.

"Yes."

"Well, Declan and I have been talking about it, and we've come up with a great solution. A perfect solution for all of us, actually."

My eyes narrowed. "A solution to *what* exactly?"

She smiled. "Why, to you having to move of course. To us having to sell our home to strangers. You and Liam will be able to live here indefinitely. For the rest of your life, if you want to."

"Mom, what are you talking about?"

My mother again shot Declan a look. She seemed so pleased with herself, and maybe I was being dense, but I still couldn't figure out why. "Declan will buy me out," she said, smiling away at me like she'd just told me I'd won the lottery.

"Buy you out?" I was still confused. Maybe I hadn't had enough coffee yet.

Mom sighed, like I was being a particularly thick child. "My half of the house, Amelia. Declan will sell his place and buy out my half of the house. And then all four of you can live here together. Well, once I move out anyway. It's perfect. A win-win for everyone. Don't you agree?"

I felt my jaw drop. I looked between them, forcing my mouth to close. They were both completely serious about this. And they both looked so pleased with themselves. They clearly

376

thought it was the greatest idea ever, planning my life for me without my involvement. Like I needed taking care of. Like I couldn't manage on my own.

Fury rose up from deep inside. I had no interest in getting into this in front of my mother, though. This was between Declan and me. So I grabbed him by the wrist. "We need to talk. Upstairs," I gritted out, trying my best to control the anger in my voice.

"Why Amelia, whatever is the matter?" my mother asked.

I ignored her and pulled Declan to his feet. He followed me to the steps without a word, although I saw him look back at Mom with a small shrug. Like I was being unreasonable. Like I was a child having some sort of tantrum.

I could hear the kids chatting in Liam's room. I figured if they needed anything, they could ask Grandma, so I ushered Declan into my bedroom and firmly closed the door. Leaning against it, I glared at him as he sat on the bed facing me.

"What's wrong?" he asked. He was clearly both confused and concerned.

"What's *wrong*? I'll tell you what's *wrong*! After everything we've been through, after all our talk about honesty, you went behind my back and planned all this out with my *mother*? Without discussing it with me first? *Seriously*?" I was so angry I felt tears rising.

"But this is a *good* surprise," he said, frowning. "It fixes our logistic problems, and this way you don't have to pack up and move, or see your childhood home sold. Why're you so upset?"

"*God!*" I covered my eyes with my hand, shaking my head. "You just don't get it, do you? And of course you never even bothered to ask me what *I* wanted. Because you both just knew?"

Declan sighed. "You're right. I should've told you. I just wanted to surprise you. I honestly thought you'd be happy about this. But I can see I was wrong. Please, just sit down and explain this to me and we'll work it out." He patted the bed beside him.

Instead I shoved aside the pile of clothes on the chair and perched on the edge. Taking a deep breath I attempted to calm down so I could speak rationally.

"If you or Mom had talked to me about this, I would have realized that yes, you're right, we don't need to sell the house. Liam and I can stay here. I'm actually amazed I didn't think of it myself. But it won't be going down the way you guys planned."

His frown deepened. "What d'you mean?"

"Tomorrow I'll go to the bank and find out what I need to do to qualify for a mortgage to buy out my mom's share of the house. We'll need an estimate of the value, but I'm pretty sure even with just my earnings I'd be approved for fifty percent of it. And then Mom can transfer the house into my name." I looked Declan straight in the eyes and added, "Just my name."

Now as well as confused, he also looked hurt. He braced his elbows on his knees and lowered his forehead onto his joined fists. And I realized that, to him, this sounded like a rejection.

I sighed as I got up and moved to sit beside him on the bed. Softening my voice, I added, "Don't get me wrong. I *do* think about us living together as one, big happy family. Someday. Just not right now. Even after all these years, this is really still just the beginning for us, and as much as I'm happy with where we are and where we're headed, I'm not ready to commit to co-habitation—and especially not owning property with you—yet. Let's see how things go. Maybe in the summer once the kids are off school I'll be ready to talk about you and Alexis moving in. I'm sorry if this isn't what you want, but I hope you can try to understand."

He turned his head to gaze at me and all I could see was softness. In that moment, I understood that this would not break us. It wouldn't even scratch the surface. Because we were a team now. Nothing was going to break us ever again.

Declan

I was a complete fucking idiot, as per usual.

I'd thought I was doing the right thing for Amelia—hell, Brenda and I both thought it—but I should have known better. I should've known to talk to Amelia about something like this first, not just dump it on her and expect her to be grateful for my magnanimousness.

She was very much not. And I should've seen it coming.

Of course she would want this house to be fully hers. It was the house she grew up in. It had been her father's house. It was her legacy. Selling it to strangers would be a mistake. And I now realized co-owning it with me, which would give me claim to half the value if we ever split—not that I'd ever do that to her—would also be a mistake in Amelia's eyes. It was too big a risk for her. And, after everything, I got that.

"I do understand," I said to her. "I'm so sorry, Mel. I didn't even think of it like that."

"Well you would've, if you'd talked to me about it."

"Clearly. I promise you that's one mistake I'll never make again."

Her face was deadly serious. "Good. Because you can't shut me out of important decisions. Not if we're going to be partners."

I offered her a small smile. "That's all I want. And I won't pressure you to move in together. Not until you're ready. I swear."

She smiled back and leaned her head on my shoulder. "Thank you."

Putting an arm around her, I drew her closer. "I love you, and like I told you before, I'm not going anywhere. We can move at whatever pace you're comfortable with. I just wanted you and Liam to be able to stay here."

"I want that, too. And thank you. Because even though you didn't go about it the right way, you've given me the idea I needed to buy out my mom myself. It's exactly what I should do. So I appreciate it."

I chuckled. "You're...welcome?" Then I remembered her gift. "Hold on, let me up for a minute." She raised her head and looked at me in confusion.

I went around to the other side of the bed where I'd thrown my jacket last night and retrieved the box from the inside pocket. I'd wrapped it carefully so she could pull off the lid without tearing the paper. Coming back to sit beside her, I held it up. "Merry Christmas," I said softly as I put it in her hands.

"What is it?"

I snorted. "You'll just have to open it and see. But don't get your hopes too high—it's not jewelry this time."

She smiled, one hand lifting to stroke the ring on her pendant. Instead of opening the box, she got to her feet and pulled out her top dresser drawer. A second later, she turned around and handed me a slightly larger wrapped box. "I wasn't sure what to get you. Hope you like it."

"I'll love anything you give me," I said. "But you first."

Amelia carefully pulled the lid off my gift and peered inside. Her eyebrows drew in as she lifted out a keychain with silver music notes dangling from it. A brass key was wound onto the ring. She raised her eyes to mine. "Is this a key to your house?"

"I'd be happy to give you one of those, too, if you want. But no, it's a key to my apartment."

The vertical line between her brows deepened. "Please tell me you didn't rent an apartment for us, Declan. Especially now that I no longer need one."

I smiled. "Of course not. I actually own it. When James passed, I inherited his place in Lynchburg. I've been renting it out the past few years, but my tenant recently gave notice and instead of finding a new one, I thought it'd be great for us if we wanted a little privacy. Or for you, if you needed somewhere to go for some alone time. It's not far from the office."

"I can't accept this. You should rent it out again." She tried to hand the key back to me, but I wouldn't take it.

"Don't be silly. It was paid for when I got it, so there's no mortgage. This key is so you always have a place to go. With me or without. Whenever you want. I'll take Liam anytime you need some time to yourself. Or, if you're in the mood for a little afternoon delight, we can sneak over on our lunch or after work." I winked.

That elicited a laugh. "Of *course* you're thinking it'd be our secret sex hideaway!"

I shook my head, chuckling. "What else would you expect from me? But seriously. It's tiny, only one bedroom, so not big enough for either of us to move into, but it's perfect for some alone time. Alone-alone or together-alone."

She leaned over and set the keychain on her dresser, then flung her arms around me and hugged me tight. "Thank you," she whispered just below my ear. "I didn't give you enough credit earlier for knowing what I need. And having a place to escape to sometimes sounds like exactly what I need. What we both need."

I kissed her and when we broke apart, I said, "I kinda wish we had some together-alone time right now, actually."

Amelia smiled that wide, beautiful smile that always made my heart do strange flips in my chest. "I'm sure my mom wouldn't mind if we took a drive into Lynchburg to check it out for an hour or two."

"Oh yeah?"

"Yeah. But first things first. You still have a gift to open, mister."

I pulled her back against me, leaning in until my lips were only an inch from hers. "I already have the gift I've always wanted. Right here."

380

Chapter 35

ABOUT SIX MONTHS LATER

Amelia

It felt strange waking up in this house and realizing my mother no longer lived here. This had always been my parent's house, or my mom's house. It was going to take some time to get used to thinking of it as mine. My house. My very own house. The words brought a smile to my face.

Declan, Josh, Holly, and I had helped Mom move into her new condo yesterday. I intended to move into the master bedroom here so that my childhood room could be set up for Alexis, but we'd been far too exhausted to shift any more furniture around last night. In fact, I'd probably sleep in here for several more days.

And next weekend we'd have to do it all over again on a larger scale. Because in just under a week, Declan and Alexis were moving in. We'd need to take Josh and Holly out to several fancy dinners and offer to babysit Emily until she was a teenager to make up for them helping us two weekends in a row. But Declan's brother was about to become a dad for the first—and let's be honest, probably only—time and Ryan didn't want to stray far from Diana this close to her due date. Declan was excited about becoming an uncle, so he didn't mind, but I was concerned that other than Josh and the movers with the truck, he wouldn't have a lot of help with the heavy stuff. He kept assuring me everything would be fine, though. He hadn't sold the place yet, so if they didn't get everything moved in one day, it was no big deal.

Asking him to move in with me had been a no brainer. Things between us were even better than I'd hoped they could be. Sure, we argued sometimes, but what couple didn't? We always made up. And Declan and I made up in the best possible way, usually with trumpets and fireworks and all that sizzling-hot fanfare. At least when we could.

He'd been right about the benefits of having a little apartment to sneak off to sometimes. I'd worried it would be difficult to re-find the excitement and passion of the early stages of a relationship when there were two kids around most of the time, but having somewhere to go to be alone had made a world of difference. Our sex life was incredible. Cataclysmic, even. Just like it had always been. Being over forty had not caused any decrease to Declan's sex drive. If anything, it was higher. He claimed it was just because he was with me, and maybe that was true. I didn't know, but I didn't much care either. I was just happy to be on the receiving end.

In fact, last night was one of the very few nights we'd fallen asleep in the same bed without first making love. But there was plenty of time this morning. Liam had slept over at Marco's house last night because we'd been busy moving Grandma all day. And Alexis was at Laura's parents. Which meant there was no risk of anyone barging in on us. For the first time we had the entire place to ourselves.

Speaking of Marco, the ice between Liv and me had finally started to thaw a little. We weren't exactly making plans to go out for drinks yet, but we were talking. She would give me a smile when we met now, and ask after my mom. Our kids were best friends so we saw each other a lot more these days just with drop-offs and pick-ups. There was still a ways to go, but I had renewed hope that our friendship would eventually be repairable.

And then there was Scott. Scott wasn't angry with me at all; if anything he always seemed really happy to see me when we ran into each other. He was his usual kind, cheerful self, at least about every subject but Declan. Scott did not like Declan at all. I didn't think it was because he'd discovered I'd had an affair all those years ago either—if he'd found that out, I doubted he'd have been so nice to me. I assumed it was just some instinctual, residual protectiveness toward me, an automatic dislike of any other man in my life. Like a big brother, sort of. At least that's the only explanation I could think of. It didn't bother me, though. So Scott and Declan would never be friends. Big deal. To be completely honest, I didn't really want them to be. Them being friends would just make me feel guilty on a regular basis for things that happened a long time ago. It was better this way.

As for what I'd done to Scott way back when, I owned my mistakes, but I saw no point in confessing them. It would only hurt Scott and serve nothing but to ease my guilt. It would be all about me. So I'd vowed that particular shameful secret would stay a secret forever. It was the right thing to do for everyone involved.

Just then Declan stirred beside me, bringing me back to earth from my litany of thoughts. A moment later, he threw off the blanket and got up to use the bathroom. When he returned to bed, I rolled onto my side to face him.

"You realize we're all alone here for the first time ever?" I said.

He smiled. "I do." Stretching his arms above his head, he yawned. "It's nice, isn't it?"

"Definitely. Soooo…what d'you wanna do with our free time?"

One corner of his lips curved up. "I was thinking about going downstairs and making pancakes. Why? What did *you* have in mind?"

I grabbed the hem of my nightgown and pulled it up over my head, tossing it aside. "I might be able to think of one thing."

He arched a brow, shifting closer but still not touching me. "Just one?"

I pretended to be thinking hard. "Maybe two."

Declan growled low in his throat and it was one of the sexiest sounds I'd ever heard. And then with one swift movement, like a cat with his prey, he pounced.

Afterward, we lay on our backs and stared at the ceiling with matching dazed expressions. Blindly I reached for his hand and squeezed his fingers. We were both content to just lie beside each other, catching our breath and enjoying the right here, right now.

Out of the blue, he said, "I'm meeting with a realtor this week. I wanna get my house listed ASAP. Before July hits and all the prospective buyers are on vacation."

I was quiet for a long moment, my mind once more swirling. "I was thinking maybe you should hold onto it for a while. You could always rent it out, like you used to with the apartment?"

Letting go of my hand, Declan turned to face me. He no longer looked blissed out. "Be honest with me. Are you saying you want me to keep the house in case things don't work out between us? So Lex and I have someplace to go?"

I felt my face heat up. Reluctantly, I shrugged. It was close enough to an admission.

Declan released a long, low sigh as he sat up and leaned against my headboard. One hand clutched his forehead like a headache was forming.

"I'm sorry," I said in a low voice. "It just…it just seemed like it might be a good idea. And the rent would cover your monthly costs, so you'd basically be keeping it for free."

"This is *not* about my financial situation." His voice was hard. And hurt. "This, as usual, is about your incessant need to control everything, to have a backup plan, a failsafe in case it all goes to shit again." He turned to look at me as I shifted myself up to his eye level. "Isn't it?"

I didn't answer. But he was right. Deep down I knew he was totally right.

"Look. I know real life has no guarantees of a happy ending. And I know there's always a chance I'm gonna somehow fuck this up no matter how hard I try not to. But Mel, this is worth the risk. I have faith in us, and whatever small risk of future heartbreak might exist, you are worth it to me."

I bit my lower lip and wrapped my hand around his arm, pushing myself against his side. "You're worth it to me, too."

He turned to look at me, his blue eyes dark and burning. "Let me ask you one very important question, possibly the *most* important question: do you think you'll ever be able to trust me again?"

Of course I trusted him. He wouldn't be here with me right now if I didn't. I wouldn't have asked him and Alexis to move in with us if I didn't. But he obviously didn't believe it. Did he still think I harbored resentment for how he'd hurt me years ago?

Of course he did. Who was I kidding? It's not like I'd told him otherwise.

"I do trust you. And before you ask, yes, I forgive you. I think I actually forgave you a long time ago. And I'm sorry if I didn't make that clear before. I want a future with you. I have faith in your commitment to Liam and me. And I'm committed to you and Alexis."

His expression had softened. "Good," he said quietly.

"So go ahead and sell your house if you want to. I'll support your choices the way you've always supported mine."

For what felt like several long seconds, we just stared at each other. Then he set one palm on the side of my jaw and drew my face to his. When we broke apart, he smiled. His eyes were sparkling again.

"Marry me," he said suddenly.

My brows flew up. "*What*?"

"You heard me. I love you and I want you to be my wife. There's nothing stopping us anymore. So marry me." From the look on his face, I knew he was completely serious.

I was thrown for a loop, but I didn't want him to notice. I couldn't stand the thought of hurting him again if he assumed he was being rejected. So instead I smiled, and I kissed him, and I said, "I love you, too."

He wasn't fooled though. A small frown creased his forehead. "But?"

I bit my lower lip, knowing I needed to pick my words carefully. "Would you be okay with us living happily ever after, for better or worse, for richer or poorer, in sickness and health, 'til death do us part, without a piece of paper to prove to the world that we're a real family? Because we are. A real family. And I don't need a certificate to feel that way." I reached behind my neck and unfastened my necklace, removing the ring and handing it to him. Sticking out my left hand, I wiggled the fourth finger. "I promise to love you, Declan Kavanaugh. Forever."

Declan smiled as he took my hand and slid the ring into place. "I swear to always love you, too, Amelia York. You and Liam both. 'Til death do us part."

A lump formed in my throat. This was a hugely significant moment and I hadn't seen it coming. Yet I knew we'd remember it for the rest of our lives. I threaded my fingers through his and stared into those mesmerizing blue eyes that I was going to be lucky enough to look into every day. "I'll wear this ring you gave me and we'll both always know what it means," I told him. "Because it's a Mobius strip. It has a never-ending surface. Which means forever. Or, like you once promised, for the rest of ever."

"For the rest of ever," he sang softly back to me.

I realized I'd been wrong before. Maybe once in a blue moon, once all the messy, jagged pieces finally fall into place, real, honest love actually can conquer all. My own personal fairytale was finally coming true. This Queen and that King were going to get our happily ever after, after all. And our little Prince and Princess right along with us.

About the Author

J.S. Eades lives in southwestern Ontario, Canada, with her family. An avid traveler and scuba enthusiast, she can often be found under the warm waters of the Caribbean.

Connect with Me
Website: www.jseades.com
Facebook: AuthorJSEades
Twitter: @JS_Eades
Instagram: @jseadesauthor

Dear Readers
Thank you so much for reading my novel. If you enjoyed it, would you please take a moment to write an honest review on Amazon or Goodreads.com so other readers can find and hopefully enjoy it, too? Even just a few sentences would mean a lot to me.

Thanks!
J.S. Eades

Other Books by J.S. Eades

PROMISES AND OTHER BROKEN THINGS
(Amelia and Declan book 1)

Amelia York seems to have it all: a great career, good friends, and she's married to her high school sweetheart. Starting a promising new job is just another step in the life she has all figured out. The intense connection she develops with a handsome co-worker, however, threatens to derail all her well thought-out plans.

Declan Kavanaugh's whole world revolves around his daughter. Overworked and under-appreciated both by his wife at home and his colleagues at his family's firm, the stress is starting to get to him. Making friends with the pretty new accountant comes as a surprise, but he finds time spent with Amelia is like the breath of fresh air he so desperately needs.

Neither of them wants any complications in their lives—and the last thing they want is to fall in love.

But as they discover, sometimes no matter how much you fight it, life has other ideas.

DEATH DEFYING

What happens when you discover nothing you'd believed about yourself is true?

All Genny Dupont wants for her 21st birthday is to sleep in, eat a great breakfast, and go out dancing with her best friend. At first, it seems like her day goes exactly to plan. She even meets a cute guy at the club. But when they get together for coffee the next afternoon, she realizes she's made a huge mistake.

Because the story JP tells her, that she and her sister are the only remaining descendants of a family of immortal vampire slayers, is completely insane. He's obviously a lunatic. Disappointed, she walks out, but Genny can't quite shake the idea he's planted. Could he possibly have been telling the truth?

Learning about her family and how they died opens the door to a world she'd thought only existed in fiction. Sure, this world includes enemies that want her dead, but it's not all doom and gloom. As Genny starts to embrace her legacy, she and JP grow closer.

She's a slayer. JP insists vampires are evil. But when she strikes up an unlikely friendship with Quinn, a vampire who risked his own life to save her, she comes to understand that not everything—or everyone—is how it seems.

AGAINST ALL ADVICE

Giving advice is easy; taking it, on the other hand…

Evie Colville has one goal: earn a college scholarship to escape from small-town Sutterton. Between studying and working in her dad's coffee shop, she doesn't have much free time. None for a boyfriend, that's for sure.

Then she meets Alistair.

Alistair fled to his uncle's after the woman he loved brutally betrayed him with his own brother. The last thing he wants is another relationship. And after what he's gone through, he has zero tolerance for lies.

Evie, however, is keeping a big secret, not just from Alistair, but from everyone in town. Along with her other responsibilities, she's also the clandestine author of the local paper's Miss Lonely Love advice column. And recently she's been corresponding with a frustrated young man who has sworn off women for good.

Falling for each other is the *last* thing either wants. There's no possible way they could make this work.

Is there?

Read Chapter 1 for free, starting on the next page.

AGAINST ALL ADVICE

Chapter 1

Evie Colville has a secret identity.

She may be a lot of things to a lot of people—dutiful daughter, loyal best friend, hard-working waitress at her father's coffee shop, just to name a few—but one thing she absolutely *isn't* is even remotely qualified to write her weekly 'Miss Lonely Love' column for *The Sutterton Herald*.

At least she doesn't think so.

Luckily, no one but her editor, her dad, and her best friend, Grace Bryant, know Evie's secret. The byline of her column is credited to Shara Strong, Evie's carefully crafted, fictional alter-ego. Shara is basically Evie's opposite. She's definitely *not* an eighteen year-old senior at Sutterton High. She's a Grown Up. And she had plenty of dating experience before she married the Man of Her Dreams. The regular readers of 'Miss Lonely Love' know Shara is neither a Miss nor Lonely; in her column she often mentions her handsome, perfect husband. Evie assumes, correctly, that if her readers believe she's been so successful in love, they'll be more inclined to trust her advice with their own problems.

Which is ironic really, because Evie is nothing of the sort. She's never been in love. She's not even dating. She *has* had a boyfriend. Once. But it wasn't serious. Evie's not ready for a relationship. In fact, over the past year, she's barely thought about boys. Concentrating on her school work and her two jobs, not to mention taking care of her father and brother and squeezing in occasional time with friends—well, it doesn't leave much room for dating.

She doesn't mind, though. She needs to graduate at the top of her class to win a scholarship to a good college and escape this tiny town. Falling in love would only complicate things. And she doesn't want complications.

This evening Evie sits at the counter of Colville's Coffee Clutch, mug of hot chocolate in hand, polishing her column for

Friday's paper. She's just finished advising a teenage girl, whom she suspects might be her brother Dylan's friend Charlie Lancaster to stand up for herself to her controlling boyfriend.

Once Evie's happy with her replies, she emails the document to her editor. A glance toward the clock over the door shows she still has ten minutes until she can close up.

Sometimes, if she reads a message she feels deserves a response but she's already finished her column, she takes a few moments to send a personal reply. So tonight, with passing curiosity, she pulls the top letter from the bundle in her knapsack.

The writing is small and cramped, with jagged, crow-scratch vertical lines. She assumes it was written by a man.

Dear Miss LL,

I've got a messed up situation for you. What do you do when you find out the love of your life has been sleeping with your brother behind your back? You thank your lucky stars you're free of her, right?

My problem is I can't stop thinking about her. She stabbed me through the heart, and I left town and haven't looked back. But the sad truth is, much as I hate myself for it, I'm still in love with her. And I'm terrified that if she apologized and groveled, I just might give in and take her back.

Now I'm not dumb enough to think that's ever going to happen. As far as I know, she's still with my brother, and I really don't want to see either of them again.

So, my question for you is, how do I get over her?

Just Another Idiot

Evie purses her lips as she re-reads the letter. She's answered questions about cheating before, but never cheating involving sleeping with two brothers at the same time, then swapping to date the other. She agrees with the writer—that's pretty messed up.

Tapping her fingernails against the countertop, she contemplates how to reply. She tries to imagine how she might feel if she found herself in a similar situation, and how she'd want to deal with it. Tearing out a fresh sheet of paper from her notebook, she picks up her pen and starts writing.

Dear JAI,
Even though I can't include your letter in this week's column, I wanted to send you a personal reply.
First of all, I'm so sorry you went through that.
Second, you're absolutely right. You should probably get down on your knees and thank some higher power that you're free of her and get on with your life. But I know it's not that easy. Love isn't something you can flick off like a switch. It burrows deep inside and becomes a part of you. The only thing that might help lessen its grip is time, but I think you probably already know that.
Good on you for leaving town, though. Time and space away from them is just what you need right now. I recommend you get out and meet some people. It might surprise you how new friends can distract from old problems. Although you may not be ready yet, I also suggest you consider maybe starting to date again, even if it's just casual.
Be strong. Someday you'll look back on this and see that it pointed you toward the path you were meant to be on.
Best of luck!
Miss LL

Evie reads her reply over, then tucks it into an envelope and prints the local post office box return address across the front. She glances up at the clock again, and with relief sees it's time to head home.

She packs up her things, pulls on her heavy winter coat and hat, and dims the lights. The welcome bell over the door tinkles its goodbye as she steps out and locks up.

Sutterton in mid-January after midnight is cold and still. The silence is so overwhelming Evie's eardrums interpret it as a low roar, a crowd cheering off in the distance, a jet plane passing overhead at six hundred miles an hour. The emptiness feels absolute, with only the fading echo of the bell to ground her in reality.

White clouds of breath mar the frigid air in front of her and her boots squeak on the hard packed snow. She looks up at the clear night sky above the jagged black silhouette of the distant mountains. The stars seem to shine brighter than ever tonight, too frigid to even twinkle.

The buildings are dark, the snow is light, and the few streetlights cast long shadows. The vivid blue of the mailbox on the corner pops out of all that monochrome. When Evie reaches it, she pulls the letter from her pocket and slips it inside.

She takes a deep breath, her lungs filling with ice before hurrying along the frozen sidewalk, anxious to reach the warmth of home.

Friday morning's alarm is always unwelcome. On Thursday nights Evie has to close the coffee shop late, and the resulting lack of sleep tends to make her grouchy. The crash of the clock hitting the floor as her flailing hand knocks it off the nightstand only jolts her further from dreamland.

With a groan, she pushes back the covers, reluctantly emerging from her cozy cocoon. She trudges to the bathroom half-awake, pounding on her brother's door to rouse him as she passes. An annoyed groan is her only response.

Her father left nearly two hours ago to open for the before-work crowd in need of their morning fix. Every morning but Sunday it's just Evie and Dylan, fighting for the bathroom, scrounging up breakfast, and then scrambling out to the corner to catch the school bus.

This morning they manage to end up at the kitchen table at the same time, Evie with jam on toast in one hand and a mug of hot chocolate in the other, Dylan digging into an enormous bowl of half Raisin Bran, half Fruit Loops. He claims it gives him the energy he needs for the day as he's a point guard on the school basketball team. Evie just rolls her eyes.

Her phone beeps with an email from her editor reminding her of the last letter she'd included in her column last night.

"Hey Dyl?"

With barely a glance her way, he shoves another heaping spoonful into his mouth. "Mmm?"

"Is Charlie still dating Cameron Wheeler?" She tucks a loose strand of long, dirty blonde hair behind her ear.

Her brother's face twists. "Yeah. Why?" It's clear he doesn't approve.

"No reason. I was just curious."

Now she's more suspicious than ever that the email might have come from Charlie. Cam is the captain of the football and basketball teams and is, in Evie's opinion, a complete alpha-male douchebag. His ego is nearly as big as his father's. Martin Wheeler is Sutterton's mayor. The Wheelers were one of the original families to settle in this area. So were the Colvilles, but that might be the only thing the two families have in common. Tom Colville is content to live a quiet life, and though his coffee shop is moderately successful, Evie knows that some months they barely scrape by. The Wheelers have money and power—plenty of it. They live in the largest of the riverfront mansions along Route Ten, and are famous for hosting lavish parties. Since founding families are a mandatory presence at such events, Evie has had to endure every one of them.

She glances at the digital clock on the microwave. *Crap*! "The bus is gonna be here any minute!" Jumping to her feet, she dumps the remains of her chocolate into the sink and dashes for her coat.

As usual, Dylan heads straight to the back of the bus, while Evie sits near the middle with Grace. She notes her brother has taken the empty spot beside Charlie. Cam drives himself to school, so if he *is* still dating Charlie, he didn't bother giving her a lift today.

Evie chats with her friend until the bus approaches the gray stone and red brick castle that is Sutterton High. Her eyes are drawn to the corner turrets whose upper windows have an awesome view of the park and river bend across the way

The high school was built in 1915 at the height of the architectural castle craze that swept across America. Now its hulking edifice seems out of place: an embarrassment to be ridiculed by the students, a point of pride to the mayor and town council, and a roadside attraction to outsiders.

Evie thinks it's beautiful. She's loved this building since she was small—years before she'd ever stepped foot inside its hallowed halls. When she's having a crappy day, she needs only to make her way to the highest tower and look out at the view to instantly feel a bit better. It's like something clicks inside and, even if only for a moment, she understands her place in the world. Like she finally feels she's where she belongs.

After Math class, she has a free period. Normally, she spends this time doing homework in the library, but today she has an appointment with her guidance counselor.

"Good morning, Evie. What can I do for you today?" Mrs. Zeigler asks once Evie takes a seat. She's an older woman with thick red hair streaked with gray that she keeps piled into a messy bun. Evie likes Mrs. Zeigler. She treats Evie like an adult.

Evie sits with her spine straight, her legs crossed, and her hands clasped on her thighs. "Good morning. I was wondering when I should start applying for college scholarships? Are they all online now, or do any still do paper?"

Mrs. Ziegler shifts some files off a stack on her desk. "I got some paper ones for Syracuse last week. I know for Cornell, Columbia, and S.U.N.Y, you can submit online, but I don't think they're reviewing for this fall yet. It's still a bit early, as your final grades aren't locked down for a few more months. Try applying in another month, around the end of February."

"I'll take the Syracuse application then, please."

Mrs. Ziegler hands the forms over. "You can fill out most of it now, and then attach a copy of your mid-term report card once you get it. They may want recommendations from some of your teachers as well."

"That won't be a problem," Evie tells her with a self-conscious smile. She knows her teachers will have good things to say. She usually got straight As, and the only time her grades ever dipped below a B+ was in the months following her mom's death. Otherwise, she's always been a model student.

She gets up to leave, but Mrs. Ziegler stops her. "You're only considering in-state colleges, right?"

Evie sighs softly. "For now, yes. I'll let you know if I need any out-of-state information."

Mrs. Ziegler nods, and Evie walks back into the hall. She'd love to apply to out-of-state colleges, but the thought of living far away from her father and brother worries her. She wants to get out of Sutterton, that's a definite, but she also doesn't want to be too far away. Her father might still need her to work weekend shifts at the Clutch.

There's also the fact that they have no money to pay for flights or living expenses beyond the bare minimum. This limits Evie's choices, but she'll just have to do the best she can with what they can afford. And if she doesn't earn a full scholarship, she won't be going anywhere.

It's been a busy evening, but The Clutch is finally starting to empty as people head up the street to Henry's Grill for a drink, or home, or wherever else they need to be on a frigid Saturday night. As Evie wipes the counter, she glances back at the slim boy sitting in the corner. Well…he isn't really a boy, is he? He's tall and pale, with dark hair mostly hidden under a black Greek fisherman's cap. He wears tinted glasses and, as usual, has his nose buried in a book. As usual because, although Evie has no idea who he is, she knows he's been in her shop before. More than once. Always when she's been too busy to really pay him much notice. She remembers noting his cap and glasses, as well as the thick, black pea coat he wears. And that he only orders coffee, also black, which he has her pour into his own travel cup instead of a red Colville's Coffee Clutch mug.

"Excuse me, Evie?"

With a start, she turns to the elderly woman at a side table with her husband, where they sit almost every Saturday evening.

"Yes, Mrs. Clancy? Can I top you up?"

"No, thank you. It's time for us to head on home. I just wanted to say you look lovely in that shade of blue. It matches your eyes."

Mr. Clancy nods in agreement. A few weeks ago, they had told Evie they'd been married for forty-eight years. He slides a few bills onto the table, then gets to his feet to help his wife stand and ease her arms into her coat. They have matching down jackets with fur-trimmed hoods, perfect for a chilly January night.

"Aw, that's so sweet of you. You guys take care on those icy sidewalks," Evie advises.

Not long after they leave, her history teacher, Mr. Wright, also heads out. Now there's only Evie and the reading stranger.

She takes a breath, straightens her spine, and walks back to him.

"Warm you up?" she asks, holding out the coffee pot.

He looks up at her and lowers his glasses.

Evie's breath catches in her throat as she stares into the most brilliant green eyes she's ever seen. In the harsh fluorescent light of the shop they shine like emeralds— emeralds framed by thick, black lashes. And right now those mesmerizing eyes are watching her with amusement.

"-in mind?"

Crap. She missed most of that. Heat floods her face. "P...pardon?"

"I said depends what you have in mind," he repeats, one side of his mouth curving into a lopsided grin.

She flushes deeper as she realizes the double entendre of her words. *Warm you up. Oh God.*

"More c-coffee?" she stutters. Holy cow. Get a grip, loser. You left yourself wide open for that one.

"No, thanks." He flashes a real smile this time. "I should probably go. Aren't you about ready to close?"

His smile is as striking as the rest of him, and it eases Evie's embarrassment a little. She wonders how old he is. She's sure she'd remember if she'd seen him at school. No, he is definitely not a teenager. But not by a lot.

"We're open 'til midnight Thursday to Saturday," she says with a bit more assurance. "I have to stay, even if there's no one here."

"That sucks. Don't you get bored?"

She shakes her head. "Nah. If it's dead I just do homework or clean or read. There's always something the needs doing."

He looks her up and down and her temperature spikes again. "You're in high school…" Pausing, he checks her nametag. "Evie?"

"For a few more months," she admits.

One dark brow arches thoughtfully. "Huh. I pegged you for older."

"I'm eighteen. Why? How old are you?"

He looks at her for a second, his face going neutral. Then that easy grin returns. "Twenty-two. Just moved here a few weeks ago."

"Welcome to Sutterton. What brings you to our quiet little town? Certainly not the weather." She sits down opposite him. Why not? There are no other customers to serve.

He sighs, so softly she almost doesn't hear it. "That's a long story I'd rather not relive right now. My uncle owns a house on Route Ten just outside town. Used to be a bed and breakfast. I'm staying with him at the moment."

Evie's eyes light up. "Oh! Your uncle is Max Sterling! My dad knows him. He comes in here pretty often."

"Yep." His eyes shift down to the book in his hands.

Following his gaze, she asks, "What're you reading?"

He flips it over so she can see the cover.

A bright smile of recognition lights Evie's face. "*The Great Gatsby*? Cool. I'm reading that right now for English. Well, I actually got so into it I couldn't put it down and finished it in two days, but I'm re-reading at the pace we're supposed to. Have you read it before?"

He presses his lips together self-consciously. "Nine times," he confesses.

Evie's eyebrows fly up. "Woah! Maybe I should get you to help me with the five-thousand word essay I have to write on it," she laughs.

"Maybe," he mumbles, shifting around on his chair. Tucking his book inside his coat, he abruptly stands. "Hey, so, I gotta bounce. Thanks for the coffee and conversation."

Evie wonders if she's said something wrong. They seemed to be getting along fine, but now he looks like he'd rather be anywhere than here. Scrambling to her feet as well, she clarifies, "You don't actually have to help. I was just kidding."

Their eyes meet as he adjusts his cap, for a moment revealing more of that messy dark hair. A waft of fresh, light cologne hits her as they stand in close proximity, and much to her surprise, hot desire clenches low in her belly.

"I don't mind looking over your essay. As you might've guessed, it's one of my favorite novels. Maybe I'll see you in here next week. Enjoy the rest of your night, Evie."

She doesn't reply at first, frozen in thought as she watches him walk away. Just as he reaches the door she calls, "Wait!"

He pauses and looks back at her.

"I don't even know your name." Her voice comes out sounding much younger than her eighteen years.

With a small smile, he replies, "It's Alistair."

Then he slips out into the night.

Available at most online retailers.